Killers & Kings

By

Mark R Goodrum

Copyright © 2017 Mark R Goodrum

All rights reserved.

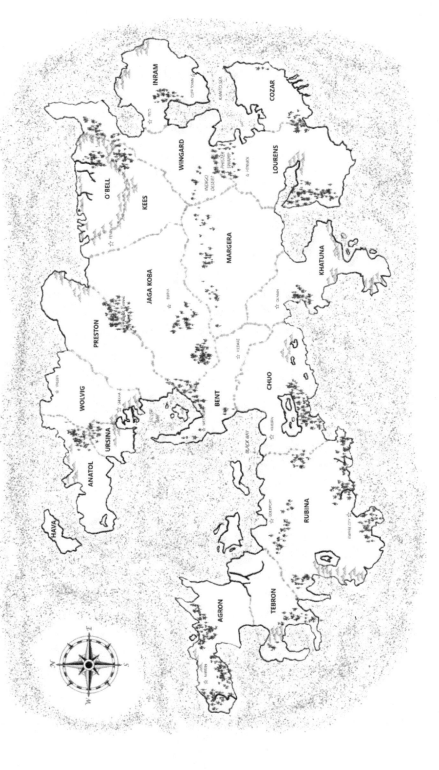

Table of contents

ACT I: The Killers
Chapter 1: The Highwayman	Page 9
Chapter 2: The Sellsword	Page 15
Chapter 3: The Traders	Page 21
Chapter 4: To Catch a Thief	Page 28
Chapter 5: It's Just Business	Page 34
Chapter 6: Genia King	Page 37
Chapter 7: The Gambler	Page 41
Chapter 8: Brothers	Page 45
Chapter 9: The Twilight Forest	Page 55
Chapter 10: The Curse	Page 60
Chapter 11: The Demon	Page 65
Chapter 12: The Movement is Born	Page 68
Chapter 13: Genocide	Page 74
Chapter 14: Ambush	Page 81
Chapter 15: Quell Expansion	Page 86
Chapter 16: The Siege	Page 94
Chapter 17: The Twins	Page 98
Chapter 18: Danika and Jorn	Page 109
Chapter 19: Awakening	Page 119
Chapter 20: The Mage	Page 123
Chapter 21: Magic	Page 125
Chapter 22: The High Father	Page 134
Chapter 23: Theocracy	Page 140
Chapter 24: The Masterless Knight	Page 144
Chapter 25: The Warlord	Page 149
Chapter 26: War for Inram	Page 160
Chapter 27: Renata Rin	Page 173
Chapter 28: Coup	Page 187
Chapter 29: The Queen	Page 193
Chapter 30: The Bride	Page 193
Chapter 31: The Princess	Page 199

ACT II: The Kings

Chapter 32: King Syphon	Page 204
Chapter 33: Trade War	Page 210
Chapter 34: Best Served Cold	Page 217
Chapter 35: The Monastery	Page 222
Chapter 36: Landis Stone	Page 233
Chapter 37: The Healer	Page 237
Chapter 38: The Prince	Page 244
Chapter 39: The Vision	Page 249
Chapter 40: Rest Stop	Page 258
Chapter 41: Wever Bran	Page 264
Chapter 42: Reinforcements	Page 269
Chapter 43: The King's Table	Page 271
Chapter 44: Herron	Page 280
Chapter 45: Landis' Story	Page 285
Chapter 46: The Road East	Page 288
Chapter 47: Gahrenna	Page 292
Chapter 48: Argus	Page 294
Chapter 49: Showdown	Page 299
Chapter 50: Opening the Door	Page 302
Chapter 51: Jarrod Stone	Page 307
Chapter 52: The Quell Horde	Page 312
Chapter 53: O'Bell	Page 319
Chapter 54: Revenge of the O'Bell	Page 322
Chapter 55: Repelling the Quell	Page 329
Chapter 56: The Princess and the Warlord	Page 333
Chapter 57: The Prisoner	Page 339
Chapter 58: Desert Storm	Page 345
Chapter 59: Calm Before the Storm	Page 349
Chapter 60: Final March	Page 354
Chapter 61: The Swamp	Page 357
Chapter 62: War	Page 365
Author's Note:	Page 374

Chapter 1: The Highwayman

Era Rutendo sat up on the high branches of a tree that lined the main road through Tebron. There were great grassy plains between the major cities, and this was one of the few areas where the road cut through a forest of any size. The men who cut the trees to create this shortcut probably never realized that they were creating an ideal place for an ambush.

Era's skin was dark in complexion, he had long greasy black hair and both a mustache and beard that looked as if they had never been trimmed. He almost always had a big toothy grin, and a couple of his teeth were gold, to match the gold rings, earrings, and chains that he wore on his exposed chest. His clothing looked new, a dark brown simple shirt and leather pants; but they did not look clean. He waved to his men who were concealed in the thick brush that lined a section of the road almost directly below him. He made motions to let them know that their prey was drawing near and to be ready to act. As the wagon train approached, he prepared himself, ready to give another of his famous monologues.

A dozen heavy wagons, pulled by two horses each, formed a train heading for Goldport in the neighboring region of Rubina. Each wagon had a driver and a security man, and there was a mounted guard on each side of each wagon. There had been an increase in highway robbery recently, and Master Trader Genia King wanted to make sure that this shipment reached port. There were finished weapons, tools, and other manufactured metal items that had been fashioned at great expense. Furs, silks, spices, and even hard currency were among the items being transported. *This is my first big shipment since becoming a Master Trader. I know this extra security is costing a fortune, but I can't afford for anything to go wrong,* she thought to herself.

The supply train approached a forest that stretched for many miles in each direction. *This smells. If I were planning to steal my goods, this is the place I'd do it.* Riding forward from her position at the rear of the train, she pulled up next to the commander of the security detail. He was formerly a knight; but now without a noble house to serve, he was selling his services to anyone needing security. Years ago, he had sold his plate armor for money to eat, now he wore leather armor and many of his men wore no armor at all, save for the odd, rusted helmet or shield. It wasn't easy, but after waving at him, she got his attention. He slowly turned and looked over to see what it was that she wanted.

"Sir Gerald, I'm a little concerned about those woods up ahead," Genia said in low tones to the commander. "It seems that a thick wood like that would be an ideal location for an ambush."

"Good observation, Madam," he replied, sitting up in his saddle and looking for signs of danger. "Yes, you could be right. I'll send out scouts to see if the way ahead is safe." The commander whistled loudly, catching the attention of everyone in earshot. He waved over a couple of his outriders. "Scout ahead along the road, look for signs of a possible ambush."

"Yes, Commander," the closest rider called out, saluting by holding his fist to his chest. Along with another rider, they went forward at a gallop and disappeared into the woods. The wagon train crawled forward at a leisurely pace till they had reached the entrance to the woods.

"Your men have not yet returned. What is your recommendation, Commander?" Genia demanded.

"Well Madam, I have to assess the risk of there being an actual risk, against your need for expediency," he said, trying not to give weight to either option.

"I'm aware of the choices. I'm paying you to make the right one!" The Commander's face looked troubled, he knew that the wrong choice could cost him his life, or worse yet, he might not get paid.

"Obviously, I'd feel better if the scouts had returned, but we haven't really given them the time to get very deep into the woods." The older man started sweating under Genia King's relentless stare. "I've brought along many good men. If we encounter some difficulty, we should be all right."

"All right. Lead us in Commander." With that, she turned her horse and resumed her place at the rear of the column.

Deep in the heart of the forest, is where the sun had the hardest time penetrating the canopy of treetops. A small ravine that crossed the path and where the woods were at their darkest, is where Era sprung his trap. He dropped from his perch a dozen feet above the ground to land directly in front of the Commander and the lead wagon. Several of his men also made their presence known, popping up from their hiding places, arrows nocked and ready to fire. He grinned widely at his intended victims, especially at the Commander whom he picked out as the one in charge.

"Good Sir, where are you about on this glorious day?" he asked brightly.

The Commander stiffened up, looking as knightly as he could. "None of your concern, brigand!" he bellowed. There were sounds of alarm all up and down the wagon train. "I know that it's your intention to steal our cargo, but that's not going to happen. I'll give you the chance to leave with your lives, and that is the best offer you'll get today!"

"You really cut to the chase, eh? Ok, we can play it that way." The highwayman put his hand to his bearded chin in a thoughtful way. "I like property, especially when it's someone else's; and yet, I have no desire to harm anyone today. I have enough boys in the trees here to wipe you out, but it doesn't need to come to that. Surrender your loot and we'll allow you all to leave our woods... un-killed."

The commander looked over at his aide, who on seeing his master's sign, pulled a horn from his waist and gave it three sharp blasts. Then the commander turned to Era, "A most generous offer, I'll counter by allowing you to run to your holes in the ground, pray to the gods for forgiveness, and forever give up your lives of crime," he said calmly. "If you do not, it's very likely that none of you will survive to tell the tale."

There was a crashing sound that came from not too far away and the commotion was quickly upon them. Two dozen additional outriders came crashing through the woods to surround both the wagon train and the bandits. Era was caught by surprise. Previous wagon trains had not had anywhere near this level of protection. Being very concerned with his own well-being, he dove into a thicket and headed toward the deepest part of the forest. The bandits found themselves left without proper leadership. One of the archers must have tired of pulling the bowstring and let his arrow fly. The arrow caught the commander between his ribs, burying itself deep in his torso. His expression was a mix of pain and displeasure. The riders immediately went into action. The archers were cut down without mercy, they then found another dozen men hiding nearby, and with their broadswords, they cut them to pieces. Soon, they emerged from the thicket and onto the road with only a few surviving bandits in tow.

Genia came up to the front of the procession in time to see the guards helping the Commander down from his mount.

Pushed down on their knees, the captive bandits looked around fearing the worst. She looked over the scene with a satisfied grimace.

"Will you live Commander?" she asked.

"I expect so, I've endured worse," he said stoically.

"Good job on hiring the extra men. I doubted your cost estimate, but you were right. I will most certainly use your services again," she said to the commander. Then she walked over to the prisoners.

"You men!" she addressed the prisoners. "Who's your leader, and how did you know that we were going to be here today?"

One of the men looked up at her, with tears in his eyes, "I have a wife and child, mistress. Mercy! I beg you!"

"Depending on how cooperative you are, I may see my way to being lenient with you. Again, who is your leader? Who told you that a prize target would be in your woods today?"

"Era Rutendo is the leader of our band. He came to us a few days ago and said that anyone wanting to make a fist full of coin, should meet here at dawn. We're always here waiting for goods ta share, so it were no problem."

"You'll not be sharing my goods. My partners will see how I handle business, and soon, these will be my woods," she boasted to the highwayman.

The Commander was being helped into the back of a wagon after having a bandage applied to his wound. Looking back in irritation, he turned to his second in command. "Neville, execute these men and get this wagon train moving again."

Genia looked shocked at the commander. The bandit's faces went from miserable to absolutely crushed. "Miss! I thought that you're going to have mercy on us, fer being helpful and all!" Genia looked troubled for a few moments, then she dug her knees into her horse's side and rode back to the end of the queue. She shuddered as she heard the wailing and screams, then... silence. The woods were suddenly quiet except for the rustle of leaves above, and a far-off bird was calling.

Chapter 2: The Sellsword

Landis looked her over again with an appraising eye. She was a unicorn, that mythical creature that men always dreamed about, but rarely if ever got to see. A truly beautiful woman working in a rundown seaside bar. She was way too good for this place. Long black hair cascaded in loose curls about her shoulders, fragrant oils causing it to shine in the dim light from the rapidly setting sun. Her top was a brilliant white with embroidered designs around the deep neckline and elbow-length sleeves that contrasted with her deeply tanned skin. A bright red sash was tied at her waist, and she wore a knee-length dark green skirt. She was not overtly exposing herself; but when she bent over to place drinks at the table, his eyes were drawn to the shadows in her cleavage. Her skirt rode up to mid-thigh when she sat, showing off her long and flawless legs. Without invitation, she sat on his lap.

"Sorry dear, what was your name again?" he asked her without taking his eyes from the curve of her hip.

She pulled him by his unshaven chin so that he had to stare directly into her blue-green eyes, "Carmen. You men never listen!"

"You're so beautiful that I can't help but be distracted," he said without remorse. He wasn't the smooth talker that his brother was, but he did all right with the ladies.

"Usually, flattery will get a man nowhere with me, but we don't get many like you in here. Buy me a drink?" she asked with a quality in her voice that sounded more like the opening round of negotiations than a simple request for a drink.

"Beer for me, and whatever you'd like for yourself. You've put me in an exceptionally good mood, and I have a bit of coin to spend." He flashed his brilliant white teeth at the barmaid. Landis Stone was a puzzle to the discerning eye. Even from a distance, he could be seen for what he was, a common sellsword. At the owner's request, he had left his longsword and shield with the doorman, but he kept matching daggers in sheaths tucked into his waistband. His plain white tunic identified him for what he was, a 'man at arms'. Men of his type were not uncommon, but he was different from most. At a bit over six feet, he was built solidly and was taller than most. He had dark blond hair that looked clean and hung to his collar. His beard came in dark and highlighted his light skin, tanned from walking the countryside from job to job. He was handsome in a profession that was usually filled with men who had lived hard lives and often bore the scars of dozens of hard-fought battles.

Leaning over, Carmen placed a playful kiss on his cheek, then bounced out of his lap and made her way to the bar. *What have you done to deserve this?* He thought to himself and smiled at the prospect of taking her to his room later that evening. *True, I have coin in my purse, but it seems to spend as fast as I get it. Curse me for my weakness.*

The open-air bar had one whole wall that faced the ocean and was open to the cool night air. Ships were tied to piers that reached out into the bay like long skeletal fingers holding them against the sometimes-turbulent currents. Sailors, merchants, and townspeople walked up and down the boardwalk on their various missions, few had the time to sit and lounge like a fighting man between wars. Landis sipped thoughtfully at his drink, enjoying the flavor on top of the lamb and potatoes that filled his belly. He had been traveling through the country of Rubina for a few weeks now and had only gotten to Goldport that afternoon. There was action to the West, and he was planning to head in that direction. Wherever there was trouble, there would be the opportunity for employment, and of course, coin. He barely took note of the men who entered the bar. When a man can handle himself, he doesn't worry about strangers. Most men who might be seeking trouble looked at him and decided it best to leave him alone.

Four sailors entered the bar, already well on the road to inebriation. They didn't wear the insignia of any noble house and weren't sailors for Rubina's royal family. When Carmen returned to his side, she put down his drink causing him to come out of his train of thought and notice the new patrons. They didn't have the look of the merchant marine either. They had the hungry and arrogant look of men who took enjoyment from making others fearful and miserable. Many of his fellow sellswords had that look too. He had spent much time around such men, and as such, quickly put them out of his mind.

Pulling Carmen back onto his lap, he gave her supple thigh a tight squeeze and managed to look her in the eyes instead of letting his gaze linger on her other attributes. Pulling her close, he whispered in her ear, causing her to give out a sensual kind of chuckle. They chatted amongst themselves for several minutes, ignoring the rising volume of the only other guests in the tavern. The other barmaid, a blonde who was a little on the heavy side, and a bit older, was ferrying drinks and plates of food from the bar to the sailor's table. She greeted them with a big smile as she tried to fill their orders; but they continued to be loud, banging on the table with steel mugs and fists. One who appeared to be the leader of the small group slapped her unkindly on her plump bottom.

"If we were still at sea, I'd settle for the likes of you; but not when there's better to be had," he said with contempt for the poor girl. Standing in the middle of the room, he looked directly at Carmen, who along with everyone else in the room, could no longer ignore him. "Come over here girl, you're too fine fer the likes a him," he said with command in his voice.

"Rowena seems to be taking good care of you," she said, not stirring from Landis' lap.

"She's fat and ugly!" he screamed across the room. "We sail with Captain Lago and we only accept the best. We 'take' what we want, and no foreigner will deny us what's ours!" He pulled a long wicked dagger from his belt. "Get over here now, or I'll take you in front of everyone, even if I have to bend you over your man's corpse."

A shiver of fear passed through Carmen. With very little enthusiasm, she climbed off Landis' lap and turned to walk over to the sailors. Before she could take a step, Landis caught her by the wrist, causing her to turn back to him. "Do you 'want' to go over there?" he asked in a very neutral tone.

"No, I was enjoying your company, good sir," she said with great regret.

"Then I 'insist' that you stay." He smiled in the direction of the sailor who had threatened them. The standing sailor turned instantly purple; his rage was immense. Brandishing his dagger, he stalked across the room, his partners stood and moved to follow him.

"She's a fine piece, but you're a fool ta die fer her comp'ny."

Landis stood up, using his arm to sweep the barmaid behind him. He'd seen their type more times than he could remember. The other barmaid ran to join the bartender who was cowering behind the bar. All four of the sailors looked up at the soldier, realizing that he was bigger than they had anticipated. Their faces showed their waning enthusiasm for a scuffle with someone large who was apparently a trained fighter. They wore loose shirts with too many chains, had too few teeth, and smelled like hot garbage. The leader of the sailors rushed forward, waving his knife around in a clumsy attempt to slash Landis' face. Landis easily caught his wrist and wrenched it backward with a sickening, bone-snapping twist. The heavy dull blade fell to the wooden floor where it stuck standing straight up in the wooden floor. Balling his calloused hand into a fist, Landis hit the injured man square in the face, sending blood flying from his nose, and sending his body to the deck.

Two of the other three let the shocked look on their faces turn to rage as they rushed forward together. Landis kicked out his left leg, the heavy steel-tipped leather boot catching one of the sailors in the gut, doubling him over. The other man he caught by the neck, his wide hand like the talon of some giant eagle, gripping the man and standing him upright. They looked at each other for a moment, the sailor knew that he was in trouble, and wondered just how bad it was going to be. Landis gave him a smile, a most unpleasant smile if you were to be on the wrong end of it. He lifted the man an inch or two off the ground, then with a move that was surprisingly fast for a man his size; he body slammed the sailor back first onto the unforgiving wooden floor. You could practically see the air flee his lungs.

Landis looked up at the remaining sailor, the joy of battle made his face practically glow with excitement. He had slain many men in service to various nobles, but he had almost forgotten how much he enjoyed a good old bar fight. The sailor surveyed the scene, and calmly put his dagger back into his belt; he held his hands apart from his weapons. Landis nodded in agreement, effectively ending the skirmish.

"As you can see, I took it easy on your boys," he said to the remaining man.

"I see that. I 'magine that it coulda been… more perm'nent for em."

"If I'd killed you all, you wouldn't be able to apologize to these nice ladies, which is what you'll do before you leave."

The sailors were recovering, and all were nervously standing around except for the one with the broken arm. The others helped him to his feet and collected his raggedy hat. "We're sorry miss," the three said to Rowena. They turned to Carmen, "and sorry to you also miss. We been drinkin all day and 'ave forgotten our manners."

"That's all well and good; but this one," Landis pointed at the man with the broken arm, "has to apologize." The man held his injured arm, his face a mask of pain and anger. "If he doesn't, none of you are going to walk out of here."

Gritting his teeth against the pain, the sailor made his apologies to each of the barmaids, to the owner, and finally to the man who broke his wrist. The owner of the bar and his wenches watched as the sailors walked off with their injured brother in tow. Landis took a healthy draught of his beer, watching the others with amusement. Violence is fascinating to those who are incapable of it themselves. When the sailors were out of sight, everyone returned to their duties and Carmen approached her savior.

"You made that look easy, usually these pirates give us a hard time till dawn."

"It was easy," he said confidently. "Having numbers is always an advantage, but to go around bullying people, you have to have at least *some* skill." He drank from his mug, "They're just lucky that being around you has put me into such a relaxed state."

"Well, don't relax too much," she said coyly. "Your real exertions are still to come."

Chapter 3: The Traders

Genia dismounted her horse and handed the reigns to an attendant. She began to climb the stone steps that led to the Goldport Trade House. After her father passed, she inherited the King Trading Company, part of the West Plains Trading Consortium. She was the youngest Master Trader in the consortium and did everything that she could to let others know that she was a serious businessman and was not to be taken lightly. Genia wore her dirty blonde hair short, cut close around the ears. Around her wrist, she wore a white gold band that showed her to be an upper-class person of Tebron. Her jacket was of the finest deerskin, and she wore a bright red silk shirt over comfortable, dark brown cotton pants. In all, she exuded confidence and wealth, exactly what she was going for. A dagger was always at her waist; but like all traders of her stature, she always had at least one security guard at her side. Per custom, the man known only as 'Naoka' walked behind and to her left. He was balding, six and a half feet tall, with light leather armor and both a long sword and a short sword. He almost never spoke, his ugly face looked like an amateur's attempt at sculpting a bust.

When she reached the top of the stairs, the guards pulled back their long pikes and the man on the right opened the door for her, all without saying a word. She was well known here, and both she and her bodyguard were welcome.

"Naoka," she said turning to her man, "eat, then come back for me here in an hour or so," she commanded. The giant man just bowed and went towards the kitchen.

Red Apna looked up from his books when the stylish young woman entered. Around him were several of the other members of the Limurca Trade Federation. They were all fifty to sixty years of age and wore only the finest suits. Red wore a white tunic and black pants; he had the equivalent of a normal person's yearly income on several of his fingers. He wore spectacles, which were thought by some to be a novelty. It was very difficult to find a craftsman able to manufacture them, and of course, they cost a small fortune. The others were not quite so ostentatious, but they too were visibly men of wealth. Setting down his pen, Red leaned back with a pleasant smile. She fully expected them to be condescending; they had made an offer for her firm before her father's body had even been put in the ground.

"Very well-done Madam King. I hear that your precautions were well founded and that for the first time in a long time, our shipment arrived at port without loss." The others clapped in approval.

"Yes, gentlemen, they were very predictable. This allowed us to deal with them without significant loss to the men that I hired," she said with a smug grin.

"Their leader got away, is that true?" he asked.

"You ask me questions that you already know the answers to? Don't I deserve better than that?"

"I didn't mean to offend you. Yes, I have been told that this Era Rutendo character melted into the woods as soon as he saw that he no longer had the advantage," he said. Red picked up a form from a basket on the corner of his large wooden desk. "This is the bill for security. Certainly, cheaper than losing a shipment, but still, that many men were very expensive."

"What do you propose I do to ensure the safety of the goods that I'm shipping? The Iron Road is the fastest way to conduct trade, but criminals know this too. This was a success, gentlemen!" she replied testily.

"Absolutely. Just to be clear, this added cost comes directly off the top. Our profit is reduced coin for coin by this expense, a cost that should not be ours to bear."

"If it's not our cost to bear, then we increase our prices."

"This attack happened in Tebron, in the lands controlled by House Sarutendo. We pay them taxes…"

"I, pay them taxes," she cut in.

"Very well, you pay them taxes; but regardless, they are responsible for the safety of the citizens and businesses that support them, and allow them to live in a well-furnished castle, with unlimited wine and food."

"So, you want me to approach my king and ask him to foot the bill for security on export shipments?" she asked, not fully believing what she was being asked to do.

"Well, yes. Or he could supply the men next time from his personal guards," he said smiling. She shook her head and left without another word.

"Genia!" he called after her. "I will be at the docks tomorrow in the afternoon to take inventory and sign for the shipment." She ignored him and continued walking.

Genia and Naoka were walking down the boardwalk by the docks. The waves rolled in lazily, and the sky was getting dark. She was ready for a steak and a pint. They were about to step into an inn when something caught her eye. Far down the boardwalk, near the warehouse where she had deposited her goods, was a familiar figure. A man with wild hair, a scraggly beard and mustache. She squinted to see better in the dying light... yes, it was him. She waved at her companion, and they walked in his direction.

Even at this hour, there were dozens of sailors and merchants going back and forth. Loading and unloading ships with giant wooden cranes, the ropes being pulled by oxen or horses. Women of both repute and ill repute walked here and there, homeless children ran about looking for things to steal, and drunks stumbled around looking for a place to lay their heads till the sun came up again. One side was full of docks and mighty sailing ships, the other side was lined with warehouses, taverns, inns, various trade shops, and even a brothel or two. Genia and Naoka stayed in the shadows of the buildings, and despite their odd appearance, they were able to get close to the Trade Federation's warehouse without being noticed. When they were close enough, she was able to make a positive identification. It was indeed who she thought it to be. The highwayman, Era Rutendo.

Her first instinct was to have Naoka eviscerate him. She liked that idea very much. Reason won out though, and she decided to watch him to see what he was up to. She couldn't quite make out his words, but she could see that he was not alone. In fact, he was barking orders at a crew of what looked to be about twenty men. He had the front door of her warehouse open; she could see the lock hanging from the door, it looked as if it had been opened with a key and not by force. Then men formed a line, carrying boxes and bales from her warehouse to another warehouse a couple of hundred yards down the boardwalk. They were very efficient, soon they had cleaned out what she determined to be every bit of the freight that she had risked life and limb to deliver safely.

Her anger had never been this intense in all her life, and it took every bit of her energy to walk away without causing a scene. That would just get her and Naoka killed, and they would still have her property. She was known for always paying her debts. That also meant that when she was wronged, she would do whatever was necessary to be made whole. She needed time to relax and think, she had until the next afternoon to do something. She collected Naoka and they headed back the way from which they came. When they were far from the warehouses, they approached a seaside tavern. Four pirates almost fell out of the place and made a straight line for their ship. The place only had a few customers, and otherwise had a friendly look to it. They walked in and made themselves at home. Genia found a well-lit table near the bar, and Naoka sat by himself in the darkest corner.

"Miss, a warm pint, and your best cut of beef. Keep it bloody, and some roasted potatoes too," she said to the barmaid. She looked the woman up and down as she left to get her food and drink. Her stare seemed a little too long for just curiosity. When she turned back, a sweaty mercenary type was looking at her with an amused expression. She was thinking of snapping at him, then the most beautiful creature she had seen in a long time came with a drink for the two of them. Because of her wealth and position, she was not ashamed to stare where most people would be self-conscious. Getting up, she walked over to the table that seemed to dominate the middle of the room. Coming withing a few feet, she looked the man over. He was handsome and exuded confidence and was neither impressed by her manner nor her apparent station in society.

"I would like to join you," she stated, looking them over from head to toe.

"Well…," he said looking her in the eyes, "I've had enough of fighting with the locals, so please, have a seat." He indicated an empty chair across from himself and Carmen. "Landis Stone and this lovely creature is Carmen."

"Nice to meet you. Genia King. I'm not a local, I'm here on business from Tebron." She took a seat. "Those pirates that just left here were looking worse for wear. You're doing?"

"They wanted my company without my consent. I pick and choose who gets to spend time with me," Carmen answered. "Thank the gods that my brave warrior was here to protect my honor!" she said, placing a delicate kiss on his cheek.

"You bested all four of them? By yourself?" Genia asked.

"Bested?" Carmen exclaimed. "They all had long, wicked knives, and my man was completely unarmed! He never even thought to reach for his sword."

"True, there were four of them, but they were clearly not disciplined fighters, I don't give a second thought to drunken fools," he said trying to sound nonchalant.

"It might be fate that we've met tonight. I just found out that my business partners are stealing from me. Tomorrow they'll tell me how my warehouse was broken into and that I should bear the financial loss," she said, contempt thick in her voice. "The highwayman that attempted to steal my cargo in transit was supervising a whole team of thieves. I need to turn this around. My partners are coming tomorrow to take legal possession of my shipment, so technically, it's still my responsibility till they sign for it."

"You must be someone important. Quite a large fellow you have there," he said, nodding in the direction of Naoka.

"I'm a Master Trader. If someone ever wanted to try and take me prisoner, they could ask for quite a bit of money from my company. It's cheaper to have Naoka there to prevent my capture in the first place." She waved for a drink from the other barmaid. "So, what say you, Landis Stone? Are your services for hire, and can I trust you with my life, and more importantly, with my goods?"

"I have to go fish my brother out of jail down in Empire City... but it might do him good to spend an extra day or two in jail. When I take an assignment, I always complete it to my employer's satisfaction. I can't be bought, and when the mission is over, I'm on my way." He gave her his wide, toothy smile. "Your situation doesn't sound beyond my abilities. In fact, I think I may have just the plan to solve your problem." He took a deep draught of his brew.

"I'm assuming that you don't come cheap, but I'll make sure that you earn every coin," she said giving Carmen another once over.

"If you don't mind my saying, I saw the way you looked at Rowena." He nodded toward the barmaid who was serving some new customers. "And then again at my friend Carmen here." He started cutting into his steak, "I have already had to defend her honor once this evening. I hope it won't come to that." His tone was lighthearted but she could see that he was serious.

Genia looked at them both, evaluating the options. She was a master at making deals and finding the middle ground. "I would never try to take your company from you good sir; but... perhaps you 'both' might like some company, this evening." She sat there smiling, letting the offer hang in the air.

Landis put a bite of steak in his mouth while looking over at Carmen, his expression didn't try to sway her either way, he left it up to her. She smiled broadly, taking each of them by the hand.

"I think that I'll like working for you, Mistress King."

Chapter 4: To Catch a Thief

The hotel room was the most luxurious in Goldport; the average person could never imagine such opulence. The morning sun was filtered through floor-length lace curtains. The sky was still light, but the sun would be fully over the horizon in a matter of minutes. The room was engineered so that it would always feel like the air was the perfect temperature.

Genia King stood naked, staring through the curtains at the seaside below and the sea beyond that. She had chosen this room not only for its amenities; but also, for its proximity to her warehouse. She was deep in thought and seemed oblivious to the pair still in her bed. Carmen was fast asleep, the cotton sheets covering her in a haphazard fashion. Landis Stone was marginally awake but kept his eyes closed, and let Genia fully explain her situation. This was by far the most comfortable room that he had ever been in, and he was in no hurry for it to end.

Without turning, Genia spoke in a low voice "I need your help."

Landis knew that she was talking to him. "I don't come cheap," he said, low enough not to wake Carmen. "And last night wasn't a down payment."

She turned around, the morning light filling the room, making her pale skin almost shimmer. She strolled over to the edge of the bed and sat lightly. The fact that the three of them had been tied in exquisite knots a few hours earlier didn't factor into her current dilemma.

"I have to get my goods back." She looked at him, anger beginning to rise again, "Business is business, and I can afford to lose one here or there; but they think they can steal from me and then get me to replace everything?" She looked Landis in the eyes. "I don't know you very well, in fact, not at all; but I think you can understand that it's the principle as much as anything."

He thought for a moment, "I am a whore in the truest sense of the word. I can be bought, my affections, my loyalty..." He sat up and looked at her "but once I accept a job, no amount of money or... temptation of any kind, can make me betray my employer." They sat quietly for a moment or two, he placed a loving hand on Carmen's thigh. "Pay my price, and I'll be your man till the job is completed to your satisfaction."

Genia and Landis were in a bakery, looking out the window at the front of the warehouse where her goods had been moved. There was a pair of large and well-armed guards standing in front of the place. It was going on lunchtime and Genia was starting to get nervous.

"We need to move, the Trade Federation will be here soon, and when they see that my warehouse is empty, that'll be it. I'll be a victim. I like being a victim even less than I like being stolen from," she said anxiously.

"Not to worry," he said with a hand on her shoulder. "I have a plan that I think will work out just fine." He paused for effect, "if not, you owe me nothing."

Landis had his winter jacket on, it covered him from neck to ankle and hid his armor and weapons. He approached the warehouse with a drunken stagger. He lurched towards the water for a few yards, then tacked back onto the boardwalk. He finally lurched towards the guards who were none too happy to have a large drunk to deal with. They tried to push him away, but he staggered back, then again fell into their arms. The smaller of the two pulled out his short sword to make a point. Big mistake.

Landis looked around and saw that no one was near and that no one was paying attention to his drunk act. Lighting fast, he punched the man on the chin, then he grabbed the arm holding the short sword, and twisted. The sword fell, and so did the man. The larger of the two tried to grapple with him; again, big mistake. Landis placed a perfectly aimed liver punch that brought the big man to his knees. He cocked his fist and waited for the perfect angle and when he punched, it was faster than the crack of a whip. With a little effort, he dragged the men into the warehouse and tied them up. Inside the warehouse was a large open area where trade goods were stored. There were offices on the upper level at the back of the building, but the front was exclusively set aside for storage.

Walking cautiously, he heard a couple of people talking towards the back of the warehouse. They were at the bottom of the stairs discussing who knows what and not actively looking out for intruders. He peered around a large stack of crates to see a cluster of five men, one of them had crazy hair and he wore too much jewelry. Landis pulled a coin out of his pocket and launched it at the opposite end of the room. The sound of metal striking wood crates and stone flooring got their attention. The one with the wild hair started giving hand signals, and three of them darted off in the direction where the coin landed, drawing their weapons as they ran.

When the sound of running feet had faded, Landis stepped out into the open, not more than fifty feet from Era Rutendo. The Highwayman looked up at the lone figure, scanned for his backup, then smiled. His trademark wide grin was meant to encourage his men and to frighten his enemies. Today it did neither.

"Get him!" Rutendo screamed at his last accomplice while running to join his other men. The man pulled out his sword and started swinging it in a wild, menacing manner. He was well over six-foot tall and had broad shoulders. His beard was spiked at the bottom with beads worked onto the spikes. All of that, along with his breath was probably enough to scare away most opponents, but not so with Landis. When the thug swung, his aim went too high, too low, too far to the left, too far to the right. Landis waited for the moment when he was thrusting and leaning too far forward and stepped to the side so that he could bring his razor-sharp blade down across both of his arms. His sword cut through both wrists and dropped them along with the sword they were holding to the dusty warehouse floor. He cried out in agony till a straight thrust pierced his heart.

Pushing past the corpse, Landis went off to find the Highwayman and his remaining crew. They were either too surprised or too stupid to try and be quiet. He followed the sounds of banging and shuffling feet till he found them trying to open the side door. A shorter, bald man had his back to Landis, desperately trying to work the lock on the door. Landis pulled his short sword and threw it hard enough that it passed through the man and embedded in the wooden door. Era Rutendo pushed the others in front of himself while bargaining at the same time.

"Who are you, friend? Why do you harm peaceful traders?" Era asked.

Landis lunged forward like a viper attacking and skewered one of the men guarding the Highwayman. "I know that you're a thief. You failed to steal these goods on the road, so now you're trying to fulfill your contract here in town." He blocked a few strikes from the last man. Landis looked at his opponent, a tall skinny fellow with dirty blonde hair and poor complexion. The man was slightly better than a common cutpurse; not anywhere in the same league as a professional sellsword. He wondered why the man would stand here, toe to toe, both of them knowing how it would end. Landis parried a few more attacks, then with a minimum effort, he thrust his sword into the man's throat. The thief's eyes bulged, and he dropped his weapon. He reflexively reached for the slice in his throat, though it became clear that he knew he was mortally wounded. He slowly fell forward onto his face, so that there was now no one between Era Rutendo and Landis Stone.

"You're coming with me," he said, his voice making it clear that there were no alternatives.

"Lead the way, ya lousy cutthroat!" Era spewed.

Landis cracked him violently on the top of the head with the flat of his sword. The man crumbled unconscious to the floor. Landis tied a rope around his boot and dragged him to the far entrance where Genia was waiting.

Cool water splashed Era's face. The shock of it pulled him out of his delirium. Looking around, he saw that he was in the back office of what he assumed was a trading company. He was dumped unceremoniously in front of a short-haired woman, smartly dressed in white clothes, tailored, tasteful, and expensive. She looked very familiar. Behind her was the lout that had knocked him out and killed his crew. In the corner was her bodyguard, quiet and always watchful.

"You again! You don't seem to know how this is supposed to go," he said to Genia.

"Perhaps I don't," she said. She walked over to a cabinet and went for a crystal bottle, pulled out the stopper, and poured some of the honey-colored liquid into a crystal glass. Era looked longingly at the beverage, but she only served herself, not offering it to anyone else. "You're alive so that you can tell me how things are supposed to go. I know you're the puppet, and I need to know who pulls your strings."

"More accurately, Miss, we are both puppets in this production." He sniffed and nodded at the glass in her hand. She ignored him and continued her interrogation. "I have my suspicions, but who precisely hired you to raid my supply train?"

"If I say anything, my life is over Miss, you must understand that!"

"This specialist behind me?" She hooked her thumb in Landis' direction. "I sent him to the warehouse knowing that there were five of you in there. He came out with you in tow in just a few minutes, and he didn't look even a bit tired." She crouched so that their eyes were now only a few inches away. "Tell me the answers to all of my questions, without delay or obfuscation, and maybe I won't ask him to skin you to make me a winter jacket."

Era looked miserable; his ever-present smile was no longer present. He thought for a moment, then his body language became one of surrender. "Apna, it was that trader Red Apna, with the Limurca Group."

"As I expected," she said calmly. She pulled up a chair so that they were in close proximity, almost like he was an invited guest. "I have a list of things to ask. If you cooperate, I'll consider letting you live." Era was truly unhappy now, his head down without the power to look up, he just nodded in agreement.

Chapter 5: It's Just Business

The carriage pulled up in front of a warehouse that was in a long line of warehouses. A large bodyguard exited the vehicle, followed by his charge, Red Apna. Even though he was spotless, he still felt the need to dust himself off. Looking around, he was obviously trying to find someone. He walked up to the door of the warehouse to find that the door was fine, but the lock had been destroyed. Pulling on the handle, he was able to walk inside without anyone or anything to stop him. The inside of the warehouse was empty, completely empty. No one was around, so he felt at ease to break out his most lascivious smile. Putting on his concerned face, he turned and walked back outside.

Coming down the avenue was Genia King, looking unconcerned and handsome as ever. She was flanked by a large man who carried himself like a swordsman of some skill, and another man who was just plain huge. Red waited for Genia and her partners to come close enough to speak. He maintained his dour look, and it bothered him that she still seemed quite content.

"Mistress King, so sorry to be meeting with you under such circumstances," he said while nodding at the door of the warehouse. "It seems that you've been cleaned out." In his most fatherly tone. "I saw the broken lock and thought it best to have a look. Not only are all the products that you transported from your recent supply run gone, but they seem to have gotten the items that you keep in emergency inventory."

"Is that so?" she asked gaily, "I just looked, a few minutes ago, and everything seems to be in order."

"Genia, I know that you are concerned about not having the capital to cover such a loss, but you must grow up and face reality. You've been robbed, and you have a commitment to the trade group that you will not be able to meet." He was in full scolding mode. "It's more than a breach of contract young lady, you will have to go before the board." He stepped a bit closer, tempting the giant behind her to make a move. "They will be fully within their rights to revoke your charter. Your protected markets will be divvied up amongst the other members." He had the slightest hint of a smile on his lips.

"That would be quite a calamity! We should check together to see which of us is correct," she said calmly. He turned towards the warehouse, while she turned to head down the boardwalk.

"My dear, your warehouse is right here!" He spoke to her like she was a child.

"No Red, my warehouse is a few buildings this way. See that sign?" She pointed to the number painted on a board that was mounted high above the door. The sign had the number '7' printed on it. "My warehouse is number '3', not '7', you silly man!" She led them all a couple of hundred feet down the road till they were in front of another warehouse that had a sign with the number '3' nailed above its door. "See, just like my charter says, I have warehouse number '3'. Let's look inside. She pulled out her key that hung from a long iron chain. It of course fit the lock and let her in easily. She walked in followed by the rest.

The warehouse was stuffed to the rafters with crates, barrels, and finished goods. "Naoka, please hand me a torch." The giant pulled a torch from a wall cradle and got it lit. She took the torch and led them down an aisle at random, putting the light close to a crate. The crate was marked with a stylized crown. "See!" she said. "This crate bears my mark! In fact, every crate in this building has my mark. I will have to redo my inventory though. It almost seems like there are a couple hundred more crates than I remember having," she laughed. "What do you expect, I'm just a girl, right?"

"This is impossible!" Red sputtered. "This is not your warehouse. Your warehouse was robbed, you are liable!" His face was turning beet red.

"Listen here Red!" she said, no longer using her friendly female tones. "This building is marked with the number "3" my paperwork all says building "3" All my stock is intact, marked with my seal." She got in his face. "I may have been born at night, but it wasn't last night. When we go before the board in a couple of hours, you will verify that King Trading is in full compliance with our obligations." He stood fuming quietly to himself, then turned and walked back to his carriage.

"Red!" she yelled after he had gone a dozen feet. He turned, "If you are thinking of tracking down and punishing that idiot Era Rutendo, start looking at the bottom of the bay." She looked in the direction of the sea. He looked horrified, then turned and walked quickly back to his cab.

Chapter 6: Genia King

Crossbow bolts easily took out the guards at the front of the property, and only the sound of their bodies hitting the ground marked their passing. The swarm of five black-clad figures double-checked that the guards were dead, opened the gate and entered silently. A long path stretched from the gate to the front of the house; there were fruit trees on either side, and the occasional oil lamp to light the way. The men kept to the shadows and arrived at the house without being noticed. Another guard stationed in front of the main entrance also fell to the nearly silent swish of a metal-tipped wooden bolt. The area around the porch and front door was well-lit and made the men stop to assess the situation. Odds were that they could enter the home through the front entrance and overcome any resistance that might lie inside but being so bold was opposite their nature. Instead, they circled around to find a more discreet way in.

It was late in the evening, so the staff was already asleep. They pried their way into a back window by the kitchen, then worked their way through the house. They spread out but were always within whispering distance of each other. They found the chef in his private room, the maids in a room that they shared, and the gardener and butler, each in his own room. They were not the reason for being there, but professionals never left any loose threads. Each of the staff got a cold, blackened steel blade to the temple or back of the neck. On the second floor, the upstairs maid met the same fate as the servants below. Last was the master bedroom. The door wasn't locked, so three of them slipped in while the others remained on watch without. In the bed was the master of the house, and president of one of the world's larger trading companies. The assassins had been so efficient that they had killed everyone in the home, and still, the master slept.

Next to her was a young man who was eighteen, give or take a year. The young man slept on his stomach, his face to the side, he was completely naked under a thin silk sheet. The man on that side of the bed circled around till he could grab a handful of the messy blonde hair. He put his knee on the boy's back and pulled back hard on the boy's hair. The boy let out a pained scream that instantly woke Genia. She opened her eyes and looked at her lover, just as the assassin dragged his blackened dagger across the boy's throat, silencing his screams.

Genia was going to call out, but a gloved hand covered her mouth. One of the invaders got down close to her so that she could look her in the eyes. The assassin was a woman of above-average height, the only part of her visible was her eyes. A black cloth covered her mouth and forehead, a hood over that. She was covered head to toe in black leather armor, a short sword at her side, several daggers in her belt, and a short crossbow strapped to her back. She put her index finger to her mouth in the universal sign for 'be silent'. When she was sure that she had Genia's undivided attention, she spoke.

"Genia King, this is your only warning. Papers will come by messenger in two days, be prepared to sign them. Do not run away, do not go to the constable, and don't think that there is any room for negotiation. If you fail in any of these demands, you will go to sleep one night, and simply never wake up. Do you understand?"

Genia was doing her best to get her heart to slow to a normal pace. She had a hard time breathing, but after a few moments, she was able to gain control, "I understand."

The woman behind the mask adjusted the brass knuckles on her hand, then gave Genia a single punch to the side of her head. When Genia woke up, hours had passed and the dead boy in her bed had long ago stopped bleeding and was now turning cold. She went from room to room to see what crimes had been committed against her household. Rage filled her, her eyes turned red as the anger she felt grew and grew. There are some people in life who take their beatings like a man. Genia King was no man.

Shaken and afraid, she stood before her king, Imanol Sarutendo. Genia King was well known to her lord; her business had helped the wealthy nation and she had personally paid a small fortune in taxes over the years. Now she needed the crown's protection.

"Sire," she pleaded, "my home was invaded, my guards and every member of my staff were murdered last night. The Trade Federation wants me to sign away my interest in my family's company. I have always supported you, my lord, please intercede on my behalf!"

Sarutendo was a tall man with a dark complexion, black hair, and a long tapered beard. He was a brooding and unpleasant man under normal circumstances, a real bastard in almost everyone's eyes. He had no friends to speak of, and he could barely stand the wife that had been arranged for him. He liked no one, and no one liked him, and he was fine with that. He was an honorable man, in that when he made a promise, he stuck to it, but he was not one to go over and above what was required of him.

"I of course value you as a loyal subject, Lady King, but I'm not sure what it is that you are asking of me. If you want extra security, I can lend you a few of my men… for a while. I can't take property from the Trade Federation and give it to you, even if I fully believe what you are saying. If you wind up signing papers giving away your company, there is really nothing that I can do."

"If I must sign away ownership of the company, and it's obviously under duress, can't you choose not to recognize it? If this type of open lawlessness is allowed, how can anyone in Tebron feel safe?"

"I don't know what you mean, Lady King. I am sorry for your loss, but this type of violence is a very rare thing here, and I am sure that most of my subjects are quite happy."

A salesman knows when the sale has been lost, and this one was never going to happen. Her rage burned, but she was able to maintain her cool till she was well beyond the castle walls. She would surrender her company, but she was young, and fortunes can be made and lost in a heartbeat. One thing was for certain though, her days of playing by the rules were over.

Chapter 7: The Gambler

Empire City was on Rubina's southern coast, a tourist area that attracted people from all over Kronos. Jarrod Stone booked passage on one of the daily carriages that brought vacationers from big cities in the North. They passed through orchards and vineyards that filled the air with their perfume. Oranges, apples, cherries, and even strawberries were on both sides of the road. The city itself was laid out in a circle with the best inns and taverns in the middle.

"Drop you at the closest inn, sir?" the driver asked.

"No, I plan to be the guest of a beautiful woman this evening. Drop me at one of the nicer taverns so I can discover her." Jarrod sat back and waited till they reached the tavern. He carried a single large pack which he lived out of. He was just over six-foot-tall, with shoulder length, light-colored hair, and a clean-shaven chin. He was broad-shouldered, built for action, but only carried a long dagger for protection. He had left home as a young man and never looked back.

"We're here sir," the driver announced.

Jarrod got out, paid the man, and stood there checking out the town that he had heard so much about. There were at least a dozen taverns in sight. There were large inns where things became boisterous at night, the quiet type where a man could reconnect with a wife or lover. There were bars just for men, where you could overdrink and not shame yourself in front of any women. There were bars where you could relax to music, and there were spots where you could be guaranteed to leave with a woman on your arm.

He found an Inn that obviously catered to a more upscale crowd. Going in, he found tradesmen, businessmen, members of influential houses, and even some lesser nobles. Leaving his pack with the doorman, he made his way to the bar. The place was well-lit and smelled of cuts of beef being grilled on the open pit. The floors were sanded wood that had been stained and oiled to a slight sheen. The bar itself was heavy, hewn from a single large log of wood, that was stained and sealed with a shiny waterproof finish. The barman greeted him as he seated himself at the bar. Jarrod ordered himself a drink, then looked around the room for an opportunity. Across the room was a group of young men, all like him, in their mid-twenties. They were laughing and drinking freely and tossing money around like it was nothing special. Two of them were playing with their daggers, getting ready to toss them at a target in the corner. Jarrod walked over with his wide, inviting smile.

"I'm just in time!" he said, walking up to the group. They all stopped their conversation to see what this stranger was talking about. "I haven't seen either of you throw, I just arrived in town today, but I'll wager ten crowns on this fellow." He clapped one of the men on the shoulder. "I don't know why, but putting a wager down makes any activity more enjoyable!" he said heartily. They warmed to him immediately, as everyone did. After hours of drinking and well-told lies, he parted company with them, pockets full of their coins. He had his eye on a lady who appeared to be cultured and far too pretty to be drinking alone. She had noticed him as well, putting a lot of effort into not meeting his gaze. Walking over to her table, he gave her a smile that could easily have been taken as overconfidence in a lesser man. He touched the barmaid's arm as he was sitting.

"Wine please, strong and sweet with a touch of earthiness." He gave her a long appraising look. She smiled coyly, pretending that she didn't love every second of it.

"Jarrod Stone. Nice to make your acquaintance."

"Sierra," she replied. "Nice to meet you." She finished the glass she had been drinking and pushed it to the middle of the table. "You made quite a bit of money over there."

"I would try to impress you by offering to spend some of it on you, but you have your own money, and that sort of thing wouldn't interest you."

"True, and true. I noticed that you play with that knife like a violin, are you a cutthroat, cutpurse, a cut… something?" she laughed at her own joke.

"Tossing knives for sport is but one of my many talents; but I assure you, I only carry a knife for self-defense. I know it's not very auspicious, but I guess you could say that I was a gambler by trade."

"You like playing games?"

"Games of chance. I don't play games with the women in my life."

"So, you're an honorable man?"

"No, not honorable. But I don't lie. Father taught my brother and me to fight, protect women, and to not lie. So no, I don't go looking for trouble. Speaking of trouble." He looked her over with no attempt to hide his lustful evaluation of her body. "What sort of hidden talents do you have?"

"Well…, I could make claims and then do my best to make you believe they're true; but a simple demonstration is always more convincing. After we drink your wine, let's retire to my suite."

"You're a breath of fresh air, my dear."

Jarrod woke up abruptly as someone was pulling at his arm. He opened his eyes to see a maid with a look of terror on her face, doing her best to not only wake him but get him out of bed. Stepping out of bed, he was completely naked; but the maid seemed far too agitated to care. She was picking clothes off the floor and pushing them into his open hands. Quickly as he could, he put on his pants and shirt and was getting ready to put on his boots when the maid started urging him to exit via the window. He looked out, and there was a large bush below the second-story window that was supposed to break his fall. That's when he heard voices in the hall. Male voices. Hoping for the best, he leaped out of the window head-first and tumbled in the air so that he would hit the bush with his back.

Somewhere, in the not-too-far-off distance, he could hear hounds barking. They were hot on a trail, and he was pretty sure that it was him that they were hunting. Hiding behind the bush, he was able to get his boots on. His pack would have to wait for another day. Not seeing anyone, he made a beeline for the nearest section of the perimeter wall. The cottage was part of a larger, very exclusive collection of residences for the rich and powerful. The grounds were meticulously taken care of, and a white plastered wall, about ten feet high, encircled the entire lot. When he reached the fence, he hit it with his foot, stepped up before his boot could slip, and grabbed a hold of the top of the wall. He lifted himself up and over in a graceful vault and was gone.

Jarrod was not a fan of close calls, and this was by far, not his first. He was dusting his hands off and had made it to the road that went around the resort before they found him. He did his best to play innocent, but a lack of concrete proof only helps in court. In the court of public opinion, he was guilty and that was enough in Empire City to get you time in jail.

Chapter 8: Brothers

Why do I always have to bail this guy out? Landis thought to himself. *I bet he took a private carriage to get here, and here I am walking. Again.* He'd been down south before, looking for work. Now he was taking a long detour to get his younger brother out of jail. He was enjoying the fragrant orchards as he walked, almost forgetting how annoyed he was with Jarrod.

"Can I help you?" the magistrate asked. He was old, too old to be a deterrent to crime. It was apparently part of his job to approach strangers. Even ones that looked like they could be dangerous.

"I am here to secure my brother's release from jail."

"You want to break him out of jail?"

"No, why would you think that?"

"You're obviously well-armed. And large." He looked Landis over, sizing him up, "And then there's the problem of your brother being incarcerated for a very serious charge."

"I thought he was just accused of some... dalliance?"

"It's not the crime so much, as it is whom he dallied with."

"Oh," *Why am I not surprised*, he thought to himself. "Is there a bond that I can post? Some way to *legally* get him out?"

"I do not see a crest on your rig. Am I correct in thinking that you are not sworn to some great house already?

"No, I have no master." He knew where this was going.

"Your brother is in serious trouble. Yep, serious trouble." The older man scratched at his scraggly white beard.

"What do you need to be done?"

"It's funny you should ask." His smile didn't hide his exuberance. "There is a merchant family just south of town that is causing a lot of the locals' problems. They're driving out the competition very aggressively and they are using intimidation tactics against many small businesses. They've brought on a lot of new men to enforce their expansion."

"How many are there, and how much force am I allowed to use?"

"Not sure of the exact number, more than ten at last count. On the positive side, there are usually not more than four of them together at any given time."

"And you think that one sword for hire can take on so many?"

"They're dangerous to shopkeepers and business people, but I'm sure they don't have near your level of training. And besides, we're not paying you."

"So, If I do this thing... my brother walks free?"

"Free and clear." He smiled generously.

They rolled into the potters like they owned the place, two men and a woman who took the lead. She dressed like a man, a ruffian with dirty low boots, brown pants, and off white shirt. In her leather vest, she wore a pair of crude steel knives. Strolling up to the counter, she smiled at the proprietor with her stained teeth and unkempt brown hair that fell to her shoulders.

"I'm Lola with House Bevin and I've come to collect your payment," she said confidently.

The owner was a short man with thinning gray hair and a slight paunch. He looked flustered as she stared him down. Landis came out from a back room, carrying a tray of newly fired bowls. The thugs looked at him and their looks of confidence faded.

"Payment? Payment for what?" Landis asked.

"Who is this?" she asked, pulling her knife, and pointing it at Landis. The owner again looked flustered and stumbled over his words.

"Not to worry uncle, I'll speak with these people." He smiled at the older man. "This is a business, we sell crockery. Are you a supplier of materials?"

"Listen here, you big slab of beef. House Bevin provides a valuable service to all the shops here in Empire City. We provide protection against unsavory types, and for that, they are required to pay a fee. We collect weekly."

"I'm not worried about unsavory types, neither is my uncle here." He smiled widely at the female thug, "We'll not be needing your service, so please move along."

She slammed the tray he was carrying, sending the pots flying. They smashed on the ground as everyone stood there watching. She held her knife out, holding it near Landis in a threatening manner. He grabbed her wrist and pulled the knife from her grasp.

"See, we don't need your help." He looked at the knife. "I'll be keeping this. You can't be trusted with a weapon."

Pulling out her other knife, she screamed with a bird-like screech and attacked. She swung her blade around wildly, though her skill was so poor that she didn't come close to connecting.

The other thugs stood dumbfounded, allowing her to make a fool of herself.

"Help me!" Lola screeched as Landis took away her other knife. "Teach this nobody a lesson!" The two men rushed into corral Landis and were met with fists. He had a couple more vases nearby that he crashed on the heads of the male thugs. The woman kept sputtering and urging her companions on.

"I don't strike women, but you two have no such protections." He went back to pounding them men with his large, calloused fists. For being in the business of intimidation, they were not very good fighters. When they were all sufficiently humbled, he spoke.

"This has been fun, but we have work to do. Please leave now before I lose my temper."

The men picked themselves up from the ground, bleeding from the nose and covered in bruises. The woman wanted more, but her companions dragged her out.

"We'll be back!" she yelled, "You'll pay for this!"

"Do you think they'll be back?" The store owner asked after they had gone.

"For sure, but I'll be here to take care of you." He looked at the mess. "Good thing you had all these damaged pots. I like the sound it makes when you smash it on someone's head."

Empire City was known for its selection of inns and taverns. Several choices for every stratum of society, from the day laborers to the rich and famous. The high-end establishments had plenty of their own security and were run by people with considerable resources. The lower-class bars were frequented by people with nothing to steal. Taverns for the middle class were ripe targets for organized crime. With a few hours of investigation, Landis had narrowed down his target to about three taverns. The sun had just gone down and at the second of the taverns, he found what he was looking for.

"Everyone, your attention please!" A twenty-something man said above the din of the evening crowd. "We are collecting for House Bevin tonight. My mates will be walking around with a satchel, please put your coins and baubles in the kitty. I am counting on you to remain peaceful." Four men and the female thug Lola, started circulating around the room, each holding out a large canvas bag.

Still no swords or armor? They are really relying on the sheep to roll over without a fight. Landis thought. Much to his dismay, everyone in the common room started handing over their valuables. Half the room had given over their goods when one of the thugs approached Landis. He held out his bag expectantly, then shook it impatiently when the tall patron made no move to contribute.

"Give it up, guv'nor!" he demanded.

"No."

"What you mean *no*?"

"I *mean*, I work hard for my money, and I have no reason to give it to the likes of you."

"We got a rebel here!" he yelled to his accomplices. He held the bag with one hand while pulling out a long knife with the other. He held the knife out trying to be threatening, but it looked more like he was trying to create distance between them. Landis had taken his weapon just as the others were coming over. When Lola saw him, she exploded in a fit of anger.

"This is the guy! The potter's nephew who assaulted us."

"He doesn't look like a potter," one of the thugs said.

"Let's teach him a lesson," another thug added. As one, they all reached for Landis, knives outstretched. He easily blocked their clumsy attacks, slicing at a couple of forearms and kicking a couple of them. Within seconds, all were pulling themselves off the ground and licking their wounds.

"This is what you're afraid of?" he said to the other patrons. "As you can see, they're not so tough. You outnumber them twenty to one. Let them know how you feel about their intimidation and theft of your hard-earned assets."

The crowd turned ugly in a flash. They descended on the thugs, pummeling them with fists, boots, and even heavy wooden mugs. After several minutes of beatings, Landis had to save the thugs from certain death. The crowd was full of adrenaline and had the rush that one gets from a confrontation. With help from a few good-sized men, Landis dragged the thugs the few blocks to the stockade. The constable accepted them with a huge smile and locked them away to await justice.

Landis was eating at an outdoor café when the ground began to shake. Not only did the ground shake, but he also felt like the air itself was vibrating. The light of the sun dimmed, flashed, and then returned to normal. He realized that he had stopped breathing and sucked in a lung full of air. He thought to himself, *the gods must be fighting, perhaps they're ready to punish us and destroy all of Xoran!*

Everyone around was having the same reaction. The waitress was on her knees, clutching at her throat. Other diners were looking around with panicked stares and were picking up their mugs and plates. A passing horse was whinnying loudly and had reared up on its hind legs. A handful of birds had fallen out of the sky and were trying to pick themselves up off the dusty street. And just like that, it was over. *Whatever just happened, I can't help feeling like something important has just occurred. Maybe I'll never know exactly what just happened.*

Landis woke to the sound of someone pounding on his door. *Who the hell is banging on my door in the middle of the night?* He was dressed only in his night pants, but he held his sword as he opened the door. The son of the inn owner was standing in the hallway, out of breath and looking distressed.

"Come right away, sir! The Bevins clan is breaking their men out!"

Landis nodded and picked up his clothes and started dressing. *This is coming to a head faster than I thought. Thank goodness. It's time to get out of here and start making some money again.* He thought as he quickly donned his underclothes, and armor, and then strapped on his weapons.

The jail was on fire and a bucket brigade had formed to try and put it out. Between the townsmen and the conflagration stood a dozen armed men, four of whom wore armor, not unlike Landis'. The crowd was yelling and demanding access, so they could not only put the fire out, but also to keep it from burning down the rest of the town.

Landis approached the wall of men, his self-confidence lending spine to the men who fell in behind him. When the mercenaries saw him, they ignored the rest of the townspeople. Professional fighters recognized each other. It had been a few days since the people revolted against the Bevins in the tavern. The four men leading this jailbreak had clearly been brought in from out of town to help solidify House Bevin's hold on Empire City. He had tried to take it easy on the low-level gangsters, but these were professionals, and they would surely not take it easy on him.

"I know you men were hired to stir things up a bit, but let me give you the opportunity to leave, with your lives."

"That's big talk from a single sellsword. We are four, along with a dozen men from House Bevin," one of the mercenaries said confidently. He was a dark-skinned man of forty, with armor that seemed to have been repaired multiple times.

"Last chance," he said. "I don't want to kill you, brothers."

They charged, feeling confident in their superiority. A rain of fruit and vegetables pelted them from the hundreds of shop owners and tradesmen. They were distracted long enough for Landis to strike first. The man who spoke up, who seemed to have the most experience, was the first to die. Landis moved forward as the rain of produce struck the mercenaries, and skewered the speaker, through and through. The man died instantly. Landis dispatched another of the sellswords before he knew what was going on. The townspeople advanced, some pelting the Bevins' with produce and others striking them with clubs and cudgels.

Landis lifted his shield to deflect strikes from the two remaining professional fighters. He thrust his sword but was blocked. Back and forth, he parried with the two, looking for any edge. They were competent fighters, bearing the scars of many encounters. Just being alive and having a few years on you is a testament to either your luck or your skill. He was a few inches and twenty pounds heavier than either of the other men, and he used it to his advantage. Using his shield like a battering ram, he knocked both men back on their heels and attacked. He disarmed the man on his right, then slapped the other viciously with the flat of his blade. The unarmed man dived for his sword, moving faster than Landis had anticipated. He came up and slashed at Landis' chest, ripping through his tabard. He smashed the other fighter again with his sword, knocking him unconscious. The last man came at Landis with renewed vigor, pounding away at him, connecting with his shield and his sword. The blows came fast and furious, and Landis found himself hopelessly on the defense.

"They're not paying you enough," Landis said, trying to hold his ground.

"You don't know how much they're paying me," he replied.

"No matter how much it is, it's not enough. You're good, but I'm better." He dropped on his back and hacked at the mercenary with a horizontal slash. He didn't get past the leg armor, but it was a painful strike. He kicked at the knee and the man went down hard. From his back, he stabbed through the man's neck. By the time he got to his feet, he looked around to see that the action was over. The townspeople had risen up and dealt harshly with the Bevin family's hired muscle.

"You've dealt the Bevin crime cartel a huge blow, but they have money, they can recover," the constable said. He was cut and bleeding and his left arm was set into a sling. "We need to eliminate them. Kill every last one so that they can't come back and threaten the people of this town."

Landis looked at him for a few long moments, "I'm a sword for hire, not an assassin." Landis cleaned his blade and returned his sword to its scabbard. "Free my brother. You can go collect the Bevins family on your own."

"We hired you for a job. Your brother will be free when the job is completely done."

"I completed the job. The extortion crew is dead or in jail. You saw me defeat four other sellswords. Do you really want to get on *my* bad side?"

Chapter 9: The Twilight Forest

The Twilight Forest was the largest forest in all of Kronos and it straddled the border between the countries of Preston and Jaga-Koba. It was called the Twilight Forest because, even on the brightest of days, when you were deep inside, it always looked like the sun was setting. Besides being dark, it gave off a negative energy that caused most people to take an extra day or two to go around. If one only ventured into the forest for a few hundred feet, they could usually find their way out; but history was full of stories of those who had entered, traveled too far in, and were never seen again.

Near the center of the forest was a mighty tree, perhaps the tallest in all of Xoran. It was a tree that had never been seen by any man that lived to tell about it. The bark was black and wet, and it smelled of moss, mold, and death. The tree's lowest branches were far up, lost in the forest canopy. What could be seen from the ground was a massive trunk, easily as big around as a king's tent. There were the usual creatures in the forest, deer, squirrels, birds, and lizards; but there were also unusual creatures, those that were thought by many to be extinct. None of the creatures, no matter how docile or how dangerous would approach the tree.

No one was present to feel the wave of energy that passed through the forest. The ground shook, the air vibrated and it grew even darker for several minutes before things returned to normal. The trunk of the tree cracked, and the crack started spreading. The base of the tree just below ground level started to rip upward. It opened like a wound received in battle, three feet wide and about eight feet up from the ground. Blood-colored sap ran from the gaping wound, pouring out onto the moss-covered earth. From the void came an old woman that seemed not quite human. She emerged from the prison of the mighty tree where she had been trapped for a dozen lifetimes. She climbed out slowly, like a person waking from a long sleep.

She was ancient and her vast age showed in the many wrinkles on her face. Her body had skin, but almost no flesh beneath. Her bony old fingers clawed at her eyes, clearing away the thick muck that coated every inch of her. When she could see it again, she looked around at her surroundings, and a nearly toothless smile broke on her wretched face. The crone remembered Xoran as it used to be hundreds of years ago. The world had been wild and untamed. The old gods had grown tired of the beasts that filled their creation and longed for a change. They spawned the seven races and gave them dominion over the land. She had been a creature of the old world, and when it was time to end the 'age of magic', she was no longer welcome. For centuries she had been in a dream state, her body held in a prison that was protected by an immensely powerful spell of binding. She couldn't sense the old mage that had trapped her, but no matter. She would seek out her sisters, and then she would have her revenge.

Not only could she not sense the mage that had trapped her, but she couldn't feel the presence of her sisters either. They might be on the other side of the continent, or they might be on the other side of the world for all she knew. The old crone sat on a log before a raging fire, soaking in its heat and energy. Closing her eyes, she began chanting the ancient words. Words that had not been spoken aloud for thousands of years. She went into a trance that lasted for hours. The whole night passed, and the sun was starting to rise when she finally finished her conjuring. Despite not feeding it, the fire continued to burn and even grew in intensity till it was blasting her with its heat and threatened to escape the boundaries that she had set for it. The fire was the doorway for her spell of summoning.

The creature walked through the flames, pleased to be in the world of man again, but was indignant that he had been summoned. Demons hated that they could be summoned and be bound into service. Demons see all men, even those that worship them, as being no more significant than the ants beneath their feet. He looked at the crone who brought him to this world of man, this plane without magic. His first instinct was to strike her down and return to his eternal flames, but he couldn't. The same magic that had allowed him to cross worlds, also made him her slave. The only thing that demons hated more than being summoned, was being enslaved by mere mortals.

"Why have you disturbed my reverie... human?" The last of his words clung to his lips like a curse. From his hooved feet to the ram's horns on his head, he stood ten feet to her barely five and his skin was covered in black and red scales. His long, spiked tail waved from side to side as he stood there in the forest, looking down on his new master. He exuded contempt for this world and most especially for the witch that had brought him here.

"You may think that you see a weak human before you but use your senses demon! You should be able to sense that I'm much more than a mere human. This world is called Xoran, created by the old gods. This was once home to every manner of monster. Creatures that men call mythological were common just a few thousand years ago. The Emar, the Telnor, Goran, and Vinkul; all of the ancient races were masters in their own lands. The forests were filled with Elves, Sprites, and Dryads, all the faerie folk. The skies were filled with Griffin, Roc, Harpies, and Dragons." Her eyes shone brightly from the firelight. "All that changed when the gods themselves made war on each other. Magnus, the father of the gods, was very proud of this world. It was his personal creation. He germinated the seven races and split off Xoran into parts, making it safe for his chosen and casting off the supernatural."

"Why do I care about all of this, witch?" the demon asked, plotting her demise.

"I've been held in a trance, buried in the world tree. For centuries I was like an insect stuck in amber; but now I am free. Even in my comatose state, I felt the shudder. There are many worlds existing at the same time, in the same place, overlapping but not touching. They are as ephemeral as a reflection on a still pool of water, as elusive as wisps of smoke. I know not the cause, but the worlds are trying to merge, to become one again. As they reunite, magic will come again to Xoran. With the return of magic, my sisters and I will build our armies and launch an all-out war on the works of the old gods. With demons like you at the head of my army, I will be able to reclaim what should have been mine all along. Xoran will come under my control, and you will be the weapon I use to aid in the destruction of mankind."

"I am no friend of the old gods. If I can destroy what they've made while collecting souls, so much the better." He leaned in to look the crone in the eyes, "Do not forget that I will kill you at the earliest opportunity. I do not like being summoned like some lower demon."

She mixed ingredients into a pot near the fire, "They will fear you, they will fear your physical might, but these 'men' have no idea of the power you possess." She slowly poured a cup of the mixture and offered it to the demon. "Drink," she instructed. "They have no respect for the *old ways*, or for those that walked this land when they were still just clay on Magnus' work bench. There are those that would embrace you and call you 'God'. Men are full of fear and anger, and they need one such as yourself to lead them. There are the thousands of these humans that are cast out by their own kind and shunned. These outcasts will resonate with your promises of power and revenge. They will risk all to follow a charismatic leader that promises them women and power. We will select one of them, a man with a black heart, but enough charisma to get these dregs of society to follow him. You will present yourself as a God and command him to gather a following. I will feed you poisonous words, commands to do the most hideous acts. Our puppet will create chaos from order, and you will have thousands of souls to fill your dominion in hell. As you belong to me, they will belong to you."

"What is in this for you… master?" he said through gritted teeth.

"My god is chaos. I sow the seeds of dissension whenever and wherever I can." She stood painfully, then paced back and forth, staying near the fire. She turned to the demon "You must multiply the chaos. You relish evil and yet it's pandemonium that you seek. I will give you followers who will worship you and help to spread your disease. Unlike the gods that these humans pray to, you will be of flesh and will walk the land." Her eyes burned like coals in a cookfire.

Chapter 10: The Curse

Oscar was desperate. He was a lumberjack by trade, but it seemed that every tree in the world was owned by someone, and gods help you if you are caught on land owned by some damned noble house. They claimed whole countries by divine right, then sold rights to the land. If he had the money to pay for a *license*, he would be working his own land. And why should he be expected to give half of the fruits of his labor to lords and to the Church?

There was talk of a forest, a large and unmapped forest that straddled the lands of Preston and Jaga-Koba. A place where he could conduct his trade without eyes looking over his shoulder, counting the logs he cut, and demanding their share. He took his crew, a dozen good and strong men, to the edge of the Twilight Forest. They stood on the road that led into the far Eastern edge of the forest, the sun itself seemed to avoid the place. It was dark and foreboding, but it also called out to his pioneer spirit. Only a man who was willing to sacrifice his life for riches was worthy to work in a place like this.

His men all stood behind him on the rocky road that was not well traveled. It looked as if no man had taken this road for a generation, and in Oscar's eyes, that was both a warning and a blessing. He needed virgin woods, a forest with dead trees that they could harvest without undo effort. Taking the dead trees was the gravy, felling the live trees that were still a vital part of the forest would be more challenging and time-consuming. No one said anything, though they all shared the same reservations. These woods were practically untouched and there was a reason for that. They didn't want to tempt fate, but they all had mouths to feed and bills to pay. Following their 'Uncle' into the forbidden forest was the price they knew had to be paid.

"Stay together, let's form groups of four men each. For now, we scout for the low-hanging fruit. Count your paces and mark the location of logs on your maps, so that we can recover them easily." The men nodded. "No cutting today. Today is just about marking logs for later." They started walking into the woods, two or three abreast. A mile or so into the woods, they came to a fork. The trail was divided into three paths, one to the left, one to the right, and the third, going on straight.

"I'll take you three," Oscar pointed to three men near him. "Jonah, you take those three and go that way. Scarn, you take the rest and go right," he instructed. They all nodded, and the group split into thirds. For quite a while, they trudged on, still able to hear the other groups off in the distance; but after another half mile, there was a disturbing lack of sound. Without saying anything, all of them felt that something was amiss at the same time. They were following Oscar's lead until he came to a stop. He looked around and seemed confused.

"I would have thought by now that we would see some dead trees, something that we could easily saw and pull out of here."

"Your right," one of his men replied. "Every little branch had a leaf, some are black, but there are no dead leaves, much less, dead trees." The man looked around, "No birds, squirrels, nothin'!" they all stood frozen and just listened. There were no sounds save for a quiet rustling of branches far above.

"This is mighty odd," Oscar commented. "If we can't pull out any trees that are already dead, we might have to cut green ones. If that's the case, we need to start at the forest's edge. The outer edge of the forest has some good trees for lumber." He looked around, "Let's head back." They felt relieved that the boss was ready to lead them back out into the sunlight. This forest felt evil, and being so deep in it, they were all on edge. They allowed their mood to lighten for almost a minute; before they heard a woman's voice.

"Who are these men? These invaders, who trespass where they are not wanted?" The voice was thick with scorn and revulsion. They all turned slowly toward the sound that was now behind them. An old crone stepped out from behind a tree, the largest tree that any of them had ever seen. The ancient woman was covered in black and red slime. Her long white hair was matted with gore. Grime and filth covered every square inch of her thin, wrinkled frame.

"We're just leaving old woman," he said, looking at her in horror.

"You are trespassers!" Her voice cackled when she spoke, "You have wronged us, and now you must pay a price!" She shambled forward till she was only a few feet from the woodsmen. They all towered above her, but they feared her just the same.

"We are sorry for entering your forest without your leave," Oscar said with real contrition in his voice. "We wanted to see if there were dead trees that we could harvest. It helps the forest to remove them, and we'll have a product that we can sell to put food on our tables."

When the old crone smiled, it sent shivers down their spines. Her teeth were ragged and the few that remained were sharp as cat's claws. Her tongue was longer than it should have been, and it darted out like a lizard. She looked at the men and licked her slimy lips. She took a step forward and placed her foul hand on Oscar's forearm. "Too late!" was all she said. Oscar fell to his knees, screaming in pain; he couldn't shake the old woman's grip. "I curse you! From now on, you are Gharenna!" she said to him. The color quickly left his face and hands; his skin took on a corpse-like appearance. The other men didn't need an invitation, they turned and sped down the trail as fast as their feet would allow.

Two-inch-long, razor-sharp fangs ripped at his throat, and his lifeblood sprayed everywhere and splashed on the ferns that covered the forest floor. He landed on his back, just as the creature leaped on top of him. The air was knocked out of his lungs, and he grew dizzy from the lack of blood. The last thing he saw as he lay prostrate on the ground was the creature that nearly killed him bound off down the trail after the others.

The Gharenna was taller than it had been when it had been a man, it stood at about six feet, and weighed in at two hundred and fifty pounds of solid muscle. Six-inch-long, wavy brown fur coved the man-like creature from head to toe. One of the lumberjacks was running through the woods as fast as he could, but the creature dropped to the ground in front of him. It looked vaguely human, but the jaw was long and tapered, like that of a wolf or bear, and the mouth was full of sharp dagger-like teeth. Its yellow eyes were intense, and though they seemed fit for a beast or demon, there was enough humanity left in them that he knew the agent of his demise had once been a man.

The lumberjack had no weapons on him, not even the axe which he usually always carried. This was supposed to be a scouting mission through the woods, and now he was face to face with a savage creature from his worst nightmare. It had once been a man, but the blood-soaked jowls and claws made it seem more like an animal than anything else. The Gharenna leaped and landed on him, jaws snapping, drooling, claws raking his skin, and drawing blood from half a dozen wounds. When the jaws clamped down on the side of his neck, he knew that his life was over. There was no pain, dying was not anything like what he was expecting. He was looking up at the tops of the trees far above, he felt the warm blood flowing down his neck and onto his chest. In that moment, he was calm.

The beast came out of the forest to look up at the setting sun. He stood like a man but hunched over as if with age or pain. The blood on his jowls was drying, and the flesh hanging on his claws was already darkened and turning sour. From behind came another and then others of his kind. They emerged from all along the division where the forest met the plains.

The first beast out sniffed the air and found only his own kind left. As more of the Gharenna emerged from the woods, he became emboldened and let out a spine-chilling howl. The sound was echoed by his brothers, and soon there were a dozen of them. They howled in reply to their leader, the first of their kind, and gathered around him. He stared at them with bloodshot eyes and a furrowed brow. Any trace that he had once been a man was gone. Now they were killing machines, controlled by all new instincts. He howled and barked at them and then turned to the trail before them. He ran mostly on his legs but kept switching to a four-legged running posture for additional speed, as his body was almost parallel to the ground. He looked like an emaciated greyhound as he ran, the bones in his back causing the fur there to stand up where the bones protruded. They formed a pack, following their leader along the edge of the forest. He ran them as fast as they could go, their bent over deformed bodies adapting to this new reality. They ran all night, following the scent of man. When the sun came up again, they buried themselves under logs and roots, piles of leaves, and patches of sod. There they slept and waited for the sun to set again.

Chapter 11: The Demon

He stood in the field and watched his house burn. He was in his late twenties and until minutes ago, had lived with his parents. Now, they were lying in pools of their own blood, inside the house that his father had built thirty years ago. He would have inherited the farmhouse as he had no siblings, but he had no desire to become a farmer. He was an ambitious man, yet he lacked the discipline and work ethic to achieve his lofty goals. His immediate goal was to get out from under his father's heavy thumb. He hated his mother just as much, perhaps even more for letting it happen. He had lost count of the beatings he'd received over the years, though he wouldn't acknowledge that many of them had been deserved. *Am I good for nothing? Well, I killed you and Mother, burned everything that you've created in your entire miserable life.*

He was mesmerized by the flame, it danced across the roof tiles as it quickly consumed his home. He could smell the stench of burning flesh and it didn't both him in the least. He wasn't sure what he would do now, or where he would go, but he felt free for the first time in his life, and it felt... good. He was in a trance and didn't hear the other person approach. A hand landed on his shoulder, bringing him out of his fixation on the fire. He looked around, then upward at one of the most beautiful faces that he'd ever seen.

"Lem Lothe, did you summon me?" the man asked. He was well over six feet tall, with pale white skin and golden hair that fell to his shoulders.

"Summon you?" the young man asked dumbfounded. He looked at the beardless face and the long, flowing silk robe that the man wore. Everything about him led Lem to believe that he was a person of wealth and influence. "No sir, I didn't summon you."

"This fire, this cry for help." He pointed at the conflagration, "This is you, summoning me."

"Who are you, friend?" Lem asked, feeling uneasy in this stranger's presence.

"I have many names, but you may call me 'Quell'. The old gods envied me and hated me for how much I loved mankind. They disapproved of my willingness to interact directly with my followers. I rain blessings and gifts on my believers and because of that, they cast me out of their ranks. I seek to build my own kingdom here on Xoran."

"Out of their ranks? You are one of the old gods?"

"I've been around for millennia; I sit on a throne and thousands kneel before me." He placed his hand on Lem's shoulder, "What do *you* think?" Lem fell to his knees and bowed before Quell. "Rise my son. If you desire power, if you want women and riches, you must follow my every command without question."

I know he's a god, but how can he read my mind? Of course, I want power, riches, and women that I can use and throw away. I doubt he knows how much I want those things, how much I need those things. Lem thought to himself. He rose and tried not to look his god directly in the eye. Quell radiated power, his very skin glowed and it was blinding to stare at him.

"Did you feel that disturbance yesterday? A shaking of this very world?" Lem nodded in the affirmative. "That was the old gods, playing their games. It's happened before. They get bored with what they've created and allow it to burn, then they start something new. Is that what you want for this world? If they rip Xoran apart, you will surely lose your life, but worse yet, you will never enjoy all the pleasures that are due to a man of your ability.

Damn right!

"As my agent in this world, you will of course be greatly rewarded. I know all things, I know that you have never laid with a woman, that no matter how hard you try, they continue to reject you. As a disciple of mine, you will be allowed to *take* what you want. I know that your peers see your slight frame and your social awkwardness, and they torture you for it. No more! As a high priest in the church of Quell, you will be untouchable. You will be second only to me. If a man speaks against me, smite him! If a man denies the authority that I've given you, smite him!"

This seems too good to be true, but I don't care. I'm so tired of being a nobody.

"Gather men to you. Speak the words that I will impart to you and make them your soldiers in the coming holy war. In my name, I command you to revolt against royal houses and governments. The time of the old gods is over. It's time for the followers of Quell to sweep across the land and crush all those who will not subscribe to these truths." They sat talking for a long time by the light of the burning house.

Chapter 12: The Movement is Born

Lem Lothe walked into Galena with two dozen of his loyal followers, they had left their makeshift base a couple of days ago on foot and they were ready for a break. They were chanting loudly so that everyone in town would stop what they were doing and look up as they passed. Galena was a small town, with only a thousand people or so. They were loyal to House Cadmus and to Delph, the God of travelers and the forest. The main part of town was a straight road that passed through town heading East-West. A mill, a livery stable, and a temple dedicated to Delph were located on the main road. Most of the trades were relegated to the smaller alleyways running perpendicular, north and south of the main road.

They came across a street musician who was standing on a bucket, playing a guitar and singing for tips. They were drowning him out with their chanting, but Lem raised his hands when they were just across the square from the singer, and they went silent. With a look of relief, the singer again began singing in earnest. He played a song that would work well in this city; a song glorifying Delph and his works. A couple of people dropped coins in his hat, and this encouraged him to sing louder and with more conviction. What he did not pick up on was the sour looks from the followers of Quell.

The singer was smiling at a young maiden passing by and was caught completely by surprise when the fist-sized stone crashed against his uncovered head. Several more rocks followed till he was a quivering bloody heap on the ground. Lem strolled over, pulled the guitar from the singer's grasp, and used it to beat the man till he stopped moving. The guitar broke on the third or fourth swing, but he kept hitting the man till he had nothing but a bloody handle in his hand. Blood was everywhere, covering the stones of the village square and Lem was covered to the waist.

He tossed the broken instrument on the corpse that a minute ago had been a living person.

Stepping up on the bucket, he looked out at the hundred or so horrified faces. They had witnessed what to them was a senseless murder, and they were too stunned to act or react. A tall man was standing on high with a bright white robe that was soaked in the fresh lifeblood of one of their citizens. "People of Galena!" he bellowed. "This man was wicked and blasphemous! There is but one God, his name is Quell! To follow any false gods is to incite His wrath!" He waved at the pool of blood near his feet, "This infidel deserved what he received, for it is a sin punishable by death, to worship false gods!"

The people were angry and horrified, but they were not sure what to do. They crowded closer to the action, but no one was willing to confront a man who had just beaten another man to death in front of their eyes. Around him were his acolytes, they were all young men, also dressed in dirty white robes. They were not clean, and their hair was wild, their beards were long and greasy. They shook their fists at the townspeople and waved bricks and clubs at those around them.

"We do not worship your false God!" a man called out from the crowd. Lem's eyes lit up, he tried to hide his delight behind his yelling of curses.

"Grab him! Grab the unbeliever!" he yelled, pointing at the man who had spoken up. A handful of his men waded into the crowd, knocking aside those in the way till they were able to lay hands on the man who had spoken. They pulled him from the crowd and dragged him to the open space between the followers of Quell and the horrified crowd. When he was in the open, the followers of Quell rushed up and struck him as hard as they could with long canes. His howls of pain just made the crowd even more nervous. There was a disturbance, and from the back of the crowd came the constable and his deputy. They both wore tunics that reflected their position and carried short swords. They ran out to protect the man being caned, their swords drawn.

"Cease this behavior right now!" the constable demanded. He was a man of medium height with a stout frame. He had no facial hair and the hair on his head was turning grey. He was about to issue more demands when a brick flew in a short arc and hit him in the eye. Blood gushed from the broken orb, and as he screamed in pain, the crowd of onlookers began to nervously disband. The air was suddenly full of stones and bricks, and in a minute or two, there were four bodies on the ground. Lem told his men to get the injured men to their knees.

The three men still living were lined up and forced to kneel before Lem. They were gravely injured and drifted in and out of consciousness. Lem Lothe stood behind the first man, the one who had questioned the validity of Quell. He went on and on with his rhetoric to a crowd that could sense what was taking place and was starting to panic. When he had finished his manic diatribe, he sentenced all three men to death. Lem Picked up a stone that was about the size of a small watermelon, and with a thundering prayer to Quell, brought it crashing down on the man's head. His skull caved in, and his blood and brains splattered for several feet in every direction. The headless corpse fell to the stone-covered street. He then did the same for the next two men.

The women in the crowd screamed, then wept at the horror of it all. Children cried incessantly as their parents tried to drag them away. Now that the citizens were prepared, Lem Lothe laid down the law. His men cut off the roads in and out of town, trapping a hundred people in the town square with four dead neighbors and a pack of bloodthirsty intruders.

"There is evil in this town!" he screamed. "Praise Lord Quell that we have come to cut out the decay here and save your eternal souls!" He then directed that the men and women be separated. He stood over the men who were all made to go down on their knees. For an hour, he preached about the virtues of the one true God, Quell. He showed them proof that the Old Gods followed by most of the people of Kronos were not real. That in fact, to follow them was one of the worst sins that man could commit. The men all looked terrified. Only feet away were the battered bodies of the Constable, his deputy, and two other men who had no idea that today would be their last.

"Now it the time for each one of you to make a decision!" he spoke even louder now. "Time to decide if you will join us as brothers... or remain the sinners that you are today!" He walked up to the first man in line. He lifted the man's chin with his dusty boot. "Will you now swear your life and allegiance to Quell?"

The man didn't have to think about it. "No, I will not!" defiance in his voice. From behind, Lem's second in command pushed the man over so that he lay flat on his stomach, his face against the paving stones. He put his knee in the center of the man's back, and two of his men circled around and grabbed each of his arms. Lem walked up, picked a large stone from the pile, and held it high above his head. He turned from side to side so that everyone present could see the heavy object.

"In the name of Quell, I sentence you to death!" He brought the large stone down squarely on the side of the man's head. Crushed between two unyielding surfaces, the top of his head exploded, shooting brain and blood out like a cannon. The women in the crowd screamed a few swooned at the violence. Lem smiled at his vicious act, and his men all hooted and hollered like he had done some great thing.

Walking to the next man, he asked the same question. "Are you ready to swear your life and allegiance to Quell?" The man looked at the bashed skull only a couple of feet away.

"Yes, yes I will!" he said, not taking his eyes off his fellow Galenite.

Lem looked at him with disapproval, "No, I don't believe you." Dellan pushed him in the back, and another townsperson went face-first on the street. Hefting his rock up again, he brought it down with all his strength, crushing the skull of another heathen. "There was no conviction in his voice, was there my brothers?" he asked Quell's followers. They all agreed.

Lem walked to the third man in line. "I ask you the same question as I did these infidels!"

The man was in his late twenties, good-looking though scared out of his mind. "Yes! Quell is my Lord, my God!" he raved. "I piss on the false God, Delph!"

"Very good, stay where you are." He continued down the line. The rest had learned their lesson. A dozen or so men were now enthusiastic converts to Quell.

Lem now walked over to the women. He looked them over like he was grading cattle. Pointing at the oldest woman, he waved for her to stand. When she did, he directed her off to the side. He went through, picked out all the women who were forty or above, and added them to the group with the older woman. When he was done, there were women and girls in front of him, all on their knees. Some were as young as ten, the rest were as old as their mid-thirties. There was one girl in her early twenties, that was not exactly deformed, but most men would find her to be very unattractive. He motioned for her too, to join the group that was standing. When he was done, he had a very pleased look on his face as he turned to his men.

"Brothers, praise be to Quell! He has blessed us with wives and slaves to satisfy our every need. Each man will pick a woman, starting with my trusted brother Dellan Crys, and then by rank. Do not fight over these women, there will be more," he said as he was grabbing the arm of a girl who was maybe fifteen.

"What of these others?" one of the brothers asked, pointing at the group of women that had been sorted out.

"Kill them," he said simply as he walked towards a shop dragging his prize. She yelled and squirmed and cried, but he slapped her severely and she whimpered, crying a river of tears. The men all cheered as they divvied up the most desirable women. The lower-ranking brothers drew their short swords and executed the standing women with no preamble, just chopping them till they stopped moving. As he was entering the candle maker's shop, Lem turned to his people. "Tie up these new brothers, let them watch as you use the women of this town. At the next town, they will be the first to draw blood, and then they will be ours forever."

Chapter 13: Genocide

The Emar preferred the nighttime, and on rare occasions when they were found outside, it was usually a stormy day, when it was dark and rainy. They founded the city of Shikha in the Wolvig territory by agreement with House Cadmus. The city was essentially a series of caves built into the Blue Mountains with a deep and intricate system of chambers underground. For the most part, they kept to themselves and very rarely mixed with humans. The Cadmus family was well known for being fair and friendly to all people, and they welcomed the Emar with open arms.

The Emar were one of the seven races created by the Old Gods, and were distant cousins to humans, having large eyes and entirely too much hair. They generally had weak chins and were long and thin. Many called them Shades because of their ability to become invisible in shadows. In the daytime, they were easy to catch; but at night, they were practically impossible to find. They had their own whispery language, but many were able to speak the common tongue. They didn't subscribe to the Elder Gods as did a vast majority of humans. Neither did they follow the other beliefs common to humans, including Ammon, Panist, and the Quell. No human in Kronos could say that they were very familiar with the Emar and their ways. They were peaceful and kept to themselves, and everyone was happy with that arrangement.

House Cadmus was a gods-fearing noble house whose patron god was Lahni, goddess of love and the moon. This helped them to be generous and caring. They allowed anyone to travel through their territory, and even to settle in their lands if they wished. They were open to the request when approached by the Emar to settle in a land that was to humans, essentially worthless. They allowed the Quell in their country, and despite their odd ways, they didn't discriminate against them in any way. The lord of House Cadmus, and by extension, most of their citizens believed in the goodness of all men and non-human races. They went out of their way to accommodate all comers, even at the expense of those who called themselves Wolvig natives.

Anatol and Ursina lay to the West, and Preston shared Wolvig's Eastern border. These neighbors were not anywhere near as accommodating, and they knew from experience that House Cadmus could not be counted on in times of war. They had no respect for the confirmed bachelor Miles Cadmus, who along with his Steward, Burk Stiofan, ruled the land with a velvet glove. The only thing that kept them from invading his lands and taking them for their own was that he was harmless. More importantly, if one of them did invade, the other two countries would be forced to react. They were like mongrels, staring each other down over a juicy bone.

The Quell claimed that they had been around for ages; according to them, Quell was older than the Old Gods themselves. They believed in Quell, their one true god who ruled every aspect of their lives. He was the opposite of the elder god Lahni. Quell demanded absolute devotion, and anyone who didn't follow him was a heretic, an infidel. Outsiders were to be feared and hated at the same time, and if the opportunity ever presented itself, to be sacrificed for Quell's glory. Followers of the religion never mixed well with the citizens of the countries where they found themselves. When they were in the minority, they cried discrimination and expected protection. Once they had achieved sufficient numbers, they would start making outrageous demands and any slight would cause them to turn to violence. Only with an extraordinarily tolerant king like Miles Cadmus were they able to exist and grow. Showing weakness in the face of men like these was a recipe for disaster.

It was a sunny afternoon in a place that had rain more days a year than it had sun. The caves of the Emar appeared deserted because, during the day, they were sleeping deep in their caves. The Emar hated the sun, and they avoided it at all costs. The upper caves were usually abandoned till later in the evenings when the sun would go down and the temperature would drop to where they felt comfortable roaming from their subterranean homes.

I saw an Emar when I was a child once, they're creepy. I've heard that they are passive and non-confrontational. They are certainly not followers of Quell and wiping them out will serve as a warning to House Cadmus that their peace-loving ways are going to be their downfall, Lem thought. Years of beatings and long periods of near starvation toughened him up, gave him the spine to kill his parents, and now, to lead a band of religious fanatics. He was so full of rage that only spilling the blood of non-believers would help him to sleep at night. The thought of the rewards to come in the afterlife made it possible for him to perform the most horrible atrocities in his god's name. Quell demanded that everyone conform or die, and Lem found that he was very talented in getting young men who grew up as he did, to sacrifice themselves to appease him.

Ahead lay the only colony of the Emar, they inhabited islands somewhere across the sea, but this was their only outpost amongst the lands of men. He guessed that they didn't have a standing guard, as they had never fought with men. The rest of society found them to be an oddity that was tolerable. Lem hated their non-conformity and their strange ways. *If they refuse to bow to Quell they get what they deserve.*

Lem turned to his second in command, Dellan Crys, to carry out his attack plan, "Take a dozen men, and circle around the main entrance so that you can approach it from behind. We'll march right up to the front entrance and wait for when your men are in place," he commanded.

"Yes brother Lem! May the vengeance of Quell fall upon these heathens," Dellan said before galloping off. A dozen or so men followed him as they went up and around the hills behind the cave entrance where their mounts could more easily ascend. Lem watched them with pride. His followers were so willing to die for the cause that had dominated his life these last few months. He would never go off on a suicide mission; the movement needed leadership and he was the only one with the vision to carry out Quell's will. His followers were for the most part unwashed, uneducated, and unsophisticated country folk. Unlike his men, his long hair was pulled back in a neat ponytail, his beard was trimmed close, and his attire was reminiscent of a nobleman's day clothes. He sat high on a brown stallion so that he could rest his legs and look down on his fellow believers.

Peering through a collapsible telescope, he watched as Dellan and his men came up the backside of the hill where the cave entrance was located. There were no guards to sound the alarm. In all human history, no one had ever attacked the Emar. Dellan's men entered the cave, while others gathered dry brush from around the hilltop. Soon they had a fire started in the mouth of the cave, and Dellan's men just kept piling on more and more dry material till the scene was obscured by clouds of billowing smoke. The smoke was so thick that they had to retreat down the hill.

Just watch how this will smoke out those bug-eyed bastards. Calling out to the rest of his troops, Lem called for them to gather at the base of the cave system and wait. There were enough of them to form a semi-circle that blocked any possible retreat from the smoky caverns. Within minutes, the Emar started flooding out. They were coughing violently, some were throwing up, and at the same time, shielding their light-sensitive eyes. They looked scared and confused by the sudden intrusion. Some of the older Emar looked over the ring of humans who were apparently the cause of their predicament, and they understood.

"Who is the elder amongst you?" he asked the Emar. They looked around at each other, not all of them spoke the common tongue. After a few uncomfortable moments, an older male Emar pushed his way through the crowd. He looked up at the human atop a beautiful brown horse. He said nothing, it was obvious that he was their leader.

"Men, look at this heathen, this devil creature from across the seas," he shouted so all of his people could hear. "They come to this land, and refuse to bow before Quell, the one true God." His voice was smooth and powerful, persuasive and commanding, "What shall we do with you, devil spawn?" he asked of the elder.

The man looked tired. "We are no threat to you, we keep to ourselves and stay in our isolated community."

"I know that you are not a threat to us. Quell be praised! You aren't even human, so there is no way that we can convert you." Turning to the crowd, "What can we do with these demons? They're impure, not children of Quell!"

"Kill them!" they all yelled in unison. The Emar understood not only the words but the body language of the crowd. There were over a hundred of these crazed acolytes who were brandishing farm implements that would be very effective as weapons, "Send them to Vanya, kill them all!"

Lem was one of the few in the group that had actual weapons. He pulled his longsword to the cheers of the crowd. He looked down at the old Emar who was looking down to avoid the direct light of such a sunny afternoon. "In the name of Lord Quell,

I send your devil's soul to Vanya!" With that, he swung the blade from his mounted position. The blade bit deeply into the creature's neck, cutting about halfway through. The elder Emar fell dead to the ground. The women and children screamed in horror at the sight. They were peaceful people and never died violent deaths. Their instinct was to flee, but they were completely encircled by the humans, and they could not retreat because of the smoke that was rolling out of all the entrances to their caves. A few still ran in while the rest waited like sheep for their deaths. The humans waded into the Emar with clubs, smashing the large skulls of the Emar, their red blood flying everywhere. Others with homemade spears were stabbing men and women from a safe distance. The followers of Quell used knives, scythes, shears, and every type of implement that could be used to kill. The Emar adults fell, doing very little in the way of defending themselves. When the Quell followers had finished massacring the adult Emar, only the children remained. The Emar children, including the babies, had their heads bashed on the rocks that surrounded the base of the hillside. The peaceful Emar were completely wiped out; their bodies looked more human in death than when they had been alive. Blood was everywhere, the fanatics were covered from head to toe in gore. They laughed and cheered at their victory, praising the leadership of Lem Lothe and of course, praising the wisdom of Quell. Bodies that had been living creatures only minutes before meant nothing to them, and they left them where they lay.

Lem exited a tent that had been erected near the scene of the massacre. Everyone stood around eating and joking while their leader could be heard praying inside his private tent. *Lord Quell, please guide me. We have fought the inhuman Emar and purged your world of their presence. What now would you have me do?* He prayed. The prayers were loud and went on for a long time. When he showed his face again, everyone stopped what they were doing and gathered around to hear his proclamation.

"I have prayed to Lord Quell, and he has given me a vision. A vision of our next task, and the next and the next..." His words were met with roars of approval, "We shall take this victory and build upon it. We will take over this land, usurp the royalty and punish the unclean, the apostate. This victory shall be the cornerstone of our future empire!" The men hooted in agreement. "We'll make a temporary camp here, and in a few days, we will march on the nearest human village. We will take their men as prisoners, we will take their food, we will take their women for our pleasure." This elicited a round of cheers, "We will sweep across this land till all bow to Quell or die for their heresy!"

Chapter 14: Ambush

The House Cadmus guard marched in step to the cadence called by their commander. The marshal along with the king's counsel, Birk Stiofan, and the Emar assassin, rode about halfway down the column. Timo the Invisible had been dispatched from the Emar homeland to assess the situation and report back to his people.

The Emar colony of Shikha had been wiped out and now the Quell zealots had taken several small villages and the large trade city of Ingar. The city was no longer considered to be under the rule of House Cadmus. Having a handful of creepy, inhuman colonists getting wiped out was one thing; but when the same religious zealots murdered and raped their way through one of the main cities of Wolvig, that was an affront that could not be ignored. At the insistence of the Emarian representative, the king dispatched a respectable force to deal with the uprising. One hundred soldiers, led by his councilor and lover, Sir Birk Stiofan.

"What do you know of these 'Quell' followers?" Birk asked of the assassin.

"I have not personally encountered them. All I know is that they murdered everyone in Shikha. A colony that existed with your king's blessing and was supposed to be under his protection," he said bitterly. "We are generally a very peaceful people, and the colonists were no doubt lulled to sleep by the good people of Wolvig. Without warning, they were attacked and weren't able to defend themselves. Every man, woman, and child fell beneath the invader's blades and cudgels. Not a single soul was spared."

"I am very sorry for your loss. Miles... I mean the king, was in full agreement with his father's and his grandfather's policy of living in harmony with your people," Birk replied.

"That is the only reason why we have chosen to work with you," Timo said with acid in his voice. "What we are furious about is, it's not how you treated our people. It's how they were slaughtered without consequences. They swore allegiance to your king, and he did not protect them as equal subjects." His over-large eyes looked out from the darkness of his hood. "If your king cannot avenge my brothers and sisters and assure the captain and me that this will never happen again, we will be forced to land our troops in Kronos," he said to the nervous human. "The men that will come here will not be the passive farmers and merchants that you were used to," Timo threatened.

"Well... that's what we are here for today, let's hope that I didn't get dressed up for nothing." Birk smiled nervously at his companion.

The company worked its way into a ravine that ran between two steep hills on either side. The water in the ravine was shallow, so they proceeded to march straight through. There was an almost eerie silence as they trudged along, the whisper of the water, the sound of two hundred feet splashing as they marched. There were no animal sounds to be heard anywhere. The Emar started looking around, his senses told him that danger was near.

"Did you send out any scouts?" he asked Birk.

"You've been here the whole time; you know that I haven't."

Timo's next words were cut off by a thunderous sound coming from above on both sides of the narrow canyon. From both sides, dozens of boulders were either rolling or bouncing their way toward the column of troops. The first men were struck before they even knew that they were in danger. Boulders, some the size of farm animals, were rolling through their ranks at high speed. The sound of crushed armor and cracked bones filled the still air. A second and a third wave of boulders crashed through the helpless troops before it was over.

Timo jumped off of his horse; being that high above the rest just made him an easy target. A large rock came directly at him, missing him by a fraction of an inch, but crushing the neck of his mount. The assassin looked around at the mayhem now that the smoke had cleared. About half of the men were either killed outright or injured and in need of assistance. The king's councilor was laying on the ground with a couple of large rocks pinning his right leg to the ground. Men started approaching from both ends of the small canyon; they were not armored but they carried a makeshift collection of weapons.

The commander seemed to be unharmed, and he was still atop his horse. "Men, form up!" He pointed to a group. "Shield Wall, now!" He rode to the other end of the broken column. "Shield wall, form up!"

At about the same time, the attackers hit both shield walls. The attackers were probably two hundred men strong and approached from both the front and rear. The Quell soldiers were poorly trained, but they were filled with religious fervor, and they had superior numbers. The soldiers fought valiantly, but they never stood a chance.

Towards the end, the commander was backed up against a tree, three men attacked him at the same time, two thrusting their spears, and the third had a sword. He managed to cut down the man with the sword; but a spear tip punched through his armor, ripping into his intestines. Two more men came from behind, each grabbing one of his arms so that he was now completely spread open, helplessly pinned to a tree. One of the crazier members of the group, apparently their leader, approached the helpless officer. The man screamed some praises to Quell, and insults to the man, his king, and everyone else who didn't happen to be a believer. Then he stepped right up to the commander, pulled his rusty-looking knife, and proceeded to slowly saw the commander's head off.

Timo had seen enough. The canyon was dark on even the brightest of days, and he easily found a shadow to melt into. When the opportunity presented itself, he used his ability to 'jump' from shadow to shadow, until he was far away from the bloodbath. These humans were doomed, and instead of throwing his own life away, he knew that it was much more important to report to his commander.

"Sire!" the valet squeaked at his liege lord. When Miles looked up, the old servant went on, "There is a delivery, a wagon has been sent to your highness' attention. For his majesty's eyes only."

The king followed the old clerk through the maze of hallways till they reached the courtyard. Halfway between the gate and the main castle entrance was a large wagon, piled high and covered with a bison skin tarp. The wagon was pulled by a pair of tired asses and driven by an old man with the mark of Galena on his jacket.

"You there!" he yelled at the driver. "What load do you carry?"

"It is for your eyes-only Sire. I was contracted to deliver this wagon to you and to no one else. No questions asked, and I was not to peek at the contents upon pain of death."

"Who put you on this mission?"

"The Prophet himself, Lem Lothe," the man said plainly.

King Cadmus looked at the man who was old and didn't pose a threat. The wagon though could have armed men, waiting to spring into action. "Guard, open that wagon, let us know what is carried there."

Two of the guards sheathed their swords and jumped up on opposite sides of the wagon. They undid the simple knots, and then together, pulled back on the cover. A terrible smell assaulted everyone in the square. In the wagon were the heads of the hundred or so troops that he had sent to put down the Quell insurrection. The king looked at the bloody mess with growing dread, after a minute he saw the head that he least wanted to see parted from its torso. His confidant and lover Birk Stiofan was among the trophies in the wagon. Try as he might, he could not contain his grief and let out a terrible wail, followed by heavy breathing and uncontrollable sobbing. Two of his man servants pulled him away from the scene and ushered him to his quarters to rest and collect himself.

Everyone else who had witnessed the complete exchange knew that they were in trouble. One hundred of their best warriors were butchered and sent back home in pieces. This could not and would not stand. A much larger force would be required, more men, more weapons, supplies, and untold casks of coin would be required to bring these heathens to heel. The worst part was that no one was sure that this king had it in him to take the necessary steps, to make the necessary sacrifices to save their country from becoming the property of the Quell.

Chapter 15: Quell Expansion

The scout rushed up to Grand Leader Lem Lothe with his report. House Cadmus sent a small force outside of their city walls. The Quell fanatics were nearing the capital, so this small army of professional soldiers was being sent as a show of strength on behalf of the crown. The scouting report came back that there was a respectable count of knights, and the rest were regular army. No conscripts. He counted the number of tents and horses and came back with approximately five hundred souls. The king was of course not with them, as he was such a delicate and sensitive man; but his Command General was with the army.

Five hundred troops were enough to scare away most Quell attacks, but today they had come in force. *I believe in you Lord Quell, my master. This is the toughest test of your followers yet. Five hundred knights and professional soldiers await us. I know that many of your followers are weak men, men who have many flaws. With your blessing, I will lead them to victory. With your blessings, we cannot lose!* He prayed to the idol he carried with him always. Instead of the small raids on the neighboring villages here in Wolvig, and Ursina to the West, he had built his first army. He had fully five thousand men, all longing for spoils in this life as well as rewards in the next. They valued their mortal selves very little after being converted to Quell. Despite their lifetimes of failure, they still saw themselves as noble warriors for their god.

The warriors of Quell were rabid dogs, and only the firm hand of Lem Lothe prevented them from implosion. To keep their faith, to sustain their fervor, he had to constantly either punish them or reward them. There of course was only one punishment recognized by Quell, death. The crimes could be murder, rape, or other high crimes, and the culprit would be disemboweled or decapitated in front of his brothers. The crimes could also be as mild as not being able to recite the holy psalms of Quell or showing mercy to a non-believer. These crimes also led to very public, and very painful deaths.

On the reward side, they would be allowed to take any woman, of any age that was not a believer in Quell and use her as either a house slave, a sex slave, or both. Wives were often raped by a group of men, only feet from the corpses of their husbands and children. Food, weapons, and of course any gold or silver was snatched up by the victors, and the disposition of certain valuable items often lead to fights amongst themselves.

Lem knew that he was the leader of thousands of disaffected losers; but they were the sort that with just a little hope and a taste of the things those other men had worked for, they would gladly do whatever was asked of them. Every time that he won a battle, and took over more land, the recruits would literally come out of the woodwork. Third and fourth sons who would never inherit, men who were poor or unattractive and knew that on their own, they would never be a husband or father. At first, they had to threaten their captives to join them; but as their fame grew, volunteers poured in from every corner of Kronos.

"What do you say, Great Leader?" Dellan Crys asked him with excitement barely hidden in his tone.

"Are the men ready to take on this 'Army' that has been sent out to fight us?"

"The men are so ready, they are near to bursting!" he said excitedly. "The honor is yours Great Leader."

Lem looked down from his horse, and a vast ocean of faces looked up at him. They all had the same expression, the same desire. They wanted to be set loose to kill and inflict pain and death on anyone they were aimed at. Moreover, they wanted revenge for lifetimes of being bullied and abused, ridiculed, and laughed at.

"Commanders! Launch your attacks!" he commanded, and his words were passed down the lines. Five brigades with a thousand men each marched off to their designated locations. Three would attack from the front, and the other two would circle around to flank the Wolvig troops from each side. The idea was to basically envelop the enemy so that there was nowhere to run, no avenue for retreat or resupply.

The king's army sat on top of the biggest hill in Wolvig. The sky was cloudy, with rain being almost a certainty. They didn't anticipate an attack, at least till the rain stopped, and that might be a day or two away. Sir Den Scott stood at the highest point, looking south. He had his cloak pulled about him to help ward off the evening chill. It was almost dark, and he was wishing that he was back at the castle, in bed next to Celia. The wind was blowing strongly now, it made strange noises as it battered tents and the few trees that were there. He looked towards the bottom of the hill; the downgrade was a quarter mile long and was not very steep. Climbing it would be torture on the legs, but there was no fear of falling. Out of the growing mist, he saw them approach. Dozens, perhaps hundreds of men working their way up the hill. They had no helmets or armor of any kind, but each had a sword or long knife, some had clubs or chains. He looked to the East, then the West, and saw the same thing. The attack was happening now, and their numbers were far greater than the general had predicted.

Den ran the short distance to the command tent and rushed in without being recognized or gaining permission. The general was taking his evening soup, and a couple of the senior knights were with him, chatting over tea and strategies. They all halted what they were doing and looked up at the young knight who so rudely burst into the tent.

"General, they are here! The Quell are at the base of the hill and are working their way up even as we speak!" he choked out.

"Which side are they coming from, son? I need to deploy the shield wall!"

"I'm not certain Sir, but I think that they are coming up from all sides. From the South, East, and West for certain. Your prediction on their strength was off milord. There are thousands of them, several thousand."

The general pushed over his meal and quickly grabbed for his sword. No time to put the full armor on. He shouted at the others to ready their troops for a charge from the enemy and then ran out to find his runner. He was getting ready to send a message to the king; but when he found out that they were completely surrounded, he knew that no messenger would make it out alive.

He shouted encouragement to his men and had them establish a modified shield wall. Their number was not enough to form a double layer of shields around the whole circle. They would make a single ring, and each man would have to do his part to keep the ring intact. They had barely formed when the first wave hit. Crazed, tired, and dirty men reached the top of the hill and met firm resistance from trained troops. Each defender held a large four-foot shield made of Blackwood from the nearby Yuna Forest. Each man also had a dagger at his side and a long sword drawn and ready.

The first wave of invaders fell on the defending swords like lambs to slaughter. They practically threw their bodies on the sharpened points of the defender's swords. Most died right there, blocking the path of those behind them, others found themselves skewered and stuck to the defending knights. They knew that they were not going to survive, but you could tell by the looks on their faces that they welcomed the role of martyr. A few were able to strike down a defending soldier with actual fighting techniques; but most of them were completely unskilled and lashed out, swinging wildly and just trying to land a lucky blow. The second wave was a continuation of the first. If the king's men had spears, they could have killed four or five at a thrust; but they didn't, and as soon as they hacked an opponent, another filled the void, and then another after him. There was no real strategy; they knew that they had far superior numbers and their leader had decided to expend as many men as necessary to take this objective.

Den Scott was the youngest knight present, he had just been knighted by the king a few weeks earlier and still was not used to being in charge of a group of fighting men. He stood just behind the circle of infantry, and when he saw a gap, he pulled someone, with or without a shield to fill the gap. He knew that if even a few men got inside their wall, they would have free reign at the unprotected center. He wanted to be nervous and second guess himself, but there wasn't time for fear or doubt.

An older fighting man to his left took a club to the side of his head. Blood flew everywhere, and Den could almost hear the sound of crunching bone as the side of his head was caved in. The background noise of the wind and rain was almost drowned out by the clash of steel and the screams of men dying. A large man pushed his opponent down in an attempt to breach the defenses. He was a huge, and just by the way he carried himself, it was obvious that he had spent a long hard life tilling the soil or raising cattle. His square face was twisted into a mask of unhinged contempt. In Den's eyes, he could have been the Herald of Death himself. Seeing the young knight standing there, a look of fear on his face; he charged. He wore a dirty robe, the type that the Quell had taken up as a pseudo uniform. It was dirty long before the layer of blood had been applied. He carried a war hammer that was too large for most men to wield but was a good fit for him. He raised it up to crush the skull of the little puppy in his way, leaving his torso exposed. Den swung his sword with all of his might in a side-to-side motion. The blade was sharp as a razor, but it still had difficulty cutting through the giant's tough hide. The man froze like a statue, hammer high above his head as his innards poured out through the huge gash in his gut.

    The battle was fought by torchlight, the flames flickering madly in the strong breeze. Den looked around at his fellow knights. They were strong and skillful, and in front of each of them, a pile of bodies was growing; but there was no end in sight. For hours they defended their superior position, which had no escape route. The ground was slick with blood, and the never-ending cries of the wounded made it hell on earth. The ring had contracted and now the king's men were half their number, and still, the Quell came. A good fighter who was to Den's left fell to a hatchet blow; the rusty blade buried in his shoulder and driven deep into his chest. Den used his shield to bash the knight's killer as hard as he could in the face while still blocking the advance of his own foe. The one-on-one fighting was becoming two-on-one, and soon it would be over.

    From somewhere behind and to the right, a couple of quell fighters broke through and got into the hollow center of the ring. There were two of them carrying a large pig skin sewn into a bag. They stabbed the bag releasing the foul-smelling liquid inside. Grabbing a torch, they tossed it onto the spreading pool. The liquid instantly ignited and caused a huge fire to explode in the middle of the defender's position. The men who had delivered the fuel were the first to be consumed by the fire. They screamed in pain, but their faces seemed to convey that they felt victorious. As their flesh melted and their rags burned, they grabbed fighting men from behind and dragged them to the ground. Three or four more fuel skins broke into the clearing and soon, the whole top of the hill was ablaze. The king's men now showed real fear, many of them had flames already burning their feet and legs. The general called out for them to stand strong, to double their effort and if possible, push down the hill.

Den thought to himself that what he was asking was impossible, he peered over the edge and there was still an ocean of enemies waiting for their chance to kill him. Out of the corner of his eye, he caught a tall lanky Quell in a burning robe, who was trying to grab at his shoulder. Taking a chance with the one in front, he turned and swung quickly, nearly cutting the man in half and avoiding his fiery grasp. There was a sharp pain in his side, he turned back to find a raggedy man, not nearly as tall as he was, with a short but sharp dagger buried in his side. His sword was starting to get very heavy as he chopped at the man who had stabbed him; he was barely able to bring the blade around again. The man fell forward, gushing blood on Den's chest and stomach. Behind him was another, and behind him, another. The defensive line was disintegrating, and only the fire prevented the Quell from completely overrunning their position. Den was bleeding from the knife still in his side, but he couldn't tend to it with three men trying to get at him. He blocked the two on the left with his shield, and the one on the right he defended with his sword; a sword that had been in his family for four generations.

They surged forward and caused him to trip and fall backward on the burning ground. Their bodies fell on his and their weight kept him from being able to get up. The fire caught his hair, and he could feel his scalp and the skin on the back of his neck burn. The smell was horrible, and the pain was indescribable. He blacked out and soon joined his comrades in the Hespian Gardens, his last thoughts were about reuniting with his father and grandfather in the hall of fallen knights.

Chapter 16: The Siege

Lem Lothe was riding his horse along the main road that led to the city of Vallen, Dellan Crys rode at his side. They had been riding most of the night since the battle at Overlook Hill, and behind them were the remains of their army. The men were tired, but they were overjoyed to have survived a meat grinder of a battle. Their heavenly rewards would have to wait just a little longer.

"Did you get the count yet?" he asked Dellan.

"Yes, my lord. Roughly three thousand Quell souls are still with us. Quite a costly battle, but the men are happy with the win."

"Good, very good. We are almost to the city, we should make camp here, I want to be at the castle gates by nightfall."

"Of course, I'll spread the word."

The men put up a large command tent for Lem and a few smaller tents for the command staff. Afterward, they put up their own tents. They lit cookfires and made hot ale and eggs with venison. Soon, the majority were sleeping as the sun was starting to rise. Guards circled the hundreds of small tents, looking for any signs that more troops might be coming from the castle. Lem was alone in his tent and fell to his knees. *Mighty Quell, thank you for our victory. Your victory. We now go against the king of Wolvig. If we are successful in flushing him out of his castle, you will have your first country, controlled solely by your followers. Please give me guidance and watch over us as we spread like wildfire across this land.* Satisfied that his god was appeased, he allowed himself a quick snack before taking his rest. He dreamed of towns on fire, and of Quell himself coming to Kronos and wiping out all the unbelievers with a single blow. He slept well.

The castle was on the far side of town and belonged to House Cadmus. He looked across the marshy plain that led to the thirty-foot walls. Even with three thousand men, taking the castle would be a chore. He met with his generals to decide on the exact strategy. They concluded that a siege would be the best route to take. They made several camps around the castle and had constant patrols so that no one could enter or leave. They settled in for what promised to be a long, dull wait for the residents of the castle to run out of supplies.

The main portcullis was raised, and the entrance was wide open for the first time in weeks. The Quell swarmed through till they filled the inner courtyard, and there were still many hundreds outside. The king stood there with his remaining staff and family, they all looked tired and weak from hunger and thirst. The Quell had cut their water supply over a week ago, and now faced with a long lingering death, they surrendered unconditionally. They were hoping that by not demanding any terms, that the leader of the Quell would show them mercy.

Lem looked down on the prisoners with bored contempt. The Cadmus family had ruled Wolvig for a dozen generations, but now the land was the property of the Quell. When he saw how few of them were left after sending the bulk of their forces out to meet him, he regretted not trying to storm the castle a couple of weeks ago. He would have lost hundreds, but that would have been a small price to pay for losing the last couple of weeks.

"Where is your queen?" he asked aloud, already knowing the answer.

"I am unmarried."

"You don't want a wife, do you? You prefer to share your bed with other men?" he asked, revulsion in his tone. The crowd of Quell followers jeered and hissed at the king.

"What a man does in his home is his business, not yours!"

"You're no man! Certainly not a king!" He edged his horse closer, "I sent your lover's head back to you a few months ago. I thought you might want to see him one last time."

"What kind of creature are you?" the king spat, "You kill men and women and even children. Does your 'God' tell you to do these things? If so, I spit on your god Quell. Magnus will find him, and with his bare hands, he will end your demon's miserable life!"

The mass of invaders screamed "Infidel!" and "Blasphemer!" at the helpless king. They surged forward, intending to rip him limb from limb. They were only stopped by their leader's voice.

"Your Old Gods don't exist. They never have," Lem said to the prisoners, "but Quell is very, very real! He speaks to me and through me. His will is to convert everyone in Kronos. That is our calling, and our campaign of conquest begins here today!"

"What shall we do with the unbelievers Lord?" Dellan asked.

Lem thought for a moment, he absorbed the energy and violence from his men. "Do what you will with the women, the children. The men? Cut their heads off and mount them around the perimeter as a warning to the townspeople." The king was crushed, why he even dreamed of mercy and was too cowardly to take his own life was a mystery to him now. "The king is a special type of sinner. Strip him, remove his manhood. He doesn't deserve it. Tie his hands and feet and burn what's left at the stake." King Cadmus began crying as the filthy invaders swarmed forward to carry out their mad leader's orders.

Chapter 17: The Twins

The sea was rough and had been for the last four hours. There had been a shock, a darkening of the skies for no reason. Everyone seemed to catch their breath at the same time and the boy in the crow's nest nearly fell out. Waves were stirred up and grew to enormous proportions, tossing the ship around like a leaf in the wind. Minutes later, things again returned to normal, and the sailors took the whole thing in stride. The passengers lined the decks so that they could vomit directly into the waves. The journey was only a week-long, and they were still a day away from their destination when the storm hit. Jokub and Gaila Anant were moving to get a fresh start in the South and brought with them their twin children, Danika and Jorn. The children had emptied their stomachs hours ago. Jokub still had some left to contribute to the sea, Gaila's stomach was empty, but it didn't stop her from trying.

"Look at them!" Captain Nives said to his first mate. "I've been in worse conditions and still had the fortitude to take my daily ration." Jokub looked over his shoulder at the captain with dull hate in his eyes. "How about a greasy pork sandwich friend!" the captain yelled to him. The idea of a greasy sandwich sent the landlubber into another fit of coughing and spewing.

"All well and good Cap'n, but we should be getting ready to make for the shore," the first mate said to his Captain. "These waters have more than their share of pirates, and we don't have the right crew for a scuffle."

"I've heard that too, but you can't believe everything ya hear," the captain replied. "It would take us almost an extra day, if we follow the coast instead of cutting across the Emerald Sea." The captain looked again at the passengers in their misery, laughing a little. "Full tilt, matey. Cut the corner and get us there for ales before midnight!"

The storm had calmed down considerably, most of the passengers were now below decks. Jokub huddled behind one of the bulkheads with his wife and children. They all looked at father with reverence, for he was a serious man who's love for them was unquestioned. He had aged terribly after years of working the land and being outside in the sun all day. He was around forty, but he looked sixty. He was under six foot with mostly gray hair and skin that was darkened by the sun and years of neglect. Reaching in his old worn vest, he pulled out a small leather bag with a drawstring. Before speaking, he looked around to make sure that only the family was able to see what he had, and to hear his words. With weakened hands, he pulled at the knot, and finally got it open, stretching out the opening, he poured the contents into his open palm. Jewels rolled around his hard-calloused hand, sparkling red, green, gold and violet. There was maybe a dozen of them of various sizes, all rough as if they had just been pulled from the ground that day.

Mother gasped at the sight. She covered her mouth to silence a gasp, and her eyes betrayed her surprise. She too had of a lifetime of hard labor and privation. Strangers could tell that she was a beautiful woman trapped in a body that had been worn out by years of hard work. Her once shiny long black hair was now cut to the shoulder and mostly gray, and she had wrinkles from many years of laughing. Her life was hard; but it was also filled with the joy of a husband and children who loved her. Looking at the wealth in her husband's hand, wealth that she had no knowledge of, surprised her more than anything she could recall. She didn't feel slighted that he had kept it from her. He was the master of the house, and she served him willingly. Jokub's code was, there was no sacrifice was too great for his wife and their children.

Leaning in, he whispered conspiratorially, "See this red one?" He pointed with a stubby worn finger at a sparkling Emerald. "This one I found on the bank of the creek on the day you were born," he said looking at the twins. "It's my favorite." He was choking up, "This is the final tally of a life." He turned to his beloved wife, "of two lives. This is the sum total of countless hours of backbreaking labor and years of trying to make things grow in poor soil. I wanted us to move, to find a place to start over. I wanted a change that would improve our lives. I want you children to achieve more than what your mother and I have achieved," he said fighting back tears. "When we get to Aragon, House Klaas will allow us to settle there. For half of these, they'll educate both of you." He was becoming emotional. "I want you to have a life that is as filled with love and laughter, as much as your mother's and mine have been. As good as it has been, I know you two are meant for much bigger things. Things that my simple mind can't even comprehend." This had all of them in tears. He put the gems back into the pouch and returned it to the pocket on the inside of his vest, near his heart.

"Wife, children," father whispered to them. "This is my gift to us. Every moment that I was not tilling the earth or herding the stock, I was looking for more of these. I am not sure what they are worth, but I know that it will be enough for us to relocate to the South. There are open lands, and the king is welcoming people like us who will work the land and provide him with taxes and goods. Mother was fearful that we didn't get enough for our rocky little patch of land and our last few scrawny cows. I show you this to put your mind at ease. We have suffered a hard life, a tough life these last few years; but things will be better in this new land." Father beamed with pride that he was able to improve the lives of his loved ones, "Life will still be hard, but we'll reap even more for what we sew. My dream is that you Jorn will inherit the farm and that we can find a worthy husband for you my beautiful Danika."

Jorn turned to Danika after their parents had succumbed to the lack of sleep and the turbulence. They were twins, about thirteen and a half, and very different in how they looked at the world. Jorn was a thoughtful boy, very controlled. He held his emotions in check and tried to always see the middle ground in any argument. He was the same height as Danika, which troubled him to no end. They both had dark hair and blue eyes, but she was starting to blossom into womanhood, and he was still clearly, still a boy. Even though she was starting to change, he was stronger and faster. She knew that he would soon become a man and dominate her physically, so she used her intellect and wit to completely control him.

"Did you know that father had such wealth?" he whispered in her ear.

"Of course not, how would I have kept that from you," she said with her usual aggressive tone. "He said that he found the first one on the day we were born. He must have found one a year, give or take."

They never imagined that their parents had already planned out the rest of their lives for them. Jorn was not thrilled, and Danika was terrified. She kind of, sort of, knew what things wives were expected to do, and she was not even remotely ok with that.

Without warning, there was violent jarring of the ship, throwing everyone to one side. At first, there was a lot of yelling and screaming, and then there was the sound of metal swords clashing. Father circled them all with his thick strong arms as they tried to be inconspicuous in their corner of the hold. The sounds from the deck above were horrible, and mother cried into father's shoulder. Danika and Jorn looked confused and scared, they looked to each other for answers, but neither one had any idea what was going on.

"Captain, there is a ship to our rear, closing fast," the first mate shouted to the captain, even though they were only a few feet apart.

"What kind of ship? Can you identify what flag she flies under?"

The first mate looked terrified; he spoke to his captain without the usual respect, "She's not flying the flag of any nation; she's marked by the skull and crossbones." He moved closer, looking up at the captain who was instantly concerned. "God's help us... pirates!"

"Pirates? You think that they would dare attack a ship flying the Rubina flag?" he scoffed. "To attack us is tantamount to declaring war on House Vosbarra!"

"True, if anyone finds out," he screamed at his captain. "If they take all that we have, and send us to the ocean floor, the Vosbarras will never know that their citizens have been wronged."

The captain thought about it for a moment, "Your right, sound the alarm, battle stations!" he said with great flourish. "It seems like we can't outrun them, so we fight them off. Protect ourselves and our cargo."

The pirate ship was smaller and built for speed, not for the ability to haul cargo and passengers for long distances. They closed the gap in what, for the larger ship, would be an unattainable speed. As soon as they pulled alongside, the pirate ship slammed into the side of the cargo vessel. Wood crashed against wood, sending splinters and chunks of wood flying everywhere. Both crews stood on their respective decks, eyeing each other, evaluating the odds of defeating the other.

The pirate ship had a sturdy, battle-scarred crew manning it. Every man was armed with a cutlass, knife, or belaying pin and the will to kill without mercy. The crew of the freighter was mostly unarmed, some with clubs, and a few with knives. They all had the look of men who knew that they were outmatched, and just wanted to live another hour. The captain pulled his sword and ordered his men to engage the enemy. Instead of charging forth, they waited to receive the boarding pirates who bridged the gap between ships with ropes that had hooks on the ends, and boards were thrown down to form temporary bridges. The fighting went as expected. The pirates suffered a single major injury and several minor injuries. The defending crew was mercilessly dispatched.

Boyko Lago, the captain of the pirate ship calmly walked over a makeshift bridge to stand on the deck of the freighter. For him, the slaughter was just another day at work, a job that he found very rewarding. He had to constantly find trophies for his crew to capture, or they would replace him with someone who was a little more motivated. Piracy was a profession for men that loved money and the earthly pleasures that it provided. He hadn't even gone below; but he knew that the haul would be enough for his men to spend three or four days drunk, stuffed to the gills, and satiated by the local women. No one retired from this business. Eventually you lost your edge and got killed. Old pirates were unheard of.

"Roy, head down below, take a quick survey of what we got, how many it will take to transship their valuables," he said pulling out a cigar and lighting it.

"Aye aye, cap'n," the first mate said while hopping to the ladder that led into the hold. Roy scooted down the ladder with practiced ease. He was in his early twenties and medium height, muscular and lanky at the same time. His blond hair was tied back and covered by a foppish hat that had probably belonged to a dandy at some time in the past. In the hold were dozens of barrels and crates, all meant for some waiting customer at their port of call. Walking towards the back, he came on a dozen people who were quite clearly, not crew. Pulling a long knife that could have doubled as a short sword, he motioned for them all to head towards the ladder. "Up to the deck with all o yeh."

They formed a single file line and made their way through the storage and up the ladder. Shortly, they were all lined up on deck facing Captain Boyko Lago. He was the tallest person still alive on the two ships. He was a light-skinned black man with kinky light brown hair. He smiled at the prisoners with his big bright teeth. His clothes looked almost picked at random because of the clashing styles; but unlike his crew, he seemed clean. Even his three-day shadow looked to be groomed to give a carefree look to his otherwise cruel countenance. His black eyes looked at them deciding if they were potential profit or if they were expendable.

Walking up and down the line, he inspected each of them. He stopped at Danika, she was just starting to become a woman and he liked them young. He pulled her out of line, then proceeded till he reached the end, "Roy, check them up and down, get every coin, every ring, every hunk of cheese or bread, anything that's of use." He turned and walked towards Danika. "You know what to do to the rest." Pulling her close, he sniffed at her and touched her all over.

"Stop that!" Jokub screamed as he stepped out of line and lunged for the captain. Before he could cover half the distance, Roy had shoved his pig sticker deep into Jokub's side.

He was essentially dead, though it took him more than a minute to drown in his own blood. Mother screamed and fell to the deck in a sobbing mess.

Roy and another sailor quickly went down the line, roughly searching the bodies of the passengers. Whenever they came upon a coin, bit of jewelry, or anything of value, they would toss it to the deck, forming a very small pile of wealth. When they had finished, they pushed everyone to their knees. Roy went behind the first man, grabbed a handful of hair, pulled his head back and slowly slit his throat. Everyone in the line started crying uncontrollably and he moved to a woman who was next in line and slit her throat. When he reached Jorn, Danika's screaming became deafening.

Roy put his hand on Jorn's head, digging his fingers into the lush straight black hair. Gripping it painfully, he yanked back on the boy's head. Jorn's childish crying scream changed in tone at that moment. His voice became deep and penetrating, an electricity seemed to fill the air around them. With a booming voice, he yelled "NO!" and Roy let go instantly. Jorn stood up, turning to his would-be executioner, grabbing the man by the arms, he screamed into his face, "No!" Roy was paralyzed and his skin turned blue as ice filled his veins. Ice crept up his arms, down his body, and finally petrified his whole body. In an instant, he had frozen into a block of ice. Jorn pushed him over easily, and Roy crashed to the ground where he shattered into a hundred pieces.

Jorn turned around, he was not the only one on deck who was in a state of shock. His blue eyes seemed to be filled with ice, and they could all sense the great energy that was flowing in and around the boy. He ignored the blood-soaked deck and the pirates that were standing around in a state of shock. Jorn focused in on his sister and started walking slowly, menacingly, towards her and Captain Boyko, who still held her captive. The captain had his long knife out and held it to Danika's throat.

"Take not another step, demon!" he yelled. "I was going to fuck this little one all night, but I'll slit her throat if you take another step!" the captain screamed.

The sky grew dark and the energy in the air increased by a quantum leap. Jorn's frozen persona faded as intense heat filled the air. It was as if the air around them had suddenly been superheated and was just waiting for a spark.

"You won't have me, you pig!" Danika screamed. The spark had been lit. The very air around them burst into flame, a wave of fire emanated from Danika and swallowed the whole upper deck of the ship where everyone was gathered. The hair went first, then the clothes, and finally the flesh. Danika and Jorn stood there watching as the skin melted off the pirates and the few remaining prisoners. When the flames died down, Danika and Jorn were there alone, naked, looking in horror at what she had done.

Jorn rushed over to his twin and held her in his arms, trying to comfort her. They stood there, alone as the ship started to burn and smolder. The smell of burning flesh filled the air and made them both sick. Danika looked first behind her; the pirate captain was curled in a smoking ball of melted flesh. He was closest and had been the target of her rage. Then she broke from her brother's embrace to run over and attend to their mother. She was burned almost beyond recognition and was very near death.

Taking her mother in her arms, Danika cried while trying to speak. "Mother! I am so sorry!"

The older woman was near death and was in a place where her pain had mercifully subsided. She held her blackened hand out to caress the cheek of her only daughter. She looked at the girl who was on the cusp of womanhood, "No dear. Thank the gods that you are blessed with these gifts." She choked a little, "Take care of your brother, you need to find your own way now." She was trying to cry, but she was burned beyond being able to produce water. "Don't blame yourself for this. We knew that the two of you were different, and I'm glad that you both will live and that your lives will be better than what your father and I had planned for you."

"Mother!" Jorn called out, touching her scorched cheek. "Hold on, we can help you!" his voice was almost frantic. Life left her eyes and she exhaled her last.

"She's gone, brother. We're alone now." She laid her mother's head down on the blackened deck, "We need to get off this burning ship before we become victims too. Go downstairs and grab our clothes, I'll look for a lifeboat."

Jorn took off amid the chaos, and down the ladder to collect some of their things from the hold. Danika went to the pile of coins and the small satchel that had their father's gems. Collecting them all, she found a lifeboat that was near the stern of the ship. *Jorn is so attached to mother, I hope he can put aside his grief till we get off this burning ship. I don't know how I did that, but this is not the time to think about it,* she thought to herself.

Danika and Jorn were dressed, and they were able to get the lifeboat in the water as the fire spread across both ships. Jorn was paddling as best he could to get them headed toward the shore. Behind them, the two ships were parked and burned down to the waterline. They would both soon be headed to the bottom of the sea with only the twins as witnesses to what had happened. As Jorn rowed, Danika patted the inner pocket where she had hidden their coins and the gems that their father had collected over the length of their lifetimes. She tried not to blame herself for their mother's death, but she still felt guilty.

"Did you know that you could do that?" she asked.

"Of course not," he answered peevishly, "I can never hide anything from you. It was as big of a surprise to me as it was to you." He continued rowing. "How about you?" he asked. "I hope we're not cursed. What if we're demons?" he yelped.

"I'm not a demon, and neither are you. Quit talking such foolishness!"

"Somehow, we have some kind of magical ability; but what you did was much stronger than what I was able to do. Maybe it's cuz you're changing already," he said plainly.

She started to blush, then dove in, "Yes, I'm going through the change. Mother said that girls often go through it earlier than boys do."

"So, because you have boobs and... hair, you have stronger magic than I do?"

"Probably," she replied. "All I know is, you won't be a farmer, and I won't have to marry one."

Chapter 18: Danika and Jorn

The twins left their room at the Inn and took the road heading east from town. They had no idea where to go or what to do when they got there, but some vague sense told them which way to go. As they were heading out of town, they joined the dozens of travelers, leaving Goldport for destinations to the East. The country of Chuo was in that direction, and from there, the whole of Kronos was accessible. The majority of people walked from place to place. Traders had their horse-drawn wagons, and knights and the wealthy all had horses, but most people walked their whole lives and were fine with traveling on foot for days or weeks at a time.

Danika looked over at her brother as they walked. He was unusually quiet, normally his nature was very upbeat and to be honest, very annoying. Not today though. He was downcast, and she could see tears forming in his eyes. He tried not to cry because that would be unmanly, but he still mourned the loss of their parents. He loved his father as all boys should, but he was so very attached to their mother, and Danika knew that it was her loss that weighed on him the most.

It wasn't that she didn't grieve as much as her brother, indeed, her feelings were as deep as the ocean itself; but it was her nature to bottle up her feelings, to lock them inside. She felt the fear of them being alone, the anger at the greed of pirates to rob and kill her parents without thought or the slightest pang of guilt. The fire in her was always burning, and everything that had happened was just fuel to feed that fire. Literally. She had torched the two sailing ships with some power that she had never had before and she had no idea where it came from, or how to control it. After their experience, she could now feel the power within her; but that first time was just the release of all her pent-up hatred and frustration. Her desire to kill the pirates was expressed as fire in her mind, her natural ability made it become reality. Jorn was draining his pool of anger a tear at a time, she was saving her anger for a rainy day.

"What do you think we should do now?" she asked.

"I don't know." He thought for several seconds, "Not farming. That used up Mom and Dad and left dried-up old people in their place. I don't want that."

She was surprised by his reaction. They had never really talked about grown-up things like this before. "I thought you were looking forward to being old enough to really help Father with the planting and harvesting?"

"I was. That was the old me. New me has other ideas." His face was showing the anger and frustration of being a victim. "This world is filled with bad people, evil people. I don't know how we can do the things that we did, but I'll learn to control it. The next time someone tries to harm either one of us, I'll make them very sorry."

Landis Stone was walking along feeling pretty good about himself. He had made a tidy sum by taking out Era Rutendo, though he had to spend most of it to get his brother out of jail. The great part was, he didn't need to find anything immediately. He had enough to last for a couple of months unless he got too lavish with the wine and women. He made it clear to Jarrod that he was done supporting him, and that if his little brother ran out of money, he would have to earn it himself.

The Stone brothers enjoyed their time in Rubina, and there was much there to like; but there was a storm brewing far to the North, and where there was conflict, there was the chance of getting paid. Rolling hills and frequent farms were on either side of the main thoroughfare that led towards the border with Chuo. On one side was a steady stream of people walking, the other side was set aside for horses, carts, and carriages. The system worked well, and everyone respected the unwritten rules of the road. Being tall and physically active men, they set a pace that was faster than your average pilgrim or merchant. Jarrod was humming a cheerful tune to himself and passing people quite regularly. Despite the warning from Landis, he was always on the lookout for someone he could hustle. They found themselves coming up on a bit of congestion in the road, a couple of children were being accosted by older men who looked like the type that would only fight when the odds were clearly in their favor. When they got within a few paces, they could hear their conversation.

"Just give us your shiny bits! We are not trying to harm ye! Coins? Ye gotta 'ave coins if ye be travlin the Iron Road!" said a nearly toothless fellow. His stringy hair looked as if it had never been washed, his face was equally dirty. He wore rags and carried no weapons, so picking on children was his only way of getting by. His partners were likewise devoid of any social graces or hygiene. They hovered over the boy and girl, roughly blocking their progress, which Landis was not going to allow. The lead thief put his hand on the girl's arm. "If ye have na shinys, I'll be thinkin ye have other that has value!" His look and his hand on her arm made his intentions clear. Landis had his hand on his sword's pommel and was now close enough to be considered part of the conversation. He was ready to act when he was stopped by the boy, who caught them all by surprise.

"Unhand my sister, or by all the gods, I'll fucking kill you where you stand!" The strength and conviction in his voice caught everyone by surprise, even his sister, "I've killed men before, and I liked it! I am blessed by the gods with unholy power, and if you subject my sister to one more second of mistreatment... I'll kill you. No discussion, no pleading for mercy.

One second alive, the next second, dead!" His look made it clear that he completely believed that his threats were within his ability to accomplish. The bandits looked down at the boy with fear starting to build in their eyes. He was deciding whether it made sense to press the issue and find out that somehow this boy indeed had the ability to defend himself and his sister. He was not a bright man, and to his credit, he knew he was a brick short of a load. Landis took this hesitation in the action to step in.

"Nephew, are these men bothering you?" he asked in a friendly way. The children and the thieves turned and looked at him from head to toe. He was obviously a professional soldier and a near-perfect physical specimen. Behind him, another man who was nearly as tall; and just as confident.

"Yes... uncle. If you could please ask them to leave sister and me alone, I would appreciate it," Jorn said, his anger cooling.

"You men shouldn't be bothering travelers. Can I count on you to behave?" he asked while stepping within inches of the three men. "Since you've not yet crossed the line, I can let it go this time."

"Brother, I think you're too kind. These chaps haven't learned a lesson at all!" Jarrod butted in, flipping his knife high in the air, and catching it without looking.

The bandits looked at the terrifying boy, and his even more frightening uncles, and there was really no alternative. "Thank you, Sirs, we meant no harm. We'll not be bothering you nor any of the folk travelin' this road." He turned and ran forward a few steps, the others jogged up to join him.

"No!" Landis' voice rang out, almost stopping traffic in both directions, "We're going this way. You, go the other way," he said plainly. The bandits looked at him, then at each other. They were at a loss. "You have scared my niece and angered my nephew and frankly, I'm not too pleased with you either." He took a step closer, his hand resting on the hilt of his sword. He pointed in the other direction. "You go that way. Understand? If I see you again, you'll not live long enough to regret disobeying me."

All traffic on the road had temporarily stopped to observe the drama. The bandits, like whipped dogs, turned to go in the other direction, their heads were hanging, and they refused to make eye contact with anyone. Landis stood there and watched them till they were out of sight. He turned and caught up with the twins.

"Hope you don't mind our intervention. I hate to see people being victimized... though I wonder who I actually saved?" he said smiling at Jorn.

"I am Danika, this is my brother, Jorn," she said to the brothers as they all started walking again in the direction of Chuo. "Jorn's very protective, though we're the same age. He would kill or 'gods forbid' die for me, and I love him for it." She put her hand on her brother's shoulder.

Jarrod stood next to his brother, "Mind if we walk together for a while?" he asked. Jorn nodded, his face still flush with anger. "Great! Company makes the journey seem shorter!"

"It's great that you take care of your sister as you do; but how by the gods were you going to fight off three grown men like them?"

"As I said, I have been blessed... or cursed, with great power. I could have killed them, and everyone on the road." His anger was giving way to fear, "I don't know how strong my power is, but I could have easily killed them, and you." His demeanor said that he didn't have a bit of braggadocio in making the claim about how dangerous he was.

They walked in silence for more than a minute, till Landis' curiosity got the best of him. "What kind of power are you talking about? Are you a freakishly strong farm boy?" he asked. "I've seen that before."

"Can you turn into a wolf? I've heard of that," Jarrod asked.

Jorn looked around at the other travelers. It had been a couple of minutes since the bandits were sent packing, and seemingly everyone around them had gotten over the incident. When they were a dozen paces ahead of the closest traveler behind them, and even further from someone coming from the other direction, Jorn put out his hand, palm up. Even though it was a hot day, a feeling of energy was localized around him. The air in their immediate vicinity suddenly felt cool, despite the sun beating down on them. A small cloud formed over the boy's hand, the size of a grapefruit. as it sucked all energy from the surrounding area. The micro storm started to solidify till he was holding a snowball in the middle of summer.

Landis looked at it and was amazed, "Remarkable! I've been to every corner of Kronos, half a dozen times, and have never seen anything like that!" He had a joyful expression, then composed himself, "How would this beat someone intent on pillaging your sister?"

Jorn squeezed the snowball, the energy again crackling in the confined area so that it would not attract attention. When the fog cleared, the snowball transformed into a ten-inch icicle. The midday sunlight shone brightly on the razor-sharp point.

"Oh! That's great, Jorn! When did you learn to do that?" Danika asked.

"Just now. I willed it to happen, and it did."

Landis was suitably impressed, he took the ice dagger in his hand, spinning it around to test its balance. He looked at the boy, "This is what you would use on those men?"

"No," Danika answered for her brother. "He froze a man solid when we were attacked on the ship that brought us here," she said with sorrow in her voice. "He froze the pirate in the blink of an eye, and when the man fell over, he shattered into a thousand pieces. You could see his insides!"

"That's... terrifying!" Jarrod looked horrified. Then, after a respectable pause, "I bet we could make some money with this. Just think of the possibilities!" He lifted his head to the heavens, practically counting the money he could make with Jorn's gift.

Landis on the other hand was concerned. *I've fought men face to face, often with the odds against me. If what these children are saying is true, no degree of skill with a sword would save me. I would hate to wind up on the wrong side of people like this boy.*

"Does it frighten you to be around your brother and this... power of his?" Landis asked of Danika. "Aren't you afraid that he might lose control someday?"

"Oh no!" she laughed at him, "What I can do is many times worse!"

"Danika!" Jorn yelled at his sister. "Keep quiet, girl!"

"Worse?" He was incredulous, "What is worse than being frozen to death?"

She looked around like a true conspirator, "What can you imagine that would be a worse way to die than to freeze solid?" she asked the sellsword.

"Well, being eaten alive, of course." He looked at the girl. She laughed and shook her head 'no', "I guess, being burned at the stake." She nodded in the affirmative.

"I can summon fire, far worse than the cold that Jorn can summon. He's already learning to control his ability though. I'm proud of you brother," she said. "I can't show you without setting everything, and everyone on fire," she said as if it were a common thing. They walked without speaking for a bit.

"In advance, let me pledge my lifelong friendship to the both of you," Landis laughed.

"I second that motion. I can't even handle a testy constable, much less an angry mage," Jarrod chimed in.

"I am Landis Stone. A soldier of fortune if you will," he said, taking a carrot from his pack. He offered it to Jorn, who declined, then to Danika who gratefully accepted. He pulled out another and began to snack on it. "This is my younger brother Jarrod." He pointed at his brother who gave a casual salute.

"I guess you could say that I survive on the good graces of those I meet. I'm a master at games of both chance and skill. My serious older brother brings only pain and misery."

"I am about a dozen years your senior," Landis said to the twins, "and in my time, I've seen an ocean of blood. Diplomacy often fails… and that's when normally peaceful people need someone like me." They walked quietly for a bit.

"Really?" Jorn asked. "How do you get over the taking of a life? I am finding it… difficult."

"I did too, but when I found out that everyone that I killed was either trying to kill me or was in the habit of killing innocent people, it got easier," he said in between bites. "My loyalty can be bought, but I do not kill women or children. It's always some bandit, pirate, politician..."

"A soldier of fortune!" Danika said with a touch of stars in her eyes, "How exciting!"

"Exciting? Yes. But I haven't saved any money for my old age." He looked her in the eyes, "For an old age that I'll most likely never see." He crunched his carrot and looked at the road ahead. "War is easy for me now, but this is and always has been a young man's game. Someday, someone will be faster or more skillful, and that'll be the end of me." He looked at his traveling companions, "That is, unless I meet someone who can freeze me or toast me before I can draw my sword."

"I will treat you as a friend, till you prove to be otherwise," Jorn said. "Can you tell us stories of war, and... women?" he asked on the sly.

"Better yet, Jarrod can tell you why I just had to bail him out of jail in Empire City. My younger brother knows two things above all else; games of chance, and women." Jorn looked at the Gambler, who smiled and shrugged his shoulders.

They had been traveling most of the day without incident. It was clear that Landis and Jarrod saw the twins as their younger brother and sister, and the twins saw the Stone brothers as older brothers, or perhaps as wise uncles. They were again on the road after stopping at a roadside stand for soup and spring water. A black object flashed down from somewhere high up in the sky, blocking the sun for just a second before landing on Jorn's shoulder. The raven had a note tied to its foot. Jorn held his arm out like the bird was going to infect him with some kind of disease. Danika yelped in shock at how quickly the bird had swooped in and taken residence on her brother's left arm.

Jarrod reached out and undid a tiny note that was attached to the bird's leg. As soon as it was relieved of the message, the bird took off, flew almost directly upward, and then disappeared into the Eastern sky. He unrolled the note, then handed it to Danika. "Can't read," he said sheepishly.

She looked over the note, her face showed that she was not fully understanding the message. She handed it to her brother. Jorn looked it over, then pocketed it and turned to Jarrod, "Seems that someone named Argus wants to meet us at the Hilltop Inn at Clearlake in Chuo," Jorn said with a troubled look.

Without hesitation, "Good thing we're heading that way!" Jarrod said cheerfully.

Chapter 19: Awakening

The shockwave passed through the solid stone as if it were not there. He opened his eyes. The chamber he was lying in was completely dark. He blinked to be sure that his eyes were actually open. There was a deathly stillness in the chamber, the tomb where he had been slumbering for the last two hundred years. Without having to think that hard, the word for light came to him, he spoke it despite his mouth being as dry as sand in the desert. "Lumo," he whispered. A small ball of light appeared a foot above his head, precisely where he had wanted it. The light was dim, all the better. His eyes had not been open for a dozen generations; they would not like being assaulted by the harshness of a stronger light.

He could see the top of the cave, ten feet or so above where he lay. The naturally occurring ceiling was rough and craggy, made of a very dark stone with seams of a honey-colored stone running through it. He willed his eyes to pan the room from left to right, then back again. The cave was small, with just enough room for the dais that he was lying on, and storage for a few of his personal items. There was no door. With great effort, and a lengthy amount of time, he was able to sit up, and with much effort, to stand. The dryness in his mouth was outweighed by the emptiness of his stomach. He had never been one to eat much, even in his youth so many centuries ago; but right now, his hunger was intense and dominated his thoughts. Again, the word came to him as naturally as if it was his first language. "*Aqua,*" he whispered, and a skin of cool water appeared next to him on the dais. "*Victus,*" he spoke, and a loaf of fresh bread appeared. Allowing the cobwebs to clear from his thoughts, he sat and chewed the bread, washing it down with the water. With every bite and sip, he felt more energized, his thoughts becoming clearer, and his vision was now coming into focus.

Checking himself out, he was amused that his beard had not changed during the long period of his death-like sleep. His clothes... his once sparkling blue robe was tattered and torn and appeared black. He realized that every inch of both his clothes and his exposed skin was covered by a thick layer of dust. With his renewing vigor, he whispered in a more powerful tone, "*Retituo,*" and the cloth of his robe began to reweave itself, in seconds it was perfect in strength and form. He spoke the spell "*Purus,*" and the dirt lifted from him. His hair, including his beard, was separated strand by strand and each was wiped of the filth. Water appeared in midair, dousing him from head to toe. He closed his eyes, allowing what felt like invisible hands to scrub the dust from his aged pores. The clothing that he wore was likewise scrubbed vigorously to remove the ages of neglect. Dirty water lifted off him and formed a ball in the air, then folded in on itself till it was gone with a quiet slurp.

Looking down at himself, he seemed quite pleased with the results. He was once again himself. He would be standing a few inches short of six feet if not for how bowed his back had become. His age was beyond guessing, his white beard was two-foot long and complimented his long white hair. His floor-length robe was bright blue, made from the finest silk and every inch had some rune stitched into the material with both gold and silver thread. No such garment had ever existed, it was literally priceless. He picked up his bag that was next to the dais where he had left it hundreds of years before. Hefting it over his shoulder, he raised his hand and drew a rune of power in the air to go along with his incantation. "*Ostium,*" he spoke, causing a door to appear in the solid stone of his chamber. The walls were thick, and it took more energy than conjuring food or water; but in a short time, there was a wizard-sized hole in the wall, which he used to make his exit.

He looked around in every direction and found that there was no one in sight. It was nighttime and he was at the top of a mountain, on a small island in the middle of a large lake. He had known that he would be helpless if caught while sleeping, so he picked the most remote place that he could find. He gathered up a few sticks and stacked them for a fire. "*Incendia*," he said to the wood, then watched gleefully as it caught fire and gave off both heat and light. He would need something more substantial than a loaf of bread, but he wasn't sure that his stomach could take meat yet. If there was a town nearby, he longed to purchase a pudding or a pie of some sort.

Sitting on a rock outcropping, so that he was very close to the fire, he pulled his bag next to him and rested it against his doe leather boot. There was a metal buckle on the front that he opened and flipped back the covering flap. By the light of the fire, he dug around the old and odd-smelling contents till he found what he was looking for. He took out a small leather bag and set it on his knee, then he pulled at the drawstring. Pouring the powdery contents into his hand, he seemed displeased that there was only a pinch of the substance remaining. Shrugging his shoulders, he tossed the powder into the roaring flames. There was a feeling of energy in the air, emanating from the fire. He leaned in, straining to see the visions he was summoning.

In his vision, there was a young man and a young woman, and he could see that they were just children. He guessed their ages to be between thirteen to fifteen. The girl was a beauty, her long wavy black hair was contrasted by her bright blue eyes. She was well over five feet tall and was just starting to blossom. The boy had thick black hair and blue eyes and bore a slight resemblance to the girl. He was leading her by the hand, though she seemed quite capable of walking through the city by herself. He appeared both afraid to be separated from her, and proud to be her protector.

He wondered to himself if they were the reason that he had been roused from his hibernation. He watched them as the boy lead his female friend, no... sister, through a busy city populated by people of all stripes. He watched them for a while, till his fire started to fade. He was worried that he would lose the vision prematurely, till he saw a sign, 'Goldport Trading'. So, they were in Goldport. That was in Rubina, the neighboring country. He smiled at his good fortune. He pulled a small package out of his pack and placed it on the ground. The spell was automatically activated, and the package kept unfolding till it was a complete tent, erected and waiting for an occupant. Despite his long hibernation, he decided to head down the mountain first thing in the morning. He entered the tent, closed the flap behind him, and in a matter of moments, the air was polluted with the sound of loud snoring.

Chapter 20: The Mage

Argus rode an old ass that he had purchased, and now along with his new manservant, was heading West through Chuo towards the Rubina border. Though he was anxious to see the subjects of his vision, he was in no great hurry. He could sense that they too were traveling and that they were headed in his general direction. He was no big fan of riding creatures and so the slow, deliberate pace of his ass, which he had named Elo, suited him just fine.

His manservant was a Telnor. The giant humanoid rode a draft horse and kept pace behind his master. His seven-foot frame was covered by a dark green hooded robe. No one on the road would make eye contact with either of them and because of his size, they often stepped off the road and into the fields, to allow the mage and his servant to pass. Telnor were so few in Kronos, that most people thought that they were mythical creatures. Without exception, they had mottled sickly yellow skin and white/grey hair. Their ears are pointy both on the top and bottom, and they never had facial hair. Most had sharp features, with high cheekbones, and long sharp noses. Their most noticeable feature was the extra set of arms. Having four arms made them excellent warriors and their ability to do skilled work was incredible.

"Riken, when we meet the children, please wait to be introduced. I think that you might startle them," he said to his tall companion.

"They may be startled by my appearance," he said in his clear deep voice. "But I think they will be more afraid of you, my lord," he laughed at his own observation. "I think you may be the only mage in all of Kronos; your legend is well-known among my people."

"The memories of the Telnor are much longer than those of men. Your people live for two or three hundred years, men only live a fraction of that, and they don't respect their ancestors or their traditions."

"If what you told me is true, there is a new awakening. You are no longer the only one of your kind and perhaps many more like you will emerge," Riken said to his charge.

"You are more correct than you know Riken. A shock wave woke me from my centuries long slumber. I can sense the children, even from this great distance. Magic is again returning to Xoran."

"So, you think that these children are important?"

"They are very powerful, only a true mage could be sensed from this distance. There are two of them, and there may be more across the seas." He looked over at his servant, "Do your people resent the rise of man?"

The cloaked figure chuckled, "No, we had our time here." They rode in silence for a minute, "Men have named this land 'Kronos', and they think that it is the whole world. There are many lands that lie far over the horizon, both to the East, West and the North. In some of these lands, men are not even known. In the land to the North, my people are many and they rule the land. Magic still exists there and is accepted by everyone."

"Perhaps when my final duties have been discharged, I can travel with you. There is much that I need to catch up on."

"I would welcome you to see how big and diverse this world really is." Riken smiled his hideous smile at the mage.

Chapter 21: Magic

"I see the smoke from a dozen taverns. Kilburn is close now," Jarrod said to the twins. He was older than they were, but he was always in high spirits, and they took to him like ducks to water. After two weeks on the road, they were now like one big family. Though there was no relation, the twins regarded him and Landis as older brothers or uncles. Where Landis was the one true adult in the group, Jarrod had the stories that captivated the young man and made his sister blush. As they were close to a major city, there were quite a few fellow travelers on the road. Jarrod was starting to feel the need for a drink and a game. Landis wanted to deliver the twins safely to their mysterious meeting.

"Is it as big as Goldport?" Jorn asked. "Those are really the only two cities that we have seen."

"It's on the coast, so it is a pretty large city, not as much sea trade as Goldport. South of here is a little dicey, so most people stay on the Iron Road, and it takes them right through Kilburn." He slowly lost his smile as they walked along, "It's mighty expensive in a big city like that. You still have money?"

"Enough for a while, but we should probably look for work," Jorn replied. "I don't love farming. That would be my last resort."

"Jorn, if you go work someone's farm, there is no telling if they would take me too! Would you leave me to go till a stranger's land?" she asked, very concerned.

Jarrod got a devilish grin on his face, "You're almost marrying age. Bet you could get quite a nice dowry for her!" he said to Jorn.

"What!" she practically yelled. Both Jarrod and Jorn saw the mystical flame just behind her eyes. They both rushed to put their arms around her.

"Just joking, little sister," Jarrod said in a calming voice. "You won't be ready for several months yet."

"Not funny uncle," Jorn scolded. "She's never had a boyfriend and she's a little sensitive about the whole thing."

"She's not experienced... like you?" Jarrod laughed.

"Experienced! He's only kissed two women in his life, mother, and me!" Danika shouted, pointing to her cheek.

Now both the twins were sulking, and Landis was trying not to laugh out loud. They walked along, now starting to pass livery stables, hay and grain sellers, and shops of every kind. The city lay before them like a man-made forest, placed directly in their path. Danika started looking around; she had a nervous look on her face, then it spread to Jorn, and Landis could see the tension that clouded both of their expressions.

"What is it?" he asked them.

"Magic!" she whispered. "There is magic somewhere nearby. Strong magic."

"How can you be sure? Didn't you just learn that magic existed a couple of weeks ago?"

"She's right, I can feel the energy in the air. It's like the smell of burnt flesh and hair. Once you experience it, you can never 'not' notice it," Jorn explained.

"I don't know if it comes from a person... or an object...," she said hesitantly.

"Or a creature, some magic-using race...," Jorn added.

"If what you are saying is true, then the source of this magic can probably tell that you two are nearby. It may come looking for you," Landis said to them. They looked at each other, realizing that he was right and that they might be in great danger. "Of course, as your protector, I'll do my best to defend you. You may not know it to look at me, but I'm handy with a sword." The twins both looked at him. He was clearly a soldier of fortune, and still being alive with a minimum of scars spoke to his ability. They allowed themselves a nervous laugh. Jorn and Jarrod started looking around.

"Can we stop for food?" Jorn asked the others. "I'm starving!"

"Didn't I just give you a piece of bread?" Danika asked, looking exasperated.

"That's long gone, and it was a small piece. I'm so happy to be in a city... I think we should celebrate with chicken or pork, potatoes, corn, more bread..." His eyes began to glaze over.

"I think he's going through a growing stage. Needs the extra food," Landis said to Danika. "I swear, he looks an inch taller than when we met you two!" They walked the main street, and when some especially good smells hit them, they allowed the shop owner to drag them in and seat them. Danika had a lady-like meal, Jarrod had a normal portion, and Jorn and Landis both ordered manly portions and attacked them vigorously. Landis was surprised when his adopted brother was sitting there with an empty plate.

All eyes turned as a seven-foot cloaked figure approached their table. With his upper arms, he reached up and pulled back his hood, revealing his sharp yellow features. His eyes were red and focused, his fangs were short and needle-like. His long white hair was pulled back in a long ponytail that was tied off with a silver clasp.

"Are you a Telnor?" Landis asked him, hand on the pommel of his sword, ready to spring into action.

"Is this the magical creature that you were sensing Danika?" Jarrod asked.

"I'm not magical," the Telnor replied. His voice was deep and resonated. He turned back to Landis, "I have come to invite these two to meet my master."

"What if they don't want to go, what then?" he asked the giant.

"They want to meet him, in fact, they need to meet him," he said smiling at them in what he surely thought was an inviting smile. "He is a magic user, like them... he has knowledge that they desire."

The twins looked at Landis, he looked at them.

"We'll meet your master," Jorn offered, "if we can take our friends," he said, indicating Jarrod and Landis.

"Follow me," Riken said, drawing his cloak around him. The giant lumbered off towards the door, Jorn threw some money on the table, and they all took off after him.

The old man leaned over the table and poured each of his four guests a cup of tea. The twins sipped politely and had difficulty looking up at their host. He was staying in the Blue Mastiff Inn, and he had paid for every room and then sent the staff packing. They sat together at a large table in the center of the dining room. The dining area was dark and only their section of the room was illuminated. The Telnor was off in the shadows somewhere, the old man seemed more at home in the near dark.

Landis drank the tea, "That's quite good, milord." He set the cup down, "The children are not really used to such fanciness. They were brought up on water and milk."

"I have had tea before!" Danika replied like a spoiled child, "Once."

"Why have you asked us here?" Jorn asked, looking the old man in the eyes.

The old man smiled at the boy as he took his seat. "My name is Argus, I've been called 'Argus the Ancient', 'the mage', and I've gone by a few other names. I have been in a deep sleep these last two hundred years, and then a shock wave woke me from my death-like slumber. You don't know it yet; but when you are able to control magic, it gives you a sixth sense. I can see power radiating from both of you as if you were coals in a smoldering fire. I know this is all very new to you. Please tell me what you know about your abilities."

"I can show you," Jorn said "Danika is still having problems controlling her... abilities." Danika gave her brother a look, her fiery temper flaring, but she changed her mind and said nothing. Jorn stood up and held his arms out like he was holding something. The air in the room suddenly seemed to overflow with energy; the temperature dropped so quickly that it even took even Danika by surprise. Between his hands was a tiny storm, a storm that raged and folded in on itself. Ice crystals fell into place and in a few seconds, he was holding a clear dagger made of ice. It was long, wide at the base, and tapered to a thin, sharp point.

The old man's smile became a friendly chuckle. For the first time, his eyes took on a grandfatherly twinkle. He nodded and held out his hand for the blade. Jorn passed it around to him. Argus rolled it in his hands, the dim lantern light gleaming off the frozen blade.

"Very good! You did this with no training? You are more than I was hoping for." He ran his wrinkled old fingers along the handle, then the blade. They all sat in silence, watching the old man admire Jorn's work. His movements were slow, and he caressed the blade lovingly. Then with a speed that none of them thought him capable of, he cocked his arm back and flung the knife at Danika.

The knife crossed the room and got within arm's length before it vaporized in a wave of white-hot flame. The light was blinding in the inky dark room, and the heat dwarfed that of noon on the hottest day of summer. The flame was a huge hand that grew and pushed forward, the heat became dangerously hot. The light it produced was overpowering and it threatened to fill the room and consume all within it. Then it was over. Quickly as it had appeared, the ball of flame was gone. Danika stood there breathing hard, her heart racing like a freight train.

"I was afraid that your flame might get away from you, I'm glad you were able to stop it!" Jorn said to his sister.

"I didn't. I didn't stop it," she said breathing hard and looking at the old mage. The old man chuckled out loud now, he looked at the twins with a look of satisfaction and pride. He sat in his chair and the others all turned towards him.

"I stopped your fire, girl," he said. "So powerful! You are as powerful as your brother is controlled. What a fine pair you are."

"You can use magic too?" Jorn asked.

"I am what you can become. Are you hungry?"

Jorn nodded. Argus leaned forward and began to make a show of it. His old bony fingers danced in the air between them, the energy growing and collecting, then he added the incantation, "*Victus.*" The smoke cleared, and there were piles of food covering the table. Fresh loaves of bread, a basket of apples, pears, peaches, and cherries, there were baked chickens, a leg of lamb, and various sweets. Everyone was startled, and despite having eaten recently, they dove into the feast, piling all their favorites on their plates. The kids dug in lustfully, trying new foods that they had never even heard of before. Never had they seen so much food in one place. Landis too grabbed at the food with gusto. Jarrod went for the jug of wine and poured himself a generous glass. Argus just watched with a pleased look on his face, as if they were admiring his cooking and not his conjuring.

"Children, this is a bit advanced; but conjuring food is one of the first skills that I will teach you. A mage needs to be able to provide for himself or herself. Save your money for things that you can't make yourself."

Jorn looked up from his full plate, the chicken still filling his cheeks like a chipmunk, "Sir, you mean that Danika and I will be able to do this? You're willing to teach us these things?"

"Conjuring food is, like I said, one of the first things that I'll teach you. I'll help you to control your fire and your ice. I will teach you a great many things if you agree to become my apprentices. I warn you though, this is a commitment of many years, and you must see me as your master, and follow my every command." His look made it clear that he was deadly serious. The twins looked at each other, then at Landis, they were undecided and wanted his opinion. He stood up, dusted himself, and straightened out his tunic.

"Can I be assured that you'll treat these young ones kindly and won't abuse them or let them come to harm?"

"I can assure you that they'll live, other than that, it is up to them. I'm not teaching them cooking. The use of magic is inherently dangerous." He looked the soldier in the eyes, "I will use every bit of my considerable skill to protect them as they develop."

"Very well then. I give my blessing." He sat and pulled in his chair. "Where do you live, good sir?"

"I have land in South Chuo. We'll travel there tomorrow."

"We'll go with you, I need to know how to get there, as I'll be checking on them every so often... without notice."

"Very well," the old mage said smiling. "I have not been awake long, but I know your type of man, and having one such as yourself that these children can call 'friend' is truly a blessing."

The windows were covered so that the room was almost black except where the curtains met, spears of bright light pierced the darkness. Landis and Jarrod stood at the front desk that was just inside the main entrance. They had their packs with them and were getting ready to leave. Argus and his Telnor were nowhere to be seen, only the twins were present to see them off. They both looked sad. In the weeks that they had been together, Jorn had started to see the lone mercenary as an older brother, and the gambler as a troublemaking uncle. They were totally different male role models than his father. Danika too looked at Landis like an older brother; but as he hefted the pack onto his broad shoulders, some other emotion flickered in the depth of her eyes.

"Where will you go?" Jorn asked them.

"Don't laugh at me, but I thought that I would visit our father. He is getting old, and seeing you two, recently orphaned, makes me think that I should spend the time now before it's too late."

"That's a grand idea!" Danika cooed. "If my parents were still alive, I would tell them every day about how much I loved and needed them."

"I saw a few nice taverns back there in Kilburn," Jarrod said. "It's hard to make any money with this stiff around." He nodded in his brother's direction.

"Thanks a lot. I'll be going to Anatol, it's a country far to the North of here. By land, it could take weeks or even months. I'll head back to Kilburn and book a ship. I think it's only a week by ship."

"Just beware of pirates. They are thick in the Inland Sea," Jorn warned him.

"Don't you know by now? Pirates should beware of me!" he laughed out loud. "I may not have magic like the two of you, but the man I fear has yet to be born." With that, they walked from the hall. The twins stood in the doorway and watched till they lost sight of them, far down the road. They knew that their paths would cross again.

Chapter 22: The High Father

Bhava Fon, the High Father of the Panists, lay dying. He had been the titular head of the world's main religion for almost twenty years, and his strength had kept the peace while also growing the mother church in both wealth and influence. He had as many enemies as anyone who reaches the top does. Though they wouldn't take him on while he had a firm grip on the heart and souls of the populace, they were more than ready to pick at his corpse. A couple of different factions now met at the temple of Magnus, which served as the headquarters for the religion. His illness came on suddenly, but it allowed enough time for the Regent Fathers to pour in from all corners of Kronos to the country of Lourens. Lourens was House Odila's Kingdom; but the real power was held by the church that was based in their largest city, Corbinus.

Wever Bran sat in his carriage with his chief advisor, Lehna Miraslav. Wever was tall and thin with an almost starved look on his long pale face. Like all priests, he had his light brown hair cut almost to the scalp and no facial hair whatsoever. Unlike average monks that wore simple brown robes, he wore expensive golden robes with fancy piping and hand-sewn designs. His assistant, Lehna was an attractive woman in her late twenties with long curly hair, swarthy skin, and a bit of a long nose. They had traveled from Inram, a kingdom just a few days' ride away. The Laima family ran Inram, but the king was seen as being weak, and it was well known that the wolves were at his door. The church had been a minor force in their kingdom; but under the steady hand of Father Bran, it had grown in influence. Now that Father Fon was finally dying, he would be considered a prime candidate to become the next 'High Father', or at a minimum, have some of his reforms implemented. *I've been waiting for years, looks like he's really going to die this time.* Wever thought to himself.

The healer held the old priest's hand and mumbled some mantras over the prostrate form. There was a feeling of energy that flowed through the air and concentrated on the priest's head and chest. The old man's ragged breathing went from a death rattle to a soft rumbling. He turned to the senior priests in the room.

"I've done all that I can for him."

"You were able to heal him?" the housemaster asked. He was older than Father Fon and had been through several High Fathers in his lifetime of service to the Corbinus temple. The members of the senior council leaned in to hear if there was a cure in the works.

"No fathers, he is already on the road to the next world. I just eased his pain as much as I could. I think that gods willing, he'll not see another sunrise and will pass quietly in his sleep." He was a renowned healer and had performed near miracles in the past, but old age was beyond any man's power to fix.

The council members filed out of the room, a collection of old men and women who held the power over the church that encompassed all the known gods. They had suspected that the end was near, but they now knew that the High Father was as good as dead. Very soon, it would be time to begin the process of choosing his successor. Most of them were too old to want to take on the added burden of leadership, their days of politicking were behind them. After some haggling and a little bit of informal negotiation, the field was narrowed to two who were young enough and still had a fire in their bellies. Wever Bran had a strong following; but his only rival, Felica Marten was the odds-on favorite. Her leadership would take much the same form as the current High Father. She stood for strong adherence to the scrolls that by legend, had been handed directly from the Lord God Magnus to the first High Father, Silas Ameron. Wever on the other hand was a reformer and wanted to bring major changes to the religion.

The housemaster climbed onto a chair so that he could address the crowd. When they saw him, everyone turned and stopped their conversations. "Brothers, sisters... if it is indeed the case that our master will pass this night, we all need to be prepared to move forward in the morrow." He was fighting back tears. "I will stay with him till the end, the rest of you, get some rest and we'll begin deliberations in the late morning." He stepped down, and without another word, went back into the sick room to be by his master's side. Wever looked around, finding his assistant, he called her over. He whispered in her ear for a good long time, then smiling, retired to his cell.

The morning was bright, the start of a beautiful day. The priests entered the meeting room where the haggard housemaster awaited them. He looked like he had not slept in a week, and he didn't try to hide his sorrow. The High Father died in the middle of the night, going peacefully thanks to the healer's pain-relieving spells. When all were present and had taken their seats, he stood before them and called the meeting to order. After words of tribute had been said, and a few tears shed, they moved on to the new business.

"Now we are tasked with selecting a replacement for Father Fon. "Do we have any candidates for the position of the next High Father?" he asked the room. Wever looked across the room. *You better do as I told you Njord, or I'll crush you. I'm not about to let that tired old spinster take what is rightfully mine.*

"I nominate Wever Bran," Njord Luca said to the gathering. He was a longtime associate of Wever. The nomination was met with a mixed reaction. There were some positive rumblings and a few negative grumblings.

Jet Callum stood, and turned to the group, "I nominate Sister Marten." This was greeted by near silence. Several of the members looked at her, then looked around at each other. *Silence. Looks like my little birds have flown around and chirped in more than a few ears.*

"Anyone else?" the housemaster asked. No one replied.

"Then it is between Mother Marten and Father Bran. Who would like to speak?" There was a long silence, then Father Luca stood.

"It pains me to bring this up in public, but I heard a most disturbing rumor about the good Mother. If it's true, then I would think that she could not be considered for such an important post. Perhaps not even for the office that she now holds!" he said, then sat quickly.

Another priest stood, "I too have heard the rumors that you speak of." He paused for emphasis, "If they are true, I find this most disturbing." Most of the priests looked around, confused by the lack of decorum.

"What accusations have been made against me!" Mother Marten demanded.

"That you have been planning to recognize the Quell!" a priest exclaimed. "They are a death cult and not a true religion. They should be exterminated, not bartered with!"

"They claim to be a religion, but they execute anyone who refuses to convert! We can't deal with these animals, only putting them down like the rabid dogs that they are is acceptable," a mother called out.

"I am not in league with the Quell, I hate them as much… more than any of you!" Mother Marten exclaimed. "Under my leadership, we would conscript an army to quash this uprising. We would seek them out and destroy their leaders and burn their places of worship."

Wever stepped forward; a hush fell on the crowd. "You say what you must, Mother Marten, in order to win our favor; but we will not be fooled by your pleasant features and your honeyed words. Someone in league with the Quell can never be trusted." *I almost feel guilty about this. Amazing how you can start a rumor, with no proof at all, and if it's repeated often enough, it becomes the truth.*

"True!" Njord called out. "There can be only one choice! We must have Wever Bran as our next High Father!" He dared not look over at Wever. The man was cunning and vengeful.

"An accusation has been made, but not a scrap of evidence has been presented. I completely deny these false claims against me, and demand that proof be brought forward, or those who made these false accusations be sanctioned!" she demanded.

"Just what you expect the guilty to say. She is in league with the Quell, of that there can be no doubt," Father Luca yelled across the table. "Only Father Bran can save us from the influence of false prophets and false religions!"

There were cheers and hoots in favor of Father Bran. When it came time for the voting, it was already a foregone conclusion. Wever Bran became the next High Father. After the council broke to return to their various lands, the new High Father pulled his assistant aside.

"Prepare the proclamation, we need to increase taxes drastically. The people have too much comfort and the church is barely getting by. We need to prepare for my initiatives." She nodded in agreement and went about the church's business.

Chapter 23: Theocracy

Wever Bran was furious. He sat in his elevated chair that was cushioned and covered with the finest animal furs. With his fancy robe and propensity for golden jewelry, he looked very much like the king that he imagined himself to be. The room was long, and the council of priests was milling about on both sides of the main hall that terminated in front of his throne.

"Tell me again, what this 'king' has said to you concerning my right to levy and collect a tax?" he asked the priest. The man trembled before the High Father, especially knowing that he was the bearer of bad news.

"Father, he *is* the king. Lourens is his land, and we are, because of geography, his subjects," the priest whispered to his master.

"This land and all lands are the property of the gods. We worship Magnus, the king of the gods, do we not?"

"Of course, Father; but he has been very generous to give us monies to fund the church and to provide us with security and comfort. If we go against his wishes, we risk losing his favor, and that includes losing his patronage."

"That is why we need to collect our own taxes. If we are beholden to any earthly power, be it king or country, we lose our ability to faithfully carry out the master's wishes." Wever was frustrated by these nobles who thought that they had any power in the dealings of the church. The High Father paced the room, then returned to where the priest was waiting. "I need to call a meeting of the council. Make sure that they all know that attendance is mandatory."

"Yes, High Father. Your will be done," he said before scampering off.

There had been upgrades to the council room since the last meeting of the priests. Where there was once simplicity, to accentuate function over form, now there was an open show of wealth. An outsider would see the fancy and expensive trappings and be humbled by them. Countless courtiers and sycophants were present to usher in the council members, some of whom had traveled weeks to be present. The High Father watched with pride as his staff carried out their tasks to perfection; anything less would be dealt with harshly. The council members shuffled into the meeting room, breaking apart from their clusters of two or three, to take their assigned seats at the great table. When everyone was seated, and the meeting had been called to order, the High Father stood to address the group.

"Brothers, sisters, I have prayed on this long and hard. I have spoken directly to Magnus and asked for his guidance," he preached to the priests. He had reached his position by questionable means, but no one doubted his ability to grab an audience by the collar and lead them where he wanted them to go. "The king of Lourens has tried to deny the Holy Church the right to tax its people. Our people! Do we not pray for them, and cater to them when they are sick or when they have a crisis of faith? These people are the servants of the faith, they are the followers of Magnus and the Old Gods!" he said, storming down the hallway behind the row of seated priests. He stopped behind an older woman with mousy features and brown hair that was quickly going grey.

"Sister, are you not from Kees to the North?"

"I am, High Father," she replied.

"And the souls that are entrusted to your caretaking, do not most of them pray to Reina, goddess of children and of life?"

"And to Magnus, in Kees, it's almost evenly split," she replied.

"Would you not agree, that the will of kings is subordinate to the will of the gods; from whom they derive their authority?" he asked the priest.

"I am shocked that you would ask such a question. Of course, the will of the gods is paramount. It is our task to carry out the god's will, not to obey the whims of lords and kings."

"Exactly! Well said, Mother. That's the reason that I have called all of you here today. The gods want us to spread their word and fend off the infiltration of false prophets, like the Quell. We must expand the presence of the church, not just in the eyes of the flock; but just as importantly, at the table where the power brokers make their deals." He paced back to his chair and stood behind it, hands grasping the back of the chair till his knuckles turned white. "We need to raise money and gather souls who will fight and sacrifice for this holy cause. If that means we must disobey the earthly powers that misguidedly think that they hold dominion over the people, then so be it."

They all looked at the High Father expectantly. He was new in this position, but they had put him there, and it was believed that he spoke directly with the gods. They waited for his decree, for the words that might cause them to pledge, and ultimately lose their lives in service of their faith.

"I will be the first. I am sending a letter to the king that will inform him that if he interferes with our attempts to raise funds, he will be excommunicated from the church. To be cast out of the church will make him naught but dirt in the eyes of our lord Magnus." He beat his closed fist on the table, "With the money that we raise, I propose that we recruit a security brigade to protect church property, and to aid in the collection of our levies."

"To what end?" Father Clemmons asked. "Since when are we in the business of building armies and punishing the royals that so kindly host us?"

"You know this, and if you do not, you shouldn't be here. The comings and goings of men like you or I, like every king born in this land, are nothing when compared to the glory of Lord Magnus and his children. We must thank them in every moment for our very lives, and if we must sacrifice ourselves in their service ... or anyone else for that matter, then so be it!" He was in full sermon mode now. "It takes resources to run the church, to help us perform our holy contract between the people and the gods. They always can dig deeper to tithe their share. We don't ask more than any man can afford." He stalked back to his chair.

"Each of you must inform your kings and noble houses, the church intends to exact tribute from every man, be he pauper or prince. If... and more likely when they balk, I will bring the full force of the mother church down upon them. Gods help any man who would dare to defy the will of Magnus."

Chapter 24: The Masterless Knight

Dorman Cole rode slowly on an old horse that he had owned for many years. He loved the aging mare and would never trade her for a younger stronger mount, though her usefulness in battle was questionable at this point. The road to Feld was a busy one, several small villages lay on the outskirts of the great city, second only to the capital Clifftown. House Oren was based in the city for generations; the second-best house was located in the second-best city. Dorman was called by the patriarch, Rado Oren to discuss matters of a yet undisclosed nature. He was getting paid well just to attend this meeting, so it was worth at least hearing what the man had to say.

Dorman had newly arrived at Inram and was not completely up on the local gossip, but the gist was that the ruling family was weak. The undermining of their reputation by House Oren and some of the country's other greater houses made them seem vulnerable to overthrow. No king would allow another house to build an army within their borders, but the hiring of mercenaries trained out of the country and brought in was hard for the ruling house to control.

Like most sellswords, Dorman had at one time been in the service of a king, and as go the royals, so too go their retainers and generals. For half a dozen years, he had been on his own, traveling across this great land, in search of a new master. He had lost the title of knight, and lord, and he felt that there was no honor in what he did, but he needed to support himself, and leading men into battle was the only thing that he was truly great at. Kings, on the other hand, looked at these wandering soldiers as damaged goods. They were fine to thrust into battle, but they would never become family.

The hallway was long, the stone floor had a bright red carpet that stretched from the giant twenty-foot doors, more than a hundred feet to the lord's throne. The ceiling was twenty-five to thirty feet high. One wall had windows that let in light through the expensive stained glass, the other wall had tapestries and paintings of lords long dead. Dorman Cole walked casually toward the raised seat at the end of the room. He was accustomed to being in the presence of kings, this lord with aspirations to be king was not his ideal next employer, but at his age, he couldn't be overly selective. He approached the dais, and when he was at an appropriate distance, he took a knee and bowed his head. He waited for the lord's signal to rise and approach. The man made him wait. Not an insulting amount of time, but enough to set the tone.

Stepping forward to within a conversational distance, he looked at his potential new employer. Rado Oren was not a particularly impressive man. He was overweight, as was the custom of many of the monied lords who had never killed their dinner, much less defended their walls. They relied on men like Dorman Cole, men with swords and the desire to see their enemy's head on a pike. As was the custom, Dorman waited for the lord to address him. He judged the man in his head, but his expression was completely unreadable. He waited for his interview to begin.

"I know of your reputation Sir Cole, and I have only heard good things spoken about you."

"Thank you, my lord," Dorman replied. "Your reputation and the reputation of House Oren is well known in these parts. I hope that my experience aligns with your requirements, milord."

Rado was pleased that a man who would normally be his superior was bowing to him and asking for his favor. "Yes, I can see that with a man such as yourself at the head of my forces, I could take what is rightfully mine." He leaned forward to tell the story more confidentially. "My family line is truly a descendant of the gods, yet House Laima continues to rule this land. They are weak and allow the peasants to run their own lives, when of course, they need the firm guidance of the aristocracy."

"I see your position very clearly, my Lord, and I agree wholeheartedly," Dorman said in the most believable tone he could muster. "I only hope that I can help you to right this wrong and help House Oren to achieve its rightful position."

"I have hundreds upon hundreds of men willing to fight for my banner. They of course want to be in service of the king of this land. Fortune and happenstance have prevented me from realizing my family's destiny." He was very emotional when he got to this part, "For several generations we've been denied, but no more! Inram suffers under the rule of House Laima. For the good of my country, I must seize the reins of power."

"I was a knight several years ago. My king was a foolish man who thought that he could general a battle from his comfortable throne room. If I were to take on such a responsibility again, I would need complete and total control while on the field of battle." He looked the Lord directly in the eye, so that there would be no misunderstanding of what role he was willing to accept.

"Naturally." You could almost see his mind racing for the correct response, "I am meant to lead Inram. Kings do not cross swords or... dirty themselves in combat. I need a good man; a man like yourself who can right the wrongs that have been inflicted on the people of Inram." He was starting to feel more at home in his own throne room, "I of course am preoccupied with the larger matters of state; trade, civil defense, etc."

Doorman Cole saw this as possibly his last opportunity to find a place to call home. He wasn't about to let this pompous lord off the hook without some type of commitment. "Sire, of course you wouldn't lower yourself to meet your detractors on the field of battle. That's a job for your Minister of Defense." He let it hang in the air.

"Minister of Defense?" the Lord asked no one in particular.

"Yes, my Lord. A position that is far below your lordship's but is vital to attaining the house's status and of course, maintaining it."

They shared a knowing look. The whole of the negotiations was almost instantaneous. Dorman was looking for more than mercenary work. He wanted a permanent position in the kingdom that he would help to create. Lord Oren was looking for someone to bleed for him, for a price. Knowing that he would not be able to find better, Rado Oren agreed to the unspoken demand.

"If you're able to displace the weak and shameful leadership of Inram, I would gladly welcome you as the Captain of the Guard!" He looked at Dorman who was still scowling. "And as Minister of Defense, you would be a full member of the ruling council." Dorman Cole's face finally broke its stoic façade and he allowed himself to smile.

Dorman rode his horse, sitting as tall in the saddle as he could muster. Whenever he met a new batch of troops, he always did his best to be aloof, imposing, and omniscient. They needed to know that his word was beyond question, that he was better than the best of them in every way, and that he would do his best to use their sacrifice for the glory of their lord.

None of them were men at arms, they were all conscripts, forced into service by Lord Oren. He looked at the pitiful batch of men that were to be his key to ousting the seated king and installing the insufferable Lord Rado Oren. For the first time in a very long time, he started to question his decision-making ability. The man to whom he had pledged his fealty was an insufferable worm of a man, the kind that he would have beaten to a pulp in finishing school. The men before him were at best, human shields. Though he thought that statistically, there should be a gem or two amongst the group, it was becoming evident that they were all equally useless. He valued his honor above all things, including his life. His promise to his new lord was the only thing that prevented him from leaving with all possible haste. He looked at the men, studied the sturdy, though insufficient walls that guarded his master's keep, and thought to himself, this is where my story ends. He had lived through many years and many battles, most of which he had won. Those that were lost were lost with honor. Now he felt the hand of death on his shoulder.

Chapter 25: The Warlord

Renata Rin stood around in the waiting area outside of the king's audience room. There were many others waiting for an audience, but none of them approached Commander Rin. She was in her late twenties, though her face hinted at someone who was older and wiser than her actual years. She wore her hair short, as short as the men in the guard; but her figure was still female. She had armor especially made to accommodate her ample bosom, and strong legs and hips. If a man were to look for very long at all, he might think that she wore armor for show, in some attempt to command respect; but those who knew better would never question her authenticity. Her men looked at their feet or tried to look through her face, none would be caught dead staring at her. Her deep blue tunic was emblazoned with the bright orange 'Rising Phoenix' of House Laima. She had been sold into their service when she was still a young girl of sixteen or so. Since then, she had bested both men and women to become the most feared of the king's guard, and in times of war, she was elevated to General.

She often would kill time by swinging her sword in left and right arcs around her, but not today. She was just bored. Looking out the window, she surveyed the town that surrounded the castle. Clifftown was a bustling city, filled with merchants, workers, and of course beggars, whores, and bureaucrats. She loved that she was above them, above everyone but the king himself. Like the gods, the power over life and death was in her hands. She was very judicious with her authority; but she knew, and everyone else knew, that she could strike down almost anyone in the country of Inram without consequence.

King Laima had called her to appear before him, so here she was. Despite being her only superior, she found the man tedious and secretly disliked him very much. She grew up in the country to the north and west of Inram called O'Bell. It was named after the ruling house, a country governed entirely by women. The women of O'Bell were tough as nails and despised anything that reeked of insecurity or weakness. The traits that all the O'Bell royalty had were ingrained in her. Renata had been trained by the most revered warriors in Kronos and had eventually surpassed them. She now found herself pledged to a king who would not know which end of a sword to strike with. When the inner doors finally opened, a page waved for her to enter. She let out a great sigh, then with a soldier's discipline, gathered herself and entered the chamber with no expression on her face.

Unlike many of the kings in Kronos, Ayaram Laima was not at all ostentatious. His audience chamber was finely outfitted, but not extravagant as was often the case. Everyone knew that he had great wealth, and he felt no need to display it. One place where he spent his money was in the use of spies. Only he knew the extent of his spy network, his own country of Inram was heavily watched by those in his employ. He was not vain, he was not greedy, and he was not inhumane in any way, but he was paranoid to the point of obsession. One might argue that it's not paranoia if they really are out to get you, but he saw raised daggers behind every shadow and smelled poison in every cup and plate.

Renata marched a short distance from the door to the throne. When she had drawn close, she took a knee and bowed, waiting for his leave. When asked to rise, she stood again and looked up at her liege. He was a very plain man, without any distinguishing characteristics. He wore a graying beard in an unkempt fashion with his crown matting down hair that undoubtedly, had not been washed in weeks. His skin was pale and full of various types of blemishes; signs of man who rarely if ever allowed the sun on his face. He was overweight and just conveyed a 'softness' that turned most women off and did little to inspire the men around him.

"Thank you for coming at such short notice Commander Rin," he said over a map that was laid out on the table near his throne.

"I am always at your service, milord," she said routinely. "How may I serve you and the kingdom this day?"

He looked up from his maps and papers to look her in the eye. Deep down, he knew that he was blessed to have such a servant as Commander Rin. "I know that you don't always agree with my suspicions..." he let it hang in the air for a moment. She stood at attention and waited for him to continue. "This time, I have very reliable intelligence that there is a plot brewing in the kingdom." He looked worried at his own words, like someone else was saying them and he was hearing them for the first time. "The pretender has brought a new general into the fold, and there is strong evidence that they have sent for Legion mercenaries."

"Are we declaring war on House Oren, my lord?" she asked, knowing his answer already.

The king wrung his hands and began to sweat profusely. He was torn by the decision and afraid of the consequences. He made the mistake that he always made, and that was to let everyone witness his indecision. After long minutes of agonizing, "No, we can't strike without proof of his intentions. The other great houses would see that as unwarranted aggression. Heaven knows what they would do!"

"I understand sire. I'll take a squad of my best men, and we will look around for any signs of treachery. If we find someone that means harm to House Laima, we shall quietly remove those pieces from the board, as it were."

He was visibly calmed by her words, "Yes Commander, that is an excellent strategy. Please go with my blessings."

Commander Rin rode at the head of a column of a dozen riders that pulled into a small town that didn't even have a name. Many such places existed, usually located along the main roads that connected he larger cities. Their purpose was to provide food, drink, and sometimes shelter to travelers; they rarely if ever had an industry that was not service-based. They had traveled half the distance from the capital Clifftown to the city of Feld, where the upstart House Oren was based. Dismounting, she handed her reigns to her second in command. "Get us rooms and see that the horses are stabled," she commanded. Drawing her long, riding cloak about her, she walked into the tavern that anchored this end of town.

The heavy wooden door swung inward at her push. The inside was dank and dark, even though the sun was still bright outside. It was cooler inside and there was the smell of roasting meats and stale beers. Looking around, she found a table against the right wall, well-lit and not quite in the center of the room, so as not to attract too much attention. Even at this time of day, there were many people in the place, mostly men, the kind of man that often found excuses to stop working early and start drinking in the middle of the day. Farmers were still in the fields toiling away while some of the men and a few of the women in the tavern were already too drunk to walk a straight line.

She took her seat with her back resting against the wall. She didn't even have to signal for service. Her stoic expression got the barmaid to hop off her customer's lap and scoot over to take the lady's order. She stood before this woman who was a mixture of masculine strength and feminine beauty, waiting for instruction. "Whiskey, and a beer," Renata said evenly.

"Yes, Mistress. Would you be having a cut of meat and a potato or two?" the girl asked.

"That sounds perfect. Thank you." Renata looked around the tavern as she always did. It was her habit to never be in a place without knowing where the doors were and what types of people were in attendance.

In a dark corner opposite her, three men were in a heated conversation. She couldn't quite make out what they were talking about; but even without being able to hear the words, it was entertaining. One of them was a black man who looked to be about thirty years of age. He was dressed as a smithy, and he wore the emblem of Hafza, the God of storms and fertility, and known to a lesser degree as the God of Smiths. It was a common practice for tradespeople to wear the insignia of their patron deity. The other men were dressed alike. They wore simple white and gray robes with easily, a week's worth of filth covering them. Their long hair was tucked under cloth caps, and their beards were long and had finger bones woven into them. The black man was very calm, but it looked like the others were intent on provoking him. They were screaming at him, and he answered in hushed tones. Their arms were waving with the hysteria that they were no doubt overcome by. Soon, they could no longer control themselves and they were making enough noise to disturb everyone else in the establishment. The manager timidly worked his way to them, approaching them as if they were carrying some communicable disease. He tapped the closest of the raving men on the shoulder and was rewarded with a backhand. The zealot hit him hard enough to draw blood and send the wounded manager to the floor. The other man began to grapple with the smith, the men were now trying to choke each other.

Renata had had enough. This was not her fight, but anything and everything in the country of Inram was her within her jurisdiction. After all, she represented the crown. The zealot that knocked down the manager had now fished out a wicked steel knife from somewhere in the folds of his dirty vest. He had a hand full of the man's hair and was ready to open his throat when Renata appeared next to him. He looked up, his anger turning to shock, then back to anger.

"Get away woman! I will have you when we are done with these unbelievers!" he spat in her direction. Renata kicked him in the testicles hard enough to fold him in half. She took his knife and hit him on the crown of the head so hard with the handle that he fell unconscious to the floor. She then turned to the ongoing struggle.

"In the name of King Laima, cease your fighting, or I'll have both of your heads on spikes before my dinner comes!" Her voice cut through the din. Everyone in the place froze and looked in her direction. "You!" she pointed at the other zealot, "Come here and explain yourself."

The man's face was a mask of rage and indignation, "Piss on you, woman! I am a man; you'll not talk to me like a dog!" He broke from his engagement with the smith and headed toward her. Before he could close the distance, she slowly pulled out her longsword which was always at her side beneath her stylish cape. The weapon was a real sword, a tool of battle and not a dull-edged blade like those carried by most men these days. Everyone stared at the workmanship and the fact that it was a weapon that was only carried by a true warrior.

The smith looked relieved to be unhanded, his opponent looked at Renata like she was an abomination from the lower pits. His eyes bulged and he began to froth at the mouth. "How dare you hold a weapon! You're a woman, you should be cooking and cleaning!" He started walking toward her, "Any heathen woman who is not a follower of Quell deserves only rape and death!" he was spewing madly. "I'll use you in front of all these unbelievers, and they will learn of the power of Quell!" he said as he lunged at her.

Renata never showed any fear or doubt about the outcome. Her sword swung in a tight arc that bit deep into his throat and she just stood there and waited for him to realize that he was already dead. The madman fell to the ground at Renata's feet. She wiped his blood off on his back, then returned her sword to its scabbard. Reaching down for the manager, she helped him up. "My men should be right outside your door, ask them to come in," she said returning to her seat. "Wench, where are my refreshments?" The barmaid came out of her stupor and ran into the back to fetch the food and drink. Renata caught the attention of the smith and waved him over to join her at her table. He was a large man, tall and built like the furnaces where he slaved away from dawn till dusk every day. The man would be imposing to most; but in light of the martial demonstration, he looked at Renata like she was the giant. He sat across from her respectfully, waiting for her questions. She looked at him critically, though not unkindly.

"What was that all about, what is your name?"

"Tomah, Mistress. I am a simple smith on his way to Feld."

Two large and heavily armed men walked in and stood just in front of their commander's table. They saluted, their right fist on their breast, their heads bowed. "Commander," they stated simply.

"There is a body on the floor over there." She pointed to where the man that she had slain lay bleeding. "Take it out of here. I don't care what you do with it. Then come back and arrest the other one."

"Yes Commander!" they almost shouted. In a second, they had dragged the man out and left only a pool of blood where he had been.

Under most circumstances, the smith would have been the most feared man in the room and now he just wanted to fade into the woodwork. Just then the barmaid approached with the drinks and food. "Bring some for this law-abiding citizen as well. Put it on my bill."

"You're a member of the king's guard?" the manager asked over the barmaid's shoulder.

"I am Commander Rin, commander of the king's guard," she said matter-of-factly.

"Thank you for saving my life, Mistress!" the manager said while bowing profusely. "You will never pay in this Tavern! Ever!" he said with relief in his voice. "Bring the smith whatever he wants!" he said fading into the background.

The smith sat there looking relieved to be out of danger. Renata took her whiskey in a gulp, then followed it with a healthy drink from her beer. She looked at the man, thinking that he was in no way culpable. "So, Tomah is it?" He nodded. "Do you know those men and why they were trying to incite you into unlawful behavior?" She reached for a chicken leg.

"I swear to you Mistress, I was minding my own business after a long day of travel. I was going to have a drink, some food, and then off to bed," he said as she tucked into her meal. "They saw my seal of Hafza and almost ran over to me. They told me that Quell was the only true god and that I was an infidel for praying to Hafza."

"So, they were trying to convert you?" she asked.

"I don't think that they were really trying to convert me. I think that they are crazy and seeing my religious emblem sent them over the edge. When they came in, I think they were just looking for a reason to be offended. They saw that I don't follow *their* god and decided that it was enough reason to start a fight."

Slowly chewed her food while staring at the man. Among her many talents, she had an infallible truth sense. She was very accurate at telling if she was hearing the truth. His food came and he hungrily dug in. "That was odd," she said as he was feasting on the meal that she provided. "There are many gods, and we of course do not worship all of them. I've heard only a little of this 'Quell'."

He swallowed, then looked up, "I don't know all too much madam, but I've heard rumors of a growing faith far to the west of here. Unlike the true gods, these people seek out the uneducated, the rejects of society," he stated. "Like the men that you bested, they believe that you are with them, or against them; and If you're against them, they have no problem slaying you."

"It saddens me to see this kind of cancer in my adopted homeland." She was looking off into the distance, then she remembered something, "You're traveling to Feld? Why are you going there?" she asked.

Sensing a change in tone, he straightened up, dropping the hunk of meat that was in his large strong hand. "There has been a call out for many men-of-trades, especially smiths and others who make the tools of war." He looked at her for the first time, "I make swords and spear tips, though from what I saw, nothing to match the sword that you carry."

"Who is calling for skilled men like yourself? It sounds like the drums of war are starting to beat."

"I heard from a traveler near my town that men with skill would be paid handsomely for rushing to Feld and plying our trades. I have no disloyalty in my heart Mistress, my only loyalty is to our king."

She leaned forward till they were but inches apart. She looked the man directly in his eyes, "My king thinks that there are those who would plot against him. What have you heard?" Her tone left him no avenue for escape.

"For as long as I can remember…" He looked fearful and unhappy. "Please don't hold my words against me, Mistress!"

"The only way you can incur my wrath is to withhold information. Tell me everything right now, and I mean everything!"

"For as long as I can remember, people would laugh at our king. It's not that they disliked him; but they think of him as a weak person, a man who would run from a fight." He looked up at Renata. Her lack of expression gave him enough confidence to go on. "Whenever there is a conflict of any sort, he chooses the path of least resistance. A true king, one that men will fear and follow, cares only about the State, and what's in the best interest of his subjects. The Laima family are known for caring only about their personal safety and overlooking insults that would cause any man," he smiled at her nervously. "I mean any person, to go blind with anger."

Renata took it all in, she had heard similar things over the years, but never so much in such a concise fashion. "Go on," she said.

"It's well known and has been since before I was born, that the Oren family thinks that they are a better choice to rule Inram. I have heard that the new head of their family, Rado Oren, thinks that now is the time to try and claim what they feel is their birthright."

"And you are willing to support this traitor to your king?" she demanded.

"All that I have said just now is speculation. Perhaps well-founded, perhaps not. I'm a simple man, and I go where the work is."

She thought for a minute, then turned to her dinner companion, "You will get the same terms if you go to Clifftown. I personally guarantee it. Tell your fellow artisans, that whatever House Oren offers, House Laima will match." She paused to make sure he understood, "And they will not be seen as traitors by their Lord and Master."

The Smith looked at her, then nodded. "Yes, Mistress. Tomorrow I travel to Clifftown, and you can be sure that I will make the finest weapons for our king, and his noble commander."

Chapter 26: War for Inram

The column of troops was long enough that you could stand at one end and would not be able to see the far end. At their head was the general, Sir Dorman Cole, recently knighted as part of his compensation for leading this force. He was in full plate armor, his white tunic going nicely with the polished metal. With him were maybe a dozen other officers on horseback, the hundreds of others were not so lucky, they marched with all the enthusiasm of prisoners being transported to jail.

The men were comprised of two main groups that Sir Cole was tasked with meshing together into a viable fighting force. There were conscripts that came from the lands owned by the Oren family. They had no armor and were wearing the same clothes that they had on when the army pulled them out of the fields. They were unwashed, unshaven, and uninspired; and they carried their heavy packs and spears like they were filled with lead.

The other group was comprised of mercenaries, men purchased from the Legion. As many men as Lord Oren could afford, all dressed in dark blue robes over black pants. The Legion found the down-and-out men from every country in Kronos and gave them a home, and more importantly, a purpose. They wore hoods to cover their faces and hopefully, to intimidate their opponents. Each had a short sword, a dagger, and some carried small shields. These men were infinitely more skilled than the conscripts; but they too had little or no loyalty to either House Oren or the cause. They were present for the money; nothing more, nothing less.

Next to Sir Dorman Cole rode Rokus Oren, the oldest son of House Oren. He was there to aid the general and of course, claim the credit for their inevitable victory. Everyone knew that for a house to be a truly great and royal house, they had to have victorious knights in the family. Win or lose, Dorman Cole would not even be a footnote in the history of Inram.

Rokus was a man of nineteen and was eager to take on House Laima for the right to rule Inram. Not only for the glory of his father and his own house; but like many, he didn't respect House Laima. They had a woman leading their army. A woman! They were open with their borders, allowing unsavory types to take root. Lawlessness was becoming rampant in this part of Kronos, and yet the king was often merciful, even apologetic to those who tore at the social fabric. He felt that much of the time, crime was as much society's fault as it was the criminals. Without consequences, criminals felt secure in attacking almost anyone not bearing arms. They were rarely caught, and when they were caught, many citizens felt that they were treated with entirely too much compassion. This was seen by friend and foe alike as a weakness. That is why Rado Oren was sure that his family would be a much better caretaker of Inram and its people. His son would go from being a pampered heir to a wartime prince. And of course, he was eager to have himself installed on the Inram throne.

Against all advice, Lord Oren had chosen this as the time to launch his rebellion. His coffers were running short, due to housing and feeding an army that was still in training. He knew that when he usurped House Laima, he would take their wealth and their ability to tax. Sir Cole only had a few weeks to work with his conscripts, and they were not at all eager to learn the art of war. No true military man was afraid to die, but the thing that bothered Dorman Cole the most was that he would most likely die without honor. He couldn't help feeling that he was on the wrong side in this conflict and that despite the obvious lack of leadership from the king of this land, installing House Oren would not prove to be an upgrade.

Inram was a peninsula that jutted out into the sea. It was the Easternmost of all the countries of Kronos, with only a small stretch of land connecting it to the continent. Feld was a large town not far from the border with their neighboring country of Wingard, and they tried to control traffic in and out of Inram. Clifftown was far to the South, on the Kanto Sea. Their ports served as trade hubs for the other countries that were inland. Inram was a medium-sized country of exceptional wealth, and it attracted many that refused to conform to society and became a magnet for beggars and criminals. The people were tired of the bad element that had begun to infest their homeland, but only House Oren was bold enough to use the current unrest to make a power play.

    Dorman Cole was accustomed to being a senior knight in direct service to a king. He was comfortable leading hundreds of mounted cavalry, and thousands of Infantry. Behind him was a respectable force, perhaps two thousand in total; but it still felt like a suicide mission. A true soldier can feel in his gut if the wind is blowing in his direction on the day of battle. A good soldier, knowing that the gods are against him, still marches onto the field of battle and dies for his lord. These men had no idea what was in store for them, and Sir Cole doubted that if they knew, they would be willing to sacrifice themselves so that their lord could have a higher title and a shiny metal hat. The road from Feld to Clifftown was long; but remarkably devoid of anything interesting. There were no sizable towns, no natural wonders, just a long dusty road with no cover or concealment. He knew that they would not have the element of surprise on their side. The king and his woman general were undoubtedly aware of their coming and there would be no way to hide their advance. He only hoped that the gods would somehow smile on him and allow him to die an honorable death.

General Rin stood at the planning table in her private tent. Her primary advisors were with her as they studied a map of Inram. There were carved figures on the board to represent units in her army and the units fighting for House Oren. They were discussing tactics when a scout entered the tent, saluted, and waited.

"Yes?" asked Sir Renden, one of the senior knights.

The scout stepped into the light, "Just returned from my mission to observe the advancing army. The enemy column was over fifty leagues when I left them last night. I rode all night to report." The man accepted a flagon of water from a junior officer, "They are making very slow time. Their force is more than half conscripts and Oren the younger is the only one in the whole army that looks happy to be there."

"Really?" Commander Rin asked. "You would say that they have, 'very low morale'?"

"I saw them execute two lads who were tired and tried to return to Feld." He drank some of the water, "The knight that leads them is a proud man, but his face looks like a man who is composing his will in his head."

Renata smiled at the news, "Very good. Get some rest, then join your company." An idea was coming to her, a way to win without all-out battle.

Two horses that left camp with scouts on them came strolling down the road where they met the advancing column of invading troops. They had no blood on them, and they were not winded, so they had apparently walked back at a relaxed pace.

"What do you make of this?" the young Lord Oren asked his general.

"Whenever a horse returns without the rider, it's obviously a bad sign," Sir Cole answered. "We have to assume these men were killed or captured." He rode up to one of the horses and caressed its neck. "These horses are not tired. I think the enemy must be very close."

You could see the wheels turning in the younger man's head. His wide head matched his wide frame, he was shorter than his father but was more athletic by far. A lifetime of the best food, and the best teachers had made him into a competent soldier, but only experience can make a man a leader. Dorman saw in the young Lord's eyes what he feared the most... overconfidence.

"They obviously know that we are close, it's time to charge the men! Let's press the attack immediately!" he said with a fiery zeal in his eyes.

"My Lord, we can't charge the men until the enemy is in sight." He pointed at the woods less than a mile ahead. "No doubt, they're waiting in the forest there to ambush us, and if that's the case, we'll be obliterated."

The young man was not thrilled at having his idea shot down, though he had to admit to himself that the old man knew a thing or two. Like all youth, his enthusiasm was only lessened for a moment till the next idea came to him. "They know we are here. I think that we should double-time the men so that they won't have time to set their defenses." The knight could see that his charge was determined to take a planning role in the coming battle. "Let me at least scout ahead and see where their emplacements are."

"Never! You are far too valuable; your loss would most likely mean the end of the campaign." He turned and whistled while waving to two of the mounted knights behind them. "You two, go forth into those woods and find out where the enemy is.

Return as quickly as possible." He turned to the general, "There you go, Sir Cole! Now, let's get this rabble moving while there is still daylight," Rokus Oren said, feeling very proud of himself.

The second set of guards also did not return, and like their predecessors, their riderless horses were found at the edge of the woods. The conscripts were winded and tired as they came to a change in topography. They looked up resentfully at their leaders, sitting rested atop their horses. They had marched almost all the way across their country, and the men on horseback didn't seem to care that they were tired or hungry. The Legion mercenaries were in better physical shape, but they too were tired from the quickened pace over the last mile of open land. Dorman looked concerned, but the soldier in him refused to show any fear or doubt in front of his men. Spurring his horse forward, he led the column into the forest.

As they entered the forest, they saw that the trees were not so thick, there was plenty of light and everything had a cheerful green glow to it. He was sure that he saw an enemy fighter behind every tree trunk, and up on every branch that stretched over the road. He heard noises that he feared were the sounds of metal swords on leather armor; but in the end, there was nothing. The rebels led by Dorman and Rokus Oren passed through the entire forest unscathed, and in half an hour they exited the far eastern edge of the woods. There was smoke up ahead, and the ground showed that there had been many horses here in the last hour. Sir Cole led his men out of the forest and up a small hill in the grassy plain that was on the other side. When he reached the top of the hill, he could see the enemy.

There were a couple of hundred mounted warriors under the Laima 'Rising Phoenix' banner. Behind them was a mix of about two thousand infantry and bowmen. Sir Dorman Cole sighed, knowing that today was his last. Their force was rested while his men were tired. They outnumbered his men, not even counting cavalry. Then a smell drifted over their position, and it piqued his interest. The smoke that was billowing from behind the enemy lines came from the roasting of delicious meats! Venison, he took a sniff, goat, perhaps even a steer. The smell was intoxicating, he almost forgot for a moment why they were there. These soldiers were feasting, and his men were a tired collection of starving conscripts.

Not sure what to do, he urged his men forward. They were now slowed to a regular march, the double time marching before reaching the forest had burned through what little energy they got from a breakfast of gruel. Oren tried on his own to get them to full charge, but no one seemed to be able to hear him anymore.

A group of about four riders broke from the enemy camp and approached them at a leisurely trot. This would be the offering of terms, very sporting of them, he thought to himself. More than half of the enemy's cavalry went to each side of the battlefield so that they could fall in behind the invader's column. Knowing what had to be done, Sir Cole turned to his Lord.

"Lord Oren, they are approaching with terms of our surrender. I will go out to meet them, you should stay here with the men. If they strike us down, I pray to the gods that you will take as many of them with you as you can."

The young Lord finally looked beaten. He couldn't reply, he just nodded as the older knight took his aid Sir Renden and rode out to the parlay. He could see that there was a woman astride the front horse, three men rode behind her. This was undoubtedly the woman general that he had heard so much about. She had grown up as one of the O'Bell warriors but had been traded in her late teens for gods only know what. Her physical prowess and unmatched skill rocketed her up the ranks till she was now the second most influential person in Inram. Maybe the first. When they were just a dozen feet away from the waiting Commander Rin, he reigned in his horse. He looked at the much younger warrior, not seeing a woman, but seeing a worthy adversary. He bowed slightly to her, and she returned it with respect.

"You are Dorman Cole? Your reputation precedes you, Sir," she said confidently. "I am surprised to see you at the head of such a pitiful force. House Oren has always been nothing more than a pretender to the throne. Before the next full moon, they'll be nothing more than a memory. A tale of unwarranted ambition, and of blood."

"Commander Renata Rin?" he asked.

"This is wartime, that would be General Rin."

"My apologies Madam. I assume you rode out not to make my acquaintance, but to offer terms?"

"I think if you are as wise a military man as I have heard; we can limit the loss of life as much as possible today."

"You have already drawn first blood, milady," he said, perturbed by how casually she assumed that she would win the day. "We sent two sets of scouts, their horses returned, but the men did not."

"Yes, we captured them. Do you smell that smoke?" she asked, hooking her thumb at the cloud that was to her rear, behind her lines.

"By Magnus!" He blanched at the thought of his scouts being killed and roasted.

"They are back there having their fill of meat, and some wine, corn, and potatoes that my supply train brought along. I offer the same to you, and your knights and to your conscripts."

"I am confused, General. You would feed your enemy? If this is a ruse, I will personally take your life on the field!"

"Not a trick," she said without any anger. "Your knights, your conscripts, they're all citizens of Inram. They owe fealty to the king, not to House Oren. If they drop their weapons and again swear allegiance to their rightful king, they'll be fed and sent home before this day's end."

"What of myself and Lord Rokus Oren?"

"If you insist on fighting, you'll take your chances in battle. It is my intention to take you prisoner. Oren is a traitor to the throne, an example will have to be made," she said grimly, knowing that he could do very little to stop the way things would play out. "Your mercenaries are not Inram citizens, they will either fall in battle, or they will fall to the executioner's axe." She turned to ride away, at the last minute turning her head. "You have five minutes after you rejoin your men before we commence our attack."

Rokus Oren looked at the knight in shining armor as he approached with his aide-de-camp. They rode with heavy hearts. The defeated look on Cole's face made the young lord's heart fall. He was hoping for a miracle but was now expecting a death sentence.

"They offered terms?" he asked. The man nodded as he rode in closer. "What does she offer, this woman commander."

"General Rin has offered safe passage to the knight's present, and to all the conscripted citizens of Inram. In fact, if they renounce loyalty to your father and swear allegiance to King Laima, they'll be fed that feast that we can all smell. Then they will be sent home uncharged and with no further harm coming to them." He did not shout the words; but neither did he try to speak them quietly. Some of the conscripts heard that they would eat and not be killed today. To them, this was the best of all possible outcomes.

"Let the other shoe drop, Sir Cole. I know there's more."

"According to General Rin, you are a traitor to the king and the two of us will be taken prisoner. Or killed on the field." For the next part, he leaned in, "The Legion troops will not be given any quarter."

"That's it then. I reject these ridiculous terms. Give the order, 'full charge'!" he said to the knights. Standing in his stirrups, "Take heart men! For House Oren, we'll kill each and every one of these bastards!"

There was no whooping or hollering at his attempts to rouse the fighting spirit in his men. In seconds, they had heard the choices, death or a full stomach and full pardon. The conscripts marched forward, wary that the few knights that were still on their side of the battle, would strike down any man that didn't comply. Fearing for their lives, they began marching, but they had no enthusiasm at all. They held their spears waist high and started running at a medium speed toward the line of men and horses opposite them on the field. A woman on a horse waved her arm causing the wall of men and horses to surge forward. The field was half a mile across, and there were slight rolling hills to either side causing them to be in a vast shallow bowl.

The king's mounted soldiers rode forward, metal shields on their left arms, long swords in their right hands. Even the horses had armor, covering their long, majestic faces, with horns and decorations, making them look fierce. The men wore full armor, their helmets gleaming brightly in the sun. As they picked up speed, the hooves of the horses tore at the earth, throwing patches of turf behind them. The sight was so intimidating that little notice was given to the thousand-plus infantrymen who were running in formation. They had helmets that covered their heads and cheeks, with leather neck guards. These professional soldiers wore light brown leather armor, and each man wore the 'Rising Phoenix' on his chest. The sound of all the hooves and metal boots striking the ground made a terror-inducing clamor.

From behind, Sir Cole was screaming to his men to attack. He had only a few knights to help protect the young lord. Hundreds of hungry, and tired, farmers and tradesmen ran toward the enemy, followed by a full company of Legion troops. When they were nearly in range of the enemy's archers and far enough away from their masters, the conscripts all stopped. They threw their spears to the ground and fell as one, to their knees. They held up their empty arms, beseeching their enemy to spare them. The Legion troops were not in on the deal, and they came to a halt, looking around for leadership. The king's men all came to a stop, they looked to their general who came riding up. Renata Rin looked over the tired and miserable citizens of her country and felt only pity for them.

"You men leave your weapons where they are and go behind my lines. You are again, loyal servants of King Laima." She turned to address her troops, "Let them go, the mercenaries and the rest are fair game. Bring me the brat, and all of the knights, alive if you can," she said as she rode back toward her own lines.

When the mounted troops that had flanked the position saw their comrades attack, they attacked the enemy from the rear. In the end, the Legion troops were only a degree better than a farmer with a carved wooden spear. They were cut down by the swords of the mounted knights. There were only a few stragglers left for the infantry to clean up. The battle raged on for perhaps an hour, maybe less. When it was over, the only ones on the field were the king's army, a disloyal noble, and two generals.

General Rin dropped from her horse and walked over to where the noble was being detained. She looked up at the meaty boy who would be a prince. She appraised him quickly and found him lacking. She signaled for him to dismount his horse.

"You are from House Oren, are you not?" she asked the boy.

"I am Rokus Oren, son of Rado Oren," he said defiantly. "You have won this day, but House Oren will supplant that weak master you serve. House Laima will fall."

"Not while I defend it," she said to him. "For crimes against the throne, primarily treason, you are sentenced to death," she pulled her sword. The boy went ghost white, then anger pumped blood back into his chubby face.

"Give me my sword, I'll defeat you in fair combat, and your men will know that they follow the wrong House!" He looked around for any support. Renata looked at the men holding him and nodded. They released him and one of them handed him a sword. The young man ripped it away angrily and got into a fighting stance. He looked over at Renata, fear was replaced by his burning hatred for her and her master. She pulled her sword and spun the blade around effortlessly in her grip. She walked with confidence like his sword trainer, but she was younger and faster, and her moves were smooth as silk. She had an amused look on her face that only made him even angrier.

"Die, woman!" he said, launching an ill-timed swing that she deflected easily. He went into a series of swings and thrusts, doing whatever his instructors had taught him to do. She was far more skilled, and everyone, perhaps even the mad lord himself, knew this. Dorman wondered if it were cruelty that she did not finish him quickly. It was almost like she was curious to see what his skill level was. She blocked some blows, sidestepped, or backstepped others. She expended a minimum of energy and had not even once pressed her own attack. This went on for several minutes; the only sound was the breathing of the horses, the panting of Rokus Oren, and the clash of steel on steel. Rokus was starting to get tired, and the adrenaline that had given him the courage to face his death with a sword in hand was fading. The tip of his sword could no longer rise to the level of her chest. Only his spirit kept him from dragging it on the ground. Finally, he halted his attacks and looked at her with a defeated look, "I am beaten."

"I respect that you would go down fighting, that you wished to die as a man." She spun around in a move that seemed impossible for someone wearing bulky armor and removed his head with a single slash. Her sword had been returned to the scabbard before his head had finished rolling on the ground. "Let's hope your father dies as well as you did young lord."

The battlefield was deathly quiet. When Renata killed, it was always with unmatched skill and grace. Dorman looked at her, breaking the silence. "What of me General? Should I fall on my own sword? I too would like a warrior's death."

"There may be a use for you Master Cole," the lack of 'Sir' was a stinging rebuke. "I have the proper test of your loyalty. I know that you have been looking for a home, and maybe you'll have one."

Chapter 27: Renata Rin

"General Rin, reporting as ordered," she said to her king, her arm was clenched in a fist across her chest in salute.

"Renata, welcome. You've not spent much time at the castle recently. How are things in my kingdom?" King Laima asked. "Please sit and have a cup of wine. I had some bottles brought from my personal cellar. Life is too short, yes?"

"Indeed, it is Sire," she said pulling her scabbarded sword out so that she could sit. "These Quell bastards are showing up in every country from what my sources tell me. I'm sure that you've heard that they took over several towns in Wolvig and wiped out the Emar colony there."

"Rumors. They were nothing a couple of years ago, and they'll be nothing a year from now. Are you sure that we should be hunting down these people? They don't adhere to the true gods, but I have never believed in persecuting those with different beliefs."

"We don't root them out because of what they do or do not believe in Sire. This Quell movement is more a death cult than a true religion. They have killed hundreds, maybe thousands, including women and children."

"Maybe in Wolvig they are running wild, but the ones here in Inram have not caused much trouble. They are a bit aggressive with proselytizing and seem to take offense at almost everything; but so far, not more than a few sparks. No fires."

"My lord, if I waited for your kingdom to go up in flames before fighting the fire, I would be negligent in my duties. I see a threat, and I've pledged my life to protecting your interests and that of your subjects." She leaned in, looking her king directly in the eyes. "In Wolvig, they are no longer the minority, there are thousands of them, and they wiped out the royal army. Wiped them out. I have heard that even as we speak, Castle Cadmus is being sieged. They do not take prisoners, soon that whole country will be theirs, and from there, they'll feel emboldened and launch attacks upon all of their neighbors."

"That is still very far from here, literally half a world away. I think that you overestimate these religious zealots and underestimate the royal families. Cadmus is a faggot; I mean what can you expect!" He laughed with derision.

"Faggot or not, he's a king," she said testily. "Are you ordering me to not pursue these Quell?"

"Keep your eyes on them; but yes, stop killing them just for being what they are."

"Of course, I'll obey your orders my lord; but let it be known that I do so under protest."

"I hear that you have advanced that traitorous knight, Dorman Cole to be your second in command. Is this true?"

"He was a knight without a home, and without a true king to follow. I see value in man's experience and breeding. The men hear his voice and follow his commands without question. He is now and forever my man, which makes him your man, my lord."

"I don't like it. He led an army that was sent to unseat me and bring down House Laima. Now, instead of the execution that he deserved for such crimes, he has been elevated to a position of respect, second only to you. I don't like it."

"I hear you Sire. I will take full responsibility for the man and will bear any consequences as this was 'my' decision."

They sat quietly for a full minute before the king broke the silence. "Thank you for coming Renata. On your way out, please have my steward come in."

"Of course, Sire." She popped to her feet, saluted, and left.

"The king really doesn't like you," she said to Dorman.

"So, I've heard. Funny, I have no feeling toward him either way." He accepted a crystal glass from a passing servant. "I am loyal to you, and by extension, to him. Not to worry, I know my place, and when the time comes, I'll die gallantly for House Laima."

"I can't believe how blind the man is to these Quell fanatics. They're just going to get bolder and bolder, and soon, we'll be like Wolvig."

"Fucked," he stated.

"Exactly. I have heard that there is some trouble on the border with Wingard. Let's take a few men and go take a look."

"I thought the king didn't want you chasing after these maniacs?" Dorman asked.

"Not in so many words. If we are in the area, and something goes down..."

"Whatever you say milady. I'll follow you to the gates of Hell itself."

The Great Warlord of Inram was dressed like a trading company secretary, next to her was Dorman Cole, dressed as an affluent businessman. They sat at an outdoor food stand under large umbrellas, eating grilled meat and drinking heated rum drinks. They had argued for days on their way to the small town that sat just on the Inram side of the border with Wingard. He was leaning towards lying low and following the king's commands, both in action and in spirit. She claimed to be fine with obeying the king; but in spirit, she was on a completely different page.

"Renata, can I ask you a personal question, or two?"

"Sure, but I reserve the right to slit your throat if you cross the line," she said cheerfully.

"You're a member of the royal house of O'Bell, are you not?"

"I am a distant cousin to the princess. I was sold in my teens to House Laima for… well, I'm not sure exactly what they got in return."

"Well, I'm sure it was something very valuable." He smiled at his commander. "I don't know if I ever said it out loud; but I'm very appreciative that you took me into your service. You are infinitely better than that house that shall not be named."

"That house that no longer exists." She smiled in satisfaction.

"If they had listened to me, they would be comfortable in second place. Those idiots had all the land and wealth and women that you could enjoy in a dozen lifetimes, but it wasn't enough."

"You talk about women. I haven't seen you with anyone, Sir Cole."

"I'm a knight, and part of that entails being a gentleman. I could be bedding your handmaiden, and you would never hear it from me, or from anyone who would name me as their source." He took a big bit of grilled lamb, and closing his eyes, he enjoyed the flavor of the seasoned meat. Opening his eyes, he looked at his leader, whom he looked upon as a daughter figure. "What about you, Warlord?"

"That moniker 'Warlord' is silly, and I don't care for it. I tend to be attracted to whoever catches my interest at the moment. Sometimes I'm enticed by strength, sometimes by beauty. Like you, I try to be discreet." They ate and chatted about nothing special when a messenger came running over breathlessly.

"Commander!" He spoke to Dorman. "There is a man, dressed in the robes of the Quell who is causing a stir across town, not five minutes run from here."

Dorman looked at Renata, who just nodded. They both jumped to their feet and followed the man out of the eatery and down the road. The villagers gave them hardly any information as they raced along toward the sound of unrest. When they had rounded a few corners, they came to an open area where a man was standing on a broken statue of Magnus and was screaming at the top of his lungs. There was madness in his eyes, and he was screaming at a small crowd of townspeople who had gathered to witness the spectacle.

"This is a symbol of the false god Magnus! You people are sinners, it is my right to destroy it! Lord Quell compels me to attack false gods!" he raved and looked at his half dozen compatriots for moral support.

"Heresy!" they screamed. "Those who do not worship the one true god, Quell, will be burned in a pit of fire!" one of the crazed cultists cried out.

"Magnus is the king of the gods; we only worship the Old Gods here!" a villager called out.

"Quell is false, and he has no place here in Kronos!" another screamed at the invaders.

The Quell follower, along with three others in his group attacked the last person to speak. They pulled long, poorly crafted knives from underneath their robes and plunged them into the chest of the old woman who had dared to speak up. The woman's face went white, her expression went from anger to surprise as life left her. The men then began wildly stabbing at those around her, half a dozen had been injured before Renata and Dorman arrived on the scene.

From under her cloak, Renata pulled a short sword and Dorman did the same. They were experienced warriors, and they chopped the four into bits in less than a minute. When they were done, both the innocent and the guilty lay on the cobblestones in pools of blood.

"Fetch a surgeon!" Renata ordered a large man who was a few feet away. Even though she was a woman, her tone, and her swordsmanship, left no doubt that when she issued an order, it was to be followed without question. She found one of the Quell, still clinging to life. She helped him into a sitting position so that she could ask her questions.

"Are you alone, or are the Quell moving into Inram?"

"Quell is the one true god!" the man yelled with the last of his flagging energy.

"Is there an invasion coming?" she demanded, shaking the man vigorously.

He gurgled incoherently, then died. She let his corpse drop to the dirt, then stood to address the crowd that had assembled. Even dressed as she was, something in her posture and her demeanor let everyone know that she was an authority figure.

"People of Inram, know that your king is watching out for you and that he'll not allow this type of filth to invade our peaceful country. I am Renata Rin, Commanding General of the King's Guard and I need your help to determine how deeply this weed has dug its roots into our land." She had their attention. That she was a woman was irrelevant, they were familiar with the legend of the 'Warlord'. They of course had never seen her, but her skill with a sword and her demeanor left no one in doubt. A young man in his early twenties stepped forward.

"General, I saw these men enter the town from the West just today. They seemed angry for no apparent reason, and then they became violent and attacked because the image of Magnus infuriated them so."

"I'm no expert," an older woman piped in, "but they were looking for trouble. Any reason would have suited them, any reason to pull their knives. They were going to commit violence no matter what we did or didn't do."

"I've heard similar tales in other villages. Have their kind been through here before?" she asked of the crowd.

"There have been Quell fanatics here before, preaching and pulling at people's sleeves; but they've never been as bold as these here," the young man said, pointing down at the bodies of the Quell.

"They are coming more frequently," the older lady offered. "A year ago, there was one that might pass through in a month. Now, you see them coming every day, setting up stands and patchwork huts. They compete for the land, and if they don't get it... well, everyone gives in sooner or later. They're a violent people."

An older man stepped forward, "They demand that we change to make them feel at ease, they call us all manner of names if we don't give in to their demands."

"And everything offends them. They claim to be victims of our intolerance," an older lady said, "but they have zero tolerance for anything that doesn't comply with their religion."

"Has this ever happened before?" Renata asked the crowd.

"We had a single stabbing a few weeks ago," the young man said. "Across the border in Wingard, these things are happening quite often now. I have cousins who live there, and they say that these Quell are getting bolder by the day and that there are attacks like this or worse almost every week now."

"Thank you for sharing this with us. General Cole and I will inform the king of this and of the need for heightened security." The people looked at her with doubt on their faces. They had lived their whole lives under House Laima, and they did not have high hopes that their king would grow a backbone.

King Ayaram Laima and his wife Queen Bree Laima sat on their matching thrones. The room was filled with representatives from all the country's leading families. The other generals were present, along with the admirals from Inram's mighty Navy. Foreign dignitaries were present, along with several of the local trade guilds. The king was a generally testy man, and today was no exception. He rubbed at his beard like he wanted to pull it off and throw it at his Commanding General.

Renata stood there, in the very center of the hundred-plus people, strong and regal in her full armor. The plate was shined to a mirror-like finish and the silks were bright and new. She looked every bit the warlord that she was, there was no regret on her face. Far to the rear of the room was her man, Dorman Cole. He was the only one present that she would even consider calling 'friend'. She had been summoned to appear before the king to explain why, after his express instructions to not hunt down the Quell, she had executed four of them.

"I was not hunting them down Sire, I was touring your kingdom. Not as an agent of your lordship, but as a tourist. When a crazy man attacked and stabbed your subjects at random, I fulfilled my oath and interceded. Had I not, there is no telling how large the death toll might have grown."

"Tourist? You always vacation with your sword at your hip, with your second in command at the ready?" He asked in his most accusatory tone.

"Always. I sleep with my sword, I shower with my sword," she said without a trace of humor. Looking back at Dorman, she added, "I brought him so that I could get to know him better, outside of our duties; and before you ask, no, we are not sleeping together."

The king was not amused. He waved to his steward who brought him a rolled-up parchment. With great ceremony, he unrolled the paper and held it high so that he could read it aloud. "General Rin, you have disobeyed the commands of your rightful sovereign. Considering your many years of, till now, faithful service, you shall be allowed to gather your belongings, such as they are, and leave forever the lands of Inram." When he was done, he put down the proclamation and stared at her. All eyes were on her, waiting for her reaction.

She looked around the room, many shared the same sour attitude that the king had. They believed that defending yourself, even as your enemy grows bolder, was in poor taste. Quite a few of them had blank faces. They didn't care if a military person came or went. There were no friendly faces in the crowd, no one was on her side. She had always been aware of House Laima's reputation, that they were concerned with keeping their power; but were weak when confronted. They didn't care if their subjects were suffering, as long as the suffering didn't reach the capital.

"A king's first responsibility is to his subjects, to their safety. By releasing me from your service, you only hasten your end." She turned to the crowd, "You all think that you are safe behind these walls, comfortable with your expensive food and clothing? Without our swords between you and the Quell, you'll all soon have your heads removed and placed on pikes. Good luck to you all." With that, she walked calmly from the room.

Chapter 28: Coup

Renata and Dorman were the last to arrive. Renata had been summoned from O'Bell, where she had retreated after being dismissed from her position with House Laima. Dorman was glad to be out of O'Bell where a man who was unapologetically masculine was not very welcome. They had traveled for many days and despite bouts of inclement weather, were both more than presentable when entering the inn. They were in a small village on the border with Wingard, hardly more than a church and a few shops, and the inn.

Seated at a large table that took up the whole room were many familiar faces. All of the major houses of Inram were present, except for House Laima. A dozen grizzled older men and a few ladies represented most of the power and influence in the country. They were sitting over plates of food, though most were concentrating on their cups. They were trying to ease their tension by drinking ales and beers in great quantities. When they saw the former leader of the guard walk in, many heaved quiet sighs of relief.

"Welcome General Rin, Sir Cole," one of the nobles said, standing to greet them. "A place has been reserved at the head of the table for you." Indicating two open chairs. Drinks and food were placed on the table even before they were able to settle in their chairs.

"Your invitation was urgent, and yet conspicuously devoid of details."

"The nature of this assembly is… delicate and requires the utmost discretion."

Renata looked over the assemblage, seeing who was present and who was not. "I think that I can begin to guess at the nature."

"It's these Quell bastards!" an older nobleman said from the middle of the table. "They were always a nuisance, but they are now a *real* threat. They trespassed on one of my properties and killed the leaseholder. The woman and eldest daughters are missing. You can only imagine what's become of them."

"There are dozens of stories like that," one of the ladies added. "People are getting murdered, taken prisoner, and property is getting destroyed. My own nephew was murdered not a fortnight ago for not joining this Quell religion. Something has to be done."

"We collect taxes and pay a tax to the king, but why should our subjects pay for security and get none? We've appealed many times to crack down on these deviants but to no avail."

After a long pause, "Lord Beckman, were you not present when I was publicly dismissed?" He lowered his eyes in shame, "In fact, I see a few more of you who witnessed my public firing. And now you come to me for help? The same help that was the impetus behind me being fired?"

"You can scold us, and rightly so," Beckman replied, "but you have lived more than half your life in Inram, and it's now in your blood. No one, even Laima, would claim that you weren't loyal to the people of Inram, to its people. Perhaps we don't deserve your help, but we are asking for it anyway. If you don't want to help because of us, that's fine, but do it for the people you've dedicated your entire adult life to."

"What you are talking about, is treason," Dorman said clearly, his words hanging in the air.

"Treason? Is it not treason to hide behind walls and rows of armored knights? Laima is a coward. His fear of confrontation is going to get us all killed."

"It may be treason, but I think it will be easier than you might expect. None of us would lend support to Laima, and most of his personal security were subordinates of yours. Men that respect you; the person, and the position you held."

"If I agree to this… plot of yours, won't the power struggle just move to the question of who the successor to Laima will be?"

"We have an idea about that," Beckman said with a smile.

For the second time in a month, Renata Rin stood in the throne room of House Laima. This time she wore her battle armor instead of her ceremonial set. Bodies of the royal guard littered the throne room, their blood soaking into the priceless hand-woven floor runners. A few other holdouts, those who were anticipating that their power would not extend into a new administration, joined them in death.

Renata looked at the king and his queen, their disbelief had faded and now they were filled with rage. They knew that they could be killed any instant and that the Laima line would cease to be, yet they still felt outraged and demanded answers.

"I let you live, you O'Bell bitch, and this is how you repay me?"

"You let me live, so that is why I'll allow you to go into exile, instead of facing the executioner's axe. You've betrayed your subjects; you allow them to be raped and slaughtered while taking no steps to protect them."

"I'm the king, I'm not their father! I have no duty to them. They have a duty to me! My family was chosen by Magnus himself to lord over this land. I serve him, I do not serve those who are below me, those who were born to serve!"

"I'm not sure where you get your information, but if the gods did choose your line to rule this land, you have a duty to protect it. You have to be ready to give your all, your wealth, and even your life if in the service of your subjects. A king without his people is just a man, and if you refuse to aid those who need you most, you aren't even a man."

"Damn you, Renata! There are many lords who are still loyal to House Laima, and to me personally. I'll rise again and take the crown from your lifeless head."

She looked at him, almost with pity. "If that's my fate, then so be it. You have ten minutes to pack as much as you can fit into a chest. I will have a horse and wagon waiting for you outside. If you're not out of sight of this castle by sundown, I'll go against my better nature and take your heads."

Flustered and ashamed, the king and queen ran for their personal quarters where they scooped up all the jewels and any gold that they could carry. Complying with Renata's wishes, they were packed and on their way in ten minutes.

Chapter 29: The Queen

The country of O'Bell was in the far Northern region of Kronos. The weather was cooler, and they experienced more rain and snow than most of the continent. Unlike most of the continent, O'Bell was surrounded by tall craggy mountains. The three passes that allowed entry or exit to the land were guarded by female knights, and only those with entry papers were allowed to enter.

Princess Lydia O'Bell rode up to the Eastern Gate, which lay on the border of O'Bell and Wingard. Riding alongside her was her best friend and official advisor, Meisha Bannon. Behind them were a dozen female warriors that were assigned to her and served as her personal guard. O'Bell had a very controlled society, and unlike the rest of Kronos, they regulated very strictly who could and could not live amongst them. The country of O'Bell was completely female-dominated to the point that if you saw a man within their borders, you could safely assume that he was a slave. When they were within clear sight of the border crossing, a pair of female guards came to attention.

"Welcome back, your highness," the senior guard called out. Like her partner and all the princess' guards, she wore the banner of the Virgin Queen on their tunics. Though not currently on a war footing with any country, they all wore heavy plate armor, and when on duty, they all wore polished helmets. The princess' guards all wore a long, beautiful shock of straight hair that sprouted from the tops of their helmets and were meant to look like a horse's tail. They wore white because the princess was still a maiden, unmarried, and without any children. The border guards wore bright red feathers from their helmets, and they had dark brown tunics.

Lydia was tall, even for an O'Bell, who were a country of unusually tall women. She loved to fight and had been sparring with Meisha since they were five years old. The years of constant fighting gave her uncommon strength and stamina, and she was highly regarded as a skilled warrior. Lydia was not 'unattractive' though, for most men's tastes, she was 'pretty', at best.

When they were close, the guard came to attention, faced the princess, and saluted. When the salute was returned, she spoke. "Princess, we received word from the queen a couple of days ago, she wants you to proceed directly to the capital."

"Do you know what matter commands such urgency?" Lydia asked.

"I do not your highness. I am not sure that it is a matter of urgency, per se. I got the impression that she just did not want to wait for you to take any detours on your way back to her side."

"Thank you for your candor," she told the guard. The woman and her partner worked a counterweight that raised a long steel arm that served to block the way for horses and carriages. After they passed through, the barrier was again lowered into place. The princess and her entourage rode through the countryside at a leisurely pace. She would head directly to the castle, but there was no need to rush. The Eastern part of O'Bell was her favorite. With ample water, there were lush forests separated by huge grassy plains. Purple, orange, and yellow flowers were mixed in the grasses so that from atop a horse, it looked like a vast green ocean with streaks of color woven throughout. They passed farms on the way; men were working at harvesting grapes for the fine wines that O'Bell was known for. When they saw the princess, they dropped to their knees, heads bowed, afraid to accidentally meet her gaze.

"Just looking at these... 'men'. So hard to believe that they hold most of the power in the other countries." She looked at a man with his face almost down in the mud between the rows of grapevines. He wore loose, tattered clothing, enough for modesty, but not enough for protection against the elements. "How pitiful they are. If we didn't need the labor, I would be the first to drive them out."

"They do have, other uses, my princess," she said smiling at her friend. Meisha was not as strong as her princess or as good a warrior, but her deeply tanned skin and dark wavy hair made her very attractive by most men's standards.

"What would that be?" Lydia almost spat the words.

"I know that you are still... inexperienced, but you have to know what I am talking about." Meisha loved to tease her princess, who was such an easy target for such jests.

"Oh, that again. You've only tried it the one time, and you said it hurt more than me beating you at grappling."

Meisha leaned in, "I may have forgotten to mention, milady, that I did try it... a few more times."

"What! How could you not tell me?" Lydia demanded, looking at her friend with a betrayed expression on her face.

"I know you are sensitive about these things. That's why I like to tease you about it." She leaned in again so only the princess could hear. "Truly the first time did hurt, but it was still... incredible. The second time hurt just a wee bit, and the other times, I found that it was very much to my liking."

"How could you?" the princess was near tears. "Men are useless and so disgusting!" They rode in silence for a few minutes, then suddenly. "I think the Queen would want to see me sooner rather than later. I'll ride ahead." She turned to her retinue, "I'll be fine, no need to keep pace!" and she rode off in a huff.

When she was far away and out of earshot, the captain of the guard came side by side with Meisha. She looked at her disapprovingly, "Friend or no, you go too far sometimes."

"She's obviously a big girl. If she can't take that, how will she ever be queen?"

"I heard what you said to her. You really enjoy laying with them?" the guard asked. "I have only tried it a few times, to get my daughter, and... the other one."

"Your son? Having a son is not a crime, though thank goodness you also had a daughter," she laughed at her riding companion. "If you find the right one, not a field hand like the type we keep around here; but a real man, who will dominate you and worship you all in the same night." She looked to the heavens with a smile. "That's a man that will bring you pleasure, far different than what another woman can."

"Still, why toy with the princess? Are you not her closest friend?"

"Believe me, it is nothing compared to what waits for her at the Castle."

"You know why the queen has summoned her?"

"She is turning seventeen in a few days. It can mean only one thing."

The guard looked off into the distance, no longer able to see her master. "Oh my."

The audience room of Queen Vandressa O'Bell was more of a square theatre than a long hall, that the male kings seemed to always construct. She sat on a chair with huge cushions, surrounded by silks and furs. The walls had the finest tapestries, depicting the many O'Bell conquests out in the world of man; they showed the gods and how they favored House O'Bell. There were glass vases on pedestals and almost every open area had a plant. The ceiling was high, and the walls had great folding doors that allowed in the sun and wind. A couple of small-framed men were walking about watering and caring for the plants.

Princess Lydia walked in unannounced as usual and walked to where her mother was studying a few dispatches. "Get out!" she barked without looking at anyone. The men knew that it was addressed to them, and they hopped to their feet and left the room. At the sound of her oldest daughter's voice, Vandressa looked up. She was not as tall as her daughter, but taller than most. She once had the body of a feared warrior, but motherhood and the affairs of state had caused her to let her body settle into a more traditionally feminine shape. Her long brown hair was worked into a braid with gold rope crossing down the length of the ponytail. Her dress was made of an off-white fabric that was light and comfortable.

"Come closer, Lydia dear. Let me look at you," she said with her arms out. Princess Lydia walked up to embrace her mother, then backed up a couple of feet. She waited for her mother's usual evaluation. "How lovely, you have become! You take after me I think, not too bold of me to say so." She rotated her index finger, letting Lydia know that she was to spin around. The queen looked her over with the love of a parent, but there was something else.

"Why did you call for me mother? It sounded urgent, so I rode ahead of my guard."

"Urgent? No, not urgent; but... the time has come." She looked pleased with what she saw in her daughter.

"Time for what mother? Why do you speak in riddles, you know I hate them."

"Lydia, you are becoming a woman in just a few days. You are in your prime physical condition; it is the best time for you to give House O'Bell the next generation. You will be queen after me, and your daughter will follow you," she said as if it was not even worth discussing.

Lydia turned white as a ghost and started to swoon. Her mother stepped forward to catch her before she could topple over. She sputtered, but no words left her lips. Vandressa eased her daughter onto the throne where she propped her up on silken cushions, and then took a fan from a pocket and proceeded to cool off her firstborn. She rang a bell, a man appeared at one of the side doors.

"Water," she said. He disappeared and returned with water in mere seconds. "Now dear, you knew this day would come. I have been working with a few agents to find a suitable match for you. I am looking for someone who knows that his purpose is to give you a daughter and that he is not truly getting a wife, and of course, will never inherit anything. When the princess started to get her color back, her mother sat down next to her on the wide seat and began fanning herself. "We shall have a huge feast in celebration of your birthday. Shortly thereafter, I will send you out to interview the first contender." The princess looked glum and leaning over, began to weep into her mother's shoulder.

Chapter 30: The Bride

Meisha held her sword high, almost behind her, and leveled with the ground. Her eyes were wide, and her teeth were gnashing in anticipation. She was crouching, ready to either defend or launch her own attack and strike. Lydia circled her, her sword also held high, her shield though was starting to droop. She always dominated her friend and confidant, but today she was being outworked and outclassed in sword training. For a general in her mother's army, she was showing an alarming lack of skill and concentration.

The two women were clad in only the minimum; boots, chest guards and a cloth for modesty. They were sweating profusely in the late afternoon sun on top of a hill that overlooked the sea. Though they used wooden training swords, the possibility of getting injured or worse was very real. Meisha, or whoever fought the princess always had to take that into consideration. It was better to lose or be struck, than to win too decisively and possibly harm the future queen. Today, Meisha was taking no such precautions. She pressed her attack like the princess was an actual foe. She easily fought off the princess' weak attacks and did her best to defeat and humiliate her best friend. They traded strikes and inflicted minor wounds upon each other, till with a flurry of powerful chops, Meisha forced the princess to her knees.

"Yield princess!"

Looking up at her foe, Lydia was almost in tears. She hated to lose and did so infrequently. "I yield! You win, you harlot!"

"Now princess, that's not very ladylike." She helped her friend to her feet, "More than likely, this is not the only time that you'll be yielding today." She smiled evilly at her friend.

Lydia's face went white, she began to lose her balance. Meisha helped her to a chair, "Water!" she yelled at one of the men who were always around to be of service. The water came quickly, and Meisha helped Lydia to sip from the crystal cup.

"Thank you, sister. Though your jest nearly gave me an attack. Please do not joke about such things."

"It may sound like I'm joking, but you need to hear it and to think about it. By tonight, you will be a married woman." She sat next to her friend and put her arm around her, "Trust me, it is not the end of the world. Despite their simple minds and their 'body hair', there are enough positives that you may want to do 'it' occasionally just for… relaxation."

"You say that, but just thinking about it makes me ill. Men are so useless. I mean, they are good for lifting things and manual labor; but otherwise, they are dull-witted and weak-willed."

"The ones that we keep here are. Just like women, there are men of every stripe and variety. The men that we keep here as slaves are the type that would allow themselves to be dominated. Not all men are like these, indeed, most are not."

"Still, the whole process is… revolting."

Meisha laughed, "If you think that's revolting, wait till you see what else they have in store for you!"

"What do you mean?"

"Tonight's your wedding night, you'll find out! I don't want to spoil any of it for you."

The room was lit with more than a hundred candles, there was a strong cool breeze blowing through the wide-open doors on two sides of the bedroom. The curtains were pulled back and the heavy wooden doors were pulled shut. The bed was large and dominated the middle of the room. It was plush and stood several feet above the ground, like a sacrificial altar. There were a dozen silk pillows, filled with the softest down. Strong incense filled the air and buckets of iced wine were near the bed.

Lydia stood next to the bed, standing tall and strong. Her gown was elegant with thousands of hours of embroidery to give it a metallic shimmer in the patterns of trees and storms and the beloved mountains that surrounded and protected O'Bell. Despite the intricacy of the weaving and the quality of the fabrics, or possibly because of it; she was fully exposed. Every curve of her body was not only visible but accentuated. Her bronzed skin shone through the sheer fabric, and nothing was hidden. As her husband entered the room, she was waiting for him, obedient yet strong.

Off in the corner, on a high-backed couch sat her mother the queen, and a few of her most trusted retainers. The queen sat far back in the shadows where all you could see was her bright white eyes and the coal from the long pipe that she smoked. She was not present for prurient reasons, but more to make sure that her investment was well spent.

He entered the room from the far door. Emerging from the shadows, he stood in the flickering light of the sea of candles for inspection by his wife and mother-in-law. Randolph was a fine male specimen, tall and well-muscled. He wore the formal robes of his land and the crown that proved he was indeed a prince. His beard was well trimmed, and his hair was black and shiny and hung to his collar. He looked around, seeing first his bride, her nearly naked body calling to him. Then he caught sight of his Mother-in-law off in the corner. He had faced many a man on the field of battle and had bedded more than a few women, but performing in front of a hostile audience was a first for him. He put his doubts aside and remembered his instructions.

Bowing to the princess, the groom showed his respect to his new wife. Standing tall, he went for the buttons and clasps that held his clothes in place. Before he could undress, he was accosted by the handlers. Several men, all in simple robes with the House O'Bell crest came from the darkest corners to assist him. They were all shorter than him by a head and none of them was the kind of man that elicit feelings of jealousy. They expertly undid his cape, his breastplate, and tunic, his codpiece was last, and when the prince was completely naked, the attendants melted into the darkness. The candlelight was brighter than he would have wished. It was less for setting a mood and more for the purpose of illumination.

The princess did not move, and indeed, it seemed like she had stopped breathing altogether. She tried not to even notice her husband as he stood there naked before her and her mother. The light gave a shadow to his well-defined chest and stomach. He was indeed an excellent specimen of male anatomy, perfect by every definition. He was young and some things were out of his control. As he looked at his wife of only a few hours, nature took over. She was pretty, though plain of face; but her body was tall and muscular, and her breasts were petite yet firm. Her stomach was as flat as the sea on a windless day and her arms and legs were long and lean and made a man dream of having them wrapped around his waist. To Lydia's horror, her husband was becoming aroused. The smells, the sound of the wind blowing through the chamber, the soft yet revealing lighting, and of course the nubile virgin before him was too much for him to withstand.

Randolph walked towards the bed and stopped when his face was just inches from his bride's. He looked into her tear-stained eyes, his manhood almost touching her. He turned her around, his hands firm yet comforting. He pulled at the simple knots that held her dress in place. Her gown fell to the ground, forming a pile around her ankles. He looked down at her behind, it was impossibly firm like the rest of her. In the dim light, he could see the almost invisible hairs that gave her derriere a ripe peach-like quality. He stiffened even more at the sight and the smell of her made his agony even more intense.

Turning her again, he was again face-to-face with the princess. She was like putty in his hands. Her instinct to defy his will and spurn his advances was beaten down by her mother's determination to have a granddaughter. She closed her eyes as his lips met hers. She hated every second of it. She resisted somewhere in that far-off place, somewhere deep in her being. Her husband's hand touched her waist, the other went to the back of her head and gently tilted it ever so slightly to the side. His lips were rough, rougher than Meisha's, who was the only other person she had ever kissed. His tongue lightly danced on her lips, making them want to part and allow their tongues to touch.

Her whole world was swirling around, she felt like she had had too much wine, and no longer had control over herself. The candles blurred in her vision during the few times that her eyes were open. She felt herself being lifted and placed lovingly on the bed. He continued to kiss her mouth, then let his lips travel to her ears and her neck. When his mouth found her breast, she almost passed out with the sensation. She totally forgot that this man was practically a stranger and that her mother was watching just a few feet away. Time started to lose all meaning as things happened to her and around her. She felt like a disembodied spirit, floating around, looking down at herself on the bed, under this man. There was pain. Eventually, there was pleasure, and she had no idea how long the encounter went on. Was it a matter of minutes, or had hours passed?

The candles were extinguished by unseen hands, and when it started to get cold, the same hands shut the windows and secured the doors. She knew that it was over, at least for now. She felt like she had done her duty for queen and country. Strong arms were surrounding her, and though it was a feeling that was completely alien to her, she welcomed it as she rolled to her side and quickly fell into a deep sleep.

Chapter 31: The Princess

Lydia relaxed in her private apartment, lying in a pool that was out in the open so that the sun could help to heat the water. Her quarters were extensive, and her staff was second only to the queen's. She lay naked in the hot water, salts and fragrance were added as needed to keep the water foaming and smelling like fresh flowers from around her homeland. Manservants brought her fruit, sliced and peeled so that only the most delicate and tasty bites were offered. They fanned her when she became too hot and added hot water if the pool was not sufficiently heated. Even though they were in the presence of their princess in all her naked glory, their ability to feel desire had long ago been surgically removed. They were now the perfect mirror to hold up to her prince. Randolph Landrew was a true man in all respects, the creatures that served her were far less masculine than her husband. In fact, they were less masculine than the princess herself. Their warrior spirit and their manly attributes had all been removed at the same time as their testicles. They were now calm and subservient and offered no threat to a man whose cock and balls were in working order.

A week ago, she had dreaded the thought of being penetrated by a man. Dreaded was a term that really didn't begin to describe how she had felt. She thought that the love between girls was enough for her and that the whole idea of fornication was not only unsanitary but an affront to her sensibilities. True, being made love to by a man was not the same as sharing a night with another woman; but in its own way, it was very satisfying. She was so accustomed to being in charge, not only in the bedroom but in every facet of her life. Only her mother had the authority to control her. She took her station as second in command to heart. Her troops respected her, but they did not love her. Her male servants regarded her as a spoiled brat and only held their tongues because their whole purpose was to keep the princess content.

Making love to a man? Or possibly more accurately, being used by a man for his pleasure? The thought angered her waking mind; but that part of her, deep down inside, the part that sent water to her nethers, needed that feeling of being dominated. They had made love every day of their new marriage, and now that her mother was no longer watching from the wings, her prince allowed his instincts to take over and he took command when they were in the bed chamber. He ordered her around like a common whore and pulled at her hair or gripped her arms so that her body was at the proper angle for his attack. This general of the battlefield, a killer of men, was now allowing her face to be pressed into her silk cushions as he ravaged her from behind. She felt the air growing old in her lungs, yet the pleasure was so very much worth the loss of control.

Now, only months into their union, she looked down at the man in disgust; her husband, the great prince and fourth in line to a throne somewhere down south. He had been useful for the purpose he was recruited for. He had indeed planted his seed in her, and without doubt, the child would have a fine pedigree. She prayed that the child in her womb would not inherit its father's weaknesses. At first, he had been forceful, she was not his first and he tried to put all his experience to work when bedding her. During the day, when they were not making love, she found his skill at conversation lacking, and his skill at war was even weaker.

As princess of the O'Bell clan and heir to the throne, she had only two duties. One, to bear an heir, and second, to be a skillful warrior. She would be responsible to lead the O'Bell knights in battle. She was very capable of carrying out her duties, but now she wanted more. Becoming queen should have some perks, yet she felt like she was more of a prisoner than the eunuchs that catered to her every whim. She didn't have the freedom to mount a horse and take off in search of adventure. She had heard that her five times removed cousin; Renata Rin had become queen of Inram. She had immersed herself in the world of men and come out on top.

At her feet was the man that was chosen to be her mate. Good looking and supposedly skilled at swordsmanship; yet when she demanded too much of him, instead of beating her or ignoring her, he wilted in front of her like a dead rose. She hit him and kicked him, and worse yet, impugned his manhood. Even though she was already with child, she still felt the yearning for having him make fiery passionate love to her. The more that she demanded he perform, the weaker his manhood became, till it was naught but a useless appendage.

"Get up! Take your clothes off and get in bed!" she yelled at her husband. "I'm bored and I need you to pleasure me."

He looked up at her, bruises still on his face where she had struck him earlier. He miserably dragged himself to his feet and began to undress. The whole time, he tried holding back tears that were forming at the corners of his eyes. He looked at her with a mixture of fear and hatred. When he was undressed, she sat on the edge of the bed and pointed at a pillow on the floor. Like a man heading to the gallows, he sank to his knees and went to the business of servicing his wife. She leaned back and moaned softly, partially for her own satisfaction but mostly as encouragement. As he worked, she thought to herself that one of her female servants would be much better at this, and long term, this husband just wouldn't do.

ACT II:

THE KINGS

Six years have passed.

Chapter 32: King Syphon

A half-dozen colorful tents were set up near the stream that led to the Lazy River, which emptied into the ocean in southern Chuo. The sun was nearly setting, and the campfires were roaring now. The stewards were skinning the rabbits and dressing a couple of geese while the knights and the king were taking their rest. The men of Chuo were darker than those of the Northern states, and King Kell Syphon especially, was black as night. He had wavy shoulder-length black hair and small and refined features. Without his armor, the muscles in his chest and arms were visible to everyone, and his legs were not too long but were sturdy and strong. He beamed his bright white smile as the smells of food reached him and his two best friends, Sir Kenneth Clark, and Sir Marcus Breem. The three of them spent much of their off time in the woods and plains of Chuo, hunting, drinking, and partaking of whatever else was on the menu.

Six young women came from the servant's tent where they had been changing. They now wore colorful silks, gold, and silver jewelry, and not much else. As the men settled in with pipes filled with fragrant herbs and flagons of ale, the women began their dance. A very traditional dance highly choreographed to the music of flute and strings, from a small band that had accompanied them. They spun and gyrated, almost revealing the tasty bits, but never quite showing them all. They moved their hips that were adorned with gleaming brass bells and their gyrations were almost hypnotizing. Each dancer took her turn to drift over to the king and then to the others, to tempt them with their closeness, allowing the men to feel the caress of silken scarves and long silken hair.

When the dancing was done, the women stayed in their scanty outfits and served the king and his crew. The wine flowed and the women made the men feel like men, laughing at their jokes, pretending to be shocked at their lewdness, and catering to their every whim. When the party was winding down, the king grabbed his favorite two dancers by the waist and led them to his tent. The servants sat for their own meal, then one of them stayed up to tend the fire while the rest went to sleep.

The screaming woke up the whole camp. Imelda an older cook woman was screaming at the top of her lungs causing everyone to come running out of their tents. She stood at the edge of the camp, blood all over her face and torso. She stumbled towards the center where the dying fire was slowly smoking and collapsed onto the grass. One of the king's knights was the first to approach her, he rolled her over to find that she had four large slashes across the front of her from left breast to right thigh.

"Men fetch your weapons double quick. The rest of you take cover in my tent, and do not come out till we come for you!" the king ordered. In seconds, the knights had their swords, and the servants were all huddling in a large orange and green tent.

"I am King Syphon, Master of Chuo! I demand you come forth and account for your crime!" he screamed to the world. Along one edge of the camp, there was a small stock of woods, the other three sides were open. They had planned to hunt deer or bison, both of which were rich on these vast tracks of rolling plains. The southern part of Chuo was the wilder, less populated part of his kingdom. There were stories of wild creatures that had not been seen in a generation, seemingly coming out of thin air and roaming the hills and valleys of Southern Chuo. The men all gripped their swords with tight fists, wishing that they were in full plate armor. They turned so that they were almost back to back around the fire. Each man scanned for the danger that was obviously out there. An inhuman screech assaulted their eardrums, every man winced at the loud piercing tone. Only the shadow that covered them gave them a warning that the danger came from above. They all looked up in time to see the creature descend upon them.

Its body and four legs looked very much like that of a draft horse. From its sides came wings that were very similar to the wings of an Eagle; very long and broad and covered with brown, black, and tan feathers. They blocked out the sun when fully extended. What was most horrible though, was the head. The body was a pattern of brown, tan, and black patches, which turned all black at its shoulders, where instead of a horse's head, there was the torso and head of an ape-like creature. Its long arms were covered in bristly black fur, and the hands had bird-like talons on each finger. The head was simian, with a jutting jaw and gaping mouth that was highlighted by huge white fangs. It had small ears and beady, mean little eyes.

With a scream that was neither 'bird of prey' nor gorilla, it dove down at the king. He saw the lips pulled back as it opened its mouth as wide as possible to try and bite him. King Syphon was more than just a hunter, he had led men into battle and though this creature was by far the strangest thing that he had ever seen, he would not go down without a fight. He swung his broad sword in a high arc that didn't really come close to the creature but did let it know that Breakfast was going to put up a fight. The screeching sound came again as two more of the beasts circled above, selecting which man they wanted to feast upon.

"Two more of them above us, men! Don't help me, watch for your own life!" he commanded. The creature beat its wings slowly so that it seemed to hover twenty feet above them. The ape-like head screamed at him, seemingly mad that its prey had the audacity to fight back. It dropped lower to find the king in his battle stance. Left leg forward, gripping his sword's hilt tightly in both hands, holding it high and over the right shoulder. The king also knew how to affect a war face, his handsome features twisted in anger and his bright white teeth now looked more feral than charming. When the creature dove for another attack, he swung his heavy broad sword with a speed that should not be possible when using so large a weapon. The blade neatly took off the left foreleg of the attacking beast, sending its thick red blood everywhere. The screams of pain that it made were ear-splitting.

Stealing a look to the side, Syphon saw his good friend Ken get snatched from the ground by strong, black-furred arms. He watched helplessly as huge white fangs bit deeply into his friend's neck. The knight went slack, his sword falling to the ground. The creature, satisfied with its catch, beat its wings with mighty strokes that sent it soaring upward. Soon it was just a black dot against the beautiful blue morning sky.

Even though he had been grievously wounded, the creature facing Kell again glided down to attack. He was crouched, his mighty sword cocked and ready to strike. The creature dove in headfirst, its remaining arm outstretched, ready to rake the king and rend his flesh, when it almost halted in mid-air. Kell saw that his servants had fished out a couple of crossbows from his tent and had launched a volley in defense of their king. Kell used the distraction to thrust the four-foot blade up and into the chest of the winged monstrosity. The beast let out a wail as it fell to the ground where it died.

Marcus Breem still had his hands full with his creature. He had gashes on both of his arms and was bleeding profusely. The servants were trying to load up their crossbows while the king ran over to lend a hand. The creature landed on its hind legs and reared up to strike again with heavily muscled arms. Marcus lifted his long sword to try and block the blow that everyone saw coming; but his blood loss made him weak, and he couldn't hold his weapon with any degree of strength. With its left arm, the beast knocked his weapon from his hands, and sent it flying out of reach. The other mighty paw grabbed him around the neck and lifted him a dozen feet into the air.

King Syphon charged in like a berserker of old and with a war cry on his lips, he chopped down on the creature's wing. The severed wing fell with a meaty thud on the ground. The beast screamed and used Sir Bream's limp body as a cudgel to try to beat Kell to death. Breem's legs fully caught him across his chest, sending him flying backwards. The beast dropped the dead knight and went to all fours. It charged the king with a weird gait, before tucking its remaining wing so that it wasn't completely lopsided. The servants got off another volley of bolts, most of which struck the creature in its long furry brown hide. It turned in mid charge and jumped at them, all fangs and claws.

"Fight me, foul demon!" Kell tried to get the creature's attention, but it ignored him and jumped on the servants. "Over here! Damn you creature, I'll tear you limb from limb!" he screamed to no avail. The creature destroyed the cooks and stewards with a couple of swipes of its mighty arms. Kell jumped on its back, riding it like he was trying to break a new steed. He raised up and plunged his sword deep into the creature's body. Roaring in pain, it bucked like a bull, throwing him to the ground.

Kell scrambled around till he found a long dagger that had been dropped by one of his men. The creature turned to face him, a sword still deep in its back. Reaching with both tree-like arms, it grabbed Kell and lifted him far off the ground. He punched at the huge ugly face with his left hand only to have the giant maw envelop his hand. The creature was chewing off his left hand as he swung his knife with his right. He stabbed the thick neck in the jugular. Blood poured out by the gallon, and he kept sawing till the artery was severed. He pulled out the blade, trying not to pass out from the pain in his left hand, and plunged it into the beady black eye. With a howl of pain, the creature opened its mouth and dropped him.

Kell rolled away, favoring his wound as the beast fell forward and died. Surveying the area, he saw that a couple of the dancers were hiding in the forest, not far from camp. Breem's personal manservant was still alive, though his bell had been rung. Kell found a scrap of cloth and tied off the disaster that had been his hand.

"Load everyone into the wagons, get the women to help you!" he commanded, then he laid flat on the ground and passed out.

Chapter 33: Trade War

Five Years Ago

Alarms were going off all around the warehouse complex of the Limurca Trade Federation. People were running everywhere, there was yelling and general mayhem. The duty clerk in charge was responsible for everything that happened on his watch. It was his job to notify the Master Tradesman that there was a fire in the warehouse district. A fire watch was posted at all times because fire was an unavoidable part of life, but catching it early was the key. This fire seemed to come from nowhere and it was suddenly everywhere all at once. The warehouses were completely full, and the quarterly shipment to House Sarutendo and his army was coming due. Tens of tons of cloth for uniforms, grain for bread, dried meats for rations, etc. Limurca relied on these military contracts. Four times a year they would make large deliveries; these shipments alone allowed them to meet their annual budget. They sold many other things to many other customers, but House Sarutendo in their neighboring territory was by far their largest and most important client.

Red Apna sat bolt upright after being roused by his butler. He rushed to the window to see flames shooting skyward, across town in the direction of the warehouses. The flames were a hundred feet in the air, lighting up the town with their destructive power. He rushed to put his britches on, and his servant fetched his horse; but in the pit of his stomach, he knew that the warehouses would be a near-total disaster.

When Red reached Limurca Trading's property, it was as he had expected. The bucket brigade was desperately trying to put out the flames, but even a novice could see that it was a lost cause. They soon changed from trying to save his property to trying to stop the spread to other lots. He stood there watching his profits burn away and started to wonder about his future. King Sarutendo would be furious, and he would be forced to seek his supplies elsewhere.

Red already started to think about taking a loan to cover the cost. Buy the supplies to replace what was lost and meet his obligation. Everyone would know about the fire; the money lenders would not have any incentive to give him a fair interest rate. Then he would have to approach his competitors and convince them to find excess supplies for him to purchase. They too would be able to charge usurious rates. There seemed to be no way of solving this situation without a financial setback that could take many years from which to recover.

Four years ago.

"So, you're telling me, that you'll take the entire crop at Limurca's price plus ten percent?" the wholesaler asked.

"That's right. It really doesn't get any easier than that. You do nothing. No extra work, no arguing about what you feel that you deserve. Sell to King Trading and you receive more than you were planning on."

"I know Limurca, they play rough. Your boss Regina King used to be part of their trading group. If I go with your offer, they'll come by here and break something I need, like my neck," the wholesaler said. "Your ten percent doesn't come close to indemnifying me in case they don't like me selling to their competitor."

"Ms. King knew you might feel that way," the salesman replied. "Ms. King has personally spoken to me about your concerns, and will for a brief time, hire you a small contingent of men, headed by her personal bodyguard, Naoka." He waved his hand at the giant of a man who stood silently in the corner. "Limurca will immediately respond, but our people will show them that it's more costly to try and win you back than to let you go. After the first time they are sent packing, or killed, Naoka will move on to his next assignment, the security we hired will stay until you feel that you are out of danger."

"So, King is picking up the cost of security and giving me ten percent on top of what I have been getting? How can she do that?" he asked.

"Business is war, my friend. If she is the only one selling your product, she can raise her prices, and there won't be any competition."

"You can promise my safety, me, my family, and my assets?"

"We want to do business with you for many years to come. We feel that breaking even right now suits our long-term interest."

"I always did like Regina, and that Red Apna fellow always seems a little suspect. This is an easy decision. I accept your offer. Please give Lady King my regards."

Three years ago.

"They tried it again?" Regina asked her operations manager. "Will they never learn?"

"Every time they try to highjack your shipments, all they do is lose men and credibility." The manager was in his fifties, with salt and pepper hair, and dressed smartly, though not ostentatiously.

"We have practically shut them out of Goldport, and they can't ship to Westport in Bent anymore because those damned Quell have taken over there," Regina stated. "One of these days, they're going to outsmart me and I'm going to lose money. That's not acceptable."

They sat in her office, a room one-tenth the size of her old office. Gone were the priceless artworks, the rich tapestries, and expensive furniture. King trading was like its owner, lean and mean. Starting only with what she could steal before being ousted from her company in Tebron, she moved to the neighboring country of Rubina. Now she survived on tighter margins and leveraged brute force when called for. She now realized what her opponents had always known, rules are for suckers, and only the strong survive.

"Have you spoken to our man in Limurca?" she asked him.

"Yes, my Lady. We have dates for their next shipment. They are shipping bullion for House Sarutendo, along with tons of other goods, via freight ship. The king himself is supplying extra security. Pirates would be insane to try and hijack that shipment."

"It would certainly be the prize of the year." She looked at him with an arched brow.

"Thinking of rolling the dice again Miss?" the manager, Karl Goodwin asked. He was a decade older than her; but without reservation, he respected her and deferred to her authority.

"Dice implies that chance would be involved. I never leave any details to chance."

"Of course, but I know that look on your face. The wheels are turning, and you have a plan."

"Maybe half a plan. That's why I value your input Karl, you have that frustrating, yet vitally important practical side." She picked up a decanter from the table next to her desk and gave both of them a heavy pour of bourbon. They touched glasses, then both took a gulp of the fiery liquid.

"Ok, so are we thinking... in transit?"

"That's one way to go; but like you've already pointed out, unless I had a fleet of warships, that would be impractical. Likewise, intercepting the bullion before shipping or after it arrives in Tebron are both equally suicidal."

"That's not an idea? That's not even a concept!" he laughed at her.

"Thank you for boosting my morale. Do you have anything constructive to add?"

"As a matter of fact, I might. Could top me off, please?"

She poured him a full glass of expensive alcohol. He took a big sip, then looked to the ceiling. "You know, that even if you came into possession of a hold full of bullion, you could never spend it. A chest of gold? Sure; but a dozen chests of gold, silver, copper, etc.?"

"That's true, it would be like stealing your neighbor's horse, then riding it past him."

He downed the rest of the liquor, then set the crystal glass gently on the desktop. He sucked in a reviving lung full of air to cool his pipes "Whoooo! Good stuff Miss. Now, if your goal is to improve your situation in relation to your former business partners, that can be accomplished by growth in your business, or of course, depreciation in theirs. You are doing well, and you don't really need that wealth, but it's something that both Limurca and King Sarutendo cannot do without. If that treasure sank to the bottom of Black Bay, it would cripple Limurca and Sarutendo would be in debt for generations."

Regina liked to think of herself as a cool customer, but the thought of getting her revenge on her worst enemies made her smile from ear to ear. She pushed her half a glass towards Karl "If you can think of a way for that to happen, without my fingerprints being on it, you'll be in line for a minority stake in this business. This your highest priority, make it so."

The main offices of the King Trading Company overlooked Black Bay. Regina King was observing the calm waters from her third-story patio. She sat with a strong drink in her hand while her manager Karl fiddled with the looking glass. It was an expensive toy, but she had quickly seen the value in it. When he was ready, he waved her over.

She put her eye to the lens, "What am I looking for Karl?" she asked.

"See that black dot to the right?"

"Yes, I see it. Oh! It's a ship!" she exclaimed.

"To be precise, it's the Hanover, leased by Limurca for this very important shipment."

"So, you want to show me that we have failed to stop it? Once it gets past our little protected cove, it is a short sail to Tebron."

"Keep watching Miss." he instructed.

Regina kept her eye on the eyepiece, marveling at the technology. You could see things that were very far away as if they were much closer. You could see people who could not see you. Her mind was starting to wander to other items that were on her plate when the flash of light caught her attention. The front of the tiny ship that they were tracking exploded into a fiery explosion. The flames spread quickly, growing larger by the second. The ship continued to burn, the flames working their way from front to back.

"What happened?" she asked her manager.

"What every witness will attest to, is that they crossed the path of a much smaller transport ship. The crew dived into the water just as the ships were colliding, and that's how they avoided getting caught in the explosion." He beamed at his boss. "The smaller ship was carrying low-quality but high-proof whiskey. The kind that is almost better as fuel for lamps than to drink." He looked through the glass for a moment, "The alcohol covered the front of the Hanover above the waterline, but the fire started far enough down the bow of the ship that it's very hard to hit with buckets of water. Now it's spreading both up and back, and soon the ship will be a total loss. They certainly won't notice that a couple of members of the other crew who jumped in the water have swum down to knock a few holes in the hull below the water line. Even if they can deal with the fire, they'll be taking on water, and by the time they realize it, it'll be too late."

"I gave you a very important responsibility, and you exceeded my expectations, Karl. You will still be my right-hand man; but every time we make money, you will receive a percentage commensurate with the ownership stake that we agreed upon."

"Thank you, Miss," he said graciously.

"Call me Regina. Stay loyal, and you will be rich beyond your wildest dreams."

Chapter 34: Best Served Cold

The main gates of the estate were unmanned and were built high; in better times, they would have kept a small army out. They were now rusty iron with no security detail to keep the wolves at bay. There hadn't been paid guards on Red Apna's property for almost a year now. A man who years ago would spend more on lunch than most men made in a month's worth of back-breaking labor; now couldn't afford to secure his home. His wealth at one time was such that kings were envious. He always felt that the traders held the real power in the world. Kings were just high-ranking politicians who could be bought and sold when needed and could be made to do the bidding of those who actually contributed to the economy. He had never respected the men who sweated and bled to increase his bottom line, and now his sins were coming back to haunt him.

Things were different now, starting with the fire that destroyed almost a year's worth of product and profit. That's when things started going south for him and Limurca Trading. A year or so later, he was on the hook for a lost shipment of bullion. King Sarutendo tried to stick him with full liability for the disaster, but Limurca was so deeply in debt at that time and didn't have the wherewithal to take the full brunt of the loss. Limurca was bankrupt and King Sarutendo had lost his operating capital. Limurca tried several times to get loans from the larger banks, and from private funding, but his credit was suspect, and they were too far in the hole to ever recover.

His older son, Tarren Apna was counting on having a position and sufficient funds to support his status in high society. The family business had gone bust and his father had been publicly shamed by having creditors show up to claim anything of value that was left in their estate and businesses. Tarren knew that the love of his life, the daughter of a local noble would never be seen with a man of no distinction, so he killed himself. Red Apna woke one morning to find his only son hanging by the neck in their now-empty dining hall.

A stocky man pulled out a special tool, and in a few minutes, he cut the chain, and the front gates were pushed wide open. Several men, all carrying scars and pasts that made them unwelcome in polite circles, walked through the gate with a tall woman in tow. They reached the house, and the same large fellow kicked the front door open. They walked into the sound of a woman screaming and of people scurrying around upstairs. The servants had long ago been released, so the trespassers didn't waste time and went straight upstairs. Only one room had a lantern on, they all walked down the hall and entered the master bedroom.

Crouched between the bed and the wall was Red Apna, he had his thin arms wrapped around a woman about his age and what was surely their daughter. The tall blonde woman waved a few fingers, and the members of the Apna family were pulled out into the middle of the room. When Red saw her, his face went from recognition to surrender.

"Red," she said. "It's been a very long time since you have deigned to take a meeting with me. So glad that you could make the time this evening," she said with exaggerated courtesy. "Janine, it's been even longer since we have seen each other. As I remember, we were introduced at the Limurca Harvest Ball, and you were pretty upset that your husband was working with a woman. I guess you felt better when he forced me out of my family's company." The woman looked up at her with terror in her eyes, holding back a scream that was poised to break from her throat at any instant.

"Things were very difficult for me, for a while there. That's all because of you, Red." She looked at the older man who was trying not to tremble apart at the seams, "You had more money than the king, and probably several more royal families combined. For some reason, that wasn't enough for you. When I took over the family business from my father, all you saw was an opportunity to cut out another, sometimes competitor, sometimes partner." She pulled out a rocking chair from the far side of the room and sat near them in the light.

"You not only took my business, which is the most important thing in my world, but you did it out of greed. Not only that; but you had them kill every person in my home," she spoke calmly to the cowering man. "Do you know that this is how your husband does business, Janine? That he would have professional assassins enter my home and kill everyone under my employ? Simple people who relied on me for their livelihood as well as their personal security. Did you know that? They killed the maids, the gardener, the cooks, and of course, they executed all of my guards. They killed a young man who shared my bed that night. He was such a pretty boy, in the prime of his life. Killed inches from where I lay restrained and helpless."

Janine Apna started to scream. She started at a high pitch, and as she went on, it seemed to get even higher and became even more ear-splitting. Regina waved to her man Naoka. He was as big as a mountain and as silent as the bottom of a well. He cleared the room in three to four steps, and with hands as wide as dinner plates, and arms as thick as a normal man's leg, he grabbed her by the neck and picked her up off the ground. He stood there in a room full of people, choking the wife while holding her at least a foot off the ground. He stood there calmly, but you could see the muscles in his arms flex as he held her at arm's length. The husband grabbed his daughter and held her close to his chest so that she didn't have to see her mother die. A minute later, it was over. He dropped her corpse to the ground where it landed in an awkward position, her head to one side, tongue sticking out, arms and legs all akimbo.

"You took everything from me, except my life. I guess that I should thank you for that; but since that night, I haven't been in a very forgiving mood. I wanted to take everything from you, and... well, look around. You have nothing but this loud woman, and your girl there."

"I did spare your life, Regina. I could have easily, very easily had them kill you too, but I didn't. I suppose that you are behind the warehouse fire?" he asked. She looked at him without reaction. "I don't know how you did it, but I'm also sure that you are behind the loss of my best transport ship." Again, no reaction. "Now you've killed my wife. I beg of you, spare my daughter. She is innocent, she shouldn't have to pay for my sins!" he begged Regina.

Regina waved to one of the other men that she had brought with her. He walked forward, and with a bit of a struggle, he ripped the ten-year-old girl from her father's grasp. She fought with him as best she could, which was hardly noticeable to a man his size. He threw her to the ground hard, and she lay there hurt and whimpering. Without hesitation, he lifted his huge boot and stomped on her head. A few vicious stomps and her head cracked open like an overripe melon; her limbs twitched like any dying creature. Red was screaming the whole time, and he curled into a ball, crying, and breathing raggedly. They all sat quietly and waited for him to run out of energy.

"Red, this is your last chance to be a 'real man'." She threw a dagger at him; it landed point down in the wood between his legs as he sat on the floor, "You know what to do."

"Vengeance is one thing, Regina; but what you did here tonight went too far. The gods will curse you for this!" He stared at the smashed young body. Regina remained stoic and just waited. Red picked up the dagger, put the point to his chest, and with all his meager might, plunged it into his own chest. He fell forward, life already leaving his eyes.

Regina was finally able to smile. She turned to one of her thugs, "Burn it. Burn everything," she said as she walked out of Tebron for the last time.

Chapter 35: The Monastery

A young monk ran into the meditation room where the Master was enjoying his daily communion with the eternal. A dozen other monks were also meditating there, including most of the senior members of the order. They were all working to achieve the nothingness of true Ammon. The young man had vital news, urgent news; but still, he hesitated to disturb them when they were exploring other planes. He needn't worry, the Master opened a single eye, which was aimed straight at him. Seeing the bald-headed youth with dark blue robes, he could feel the other's urgency across the great hall and decided that it would be better to meet with him out in the courtyard.

The master was old, no one knew exactly how old. He didn't seem to age, and he was able to easily recall events that happened two or three generations before. He looked like a man in his sixties, head shaved bald like all men of the sect, with the same blue robe that the acolyte wore. Around his neck was a chain of heavy wooden beads which held an intricate Jade pendant. He had no facial hair, and his thin eyes and short stature gave him a very exotic look.

"Master, please come to the observation tower. Ships have landed on our North shore and hundreds of men have set foot on our sacred island!" he said breathlessly.

"I will take a look. Please sound the bell," he told the young man.

Master Kakta ordered his disciples to their stations, then made his way to the high tower. When he got there, the view was breathtaking. Ammun had their one and only temple on the island of Varia in the middle of Silver Bay. The island had beautiful beaches all along its Northern and Western faces and had sheer cliffs dropping straight down on the other two sides. The island was perhaps a mile square, with rocky cliffs that took up nearly half the island. The Ammun temple sat atop the dark black rock of the highest peak, reaching hundreds of feet into the clear blue sky. The open-air watch tower was the highest point on the island and from there, you could see three hundred and sixty degrees. The mainland was a bit too far to see from the island, so in every direction, all you could see was the relatively calm waters of Silver Bay.

He looked where the young monk had indicated, and as the young man said, there were invaders piling out of a fleet of large boats. Some were in the long robes that were common among the Quell, the rest were wearing the rags that were on them when they were pulled off of the street. The Master jogged down the levels of the tower till he reached the lowest floor, then went out to the front gate. The brothers who were part of the guard detail stood at the wrought iron gates with their long thin halberds. The other brothers and sisters started falling into place, each with his or her weapon of choice.

They watched as the horde of Quell worked their way up the wide winding road that led from the dock to the temple. There were hundreds of them, and most had swords or other sharp metal implements. The Ammun had been in the shadow of the Quell for years now, and as a competing religion, they knew that the day would come when the Quell would be so offended by their very existence that they would have to attack. Master Kakta felt that they were ready, and he believed that their god had prepared each of them to be a temple, to be an army, embodied in a single person. Wolvig was on the far side of Silver Bay; but in the last few years, they had taken over most of Preston, Ursina, and large areas of Jaga-Koba. Though not recognized, their land now formed the largest country in all of Kronos.

"Brother! Sisters!" the Master called out. No one turned towards him, but he knew that he had their attention. "This is the fight that we have been expecting for so long, your bodies will be tested; but more importantly, your faith will be put to the test. I have complete confidence in every one of you. Some of us will fall today, but our spirits will live forever in Ammun with our ancestors. Protect yourselves, protect your brothers and sisters, and protect this holy ground," he spoke with strength, without having to yell. The followers of Ammun didn't need to be coerced or convinced to stand in defense of their temple.

The Quell marched up the hill without fear and as they approached, they greeted the monks with threats and insults. The whole temple replied to their shouts, yelling a prayer, as if with a single voice. This sign of unity gave pause to the invaders, their leaders had to crack whips to keep up their commitment to invade a compound where every single person had deadly fighting skills. There were two dozen men who were humping a heavy battering ram up the steep grade. The ram was basically a huge log with steel nailed to the front and handles hammered into the sides. In all, there were about a thousand of them descending on the peaceful temple of Ammun.

The Quell were doing well in their campaign of world conquest. The kings and lords that ruled the lands in the north were too timid to face them and do what needed to be done. It amazed their leader, Lem Lothe, that they could storm into a city, destroy artifacts that had stood for hundreds of years, and there was no backlash. They would line up the men and kill them in the most inventive ways that they could come with, and yet still there was no significant resistance. What surprised him the most was that these people who called themselves 'men', would allow their wives to be taken, and even worse, their young daughters. Young virginal girls with their innocent smiles and spirits that had never been tainted by even a coarse word, much less what the

Quell had planned for them. Those who weren't followers of Quell were offensive to them, repugnant, less than human. Any indignity inflicted on them, any suffering they endured was acceptable to the fanatics. What kind of man would allow that to happen to any child, much less his own child, without giving his life in their defense? That they would have respected, but the cowering of these 'men', as they waited on their knees to be beheaded... that was beyond understanding and most definitely not deserving of respect.

The religion of Quell was unique in that it could not stand to be in close proximity to any other belief. They encroached on a region where they were the minority, and by unfettered immigration and aggressive recruiting, they soon became a very vocal minority. They refused to assimilate and demanded more and more concessions. They would claim that the criminal acts they committed were not their fault but were due to intolerance of their religion. If you had any problem with that, you were labeled a religious bigot.

When they detected weakness, when they felt they had achieved sufficient numbers, they attacked. They were a cancer that a country would allow into its body, then was surprised when it became malignant. They could not stand the Ammun because they did not show any weakness in the face of aggression. In fact, they stood strong and dared the Quell on many occasions to cross the line. Till today, they had been too cowardly to act; but they had grown confident after a series of respectable military wins. They now felt that Quell was with them, and though the terrain benefitted the Ammun, they had no qualms about losing three lives to take down one of the unbelievers.

The temple of Ammun had stood for hundreds of years. They didn't believe in the Old Gods, but they bore them no ill will. They did their best to keep to themselves and did not recruit followers. They occasionally had converts, but they did nothing to seek them out. Instead of putting faith in supernatural beings that were credited with creating the world and all living things, they believed in an even higher force. The entire universe was a system of energy that flowed between planes of existence and defined reality. The Ammun spent their whole lives trying to let their spiritual energy travel from the physical plane to the higher planes.

"Archers, prepare!" the Master called out. "On my command, let fly!" The invaders were climbing up the road as quickly as they could, there was no attempt at stealth, they thought that their numerical superiority would support a frontal assault. They lumbered up the half-mile trail and even before they were within range of the monk's arrows, they were growing tired. Seeing this, the Master decided that they were losing their momentum and the trade for accuracy was more than enough reason to start the festivities. "Fire!" he yelled so that everyone could hear, both defender and attacker.

The faces of the Quell soldiers turned white as they realized that a volley of arrows was imminent, and they were still a hundred feet from an iron gate that would not yield without a fight. Their leader urged them to pick up the pace; they all realized that every second wasted was a chance for them to be cut down. The Ammun were far fewer in number, but they held the high ground and were prepared for this eventuality. Dozens of arrows with steel barbs sailed through the air, many of them finding homes in the flesh of the invading soldiers. A second volley rained down on them, then a third. The Quell were starting to panic, and fear fueled their run up the hill. The narrow path was becoming choked with their dead and dying. With their leaders behind them, yelling orders and urging them on at spearpoint they put their backs into the ram and struck the gate with all their strength. The massive gate was holding strong, so they backed up and struck again and again. After a dozen or so tries, the chain that held the gate gave way to the sheer force of a huge steel-tipped tree being driven by twenty or more rabid invaders. Once the gate was breached, they still had to file through the opening of the gate, and this bottleneck made it easier for the defenders. Arrows still rained down on those waiting in queue to push through the bottleneck. Several hundred had been killed or mortally wounded even before entering the battlefield proper.

The Ammun were ready, though they didn't employ the traditional army tactics that most of the armies in Kronos used. Each fighter, man or woman, was highly trained and had full control of their body, their emotions, and their surroundings. They could sense everything and everyone who entered their personal space. It was said that an Ammun could sense someone directly behind them, even if that person was completely silent. They each functioned independently and didn't generally rely on others to provide them with protection.

The monks in the front positioned themselves so that a few invaders could flow past them; but not enough to overwhelm the junior monks that stood behind them. This way, they regulated the flow and stopped the Quell from their usual tactics of swarming and sacrificing a dozen to take out one enemy. In the front line, alongside the Master was Roku, a senior acolyte. He was having difficulty connecting with the eternal, but his skills on this plane were unmatched. Unlike his little sister Melina, who was a few rows behind him, he faced the enemy without weapons. His training in the arts of unarmed combat made him a living weapon that was far deadlier than any sword or cudgel.

Roku's hands had been hardened till they were like stone, and he used flat-handed chops to bring down the first few men that dared face him. His arms moved faster than the human eye could follow, and the fighters couldn't comprehend that an unarmed man had just brushed aside their sword strike and had struck vital points in their neck, head, and chest that essentially stopped their body from functioning. He was not particularly intimidating when not cutting down foes, he was several inches short of six feet, bald with dark skin from training in the sun, and yet his frame was bigger than most men his size. What they did not see was a body under his robes that was almost completely devoid of fat. The culmination of a lifetime of healthy eating and a tortuous exercise regimen had turned him into a man with a flawless physique. He was known for scowling almost all the time, even when he thought that no one was watching. The only time he looked at peace was when he was fighting, then his exotic features took on the calm look of one who was both concentrating and allowing instinct to take over.

Roku's bright orange robe seemed almost out of place in the middle of the blood and turmoil that dominated the gate. He would grab a man, twist his arm out of place and rip through the tendons, then toss him back into his comrade's hands while he attacked the next in line. If you could remove the sounds of all the clashing of steel on steel, the screams of pain, the cries of battle; if you could take out all those sounds, you would be left with Roku's world. The sickening sound of bones breaking, knees being cracked, hands being crushed, collar bones being snapped. He could feel the vibration of every arm or leg that he incapacitated, and it let him know that it was okay to move on to the next opponent.

Roku let some fighters by him because he knew that Melina was behind and to the left, as he faced forward. She wielded twin short swords, and she had practiced with them to the point that she felt absolutely confident in her ability. She was small and her attackers couldn't reach her without her being able to carve them up first. She called them short swords; but to many, they were over-large knives. They had sword handles with a proper cross guard, and each was about eighteen inches long. She had them sharpened like a man's razor and polished them to an almost mirror finish. She was so proficient that she could block or strike with either hand. Her signature technique was to block the swing of a sword or deflect it to the side, while at the same time, chopping at her enemy's throat. Her main problem was that she was killing her opponents so fast that she had to worry about them falling on her. Her kicks were not as good as her brother's, nor was her hand speed as quick. Her claim to fame was that she was more in tune with the universe. Her consciousness could travel the planes of existence with ease, whereas her brother struggled greatly.

Master Kakta was a Master for a reason. He was the most skilled with any weapon, and perhaps the best at unarmed combat. If there were only a dozen invaders, he might have faced them like Roku, without a weapon; but there were far too many for him to take chances. Every man that he could not kill would have the opportunity to kill one of his disciples, and that gave him cause to worry. He cared for each of them like members of his own family, the children that he never had. He had trained them well, and they should be able to account for themselves, but he still felt personally responsible for each of them.

He wielded a thin long sword; the light weight allowed him to swing it with little effort and he was able to form what looked like a web of steel around himself. He only had one sword, but it seemed to be in three or four places at once. It was useless to try and hit him with any type of projectile, he was able to see it and deflect it with ease. The weapon was not meant to lop off heads and arms, instead, he gave each opponent enough slashing cuts that they would bleed to death. He did partially separate a hand or two, and he took out a few eyes, but his modus was to wear them down and make them unable to continue fighting.

Like a sniper, Yana sat on the roof of the horse stables and picked off Quell as they were pushing through the gate. Each person that she picked off fell where they stood and made it harder for the rest to enter. Almost from the start, the Quell had to climb over the bodies of their friends in order to enter the battlefield. They were tired from the hill, discouraged by having to go over the bodies of their own, and completely outclassed when they eventually faced one of the monks.

Out of their thousand invaders, about two hundred finally decided that it was a lost cause and ran back to their ships. Left behind were hundreds of dead, heaped like trash in front of the large iron gates. In the compound, there were also hundreds more of their dead, and there were dozens injured due mainly to Roku's less-than-lethal methods. The Ammun suffered the loss of less than twenty members, all of whom would be given a proper service as they surrendered their souls to the eternal.

Regarding the injured Quell, Master Kakta thought for a few moments, then made up his mind. "We must learn the lessons that our former neighbors have taught us. They were soft and showed weakness, and these evil men took advantage of it. When a dog is rabid, you can't cure it, it must be put down."

Roku and a few of the other senior monks nodded and went to work. Roku found a spear and walked from body to body, and if he saw any sign of life, he would drive the point into the invader's chest. Melina found it very distasteful and went off to her cell to prepare a bath. The younger monks loaded the Quell onto wagons and rolled them towards the far side of the temple's grounds. The back gate opened to a sheer drop into the sea. One by one they tossed the bodies over the edge and into the water, hundreds of feet below. When they started, the sea below was calm; but after several hours of dropping meat off the cliff, the usually calm waters became a feeding frenzy. Today the sea life around Ammun temple would feast, and the Quell would learn a lesson they would not soon forget.

Master Kakta sat cross-legged on his mat in the mediation room. The walls were open, and a cool breeze blew through the large open area. There was no furniture, only a small fountain in the corner, several plants, and open spaces for the monks to spread their blankets. Here they would commune with nature or the eternal, or at the very least, themselves. He had been there with all the senior monks for over an hour, not a sound was made except the slow controlled breathing of each man or woman. While drifting in and out of lucidity, an epiphany came to him. He cleared his throat which, if done by anyone else, would have been considered very rude and deserving of blows to the back and shoulders; but for the Master, an exception was made.

"Brothers and Sisters, the time has come for us to take a larger role in the outside world. Our old neighbors were fine with us keeping to ourselves and they respected our privacy. Our new neighbors are born of fear and hatred, and perhaps the worst of all sins, envy. The men who stormed our gates just a few days ago had nothing and didn't value their own lives, much less the lives of others. We thought to let the outside world solve its own problems while we maintained our neutrality, but it is obvious that this can no longer be the case."

"Are you suggesting that we take a more active role in the politics of Kronos?" an elderly female monk asked.

"We are of Kronos. We pretend that we have our own world here on this dot of land, but each of us came from one of the countries out there. I'm sure that someone here has already lost loved ones to the expansion of this cult. We should not benefit from the others giving their lives and all they have worked for, to drive out these invaders. These Quell are the dregs of society. They do not know love, have never tasted success, and they only feel alive when causing others pain and misery," he said calmly. In this place, not even the master would raise his voice. "The kings of Kronos are meeting at King's Table in Tebron in a couple of weeks. We should send a representative to learn their plans, and if we are needed, to offer our solidarity."

They all sat contemplating the master's plan, there were a variety of expressions from full agreement to absolute disagreement. The temple was not a democracy though, and the master had already decided. "Roku, I want you to go and represent Ammun at King's Table." Roku was not thrilled, but it was not in his nature to complain or even second-guess the master. He stood up and prepared to leave for his cell to collect a few things.

"Master, I will go with him. I think that it's better that none of us travel alone and I have more skill dealing with... people," Melina offered.

The master only thought for a moment, "Yes, that makes sense. You keep him out of trouble." She smiled and took off after her older brother. It had been a while since she had left the island, and she was anxious to see the outside world again.

Chapter 36: Landis Stone

Landis awoke on the ground underneath the wreckage of his smithy. The building he had built to work Iron and Steel was now lying on top of him. He felt pain everywhere, in every part of his body, but most acutely in his side and left arm. He could feel the warmth of fresh blood, but the smell was not quite overpowering, so maybe his wounds were not as bad as they could have been. He could see light through the shattered remains of the roof that he had built. It took three attempts to erect the roof, but the last version was watertight, and finishing it had filled him with no small bit of pride. He shifted his body to try and slip out from the wall that lay across his torso. It was slow and arduous, but it didn't seem like anything was broken. When the weight was finally off him, he could feel the wound in his side start to bleed freely. He worked a hand through the wreckage till he was able to put pressure on the stab wound. He cursed himself for being a fool. There had been a dozen of them, and they all had been armed. Landis had long ago given up the sword; but even in retirement, their fighting skills were still nothing compared to his. Still, it was embarrassing.

When he had crawled safely out of the wreckage, he ripped a few strips from his shirt to tie around his arm, and his side. He still had to apply pressure to the body wound, the arm would keep. He looked at what had been his life just an hour ago. A small house for himself and his family, and a shop where he could forge metal into weapons and tools. A respectable life.

The sky was still bright, there were a few hours left till sundown. He staggered over to where the house had been. It was now just a smoldering ruin. How could such horrible things happen on what otherwise was such a beautiful day? He staggered over to the house and looked down at the bodies that were left without care in the midday sun. There were three men lying there because of the fatal wounds that he had given them. They were filthy, unwashed cogs in a larger machine, dressed in robes that were meant to identify them and cause fear in those they encountered. Now they lay dead with multiple broken bones and wounds inflicted by the very weapons they had brought with them.

It was earlier that morning, well before lunch when they arrived. Landis knew them for what they were immediately. Instantly, he regretted his decision to put down the sword and pick up the smith's hammer. He had hidden his sword to keep his son from asking questions that he wasn't prepared to answer.

"Gloria, take Will and run for the hills. Go! Now!" he yelled to his wife. She ran into the house to fetch their young son.

Ten or so men came down the road and encountered Landis Stone's smithy. They were cocky because by now, the robes they wore were known to everyone in Kronos. Most people did whatever they could to appease them, giving anything they owned; including offering their wives and daughters for the pleasure of the Quell. Landis was not one to submit to anyone, much less these poor excuses for men.

He didn't wait for introductions. As they were approaching to introduce themselves and begin their well-rehearsed intimidation speech, he attacked. He struck the lead man with his hammer. The blow was partially deflected, but it still hit with bone-crushing force. The men swarmed him, to stop him from swinging his weapon. They had fists and knives, and they attacked him from all four sides. Even unarmed, he was more of a warrior than the group of them combined. He ducked slashes and thrusts that should have connected. He grabbed at a random arm and twisted it till there was a loud, audible snap. Taking the blade, he thrust it into one of the men that was attacking him. Landis stabbed the man several times till he died and fell back into the rest.

They swarmed him again, they were relentless. He felt a blade bite into his arm, but he ignored it and continued to punch their dirty bearded faces with their crazy eyes. He felt bones snap in his grasp as he pushed, threw them to the ground, where he kicked, and pummeled them. Even the greatest of warriors cannot last against odds that are so stacked against him. He barely felt the knife dig into his side as he sent another attacker to the afterlife with a sickening snap of his neck. They piled on him, punching and kicking every square inch of him until he mercifully passed out.

Gods only know how long he was passed out, but when he awoke, he saw through a fog of blood that had seeped into his eyes that they were taking his wife. She was bent over the edge of the well, and one by one, they stepped up and pushed themselves into her. He heard her whimper with pain and suffering, and it was his greatest torment that he could not jump up and kill the rest of them in the most violent way possible. Just opening his eye was almost more than he could manage and to be greeted by such a sight was more than he could handle. He closed his one good eye and focused his attention on trying to stand, but just breathing seemed like a near-impossible task.

When they were satiated, they set torches to the house, and to the smithy. The shop was mostly stone, and it didn't burn as easily as the house did. When the tons of stone and wood piled on him, he felt his lungs deflate and again he lost consciousness. The next time that he woke up, he was alone. Truly alone. The body of his only son was near the house, burned where he had been hiding from the Quell invaders. His wife's body was beaten and bloody and disrespected in the most horrible fashion. As much as he loved her, he couldn't decide if her passing was a better fate than trying to recover from the brutal treatment that had eventually led to her death.

Either way, his time as a family man was finished. Landis lay in the ruins of the smithy for a couple of days, just sleeping and trying to get to his feet. When he had enough strength to walk, he dug into the earth behind the house. There is where he tried to bury his past. In the chest, only a few feet beneath the surface was his armor; a mixture of plate and leather that allowed for protection but didn't hinder his speed. He had a knife that had been stained with the blood of many men, and his longsword. Longswords are not uncommon, but they come in all qualities. He had to defeat a very notable knight to acquire this sword, a sword that was made with craftsmanship that was very rare these days.

When he was armed and ready, he visited the graves of his wife and child for the last time. He planned to never return to his home in Anatol. His family had raised him not a hundred miles away, but he didn't have plans to visit them either. The rest of his life would be devoted to stamping out the disease that was the Quell.

Chapter 37: The Healer

Father Sebastienne looked at the sky, enjoying what had turned out to be a nearly perfect day. It was sunny and warm and there was a light breeze that made the temperature feel just right. He was on the road that followed the Southern coast of Anatol, heading towards Ursina. He joined the brothers when he was a boy of ten and now had spent his whole adult life in the monastery in the Kararatal Mountains. Now that he had become an adult, he asked permission from the church to take a sabbatical; a chance to roam and experience the outside world.

Darus Sebastienne was born in Ursina and only got as far as Anatol, the next country over. He was the youngest son of a large family, so there would be no inheritance and he would receive no help in life. The Sebastienne family was very religious, so when the Church was looking for new blood, the boy Darus was quickly given up. He had not taken any leave in the many years that he had been away and no one from his family had found the time to check in on his well-being. Darus was very well thought of among the brothers, in fact some of them knew what he could do and looked at him with the reverence due a much older priest. When he asked to have time away, they warned him about the outside world, gave him some money to pay for his bread and lodging, and wished him well.

Father Sebastienne was committed to the vows of poverty, abstinence, and chastity; so, he felt almost like a sinner in his brand-new robe. It was plain brown and had a hood to shield his face from the rain and sun. He was six and a half feet tall, so no other brother could pass down clothes to him. Every time he wore out an old robe, he was forced to acquire new clothing. On his back, he carried a pack with items needed for his holy work and items for personal hygiene. He was gifted with and carried a long, gnarled staff for walking. He had neither beard nor mustache; his hair was a mix of light brown and gold and was trimmed short in the style of monks. He was tall, thin, handsome man, with a sweet disposition and an infectious smile.

Darus had been walking most of the morning when he saw a hunched figure far ahead on the road. It was an old man whom he caught easily with his long strides. Before long, the two were side by side. Darus looked down at the old man, and the old man looked up at him with a pained face. He shuffled along so slowly that Darus had to stop, let him get a little ahead, then take another step. As he moved, the old man groaned, obviously experiencing pain with each step. Darus felt bad for the senior and wanted to help.

"Sir, you seem to be in a great deal of pain. Can I help you?"

"I can't call you father," he growled. "I'm no longer a believer."

"That's fine, Sir. Still, I can probably help with the pain if you would let me."

"I have a grandchild your age. I don't know what you can do that so many barbers and surgeons haven't been able to cure."

"Ok, grandfather let's sit for a minute." He guided the old man to a fallen log that was laying by the side of the road.

The old man even looked pained as he tried to sit without falling too fast. When he was seated firmly, the father knelt beside him. He took the old man's hand in his own and lowered his head. He began praying. The old man looked miserable and scoffed at the young priest. He had lost his faith long ago. The old man mumbled and grumbled, but the young priest ignored his complaining and maintained his invocation. Warmth flowed from the priest into the old man, a feeling of energy and life and youth. First, the pain in his hand disappeared, then the pain in his elbow then shoulder joints. The old man stopped talking and just stared at the youth who was channeling a god's given healing power. The healing warmth worked its way through him, flowing like hot wax through the old man's veins. Ten minutes later, Father Sebastienne released the old man's hand and ceased his prayers. He looked up at the senior with his sky-blue eyes.

What looked back at him was a life restored. The man was still old, but his face no longer showed the pain that one gets from a lifetime of backbreaking labor. He still had wrinkles, but his arms and legs were stronger, and his back was stretched and relaxed. When he stood, he was half a foot taller than the man who had sat down ten minutes earlier. He flexed his arms and legs, his neck and back, marveling at his body like it was the body of his youth. When he came to grips with the miracle, he looked up at the young priest with tears in his eyes.

"Will... will this last... Father?" he asked.

"You are healed, friend. The gods have allowed me to heal you and their gift will last you many years if you take care of yourself."

The old man fell to one knee, and kissed the hands of the priest, "Father... there are no words that I can say to express my gratitude. I'm not sure that I deserve your gift, but I will receive it and give thanks to all the Old Gods. May they live forever!"

"That makes it all worth it friend. Go and share your renewed faith with all those that you love." With that, he stood and resumed walking.

Nighttime was falling, as the last rays of the sun were about to disappear over the horizon. Father Sebastienne had hoped that he would find a town or some type of structure to sleep in, but perhaps this was just the type of adventure that he had sought when he asked for time for himself. He had always slept in his cell at the abbey, and never in his life had he wanted for a roof over his head. These thoughts and others like them were occupying his attention when he heard moaning from the side of the road. Walking over, he looked in the ditch to find a thirty-ish man lying face down and bleeding from multiple wounds all over his dirt-caked body. He jumped into the ditch and pulled the man close to his chest.

Through his hands, the father could feel the life waning in the man. The man was as close as one can come to being dead, and yet still be among the living. He held the man tight to his bony chest and with all his might, he prayed to the gods. He repeated his prayers over and over till his mind was hazy about how long he had been praying. He knew that he was channeling power that was not his own, it flowed into him from the gods and then out to the subject of his prayers. Somewhere during the hours of supplication, the father drifted off to sleep, the strange man whom he had yet to meet was held tightly in his arms.

Morning came all too soon, and Father Sebastienne woke up to see a man who was several years his senior, staring at him in wonder. The man looked like death warmed over; but even from several feet away, he could tell that his life force was much stronger and had become stable. He still looked tired, but he was in infinitely better shape than before the young priest's intervention.

"Good morning," the priest offered. He stood up and evaluated the bloody mess that had been his spotless robe just yesterday.

"Mornin. Who are you?" Landis asked.

"I am Father Darus Sebastienne."

"What happened? I... I guess I passed out."

"You were laying in a ditch, bleeding to death."

"Are you a doctor? You have medical training?"

"I channeled the power of the gods to heal you last night."

Landis looked very skeptical, he stared at the priest, "I have been injured before, but yesterday was by far the worst. I know that I was on death's door. I dreamt that I was in the Hespian Gardens." He was getting emotional, "I was going to look for my wife and son... and then you pulled me back."

"The gods put me on your path brother, and apparently, they are not done with you. When I see someone that I can save, I use the power given to me, and lay hands on them." He took Landis' hand and was helped to his feet. "I brought you back from the brink, now we must put food and water into you so that my efforts won't be for naught." They began walking East.

"If we come across any of the followers of Quell, I will be killing them. Please do not interfere, and do not attempt to save them." Landis gave him a look that made it clear there would be no discussion on that point.

With no money, their choices for shelter were very limited. They had walked quite a distance, and when the sun was about to set, they veered off the main trail. They came upon a large tree with low-hanging branches that formed a makeshift shelter. The benefits were that it was hard to see into and spacious inside. Too tired for a fire, they each laid out their cloaks and fell asleep. It was a hot evening and there were plenty of insects, but they were so tired, and after passing out in a ditch, lying on the hard ground was just fine.

In the wee hours of the night, a cool breeze woke Landis. Leaving the father blissfully asleep, he got up to look around. He found that no one else was around, yet he still had a strange feeling. The kind that had to be explored before going back to sleep. Outside the concealment of the large tree, he saw what he was expecting. Sparse woods to his rear, the trail several hundred feet away, thick grasses all around. Then he heard the soft babble of a creek. He walked away from the tree and headed towards the soothing sound. It was so dark that he almost fell into the water.

The clouds above parted and light from the moon gave the scene a dim glow. Sitting on a log that extended into the water was a young man, about his age, handsome and with a sly knowing smile on his face. He seemed not the least surprised to see another person wandering in the middle of nowhere, in the wee hours of the night. He looked up and said in a soft tone.

"Landis Stone. I know much about your exploits, so nice to meet you in person," he said.

"Do I know you?" Landis asked, still groggy from just recently waking up.

"You know of me, and that's good enough for now. I am so terribly sorry for what happened to your family. If I could have stopped it, I would have; but I try to keep meddling in the affairs of humans to a minimum."

"Thank you for your condolences. Did you know my wife?"

"No, I never met her, or your son. I did observe them a time or two, from a distance. You have always been a person to watch, and when watching you, I saw them and how much they meant to you."

"I can never get them back; but by the gods, I will have my revenge."

"That is why I've come to you. I come to support your war on the Quell. They must be stopped, and it will take men like you to stop them."

"What kind of support are you talking about?" Landis asked.

"There is only so much that I can do." He paused, "I have a gift for you. A gift that suits your talents and furthers our cause." Standing up, the young man pulled a sword from behind his back, still in its scabbard, and handed it to Landis. "This is a special sword, one of the six Blades of the Colossus. I have named her Soulbane, and she will serve you well. I created the swords for champions, imbued them with power to help them defeat those who would seek to destroy what I have built."

Landis took the sword in his two outstretched hands. He was still in a daze; but when he focused on the blade, he could see that it was a blessed sword, power seemed to radiate from it. The sword was a cross between a long sword and a bastard sword, pointy at the end, bladed on both sides with razor-sharp edges. There were runes carved into the length of the bright silvery blade, written in a language that died long before the age of man. He looked up to thank the youth again, but the young man was gone. Still in a fugue state, Landis wandered back to his makeshift bed and went quickly to sleep.

Chapter 38: The Prince

Gilman was a town in Northern Khatuna that was known for Randall University, which was the town's main source of income. Much of the town's population was made up of students, young men and women in their early twenties. Khatuna Highway was famous in all Southern Kronos for its clubs and bars. Every manner of worldly pleasure could be found somewhere up and down the strip. People often walked up and down the street drinking and howling at the moon until late every evening.

Gabriel Heron bent over and placed his lips around the edge of the small clear glass. The vapor from the honey-colored liquid within burned his nose, as did her perfume. The glass was wedged in the ample bosom of a young barmaid. He pulled the glass free, then tilted his head back, causing the fiery liquid to shoot down his throat. The crowd all cheered Gabe's successful shot as he spat the glass into his palm and set it next to nine other glasses.

"While I was down there, I couldn't help noticing that you are a veeeeeery pretty girl!" he said to the barmaid. She reached over and pulled his chin up so that his gaze would move from her cleavage to her eyes. "Oh, hello!"

"Another round Gabriel?" she asked him, her beautiful black eyes flashing. Unlike almost every person in the club, she was sober.

"Perhaps in a minute or two. The last one is still working its way down the old pipe." He reached for her, but she was too fast and avoided his grasp. "I think it would be wise to add some food to the devil's brew that is my stomach right now. Please bring your finest dishes, enough for me and you," he noticed a young man next to him who was an older student, "and for him too!" he clapped the fellow on the back.

Gabriel had the ability, drunk or sober, to make friends. To those that knew him, he did have the reputation of being spoiled and overindulged in almost every way; but he was generous with his purse and preferred to settle a fight with a round on his tab. Downing a large glass of water, he worked his way to a nearby table and sat in an open seat. There was a mixture of upperclassmen and freshmen, party girls, and an older man who looked like he might be a professor.

"Excuse me, is this seat taken?" he asked as he sat down.

"Usually people ask 'before' sitting," the older man sniped.

"True, you have me there, friend. I was having a few drinks over there at the bar, and I suddenly saw the wisdom in having a seat, and the sooner the better."

"Do you go to the University?" one of the girls at the table asked him.

"No, I never attended university, I had tutors. I graduated a couple of years back. What I did miss though, was the opportunity to meet fine people like yourselves," he said smiling at her with half-glazed eyes.

"I'm no learned person like yourself; but for a reasonable fee, I can teach you a world of things. Things that are useful in real life, not things that are found in books or classrooms," one of the party girls slurred. She put her arm around him and tried to whisper in his ear.

Just in time, the food arrived, and Gabriel gladly shared with the table. He hand-served all that he could reach without leaving his chair. Digging into the hearty beef stew, they all broke out into satisfied smiles.

"So, if you're not a student, then what do you do, kind sir?" the professor asked.

"At the moment? Nothing really. I come from high money and low expectations, so I have quite a bit of freedom to explore the countryside a bit and," he put his arm around the party girl next to him, "the people in it." Then he leaned in and whispered something in her ear that got her giggling. Sitting back and surveying the table, he went back to the older man. "And you, Sir, can I assume that you are a professor? What specialty do you teach these eager young minds?"

"I teach philosophy and politics."

"I take it that you are not from here in Khatuna?" he asked the man.

"No, I originate from Agron; but the weather and the employment climate are much more favorable here."

"Well, welcome to Khatuna Sir." Gabriel looked around the table, "Does anyone need another drink? I think you all need to catch up."

"I open the eyes of my students, letting them know that the monarchy system that is pervasive in almost every country in Kronos is archaic and should be a thing of the past."

"When you say, 'almost every country'…."

"Wolvig no longer has a royal family, and they are fine."

"Really?" Gabriel was starting to sober up. "I heard that everyone in the major cities has either been indoctrinated into that death cult or murdered. Literally mountains of bodies lining the streets. How are the people of Wolvig better being raped, enslaved, or killed?"

"They are better... because they are no longer under the oppressive thumb of a 'King'. They have the choice to go anywhere or be whatever they want."

Gabriel looked at him for a full minute, then "Where do you get your information?" he asked, looking none too pleased.

They all dug into the plates of food. One of the students turned to Gabriel and whispered to him, "Does he know what he's talking about?"

"If everyone listened to him... well, I can't imagine that getting raped and burned alive is better than being loyal to a king."

"I've studied the various forms of governance for over a decade now and if I don't mind saying so, am the preeminent authority on the subject."

"Really?" Gabriel asked aloud. "I'm not sure that a decade of just reading about a thing makes one an expert at that thing."

"And you think that you know more about monarchies and politics?"

"I know a thing or two," Gabriel replied, turning back to his food.

They were all joking around and drinking. The young men were trying to pick up the girls, even though the girls were 'very available'. Two soldiers in full armor came in bearing the crest of House Herron and everyone in the bar stopped talking and watched them as they looked around the place. They passed through the room not caring whom they might accidentally knock over. When they saw Gabriel, they went straight to him.

"Sire, we have an urgent message from your father," one of the men said as he took a parchment from his breast pocket and handed it to Gabriel. The room silently watched their most congenial member somberly open the letter. He read, and it seemed like forever, but he finally reached the bottom of the page and dropped his hands to his lap.

"Thank you. I'll be ready to go in the morning. You two get a good rest, ask for a room in the hotel next to mine," he said, turning back to the stew. The soldiers left, and the place slowly resumed its previous state.

He took several spoonsful before the girl to his right broke the ice.

"What was that all about?" she asked.

"Seems that there is a rather large summit at King's Table, and Father is too ill to attend, so I have to show in his place."

"Who's your father?" she asked again.

"King Herron, you know, the Lord of Khatuna, and of course, this little town." He smiled at the professor who was dumbfounded.

Gabriel turned to the girl on his right, "I am traveling by sea in the morning, much earlier than I would have wanted. If we head back to my room, that's more time that I can spend with you, my dear. Are you game?" She smiled, took his arm, and they were out the door right after he dropped a couple of gold coins on the bar. They walked out and many eyes were on them, both the envious and the awestruck.

Chapter 39: The Vision

There were creatures in this part of the world that were thought to be myths or the drunken imaginings of a frightened populace. The citizens of Chuo were right to be afraid though. The monsters that mothers told their children about were real. After the king lost his hand and almost his whole hunting party, he enlisted many more men and began patrolling the dark corners of his territory. Things were more than a little tense in this untraveled corner of the world.

Argus' estate was far to the south, almost lost amongst the hills and forests that made up much of the land. Chuo was a territory unlike any other on Kronos, parts of it were still considered wild and unexplored. The Arch Mage Argus lived in the lands governed by House Syphon, but the king wisely made no demands on the mage. The mansion was active as usual, with the servants either cleaning up after the previous meal or preparing the next. There was the groundskeeper and his staff, a small group of cooks, there were maids, man servants, and at least a dozen men who were tasked to guard the property. The only residents that were not on staff were the old mage himself and the twins.

Danika came walking down the long winding staircase, her dress was simple as she had no plans for the day. She caught the attention of Riken, as he was looking after the security of the house. 'How much she has grown', he thought to himself. Both of them had grown so much in the years since coming to study with the master. When she arrived, she had been a child. Now she was an adult of nearly twenty years, and according to the human males he spoke to, she was thought to be quite attractive.

How different the twins were, not only in looks but in power and maturity. She was the one to sleep in and crack the occasional joke. Her brother Jorn was the stoic one whose laughter was such a valued commodity that it was rarely heard. He brooded night and day, and while his sister was still trying to hold onto her youth, he was determined to become an adult as soon as possible. He studied much harder than Argus required, which by any standard was a grueling schedule. His only desire was to improve his skill in the mystical arts. He saw himself as the heir to their master's position as Arch Mage of Kronos.

"Good morning, Mistress," the Telnor called out.

"Good morning, Riken." She walked towards the kitchen, "Have you seen my brother this morning?"

"Yes, he came down almost an hour ago. I believe that he's out by the fountains."

She was not surprised; he woke up earlier than she did almost every day. He spent a lot of time outside, though he almost never left the grounds. She walked across the patio, across the lawn, and then down a hill to the gardens. In the middle of the gardens were what everyone in the mansion mistakenly called fountains. There was a large stone circle with islands and rivers, and a larger body of water in the middle. Above the stone island, spheres of water floated within inches of the surface or as high as twenty feet. Some of the spheres were the size of oranges, others were as large as farm animals. They floated up, they drifted down, some of the spheres merged with each other, while others broke apart to drift independently. The fountains contained the cleanest, purest water that was clearer than glass. At times, the wind would make them shimmer in the light of a bright summer day.

When she reached the fountains, she found her brother sitting cross-legged on a stone bench. He didn't acknowledge her presence, he just stared hypnotically at the dancing water. She sat next to him and waited. When she was tired of waiting, she broke the silence.

"Good morning brother. Have you eaten?"

"No," he answered. "I... had a lot on my mind." He still stared at the flowing water. "Have you ever had a vision?"

"Not yet. I have seen Argus do it. He stares into fire to get his visions."

"I've had dreams that woke me out of a deep sleep. They didn't seem to be dreams as much as they felt more like visions of the things that will come to pass."

"How do you know? My dreams fade before I can roll out of bed."

"I don't know for certain." He finally turned to her, "I am going to try and summon them while I'm awake. I want you to be here to... make sure that nothing goes wrong."

She looked at her brother for the first time in a long time. They lived together, trained together, and spent more time together than either of them would have liked. It had gotten to the point that they never actually looked at each other anymore. They had stopped caring about the day-to-day goings on of each other's lives. Month after month, nothing ever changed. Now she looked at him critically, not as a sister, but as a fellow mage. For the first time in several years, she looked at him and worried.

"I want you here for me, Danni," he calmly. "Just wait here and observe, okay?"

"Of course, brother. I would do anything for you."

He turned back to the water, stood up, and walked into the pond. He lifted his arms straight out and started chanting the incantation. He repeated the spell, again and again till Danika could feel his power starting to fill the air with its own unique energy. A ball of water the size of a small watermelon flowed over and wrapped itself around his left arm. He was in a trance and ignored what was happening around him. Danika watched in amazement as the water that had seemed to be flowing in a random pattern was now seeking out the young mage. Bubbles flowed towards Jorn, and as each one reached him, it stuck like a drop of honey. One of the larger bubbles came to him and merged with all the others, covering his head. Jorn was now completely encased in a sphere of water that started floating upward. All the water had now merged around him, and he was in the center of a sphere of water a dozen feet in diameter. He rolled around, his limbs fully extended and his head back. She could see that his eyes were wide open as if he was watching events unfold before his eyes.

Danika knew her brother well, he tried so hard to watch out for her; but at least as often, it was her looking out for him. She knew that if she acted too soon, he would be furious. Then again, if she waited too long, she would no longer have a living twin to be angry at her. She watched his face when he was facing her direction. When the current inside the sphere rolled him away from her, she got nervous, but resisted the temptation to run around the circle like a mad woman.

When he rotated in her direction again, she could see that his eyes were still open, and now his mouth was open. Holding her hands in front of her, she began to summon her fire. It started as heat and grew into a brilliant ball of flame between her hands. Her flames grew and grew, getting hotter and brighter. Just as she was about to launch the fireball, the giant water sphere burst, and Jorn dropped the few feet to the ground. He landed on all fours and coughed up water that had gotten into his lungs. When he was done coughing and his breathing had returned to normal, he looked up at Danika. She stood there, soaked from head to toe, just as he was. He couldn't help but laugh.

"Sorry about that Danni!" he said playfully.

"I thought that you were drowning," she grumbled.

"I thought I was too; but that's when the vision became the clearest. Let's change clothes and find the master. I want you both to help me interpret what I saw."

The three of them sat at a small table in the kitchen, it was much more intimate than the formal dining room. The servants were bringing them pan fried meats, eggs, breads with sugar and nuts, and fruit. Argus as usual was having his morning tea and today the twins also partook of the strong herbal tea. Argus knew what had transpired, even without being told. The twins respectfully waited for him to bring it up so that they could discuss it.

"You had a vision," he stated. "It was a dangerous thing to do. Was it worth it?"

"I believe so. I saw scores of events, extending forward in time for months, years and even longer."

"Really?" Danika exclaimed. "Master, aren't most of your visions just snapshots of the immediate future?"

"They usually are, often there is no context to help me interpret them. It sounds like your vision was clearer."

"As clear as the water of the fountains, master," Jorn replied. "I saw a large table, old and made of unfinished wood. Around this table were all men, and two women. They all wore their best armor, and each had the crest of a different mighty house."

"That sounds like King's Table," Argus surmised.

"You were there, master, all three of us were. There were priests, there were non-human races that resembled men, but were not men."

"A meeting of kings at King's Table is a very rare thing. It happens maybe once in a generation. If kings are travelling from all over Kronos to attend a meeting, I can only assume it's about the rapid expansion of these Quell fanatics," Argus mused.

"As the only mages in Kronos, don't we have a duty to help?" Jorn asked.

"What else do you see, brother?" Danika interrupted his train of thought.

"Our friend Landis will soon be in our lives again. I see a great battle between the followers of Quell and the men of Kronos. What I saw next troubles me the most."

"What is that?"

"I saw a deep dark forest, a place where light is afraid to shine. In the very center of the forest there is a tree, a tree so large that it must be a thousand years old, if it's a day. The heart of it cracked and bled. From the gaping wound came an old crone who looked as old as the tree that she came from." Argus leaned forward, listening to Jorn's story with great interest. "I saw a demon. It could only have been from the deepest pits of Hell, and it towered over the crone as if she were but a child. I saw packs of wolf beasts that walked like men. Far into the future, I saw a great general with the head of a Ram, and an army of non-humans. I saw a land of giants, and a great war between man and beast."

"There is much for us to consider," the old mage mumbled as he sipped his tea. He had a worried look on his usually expressionless face.

"If we are to be in time for the council meeting in Tebron, we should probably leave immediately," Danika said, trying to suppress her excitement.

"Yes child, we should leave right away. Tell Riken to harness a team of horses and prepare a wagon. This trip could take us several weeks, we can leave in the morning." Danika jumped up and almost ran from the room. Jorn sat there staring at his cup of tea. They said nothing for a couple of minutes.

"There is more, master," Jorn said, looking down at his cup. "I saw your death."

"That's alright son," Argus consoled Jorn. "After hundreds of years, I know that my time is almost at an end." Jorn looked up at him, tears forming in his eyes, "Don't worry my faithful apprentice. If I die protecting the world of men, that is a fate that I can accept."

Riken led the way as always, sitting high in the saddle. Though he covered his yellowish skin and four arms in travelling robes, he was still an intimidating figure. When fellow travelers met this group consisting of an old man, a young couple, and a Telnor warrior, little did they know that the seven-foot warrior was the least dangerous member of the group. Some curious people would ride alongside and ask a question or two; but most avoided them to the point of being rude.

They had been on the road for a couple of weeks when the Telnor sat up in his saddle, sniffing at the road ahead. "Master, a familiar scent."

"Who would that be Riken, friend or foe?" Argus asked.

He sniffed again, thought for a moment, "Friend. The sellsword from the day we met the twins." Jorn and Danika both perked up at this announcement. They started looking around for their old friend. "He's ahead of us, walking," the Telnor informed them.

Jorn spurred his horse to go faster, and he pulled ahead till he was almost out of sight. In only a few minutes he had caught up with his 'big brother', Landis Stone and his companion. He rode up alongside the two men and waved for their attention. Landis looked up, then his face broke into a wide smile.

"Jorn! By the gods! Good to see you, boy!" he exclaimed. Turning to the priest, "This is the boy that I told you about." He looked up at Jorn, "though hardly a boy anymore, eh?"

"You are a mage?" the priest asked incredulously. Jorn just shrugged his shoulders.

"Jorn, this is my savior, Father Darus Sebastienne. He literally reached through death's door and pulled me back to this side."

"To answer your question, yes, I am a mage; or mage in training to be more precise. My sister and our master are coming." He pointed in the direction from which he had come. Landis was already as happy as a person can get, and then he smiled even more, so wide that Jorn thought his face would split. They were visible now, and in a minute, all were standing around in a circle.

"Danika girl, give us hug already!" he embraced the young woman, then her brother, then both of them at the same time. He even shook hands with the Telnor, one of his four hands.

"It's so fortunate to see you both, and to see how you've grown! Gods be blessed!"

"I don't know about the god's hand in this; but I do feel that we were meant to meet you at this time, and in this place," Argus spoke for the first time. "You have a part to play in the upcoming war with the Quell, they number in the thousands, and we need every hero that we can find." He looked curiously at the sellsword, "I sense magic on you, friend Landis."

Landis pulled out his new sword. When the blade left the scabbard, there was a faint glow to it that shone brightly to the mage and his apprentices. "I received this weapon just recently. A gift from a stranger. I thought it was all a dream, but when I awoke, the sword was lying next to me where the father and I had camped out." He nodded to his traveling companion, "I am already at war with the Quell," Landis said bitterly. "If not for the prayers of Father Sebastienne, I would be feeding the worms in Anatol right now."

"I'm sure that his prayers were helpful," the old mage commented, "but there is much more to this simple priest." Everyone looked at the tall, unassuming young man. "I sense enormous power in him, not like the twins; but almost as powerful in its own way."

"It's funny that you say that Sir. I have always known that the gods were doing the healing, through me," he said.

"Perhaps. I would like to speak with you alone before this is all done." Everyone automatically looked to him as the authority. "Riken, purchase two more horses. These gentlemen are travelling to King's Table with us."

Chapter 40: Rest Stop

Princess Lydia and her friend and confidant, Meisha walked from the inn to the local tavern. They had just arrived in Bekna, and after checking into the inn, were ready for a meal and a drink or two. It's where they were to meet with the Warlord herself, Renata Rin. They were coming from the Queen's castle on the Northern coast of O'Bell and were on their way to the King's Table in Tebron. Renata came from her kingdom in Inram, to represent the country that she had taken from House Laima.

They walked into the place to find it bustling with activity. It was mostly men, with some barmaids here and there shuttling drinks and food back and forth. In the corner was Renata, sitting at table with her second in command, Dorman Cole. They walked over and sat without waiting for an invitation.

"Princess," Dorman said standing and giving a respectful bow.

"Lydia, on time as always," Renata said to the younger woman. "How's your mother?"

"She's doing well. She's very proud of the way you've handled yourself. The Laima family was weak and having them at your back was the same as standing alone."

"Well, history will decide if I was a savior or usurper. I've been dealing with these fanatics for years now, and they don't value life, not even their own lives. Their crazy religion makes impossible demands, then they murder anyone who can't measure up. I personally hunt them down whenever I hear about one being in my territory. No trial. Just a quick execution."

"I don't know as much about them as you do; but I don't want them in O'Bell under any circumstances." The princess took a moment to look around the room, "So strange how the men here think that they are the equal of women," she remarked.

"They are from a better stock than those we allow in O'Bell," Meisha commented. "There's a nice one over there," she said, looking at a tall, nicely dressed man across the room.

"Meisha, we just got off the trail, aren't you done riding for a while?" Lydia laughed at her friend.

"Not if the right mount is available," she said longingly. Meisha waved the barmaid over. "Miss, please send that man over here," she said pointing at the tall stranger.

After a minute or two, he came over to their table. He stood just over six-foot, light-colored hair, tanned skin, no beard, and he was dressed like a businessman or trader. He looked over the table filled mostly with women warriors and knew that this would be an interesting encounter.

"Jarrod Stone, at your service," he said, giving a slight bow to the table.

"I'm Meisha, this is Lydia, Renata and he's Dorman," she said going around the table. "We're on our way to an important meeting; but the road is long and tiring, we want a local's idea of something that we can do to liven up our evening."

"Well, I'm far from being a local, but some things are universal. Usually, a few bottles of wine allow one to relax, and let his or her hair down, as it were." He gently placed his hand on the shoulder of a passing bar maid, "Three bottles of a hearty red for this table please?"

"You assume that we are all drinkers of alcohol?" Renata asked with an amused expression.

"I know that at the very least, you are all soldiers, and soldiers often imbibe to forget some of the things that they have witnessed. If you find the wine not to your liking, I can have something else sent over."

"No, actually, some wine sounds good right now," Lydia added. "Please Mr. Stone, you'll join us?" she indicated an empty seat near the table.

"Thank you." He slid the chair over to an open spot at the table, "May I go out on a limb to ask... are you ladies of the O'Bell clan?"

"You're correct," Meisha answered. "What gave us away?"

"The women of O'Bell are known all over Kronos for being as beautiful, as they are skilled in war. That would seem to fit all but you, Sir." He nodded to the other man at the table.

"You're quick with flattery," Lydia interjected "but what do you know of war?"

"Very little Madam, my brother is a soldier for hire. Me? I'm the black sheep of the family. I exist, only to savor the best that life has to offer and to try and give as much as I take." The wine arrived, and the barmaid uncorked the bottles and put a fine glass in front each of them. "I'll handle the pouring, miss. Please add these to my tab." Jarrod then poured each of them a hefty glass of the wine.

"I'd like to toast," he said before anyone could take a sip. He stood, and raised his glass, "To the soldiers of this world, and the protection that they provide us. They purchase it with their own blood and sometimes, their very lives... we appreciate your sacrifice." They all drank.

"So, what mission are you all on?" he asked innocently.

"Have you heard of the Quell?" Renata asked him.

"Heard of them? They're as thick as thieves around here. I'm originally from Anatol, and pretty much all the territory between here and the Anatol, Wolvig border is controlled by them." He took a deep drink from his glass, "There are some in town here, I expect them to take over this town in the next week, maybe less. It's about time for me to leave."

"I had no idea that their territory has spread so far," Dorman commented.

"Not only that, if you get anywhere near the Twilight Forest just North and West of here, you're likely to get eaten." They all looked at him like he was crazy. "It's true. They say that there are creatures the come out from the Twilight Forest at night. They are said to be men who've been cursed. They are more wolf than man, and they crave human flesh."

"It seems like this meeting could not have come at a better time," the princess added. They all sat looking into their cups for a few moments.

"Danger is close, but you'll not need to worry tonight. So, drink deeply, my friends. I'll have some food sent over, and then I have a few games that will soothe the blood and hopefully bring smiles to your more than pleasant faces," Jarrod said to the group. He smiled broadly, and his good humor was as infectious as always.

Jarrod awoke to the sound of Meisha putting on her armor. Despite having a heroic amount of wine, he still remembered the curves of her body, strong and perfectly formed. Her tea-colored skin looked radiant by candlelight and most of all, her smile had enchanted him. She embodied all the stories you heard about the O'Bell women. Their pairing last night had been her choice, she was the one who decided what, when and how. What she wouldn't admit, probably even to herself; but she liked the sensation of being with a man who was her equal. Because she was a warrior at heart, she knew that she couldn't let things get too far; but she loved the feeling of reversing their roles and pushing the encounter to the very edge of acceptability.

She looked over at him and smiled. "Good morning, Jarrod. I assume you enjoyed yourself last night?"

"Like you need to ask? You're an incredible woman, Meisha. My only sadness is that you are leaving today."

"We can go for a walk if you'd like. I think the princess drank more than she planned to last night, and I doubt she's ready for an early start."

"Princess?" he asked.

"Yes, Lydia O'Bell. She's next in line to be queen of O'Bell. We've been friends since childhood."

"Who was the other lady who shared your table?"

"The Warlord, or I guess we should start calling her Queen Rin. She ousted House Laima, and now she rules Inram."

"You know, I'm so glad you're telling me now instead of last night. I don't usually travel in such circles," he said, looking dizzy from the revelation.

"You were quite the gentleman, aside from the hair pulling," she said with a chuckle.

"I think I'm good at reading people. I can sense what they want, what they like. If men listened to what women say and not what their body language implies, the human race would cease to exist."

"So, you're the man that I'm missing in my life; but here I am putting on the armor, and you're still in bed."

Jarrod stood up and walked over to embrace her. He put his large arms around her and looked down into her big brown eyes. "Are you saying that you are less of a woman because you can fight like a man?"

"No."

"And that I'm less of a man because I like a strong woman?"

"No."

"Ninety percent of the time, you don't need a man; but I can be there for those times when you do." He gave her a tight squeeze.

"What are you saying?"

"If you are agreeable, I'll be in the area for the near future. I'd like to see you when you have the time. I know that your people are not wild about visitors in O'Bell; but I could meet you in Kees or Wingard from time to time."

"I think I would like that." She gave him a long and passionate kiss.

Chapter 41: Wever Bran

King Bargo Odila rode alongside his brother Lon and a handful of his knights. The king always traveled with security, even on days like today when stayed within his own borders. He would never admit it, but everyone knew he was furious. He was the king of Lourens, and yet when he needed to speak with the High Father, who's church was in his land, he had to go to 'him'. A king should be able to summon anyone within his domain, but not the High Father. He semi-publicly put himself on the same level as the king, and Odila was reticent to give him the public scolding that he deserved. When they reached the front gate of the church, there were two guards manning the entrance. They made no move to allow the group through.

"Stand aside, I'm here to see the High Father," the king bellowed.

"This is the Grand Church of Magnus. How dare you make demands!" the guard yelled.

The king instantly turned beet red, "I am your king! This church is on 'my' land!" he screamed. "Knights, kill these men!" he commanded.

The guards went white with fear, they pulled their shields in front of them and held them high. The knights dropped down from their war horses and slowly drew their swords while walking towards the guards. Suddenly there was a call from within the compound. A middle-aged monk came running out and put himself between the two groups.

"Guards! This is our king! Step aside and count yourselves lucky that he is a forgiving monarch!" He turned to the king, "Forgive them my Lord, they are young and drunk with the little power that they have been given. I assure you that they will be... re-educated in the strictest manner."

"Very well. Take us to the High Father, he is expecting us after all. Magnus help him if this was set up to try and make me lose face!"

"I assure you Sire, this is just a misunderstanding. Please come this way." He led them through the now open gate. When they were inside, he had some of the younger priests take the horses, and then he ushered the king's party to the main entrance of the church. As they passed through the various chambers, the king couldn't help but look about in awe. It had been several years since he had visited the church, and it was the first time since the new High Father had taken over. The glass had been replaced by very intricate stained glass. Very expensive work. The tapestries were now violet silk with gold embroidery, each one cost what a farmer could earn in a year, and dozens of them lined the walls. At the far end of the main room was a statue of Magnus. It was thirty-foot-tall, a depiction of him giving life to the first man and woman. Many other statues and vases were distributed tastefully around the room.

The king walked through the chamber, looking at the flock of bureaucrats and sycophants, the ass kissers and boot lickers, the good, the bad, and the functionaries. He was still king and pushed past the young priest who was planning to announce him. He walked up to Wever Bran who sat comfortably in a huge chair that seemed very much like his own throne.

"High Father, it's been a long time. You are too busy to visit your king?"

"Sorry my Lord. As you can see, these people are the heart of 'our' religion, and each one demands decisions from me. I am very sorry to cause you to travel," he replied with feigned sincerity.

"Perhaps it is a good thing that I have come here to see you. So many... improvements, since the last High Father's time."

"Yes, my Lord. I have always felt that it's important to give the common people a sense of awe when they enter the temple of Magnus. They need to feel how small we all are in comparison. They need to know their place. Don't you agree Sire? I should think that the same thing applies in your court?"

"There is some truth to that I suppose; but on the other hand, they might start to feel taken advantage of when they barely have enough to eat, and the place they go to worship is so lavishly adorned."

The High Father felt that he didn't need to explain himself to any earthly king, but perhaps now was not the time to try and exert his will. He chose the path of lesser resistance. At least for now. "Your messenger didn't explain why your highness wanted to meet. How can the church be of assistance to the throne?" he asked without the theatre of civility.

"You should be glad that I'm here Wever. These Quell followers are becoming more of a threat every day. When I first heard of them, I thought that it was a passing fancy, a faulty idea that would sort itself out; but that doesn't seem to be the case. The whole of the North is either under their control or in their shadow."

"I am aware. Every time they descend on a new town, one of the first things they do is kill our priests and burn our temples." He waved away the monks around him.

"They now have armies larger than the church's or any of the southern kings. Even if you didn't tax the hell out of the people, I still couldn't raise enough money to fund 'our' defense. We need to prepare to face their hordes, not if, but when they arrive."

"You're asking for tax relief? For whom, for your house? The whole country?" he asked indignantly.

"More than that father, I need you to cough up some of the wealth that you've already accumulated. And troops. I know that against my wishes, you have assembled security forces in every country that is not yet controlled by the Quell. I will need them too."

"Out of the question! I have taken steps to ensure the security and welfare of the church. I can't go down in history as the High Father that raided the coffers and left the church destitute and unguarded," Wever said with horror in his voice.

"That's the least of your problems, and you know it. I'm asking things of you that are vital to your own survival. You know of course that they have a bounty on your head? If they ever make it to Lournes, this building will either burn or be converted into a temple to praise Quell. You on the other hand, will probably be skinned alive, then boiled in oil. The only man in Lourdes that they hate more than me... is you."

"Still, what you are asking is... too much. Maybe some kind of compromise can be made."

"With me? Or with the Quell?" The king stepped down from the raised platform where the High Father's throne was placed. "I'm going to King's Table to meet with the other kings. When I get back, I want an accounting of all the gold and wealth that you can spare, and a list of men and where they are stationed." The High Father looked like someone had just walked across his grave. "I'm asking because you are in my land and so you are my responsibility; but know this, all the kings will be demanding that the church contribute. War is upon us and it's time for everyone to make sacrifices."

With that, he walked out. The High Father stared holes in his back as he left. Deep down, he felt like the money that the tax collectors brought in for the church was his to spend. It was after all his idea to raise a separate tax. He felt personally robbed by the king's demands, and that the church's money was money that he had earned with his own hands, and it was being taken from him. He would stew and fume for days, perhaps weeks; but in the end, he knew that if he refused, he would probably not live long enough to be cooked by the Quell.

Chapter 42: Reinforcements

A fleet of ships approached the Northern coastline of Agron, the Western most country in Kronos. There were hundreds of ships, each was filled with dozens of soldiers. The alarms went up and those who were ready to settle down for an evening meal were roused and ordered to the seashore. The town of Mirren on the Northwestern most part of Agron was alive with frantic activity. As the men were preparing for a battle, and the women were preparing to hide with the children, a single rowboat struck out for the shore.

Captain Roko stood in the bow of the boat as four of his larger men rowed. He was a very intimidating figure in his long black robes that only partially hid his alien features. The sun was nearly down; but the Emar disliked the sun, and it was too bright for them to feel fully at ease. When the bottom of the skiff hit the sandy beach, he stepped out, the cool water going ankle high on his soft leather boots. He stepped out onto the beach where he was met with a hundred men in various states of readiness.

"I am Captain Roko of the Emar Royal Army. I believe your king is named..."

"We serve the honorable King Rutger Klaas, of House Klaas," offered a man in front, who might have been the town constable.

"How far is the home of your king, good man?" the captain asked.

"Half of an hour by horse, my Lord."

"I'm no lord, just a simple military man. Please take me to your king. As you can see," he waved at the fleet of ships in the ocean behind him, we have come to aid the good men of Kronos against the murderous animals known as the Quell." The crowd gave a collective sigh, and all the faces became bright and hopeful.

"In that case, please accept my horse. My oldest son will escort you and your men to the castle." He turned to the crowd, calling for his son, a young man of sixteen or so to join him. "Tomas, five horses and some wine skins for our friends, the Emar!" The crowd roared with approval.

"That's a good number of men, Captain," King Klaas noted. "I heard about the fate that your colony suffered at their hands, and I sympathize with your desire for revenge." He sat at his throne and had a seat brought for his guest. "I am king of this land; but as you well know, Kronos has nearly twenty countries, each governed by its own monarch. We are meeting at King's Table, and you are more than welcome to attend the council as my honored guest. Will you accept?"

"Yes, I think it wise to meet with all your land's leaders. There is much for us to discuss." He called over his four companions and sent two of them back to the boats to deliver his message. When that was done, he turned back to his host.

"I am leaving in two days. Until then, please be my guest."

"Thank you, King Klaas. I will let my people know that not all your kind are evil."

Chapter 43: The King's Table

The King's Table was a separate facility within the castle grounds of House Sarutendo. Like all kings, Imanol Sarutendo had his throne room and his own dining facility, etc.; but in addition, within the grounds of his castle, was a large round room which housed the King's Table. The King's Table was an actual table that was made of a light wood with a deep dark stain. The table was a long oval; but there was a definite head of the table. There was seating all along the walls, and many lamps that provided plenty of light. When in use, heavily armed guards protected both entrances, and another dozen guards were only minutes away.

King Syphon walked into the meeting room and marveled at its glory. The crest of each royal house in Kronos was displayed around the circle on the walls. He noticed the dust on the picture frames, the spider webs up in the ceiling and the general sense that the place had not been kept up for some time. He was approached by King Vosbarra of Rubina.

"He knew about this meeting for months; you think that he would have at least the top layer of dust removed," Syphon commented.

"I heard that he is having some financial problems and that none of the money lenders will touch him," Ben Vosbara whispered. Syphon's eyebrows raised. "What I heard is that he screwed over one of the major traders in Tebron. They moved their operation to my beautiful Rubina where we accept their tax payments and show them the love they deserve. Anyhow, Tebron is being pinched on every bushel of grain, every ingot of iron, so that the cost of living is now ridiculous here. The final nail in the coffin was a few years ago when they were accepting a whole year's delivery of bullion and the ship it was on hit another ship. Both ships sank to the bottom of the bay, and with it, Tebron's credit."

"That's unfortunate. The timing seems a little suspicious, eh?"

"It's a good reminder. You can be a pauper, a priest or even a king; make sure you know the character of a person before you decide to fuck them," he said while waving over one of his aides. "Grab some people and have this room cleaned, don't bother our host."

Vosbara looked down at the stump where Syphon's left hand should have been. "There's something new. I suppose there's an interesting story behind that?" he nodded at the stump.

"Indeed, there is. I'll be bringing it up at the meeting. I think the creature's that attacked me, and my hunting party are somehow part of a bigger threat." A young girl with dark hair and pretty eyes walked in, staring at the size of the building with awe. King Syphon saw her and called to her.

"Girl, clean this room as soon as you can," he commanded. The kings are arriving, and this place is a mess."

She looked at him like he was crazy, then she got an amused look in her eyes. She lifted her hands and a red energy flowed between them. She began a simple chant, and a wind came from nowhere that soon became like a hurricane. The gale blasted every inch of the inside of the room, and she directed the dirty air out of the main entrance.

"Oh! I blew out the lights!" she snapped her fingers and every light, hundreds of candles and lamps lit instantly. "There, is that what you were looking for old man?" The two kings stood in complete disbelief as she smiled at them, turned, and skipped from the room.

Syphon turned to Vosbarra, "This meeting is long overdue, I think."

"Aye, brother. I hope she's on our side."

King Imanol Surutendo entered the room last and made for his chair at the head of the table. He looked around the packed room. There were many familiar faces, and some that were new. A few were missing, conquered countries that were no longer represented. Around the great table sat all the great families of Kronos. In the back rows were people he didn't remember inviting; but more than likely they were the guests of one of the other kings. There were a couple of monks from Silver Bay; they were seen so infrequently away from their little island that most people forgot that they even existed. An old man and two children. He wanted to shout to the guards to have them expelled, but the old man had the look of one that you crossed at your peril. There was a single Emar. How ugly they were, he thought to himself.

Sarutendo took his seat, and the attendees stopped talking and turned to await their host. He saw that six of the seats were now empty, their kings, including all members of their Great Houses, presumed dead.

"We have not had this council in an age and I'm not certain of the procedure."

"We have a priest in the room," Prince Herron suggested.

"Yes, that's an excellent idea. Father?" the king asked of the priest who was in the corner tying to be unobtrusive. He stepped forward and stood behind one of the empty spots and placed his hands on the back of the chair.

"I hope you will all forgive me; I am not an accomplished public speaker," he said with a bit of a squeak in his voice. "We have in this room, the hope of a world in turmoil, on the brink of all-out war." Everyone listened somberly to his blunt words, "I see that most of us here are followers of the Old Gods; but we also have other faiths represented here. We even have those who are our brothers in this conflict though they are not technically human. All here are aware that the Quell are an enemy to our security and our way of life. Thankfully, we can put aside our differences in order to face this evil." He looked to the heavens, "The gods be praised, give these men, and women, the strength and wisdom to put down the evil that has infected this world and with as few lives lost as possible. Amen." They all answered Amen, even the non-believers in the crowd. Sarutendo stood up to address the group.

"As you can see, six chairs are empty. Six royal families murdered. Their lands are now a breeding ground for an evil unlike any we have ever encountered. With bases in these conquered lands, they will attack each of us, one by one, till no free countries remain standing. They already have a third of Kronos, and if they take over our friends in Chuo and Khatuna, the land will be split with them holding the center."

"That is why I suggest we assemble what men we can, and attack as soon as possible," Syphon recommended.

King Tomislava of Wingard stood, "If we act before we are ready, we'll be wiped out!"

"What would you have us do?" Vandressa O'Bell demanded. "This is an enemy that sees weakness, smells your fear and is emboldened."

Aretas Dara of Cozar stood, "We will have to conscript huge numbers of peasants, feed them while we are teaching them to hold a spear. It takes a surprisingly long time to turn a farmer into a soldier."

"Every day we do nothing is another hundred lives lost to these animals," King Klaas stormed. "I have invited Captain Roko of the Emar to this council. His people were the first to be victimized by the Quell, and they have assembled troops to assist us." He pulled out one of the empty chairs for the Emar. Captain Roko looked surprised but accepted the chair.

"Thank you for having me at this meeting. We are distant cousins to you humans; and yet we still feel a kinship with you and yours. We know that the men who destroyed our colony were not any of you here today; they were men driven insane by this... religion. My king sent me with five thousand Emar soldiers. We are ready to stand shoulder to shoulder with our human brothers."

The room was full of gasps, and then broke into unanimous applause.

When the celebrations had subsided, Roku stepped out of the shadows. An Ammun monk away from their island monastery surprised the kings almost as much as the presence of the Emar representative. They fell silent and allowed him to speak.

"I am Roku, of the Annum. We just pushed back an attempt by the Quell to exterminate us on our own temple grounds. At the end of the day, we threw hundreds of their bodies into the sea for the sharks and turtles to feast on." The kings were encouraged by the tale and roared in approval. "We are few; but if needed, we will send two hundred monks. Each monk is the equal of ten conscripts, or a hundred of these craven cowards." Again, cheering and applause filled the room. King

Sarutendo stood again, and the room settled down and became quiet again.

"Indeed, we are blessed to have friends like the Emar and the Ammun. I think that we must immediately put the wheels in motion. Before we leave, each kingdom must pledge a certain number of troops, supplies, etc. I hear that you've already threatened the church to ante up?" he asked, looking at King Bargo Odila.

"Ole Wever Bran, he almost cried when he heard my terms. He might have to put off getting that summer home in the country," he said to raucous laughter.

King Kell Syphon stood. His usual smile was not present, his scowl and his jet-black skin gave him a menacing look. He held up the stump where a month earlier, his hand had been. He looked around the room, connecting eyes with his peers.

"Few of you know this, so I shall tell the story," he said, holding the stump out in front of him. "I was hunting with a few of my knights, good friends of mine, in the wild areas in south Chuo. These creatures came from nowhere; they had a horse body, the wings of an eagle, and the head and forearms of some great ape. They killed my companions, and I escaped minus my left hand." The faces around the room were either fearful or skeptical. Without turning, he shouted to his aid, "Jonas, bring it!"

Jonas stepped out for a few seconds, then returned with two others, they were carrying drawings and had large bags. The other two assistants unrolled a large sheet of paper, it was half the size of the table. It showed the beast just as the king had described it.

"I had this picture drawn, and it is to scale. See how large the beast is?" While they were staring at the picture, he pulled a huge hairy hand from one of the bags. It had black fur, and each digit was topped with a razor-sharp claw. "A paw like this one killed the first of my friends, he didn't even have the chance to fight back." He threw the petrified limb onto the center of the table where it landed with a heavy thud. Next, he reached into the other bag, and pulled out a skull. Without his hand, he needed Jonas' assistance to get the huge skull out of the bag and onto the table. It was three times the size of a human skull, and it had massive fangs that held the jaw open wide. "Into one of these, is where I lost this hand!" He again showed where his missing hand should have been.

"What I say to you, my peers, all kings and queens by right; there is something amiss in Xoran. There are forces outside the will of the gods and exceeding the powers of man to comprehend, that are just now making themselves known. We have all heard about how monsters and demons used to roam these lands. A time when creatures like these," he pointed at the severed head of the beast, "controlled this world and man was the interloper. We are in the Age of Man, but creatures like these appear ready to come back and reclaim this world as their own." The hall erupted in shouts and men banging on the table, the cacophony was almost earsplitting before King Sarutendo brought the room back to order by banging his heavy pewter mug on the table.

"Are you saying that these creatures are somehow related to the Quell?" Sarutendo asked.

"I'm not saying that; but many of you have heard the stories of the men who were cursed and turned into mindless beasts of prey in and around the Twilight Forest. This... and then there are rumors of mages..." He let the words hang in the air. Everyone looked around at each other, waiting for the rest.

Argus stood with Jorn's assistance and walked slowly to the near end of the table.

"There is much truth in what the young king says. Magic comes and goes like the seasons, skipping a dozen generations, then returning for a dozen more. I woke from a two-hundred-year sleep because I sensed that magic was again to be found in Kronos."

"Who are you Sir?" young Prince Herron asked. "Respectfully."

"Who, me?" Argus asked.

"He is the Arch Mage of Kronos," Jorn told the table. "We may have many enemies; but there are many who would stand and fight for the innocent people of Kronos."

"So, the last order of business, we need to decide on a leader," Prince Heron said to the assembled royals. This brought a strange hush to the table. They all knew that it made sense to unite behind one man; but each of them was a king or queen, used to absolute rule in their own domains. None of them were too keen on the idea of serving under another. "I am of course, the youngest here, and not yet a king; but I do speak for Khatuna. We can only be successful if there is but one vision for the coming battle, one leader. Khatuna nominates King Syphon, demon slayer!"

There was a huge uproar as the various kings either supported or opposed the nomination. Sarutendo looked bitter. He was in his own house, sitting at the head of the table. He thought that he would be the natural choice for leader. The wrangling went on for a while till the call for a vote was agreed on. Along with the nomination of King Syphon, King Sarutendo of

Tebron and King Odila of Lournes were also put forth as potential leaders. In the end, it came down to who was young, not unexperienced in battle, and who had the respect of the majority of the kings. They now trusted their fates to the leadership of King Kell Syphon of Chuo. Long may he reign.

Chapter 44: Herron

Jorn walked up to Prince Herron after the council had concluded. They were about the same age, though Gabriel was a very good-looking young man with an athletic physique, and Jorn was tall, thin, and awkward in both dress and manner.

"Prince Herron, you really took charge in there. I hate speaking in public, everyone looking at me an all."

"The name's Gabriel. You were never introduced..."

"Jorn, Jorn Anant," he said as they were walking towards the stables.

"Was that your girlfriend? The one with the dark hair and the bedroom eyes?"

"Heavens no! That's my twin sister."

"Does she have a boyfriend? Do you think my being a prince would impress her?"

"No boyfriend, and no. Prince, king, I have never seen her impressed by anyone really, so I don't know what her type is. Then again, I don't know women... I mean I don't know anything about women, so..."

"Well, I know a thing or two about the fairer sex. How about I give pursuit of your sister a rest for tonight, and we go into town for a drink, or ten?" he asked with his usual charm.

"That sounds great, let me tell Danika, then I'll come back here to get my horse." Jorn ran off towards the crowds still congregated outside of the council room.

The two young men rode their horses at a leisurely pace down the well-worn road from the palace to downtown. Gabriel had removed his ceremonial armor in favor of a very stylish shirt and pants combination. Jorn still wore his simple robes from earlier in the day, good for travelling; not so good for making a favorable first impression.

"You know when we get to town, I may have to at least get you a new shirt. Women appreciate a man with style."

"If you want to impress them, you should have left your armor on. If they find out that you're a prince with a sick father, they'll be making themselves available, I would imagine."

"Yes, they would, but where is the sport in that? If you want, you can pay for a woman; but that says a lot more about you than it does her. I want to be on an even playing field with other men... perhaps tilted my way just a little." He held his thumb and index finger just an inch apart.

"So, are you going to war?" he asked Gabriel.

"Yes, I'll command the men of Khatuna; but thankfully, I'll be under King Syphon's command. That's fine with me, I've never been to war, and I don't need to be in the front on my first day," Gabe snickered at his companion. "What about you, Jorn? Are you going to be carrying a spear in the coming war?"

"Carrying a spear? No. I never learned to fight, with or without weapons."

"So..., if I drink too much tonight, don't count on you to have my back?"

"Nope, I'm not your man."

The table was one of the larger ones in the tavern. It was dark, despite several torches set in the walls. Jorn and Gabriel had many empty glasses in front of them, and Gabriel had a beautiful young barmaid sitting on his lap. Jorn looked at his new friend and wished that he had the confidence to talk to women like the prince did.

"There was a big 'to do' up at the castle today, you boys have anything to do with that?" Delilah asked. She was tall and blonde, and probably on purpose, her blouse was at least two sizes too small.

"You're not from around here," one of the young men at their table commented.

"No, we're travelling for business from back east. We'll probably be heading back that way tomorrow," Jorn replied.

"They're foreigners!" a soldier offered, coming from his seat by the door. "The fancy one there thinks he can give advice to the king!"

"Is that so?" another of the soldiers asked. "Doesn't seem like a good thing to have some young punk from Khatuna running his mouth and disrespecting his elders." They both walked over, still in their armor and fully armed. They had the smell of men who had already had many drinks, enough to make them brave, or foolish.

"We were told that our king was ready to take charge of the armies.; but you spoke up and called for a vote. Instead of our king leading the armies, we'll have to follow that one-armed bastard from Chuo."

"King Sarutendo is a fine man; but he can't even manage his household. How can I trust my life and that of my men to a leader like that?" Gabriel replied.

"King Syphon is missing just a hand. Not the whole arm," Jorn added.

"Mighty bold of you to come in here, wearing no armor, only this boy for security," one of the soldiers slurred.

"I didn't," Gabriel replied calmly. Four men across the room stood up, they were not drunk, and they had their full armor on.

Jorn looked impressed, "Wow, I didn't even see them following us. Good call."

"You may have four men, but this is Tebron. We stand with House Sarutendo, and we'll teach you the error of besmirching our king!" the man shouted. The girl slid off Gabriel's lap and into the shadows. At least a dozen men stood, they were all soldiers of Tebron. They knew their king was in financial straits, and that he had been denied the honor of leading the army. They had enough liquor in them to stir up their feelings of nationalism. The two closest to Gabriel's table pulled their swords, the four guards from Khatuna pulled their swords, and the dozen or so other soldiers of Tebron pulled their swords. Just as they were about to commit to the skirmish, Jorn stood up. Gabriel looked concerned for his new friend's welfare; but before he could stop him, Jorn spoke.

"Soldiers!" he said in a firm commanding voice. "Your weapons are getting heavy." As he said it, every arm that held a sword began to falter, almost instantly, each sword tip hit the floor, the men struggled to hold up their blades. "Your lords thank you for your loyalty, they thank you for your service. Tomorrow, you will feel fine and harbor no ill will towards anyone," he spoke in soothing tones. "Right now, you only want to *sleep*!" The last part was a command. Every soldier fell where he had been standing.

"That's impressive!" Gabriel was amazed by what he had witnessed. He looked at his friend in a whole new light.

"They are all good men; I chose not to hurt them over some drunken grandstanding." He sat and finished the ale he was drinking. "Good thing my sister wasn't here, she probably would have set them on fire. It's her thing."

Chapter 45: Landis' Story

Danika urged her horse faster till she caught up with Landis. She looked at her old friend; he looked like he had aged much more than the six or so years since they last saw each other. She had grown up, that was her excuse, but something had happened to this man who always used to have a smile on his face. She wanted to push for answers, but instead, she rode quietly next to him and waited.

"Danika, you want to ask questions. What do you want to know?"

"We've not seen you in years. You've aged," she said in her blunt way.

"Thanks a lot. I guess you want to hear my story," he said looking down towards his feet; obviously thinking of what to share and what to withhold. "As you know, I'm a sword for hire. Ever since I was younger than you are now, I walked country to country, fighting for whoever would pay me. By the time I met you and your brother, I was at the top of my profession. I was well paid because I was the best and I deserved it. All the years that I was for hire, I feared no men and loved no women. I 'loved' them, but I didn't really 'love' them," he confessed.

"About a year after the last time that I saw you, I was back up North visiting my father. My mother passed away long ago, and my father and I were not as close as father and son should be, so I went to visit. I was at his house in Anatol, and my father got me to start attending church regularly. We would go every week, then go home and talk and share a good meal. Things were good, and that's when I met her." His eyes grew cold, "Her goodness almost balanced out my badness. I told her the kind of man that I had always been, and… it didn't matter to her. She accepted me for what I was on that day, at that moment."

Danika rode alongside, afraid to upset the fragile magic of a man telling his innermost secrets. She tried to keep her face neutral but couldn't help letting her growing sadness show in her expression.

"We married and had a beautiful boy. You probably would have liked her; she could have been your older sister." He finally looked up at Danika, "Of course, now you're old enough to have children of your own." She brightened at the thought of motherhood, it made her face glow.

"It seems that no one can just lead their lives these days without being hassled or victimized," he said bitterly. "I gave up wielding a sword and took up making swords for others. Swords, knives, scythes, chisels, that sort of thing. I was terrible at first; but I learned quickly, and soon I was good enough to support a wife and child. I was content to never shed another drop of blood for the rest of my life, but death missed me and instead found my family. Now I hunt the Quell."

Danika gasped at the mention of the group. Their savagery was now notorious throughout the land, even in the countries where they had not yet shown themselves. Unlike her brother, she had empathy to spare. She easily put herself in the situation, married to a good man, with a baby on her arm. The thought of the Quell animals invading sent a shiver up her spine.

"Like so many before me," he went on. "They came to our house which was far outside of town. I always liked the solitude of being away from others; but that day, it was my undoing. There were not so many of them, but my fighting skills had eroded, and my sword was buried in the yard. I killed a couple of them, but the outcome was inevitable. They beat me to the point of death, killed my son, and raped and killed my wife," he recounted the tale in an almost detached manner like he was talking about something terrible that happened to someone else. "I was very near death and didn't have the skill to heal myself. I fetched my sword, and some water and started walking for town. I don't remember what happened next. I thought that Magnus had come to claim me, and I was ready to meet him, to join him at the table of heroes in the afterlife… when I was pulled back." He looked at Danika, then nodded his head at the priest who was several lengths back, talking to Argus. "That skinny holy man saved me. I just remember waking the next day in his arms, both of us were passed out in a ditch. Your master believes that his ability to heal goes beyond the power of faith or the science of medicine, and I believe it too. That man saved my wretched life so that I could exact my vengeance on the Quell."

When he talked of battle and killing, he was most like his old self. She looked at this man who at one time was just an older boy, like her brother but with more life experience. Now she saw that he had tried to evolve into a better man and got pulled back into the real world by fate, or the gods, or whatever. There was still very much of the free spirit that he had been before, but it would take an ocean of blood and the taking of many more lives before he could return to being that person.

Chapter 46: The Road East

The main road that ran from East to West, which stretched from coast to coast, was known as the Iron Road. Many armies had traveled that road, invading their neighbors to expand their borders, or sometimes just for sport. Once there had been half a hundred major houses and each one claimed a spot on the world map, but centuries of wars and the lack of common enemies had reduced the number of Kingdoms to a stable twenty or so. Until the Quell came on the scene. They were committed to unifying the whole world under their extremist theocracy. Such barbarism could not be tolerated.

Once again, great armies would travel the Iron Road. As the Western-most army met with the next army on the map, they would merge and march together. By the time they reached the countries under siege in the East, their numbers would hopefully be large enough to win the day. That wouldn't be for a couple of weeks yet. After the meetings at Kings Table, the kings and their escorts were making their way back to their respective kingdoms to begin their preparations for war.

"Landis, I hope that you and your priest friend can stay with us?" Danika asked coyly. "We could certainly use your protection."

"Of all the women in Kronos, you are the least likely to need protection. You were dangerous as hell when you were thirteen and untrained. Only the gods know what you're capable of now."

"I'm still a woman, and Jorn is definitely in need of guarding, and Argus is… old."

Father Sebastienne pulled up alongside. "We would be glad to ride with you. It's a long ride to Kilburn and good conversation always makes a trip more bearable."

Jorn was riding side by side with Argus. The old man seemed a bit more preoccupied than usual. Jorn was accustomed to his ways and decided to wait for his master to initiate conversation.

"Jorn, my boy. Faster than I could have imagined, I am seeing your visions unfold. You two, with your talents and your raw power, are ushering in a new age. When I sealed myself in that tomb so many years ago, I did so because I could see that the time of wizards and otherworldly creatures was quickly coming to an end. Now, much sooner than I would have guessed, magic is returning to this world."

"Is the 'Age of Man' nearly over, master?"

"Never, never give up hope!" he scolded his apprentice. "What I am saying is, there will be more people like you and your sister and this priest. People with extraordinary abilities. We must find them and make sure that they are on our side," the old man said, enjoying the sunny afternoon. "There are also many other threats that are soon to show themselves."

"You will not be joining us for the coming battle?"

"No, I am needed elsewhere. I will be facing threats that are far more dangerous than what you and Danika are prepared for. Stick with Landis and the army and stay on the Iron Road. I'll part company with you shortly after we leave Rubina and enter Chuo."

"As you wish master."

King Kell Syphon rode at the head of a dozen men. The normally approachable king was lost in his own thoughts. Commanding the combined armies of the remaining kingdoms, he now had the fate of the whole world on his shoulders. The Quell Horde was like a parasite that would infect the host and devour it from the inside. Now it was up to him to cut out the rot. He felt like no one man had ever had to bear such a burden. These thoughts of doom were eating away at his self-confidence when the young prince from the neighboring Khatuna rode up alongside. The boy was fairer by half, and he was almost younger by half. The only thing that they had in common was that they were both nobles. Born to rule, and yet, obliged to serve their houses, their lands, and their people. He looked at the young man who never had anything but a smile on his handsome face. He was spoiled, like all royals; but the way that he comported himself at King's Table showed a lot more character than Syphon would have guessed.

"How is your father, Gabriel?" he asked the youth.

"Not well my Lord. I fear we soon will be equals."

"You see yourself as being my equal?" he asked.

"In title only, my Lord. I'm not ready to be a leader of men, that's why I nominated you. I was thrilled by the story of how you killed two of those beasts single-handedly. No pun intended." He smiled at Kel, "You're the leader that I will trust with my life, and more importantly, the lives of the good warriors of Khatuna."

"Thank you for your confidence. I'll do my best not to get us all killed."

"I'm not worried milord. The gods are with us."

"I wish I shared your confidence, Gabriel. My reports have their strength at twice ours, even with the Emar."

"Well, when things get especially dicey, you can find me hiding behind my new friend Jorn." Gabe's smile gave away the fact that he knew a secret.

"Jorn, who's that?"

"He's one of the old mage's apprentices. He's a smart fellow, not the least bit intimidating, and yet he put a room full of drunken soldiers to sleep, with a single word. It was incredible, and the way he tells it, his sister is the dangerous one."

"I think I met her at King's Table. She called me 'Old Man!'" he laughed.

"That's funny. We have the Emar, the Ammun, and now with the twins, and the gods on our side, we can't lose!" He was almost standing in his stirrups at this point.

King Syphon took it all in and fed on his young peer's energy. Yes! By the gods, they would win the war and secure the fate of mankind. For the next couple of hours, his burden was lightened. Many days later, when they could see the lights of Kilburn, he was developing a kernel of a plan and felt like there might be hope.

Chapter 47: Gahrenna

Lem Lothe lay prostrate on the ground, face down. He dared not look at the demon before him. Qaumon stood over him, deciding if he should slay the human who called him Quell and created so much chaos in his name. He had felt compelled to ride out in the countryside on his own, but in reality, he had been summoned by the demon.

"Lord Quell, thank you for blessing me with your presence. Our numbers have grown a hundredfold, but there are still tens of thousands of infidels who dare to worship the Old Gods. When we tried to eliminate the Ammun, our men were defeated easily. Tell me what you would have me do," he pleaded.

"Lem Lothe, my most ardent supporter. You've shown that you care as little about the lives of my followers as I do. Still, you need to become a better strategist, or I will abandon you without a second thought." Qaumon no longer wore the costume of an Old God, his scaly hide, horns and tail had struck fear in Lem.

"Yes, Lord. I have never been a soldier and your followers have no skills at war. They are simple men, hopeless and hardly worth the food we give them. For us to overcome the unbelievers, we need your assistance."

"For your next major battle, I will gift you with my cursed ones, the Gahrenna. They are wild creatures, savage and strong. Each of them is the equal of a trained knight. Take this amulet." He tossed a silver amulet with the sign of Quell on one side and a wolf on the back, to the ground near Lem's outstretched hand, "With this, you will be recognized as their master. Their addition should be enough for you to win a decisive victory in my name."

The demon placed his heavy-hooved food on Lem's back. "Do not fail me again."

Chapter 48: Argus

Argus was glad to be home. He was the oldest person in the world, and recently, he was starting to *feel* like the oldest person in the world. He found that he slept very little these last couple of weeks, he would often go days at a time without sleep. The end was coming, and he had to start preparing for it. The children were not ready, not even close in his opinion. They were so young and so powerful! They needed many more years of training just to keep them from self-destructing or becoming the menace he was teaching them to fight. Time was up though. They might not be ready, but they would have to figure the rest out for themselves. He had many tomes, books of ancient knowledge that he would have gone over with them, but those lessons would never happen. The twins would eventually find his secret library and hopefully, they would be able to decipher its secrets.

Riken was away on an errand for his master and wouldn't be back for days. It was late in the evening, and no one was awake at this late hour except for the House Master. He asked her to wake the staff and get them out of the house at once. She had long ago learned that no matter how immense or inconvenient the request was, she was to carry it out immediately and without debate.

He worked his way down the rickety stone steps from the kitchen down to his laboratory. When he was there, he did a simple spell that revealed a hidden door. The door opened to another staircase that took him even deeper into the earth. No one had been down there for hundreds of years, and the air smelled as foul as would be expected. The stairs were covered in a thick layer of dust, cobwebs were everywhere, and the walls of the staircase were suffocatingly close to each other.

After descending several hundred steps, the staircase let out to a chamber that was immense. It was a hundred feet high in the center, and at least as big as the whole mansion above. The floor was made of the same unforgiving rock as the walls and ceiling. The far wall had rows of cages, some of them enormous, made of enchanted iron, and set firmly into the stone walls. On one side of the room was a large fountain, an angel was pouring water to the basin a dozen feet below, and it was her fate to pour for all time. The other side had a fire pit, with a fire already burning that was a dozen feet high and burned with an intense flame that would never consume all its fuel.

He looked at the fire and felt himself being drawn to it. Of the two, he felt more in tune with Danika because he too was born of fire. The way the flames danced to music only those born of fire could hear. Fire was energy, an expression of raw power. The heat felt good on his old bones, and he was drawn to the flames.

What made him climb down all those hundreds of steps in the wee hours of the morning was the boy. Jorn had a lot of potential. With so little knowledge and no personal experience, he was able to receive a vision in water. It must have been some instinct of his, to know that he would be safe in the water and that the forces that created and bound the universe would grant him the ability to see what is to come. Even though it went against his nature, he would try to emulate the boy's success in water.

Reluctantly, he pulled himself away from the fire and walked over to where the water was rhythmically pouring from the vase above his head into a pool that was carved from the very stone of the cave. This side of the chamber was cool and quiet in comparison with the bright, roaring fire. The music of the water changed very little, and it created an almost hypnotic rhythm that he at first found unsettling.

Taking off his clothes, he climbed into the large dish-like pool and sat cross-legged on the cold stone, and shivered in the cool water that came up to his navel. Closing his eyes, he willed all unnecessary thoughts and doubts from his mind and relaxed despite the numbness that was settling into his legs. He imagined the force that is water and saw it bending itself to his will. The water around him swelled up to enclose him in a sphere, formed from the ancient water.

While inside, he couldn't breathe. He forced down his instinct to panic, and let the water envelop him; he allowed himself to commune with its energy. Jorn had been open to receiving a vision, Argus wanted to have a conversation. He was seeking out another in the world, a lost soul that was as ancient as he was, part of the old world. She was playing a large part in the theatre that was unfolding, and he had to do whatever he could to oppose her. The men in the world could fight each other as they always did, but the playing field was uneven. There were evil forces that wished for the door to be flung wide open, allowing them to pour forth and be free to roam, to murder and destroy at will. He had not pledged his and his apprentices' help to the cause of defeating men. If allowed unfettered reign on this plane, the demon would create a passage for millions more of his kind.

There was a small clearing around the tree where she made her camp. The old crone was poking at a stew pot with a long branch while grumbling something for her own amusement. She was covered in grime that found its way into every one of her ubiquitous wrinkles. Around her was a pallet made of branches and leaves, behind her was the God Tree, the oldest and largest tree in Kronos. She was certain that she was alone.

"Lilith," came a voice from… somewhere. She was startled and looked around for him. A look of understanding washed over her vile face, and she turned to the fire. Looking into it, she waited. "Lilith, you still live."

"Argus? You are still of this world?" she croaked into the fire.

"Like you, I come, and I go," he said. "You know why I am contacting you?"

"Because the centuries roll on, and yet some things never change. You are still looking out for them, even though they fear and hate you," she cackled into the fire.

"We all must take a side. What do you gain by opening doors and letting those things into our world?"

"Our world? I'm not of this world and neither are you. Compared to these pitiful humans, I am like a God. I can have anything I want, but in the end; I just want to watch this world burn."

"You haven't changed Lilith." Sorrow in his voice, "Please know, that when I kill you, I'll regret it with every fiber of my being. You want to see Xoran on fire, I want to reap the fruit of the crops that I have helped to sow."

"I know, Argus. It's nothing personal. It never was."

"Can I see you once, just this one last time? The real you?" he almost begged.

"Why does it matter, you're old, you should be beyond such things."

"I deserve it, and you know that. It's such a small thing that I ask."

She sighed, then stepped away from the fire. She performed intricate hand gestures to accompany her incantation as she wove her spell. Her image blurred; it was like trying to see through a pounding rain. She grew at least a foot taller, stretched out so that she was nearly six feet tall and thin. Her hands, face, and one leg were exposed. Her skin was white as alabaster and perfect. The black gown that she wore was wispy and shimmered in the light from the fire. She had a long staff, on the top was a blade on one side, and a glowing white gem on the other. On her head, she wore a crown of blackened steel that resembled the horns of a giant buck.

What Argus focused on was her face. Lilith was by far the most beautiful thing that he had seen in his many centuries of living. Her forest green eyes were wide, her nose small and sharp like her high cheekbones. She was exceptionally beautiful, but she gave the impression of coldness and inaccessibility. She was the perfect woman that no man could ever possess.

"Thank you, Lilith, for granting me this last wish," he said choking out the words. "Goodbye."

Chapter 49: Showdown

The light was dim, but it was still bright enough to see by. The cool air was stale and didn't move at all. Argus stood on the third-floor patio of his mansion in Southern Chuo, looking at a disturbance in the flow of magic. The sky became purple with dark clouds swirling far above. The grass below looked so dark green as to be almost black, and the white marble took on a gray, corpse-like hue. It appeared in front of the mansion in the area between the back gate and the house. A wall of fire grew out of thin air, and from the fire, the demon emerged. He was as tall as the mansion and was at eye level with the ancient mage. Qaumon was the name he had acquired thousands of years ago. Though his followers thought him a god, he was a demon that they called Quell. He continued to grow till his foul red face was lost far above. When he spoke, his voice shook the ground.

"Your time has come, mage!" the demon thundered.

"I think not, demon! I know now that I was awoken from my centuries of slumber to stop you from entering this plane and inflicting your evil on this world."

The demon laughed out loud. "Perhaps in your youth; but you're a shadow of your former self. Not nearly enough to take on the likes of me. Surrender and I'll make your death quick and... relatively painless."

Argus floated to the ground and began weaving his spell. His body expanded and grew rapidly till he was the equal of Qaumon. He didn't waste energy on further talk, he conjured a ball of flame and launched it at the demon. Qaumon laughed.

"Fire? You know I come from fire! It runs through my veins!" The demon sucked in a vast amount of air and blew flames at Argus with the force of a hurricane. The giant mage stumbled backward, and almost stumbled over his mansion. He grew angry and in a blind rage, he ripped the building from its foundation and crashed it over the demon's head. The demon stumbled back, a chuckle in his throat.

"Really? Is that the best that you can do? Your name is legend, even in the deepest hells where I reign. I know that you are capable of terrible violence. Give it to me!" He launched a fireball at Argus. The fire wrapped around him. When it had passed, Argus was standing strong. Like the demon, he was impervious to the effects of fire, "If you can't beat me, I'll destroy all happiness and hope in this world. Their Old Gods will be forgotten and my name, my true name will be branded on each, and every person's soul. I'll own them in life, and death."

A bystander might think that the scene was a giant illusion. Both combatants were semi-transparent and looked like they were made of smoke and light. Argus conjured a sword in his hand that seemed to shine with its own internal light. He stepped forward and slashed at the midsection of the demon. His sword appeared to pass through the demon's fiery red skin, but it tore a gash in the hellspawn. The demon healed himself, as Argus pressed his attack. Charging forward, he lopped off the left hand of the demon, who cried out in pain before picking up the hand and re-attaching it to the stump.

Argus continued to slash at the demon, opening wounds, and lopping off hands, fingers, even horns. The demon roared with his hellish rage and reached out his arm and grabbed the old mage by the throat. He smacked away the sword, which faded before hitting the ground, and pushed the old man backward. He started using both hands to choke the old wizard. Argus was turning blue, but then he started to change.

He transformed from an old man in a brilliant blue robe to become an Agila. The Agila had the body of a horse, golden and brown eagle's wings, and the head and arms of an ape. He grew larger to become a true Titan. Rearing up, he grabbed the demon by the neck and arm. Leaning in, he took a vicious bite from the demon's neck. The bite ripped out the throat and veins in the demon's neck, soaking the ground with his black blood. The great ape-like arms grasped the demon's head, and dug its thumbs into the demon's eyes, crushing the sensitive orbs. Then, with its thumbs deep in the demon's skull, it ripped Qaumon's head apart like it was a rotten melon.

The creature's body was still standing on its hind legs, coated from head to hoof in grey matter and blood. Still possessed by the spirit of the creature, Argus used the creature's sharp claws to rip the demon apart, limb from limb.

Qaumon had been beaten in this world and as its body lay spread over an acre of land, the demonic spirit returned to the plane from which it had been summoned. Beating the demon was not the only benefit to tonight's fight; he had slowed down the witch Lilith. She loved only chaos and destruction, and she would be furious to find out that her demon had been sent back to a hell where it could not return for a thousand years. That wouldn't stop her, but he hoped that it would at least slow her attempt to corrupt this world.

Chapter 50: Opening the Door

Lilith was in her old crone form, working on a spell to summon more agents of chaos to the world of man. Suddenly she jolted upright or as upright as her ancient body would allow. She knew at once that her demon was no longer on this plane of existence. She had poured so much of her energies into creating the portal that allowed him to cross over and expended even more of herself to keep the beast in check. Demons could be summoned, and they could be made to serve, but they were highly intelligent creatures that hated being under anyone's control. The demon had fought her every minute that he was on this plane, and he didn't appreciate the thousands of souls that had pledged themselves to him. Now he was gone, and his followers would never know that their god had been banished from this world.

She knew who was responsible for the demon's departure, there was only one person capable of such a feat. Argus had confronted her champion and bested him. She had to admit that she was impressed. The mage was very old though and was a shadow of the man he had been so long ago when they had first met. He would no doubt be weak from the task. This would be the best time for her to confront him. She would miss him, but he stood against her vision of a world in constant turmoil. He preferred peace and quiet; the very thought made her shudder.

Argus stood before the fire, just staring into it. He had made his way to the mammoth cave that lay buried deep beneath his mansion. The mansion was gone, but the grounds and especially the underground lairs were all still in place. The front of his beautiful blue silk robe was covered by inky black blood and gore. His ancient eyes sparkled with the reflected light from the fire. He surrendered himself to the blaze, getting lost in the light and heat from the tendrils of flame. He was about to sink into a healing trance when her voice came to him through the fire. The voice of a woman who was ancient, a creature from another time and place. Without invitation, she stepped out of the fire and into the chamber with Argus. This was the first time that they had been in such close proximity in many hundreds of years. He knew what she had once been, and what she had once meant to him; but he was determined not to let past lives cloud his resolve.

"You've come to kill me Lilith?" he asked plainly.

"Argus, it didn't have to be this way. You could have given into Chaos, turned your back on Law," she said sadly. "You killed my servant! I envisioned a future, where he strode the world like a Colossus, corrupting all the goodness in this mundane world."

"Such a sad, yet beautiful creature you are Lilith. There was a time that I would have slain giants for you, gods even; but I could no more follow your path than the river can flow up the mountain. Now, I must do what I can to stop you. These humans deserve their time in the sun. We had our time. The days of demons and monsters are passed."

"You say that, but even you can see that magic is quickly returning to this world. Not by my hand, or by yours. The tide is shifting, and these humans will have to adapt or die. Even as we speak, the lines are becoming blurred and monstrous creatures that everyone thought were gone forever are returning. They will form great herds to hunt these peaceful plains, their kind will fill the forests and swamps, even the air, with their fangs and their claws. They are coming, not because of me. I just want to be a catalyst for the beginning of the end."

"I'm sorry to hear that, dear Lilith. I guess today is the day we part for good." He started casting a spell; but she was already prepared. The crone opened her cloak and snakes poured from within. There were dozens, then hundreds; it was like a flood of serpents had been held back by a dam and were now free to slither forth. They rushed forward towards Argus, causing him to stop his casting. They were all fangs and wide-open jaws, venom dripping from their mouths as they all tried to bite him at the same time. Argus used a spell with the fastest casting time to defend himself. He produced a wall of fire between himself and the snakes, just as they were about to strike him. They made no noise except for the crackling of their skins in the fire and the eventual popping sound as they exploded. While he was fighting off her first attack, she was already casting a summoning spell for something larger.

She waved her arms while calling out in the strange language of dark magic, and from the mist before her, a void opened to another world. A skeletal hand reached across the gateway between worlds, it was followed by a full skeleton in torn and tarnished armor. The blue-green helm sat unevenly on the fleshless skull. More of the skeletal warriors followed the first and soon there were a dozen of the undead between the crone and the old mage. They drew their swords and daggers and stumbled towards the old man, swinging their arms in a wave of clumsy attacks. Their rusty points ripped his cloak, and a few even found his flesh, leaving shallow gashes on his arms and legs.

Calling up a rogue wind, Argus let it build till it had the force of a tornado, then he willed the winds to explode in the direction of his tormentors. The skeletons were violently pulled apart and their bones were propelled back at Lilith. She ducked while at the same time creating a shield to protect herself. Bones along with bits of armor and various weapons continued to be carried aloft till they were out of sight.

Argus created a ball of light and attached it to the head of his staff. He walked over till he was right next to Lilith. The light shone down upon her pale, mottled skin and hit her like a bludgeon. She seemed to recoil from the glare. Cowering at his feet, she raised her arms up to try and block the light from touching her face.

"I'm no holy man, and yet this pure light offends thee?" he asked of her over her pained groans. "Are you really so evil that pure light brings you pain? I miss the Ice Queen that you were. This new form is weak and frankly, does you no justice," he said with sympathy in his voice.

She reached out with one of her bony hands and grasped his ankle. Because he was 'born of fire', her cold hand shocked his senses. It took a second before he realized what she was doing. His ankle felt like it was freezing, and the feeling started to spread upward from where her hand grasped him. She had him in a vice-like grip and with each passing second, he could feel his already sinking life force being drained.

Over her shoulder, he could see that the gateway that she had opened for her undead soldiers was still active. He looked into that other place and saw all manner of horrors that were eager to cross the void. His only regret was that he wouldn't be around to fight in the coming conflict of man versus monster, good versus evil. He had slain Lilith's demon and prevented it from leading the armies of darkness; but even left to their own devices, they would still wreak havoc on this world. As his life force was slipping away, he cast a spell to close the doorway to hell.

He would never see the evolution, the growth of the twins. That was his last thought as the last of his life force was drained from him. Without the spirit that powered all men and beasts alike, he crumbled to the floor of the cave like an airless balloon. The woman looked down at her hand, it was still old, but she had gained back much of her lost youth. Walking over to the pool of water, she could see her own reflection. She had gone from a shriveled caricature of death itself to merely an old woman. After a few more lives sacrificed, she might even become the coldly beautiful Winter Witch again.

Chapter 51: Jarrod Stone

Meisha had passed through the Western border crossing, out of O'Bell, going towards Kees. As always, she was in full armor, covered by a long bright Orange colored cloak. She rode into town at a quick pace, anxious to get to the inn. She entered the front door of the inn and approached the front desk. The clerk behind the desk saw her come in and looked her up and down. She came within talking distance and was about to speak when he spoke first.

"Room 9 Madam, down this hall, last on the left," he said to her, a knowing grin on his face. She just smiled back and walked off toward the indicated room. When she entered, Jarrod Stone was out on the patio in a big wicker chair, napping in the sun. The sound of her stomping through the room opened his eyes, and he looked up at her with a tremendous grin. Without speaking, he stood and met her halfway, then wrapped her up in a strong comforting hug. She started to mumble something; but he leaned down and kissed her deeply, his arms still holding her body against his. Neither of them spoke as he slowly removed her armor and clothing, piece by piece. When she was fully undressed, he picked her up and carried her to the bed.

Meisha rolled over in bed and looked out the French doors that led to the patio. The sky was getting dark, and a light rain had started. She spoke to Jarrod, feeling lazy and satisfied.

"What time is it?"

"It's dinner time, Mee. We missed lunch and I know you must be famished."

"I did work up a bit of an appetite. Do you want room service?"

"How can I make the locals jealous if I don't show you off a bit? Throw something on and I'll take you for the best that this town has to offer."

"You don't have to impress me, you already got me into bed."

"It's not about that. Life, in the end, is a series of moments. When you're on your deathbed, gods willing, many, many years from now; you'll forget thousands of dinners out, but hopefully you'll remember tonight," he said as he slipped into his best slacks and cleanest shirt.

They ate and drank, talked, and laughed for hours. There may have been other people at the eatery, but they only remembered being in each other's company. Meisha was accustomed to making decisions, and it felt weird at first, allowing a man to dictate where they would go, and what they would do; but it soon felt very natural, and she warmed to the idea of sharing control.

Jarrod was about to make a final toast before retiring back to the room when the evening calm was broken by the sounds of people yelling in fear and the sounds of fighting in the streets. Standing up, he ran over to the door and looked out. A hundred men or more were rolling through the main street like they owned the town. They were pushing and shoving and breaking anything that would make a nice sound when it was smashed. He darted back inside.

"Not sure, but I think it's a bunch of those Quell bastards. Mee, let's go out the back!" he said grabbing her hand as they went through the kitchen and then out the back. The back entrance was just across the courtyard from the Inn, they sprinted as fast as they could in the near darkness. Avoiding the front desk, they went around the corner to the patio and jumped the little wall to enter their room.

Jarrod was already dressed for the road. He stuffed his few possessions in his pack and made sure that all of his many knives were now tucked into his belt for easy access. Meisha put on her armor as fast as she could, and Jarrod helped her with some of the trickier bits. In minutes, they were both ready to mount up and ride out of town; but it wasn't quite fast enough.

The inn was filled with the sound of men going room to room, pulling people out of their beds and into the hallway. When they came to Jarrod's room, they kicked in the door and found a good-sized man, and a female knight waiting for them. Meisha didn't wait for introductions; she skewered the first man through the doorway before he could even take stock of the situation. The second man pushed past his partner to also die upon her blade.

"If only we could get them all to come in one at a time, we'd be in great shape," Jarrod joked.

"I smell smoke!" she said, ignoring him.

"I do too. Let's leave the way we came," he said pulling her towards the patio. They looked at the town just outside the Inn's yard and it was a madhouse. Men lay dead or dying in the street, women were being pulled into buildings by their hair. There were a handful of businesses on fire and everyone who normally would have been there to fight the fires was getting murdered. The Quell laughed as they destroyed yet another peaceful town.

The sight of a tall fearless man, and a woman in armor was too much of an attraction. A small group of the followers broke off from the larger group and ran towards them. The Quell fanatics had lost all semblance of their former humanity. They seemed rabid and were wildly swinging blades and bludgeons. Jarrod's instinct was to push Meisha behind him, but he remembered in time that she was probably better at this type of fight than he was. They stood side by side and waited for the onslaught.

"Die, you cur!" she screamed as she swung her longsword in a horizontal arc that opened the stomach of the lead attacker. Another man was vying for her attention but instead got a thrown knife in his eye. As a gambler, throwing daggers for sport had gotten him many a free drink and more than a few bags of coin. Now it bothered him that he had to use his skills on real people. Four more knives found four more vital spots on the men that they were fighting. His shots were not all life-ending, but his victims became easy work for Meisha. Looking over, he saw that there were six or seven corpses at her feet, and she had just gotten started.

When they were down to the last one, Meisha removed his sword hand and put the point of her sword to his throat. "How many of you are there?" she asked the man.

"Rot in hell, ya infidel bitch!" the man spat.

Meisha brained him with the flat of her sword. The man lay on the ground, clutching at the stump where his hand had been. She walked over and put her armored boot on his testicles. "Let's try this again. How many of you Quell vermin are there?"

"Thousands! You're all gonna die, we have four or five thousand of us, and a plague of demons as well. We're marching on those O'Bell bitches and were gonna kill em all!" the man screamed.

"What does he mean by *demons*?" Jarrod wondered aloud.

"No idea, probably the rambling of a dead man." She stomped on his throat, crushing his windpipe.

Another group of Quell was passing by when they saw their brothers lying dead on the ground. They pulled their weapons and started running after Jarrod and Meisha. Jarrod pulled her away from the new fight and got her around the building to where their horses were liveried. The Quell were only a step or two behind. Jarrod felt a sword bite into his left arm as he was trying to get Meisha on her horse. The pain was intense, but all he cared about was her getting her on her mount.

"You need to ride as fast as you can, tell your sisters about what is coming!" he said as a knife slid into his unprotected back. His eyes bulged as the pain hit him, and he knew that the knife had hit something important. "Go, I'm done!" She looked down at him with tears in her eyes, "Go." he fell to the ground as a few more of the Quell stabbed him. They made a point of carving him up, even though he was already dead at that point.

Meisha was a soldier at heart and was not going to be a victim of sentimentality. She felt the rush of pain and despair and loss heading for her, but it would have to wait. She rode all through the night, only slowing so as not to kill her horse. By dawn she was nearing the West gate to O'Bell, but it was too late. Camps of thousands of men surrounded the base of the hills that lead to the Western entrance. By now, the O'Bell would know that they were being attacked. She turned east and slowed her pace. When she got to the next farm, she traded horses and made for the Southern Gate.

Chapter 52: The Quell Horde

The northern parts of Kees were rural, to put it kindly. A person could go a lifetime without any strangers passing by. Lem Lothe had been lying on his cot for most of the night, staring at the ceiling. He was doubting himself after the disastrous attempted invasion of Yorah Island and the Ammun temple. A small fraction of the men he sent returned, and the ones that did return were crippled or emotionally scarred. When it was him and a few loyalists, things were fine. When it grew to hundreds, they were still able to commit their favorite atrocities without serious repercussions; but the last few battles showed the weakness in his overall strategy. If you have ten times the opponent's number, just throw enough bodies at them till they drown in your men's blood. When facing a fair fight, they either lost or barely won a pyrrhic victory.

One of the three entrances to O'Bell was within striking range. A whole country of women warriors should be an easy target; but they were highly trained, unlike the last dozen towns that he took over. It was time to tip the scales in their favor for a change. Now would be his chance to use the Gahrenna. Up earlier than usual, Lem called in his most trusted advisors. He turned to his second in command, Dellan Crys.

"Dellan, take the bulk of our northern army and move it just outside of the West Gate into O'Bell. I will meet you there when the sun goes down, two days from now. I'll be bringing the beasts that were gifted to us by Quell. They'll storm the gates for us, and we'll follow. There should be plenty of spoils for everyone."

Dellan was happy, he liked it when Lem gave him responsibility. He also liked the idea of pillaging. Where Lem followed Quell because of his deep faith, Dellan followed Quell because it had elevated him from a simple day laborer. He was a man destined to never have money and probably to never marry and father children. As a follower of Quell, and one who had risen to such an esteemed position, he had all the women and wine that a man could dream of. He walked out to address the dozen or so men that reported to him with a skip in his step.

Nighttime had never frightened Lem; but the closer that he got to the Twilight Forest, the more he started to feel his skin crawl. He hadn't seen a soul; not man nor beast for hours. The evil of the Gahrenna had spread for long distances in every direction, but at night they prowled near the forest that was their home. It was said that their numbers had grown, and now they numbered in the many hundreds. He looked down at the silver amulet that Quell had given him and took small comfort in its supposed protection.

The moon was brighter than usual, but the trail was so unused that it still was very difficult to follow. He knew that he must be getting close; the sounds of birds and night animals had ceased an hour ago. Only the wind and his own pounding heart let him know that he hadn't yet lost his sense of hearing. Then, when he was near madness, he heard the first howl. It was very much like a wolf's howl, only longer and with more... pain. It was followed by another howl that seemed very far away. Both the second and the third howls were almost subliminal in that he had to stop breathing and hold his mouth open to see if he really did hear what he thought he had heard.

A few dark shapes slowly approached him, they walked on all fours like a wolf; but when they got close, they rose up to stand on two legs like a man. The one in front turned just the right way so that the moonlight shone on his shiny black muzzle. The creature seemed to be more canine than man, and yet its eyes were devious and intelligent. The Gahrenna licked its lips like it was looking for a way to disobey the amulet and gorge on the man before him.

"You recognize this, yes?" Lem said with as much conviction as he could muster. He held the amulet out to at arm's length. The creature gave a short growl and nodded its head, "Follow me, we are going to run for two days and nights, and when we get there, you will have plenty of blood to drink. You will be feasting on the flesh of women soldiers." The beast grunted with satisfaction at the thought of ripping into the soft flesh of a woman.

Lem turned his horse around and headed northeast towards the Kees border. The lead creature reared back and let out a howl that was heard for miles. Hundreds of individual howls replied. Lem set off at a swift pace, no longer afraid of the night. In his peripheral vision, he could see the movement of several of the beasts keeping pace with him, and he could hear behind him what sounded like a stampede. The creatures came out of dozens of breaks in the forest, and they converged on the train that was heading towards a new land and fresh prey.

The various forces converged as planned, and both Lem Lothe and his man Dellan were pleased. The creatures looked at the thousands of men, and instead of being intimidated by their numbers, they saw food that they were not allowed to consume. They were tired and hungry from the journey. Dark muzzles dripped with their infectious saliva. They kept looking to their leader for permission to attack, but they were always denied. On the other hand, the Quell men wanted nothing to do with the creatures, they made sure to have weapons, and when available, shields at the ready.

"My Lord, these fearsome beasts are a great boon, no doubt; but I fear that every minute we don't use them, they are plotting to turn on us."

"I think that you might be right," he said to his second. To his left were hundreds of tents where the Quell had put up camp. To his right was the trail that led up the mountain to the Western border crossing into O'Bell. He saw at the top of the ridge, several thousand feet above, there was a notch in the rocky wall that separated the territories. There would be guards there, not more than a token force he estimated. Higher up the hill was a temple to Lahni, goddess of love and the moon, and patron god of the O'Bell women. Part of his mandate was to destroy all artifacts and temples that were not glorifying Quell.

He pointed up the mountain at the temple. "You want blood? You cannot wait? Pass through that gate up on the ridge, kill the guards. When that is done, continue on to the temple up there!" The leader of the Gahrenna watched where he was pointing and gave a short growl and nod. Like two days before, he let out a blood curdling howl that was echoed by his fellow Gahrenna. They fell in behind the leader of the pack as he dropped to all fours and ran up the trail at a pace that would tire a man in minutes. They swarmed after him till the entire pack was bounding up the trail, and the plain where the men waited was again calm and monster free.

They both watched them run up the hill towards battle, and when they were out of earshot, "Do you think that they know we see them as being expendable? I can't imagine you would shed a tear if every one of them perishes up there," Dellan remarked.

"I don't care, let them soften up the bitches, so when we go over the hill in the morning, there will be no one to stop us."

Lem stood and watched as their secret weapon ran up the steep grade.

There were a dozen guards at the entrance to O'Bell territory, and they took their positions behind thirty-foot iron gates. They heard the howling and were waiting for the creatures to arrive. A runner had already been sent to the castle. Traveling by horse, she should get there in a day or two at the most. The captain of the guard said her prayers out loud, calling on Lahni for help in the coming battle. They had set torches at intervals starting at two hundred feet from the gate. When the flood of Gahrenna came around a corner and started to sprint in their direction, the guards could finally see what they were up against. They shuddered at the number of the creatures. Each one was a nightmare come to life. The archers let loose, killing a score of Gahrenna before they got close to the gate. The Gahrenna washed up against the gate, their pushing their muzzles between the bars, hungrily snapping and trying to draw blood. Others jumped up and climbed the almost sheer rocks on both sides of the gate. With ease, they were over the top and dropping down amidst the women guards.

All of their training went out of the window as strong jaws tore through leather armor, and man-like arms with sharp claws slashed at any exposed skin. The women fought the best they could, but their cries fell down the mountain and provided amusement for the followers of Quell below. In a predictably short time, the screams were over.

"Should we go up there? I'm guessing that the gates are wide open by now."

"While they are in a feeding frenzy? No thank you," Lem replied. "There is still a several days march to the capital, and we'll have our hands full with them between now and then. Set a triple guard in case they forget whom they serve."

Lem led his soldiers up the mountain. When they reached the gates to O'Bell, there were several dozen dead men with arrows protruding from vital areas. Lem thought to himself that the curse must break on their death, and they revert to the men that they had been before. Inside the gate, there was a blood bath. Body parts of the women soldiers were flung all around the area like they had been fought over. There was a small clearing for the guardhouse, then one road went up towards the temple, and the other headed down into O'Bell territory. Both directions were heavily wooded, and he suspected that his Gahrenna allies were sleeping it off in the nearby bushes or under fallen trees.

They took the road up to the temple. It was about a quarter of a mile, with many twists to avoid areas where the mountain couldn't be tamed. The temple was typical of the Old Gods. The temples that were devoted to Magnus were designed so that masculinity was fully on display. This one was dedicated to a female god, so it was designed more in tune with nature and with beauty. The front steps of Lahni's temple were red with dried blood and there were drag marks that ran down the full length of the main hallway. There were some remains, but not much was left after the Gahrenna had had their fill. Not a soul remained, but the temple itself was practically untouched.

"Men, put fire to this building and all the buildings in the compound," Lem ordered. A few of his men rushed forward, pulled torches from the walls, and set fire to the delicate sheer fabric that covered the windows. They burned the drapes and the furniture and did their best to desecrate every image or symbol that referred to the goddess. They took to the priceless statues and tile work with heavy iron hammers. When they were done desecrating the temple, a lot of the foundation stones still stood, but every other trace of Lahni was gone.

Lem walked his horse down the steep path, taking it in and enjoying his victory. "Let's get down this mountain and make our way to the castle. Burn and pillage everything we encounter between here and there," he commanded his second. The man nodded in approval. They would need spoils to keep the men's spirits up.

Chapter 53: O'Bell

Lydia O'Bell sat in her garden and watched her children play. She had a son, almost six now, and a daughter who was just over four years old. The girl was good stock and before long, she would have to start the training that all O'Bell women received. She loved the boy but wasn't sure what to do with him. He was royal blood, so he would never be one of the neutered specimens that the O'Bell surrounded themselves with. Maybe she could marry him off to one of the other houses for some consideration. Everyone knew how little the O'Bell valued their males, so he probably wouldn't fetch that good of a price. Maybe he should be sent off to live with his father. He was actually happy that she had given birth to a boy! Men. What could she get for the boy, she asked herself for the hundredth time.

War was coming, and as a general in the O'Bell army, she intended to lead their knights and soldiers into battle. Perhaps she wouldn't live to see her children grow. That's one way to settle the problem, she thought. They had returned from King's Table a couple of weeks ago, and ever since she had been preparing a force to fight off the Quell. These women who were always in a state of readiness, were now on heightened alert. They were producing arrows and spears at a furious pace.

There was a big commotion from the direction of the palace entrance. Not a fan of commotions, Lydia indicated that the maids take care of the children while she went to see what was going on. She found the source of the noise in the queen's viewing room. Vandressa O'Bell was at her strategy table surrounded by her generals. Before her was a guard in full gear, exhausted and ready to pass out.

"My queen! The Quell have attacked our Western gate!" she choked out. "From the number of campfires, there must be five thousand or more. Worse yet, they have a squad of demons with them. Wolves that walk like men, huge bloodthirsty beasts from hell!"

"We need to go out to meet them!" one of the generals roared.

"Run them down with our Calvary! Crush them beneath our horses' hooves!" cried another.

The queen looked nervous. She was preparing for a battle several weeks from now, to take place on someone else's land. This veteran of many battles and numerous victories looked overwhelmed and confused. Lydia jumped in, "Mother, we can't handle a force of that size by ourselves. We don't need to take foolish chances like men would. We need to send word to the alliance, and then button up the castle."

Queen Vandressa O'Bell collected her thoughts for a moment and knew that her daughter was right. Men would, in service of their pride, ride out and meet the enemy on the open plains that surrounded the castle. Women were smarter and not afraid to retreat behind their walls when it was the wise thing to do. Despite the impending doom, she felt so much better having strong women behind her, and most of all, a daughter that was quickly becoming a leader. She nodded at her firstborn.

Lydia walked up and put her hand on the shoulder of one of the generals. "Send your most reliable messenger to the Warlord, Renata Rin of Inram. Let her know what our situation is and ask that the alliance come to our aid with utmost haste!" The woman bowed, then ran off towards the barracks.

Lydia turned to another of the generals, her name was Melinda O'Bell, one of her first cousins. "Melinda, send word that all of the peasants should pack as much food as they can, and that they must get behind our walls within the next twenty-four hours." The general was listening carefully as if the words were coming directly from her queen, "Second, make sure that all of the walls are fortified and that the oil is filled, the ballistae are stocked with extra bolts. There should be fire pits all around the outer wall for archers, and so on." She clapped the older woman on the shoulder. The general smiled and ran off to complete her tasks. Lydia called another woman over. "I have some ideas for traps. I will need a couple of hundred workers and several items. Get the men to help. If nothing else, they are great at labor." She sent the woman off. "I have a few surprises for our uninvited guests. I hope you don't mind Mother."

"I have never been so proud daughter. When this battle is won, you'll be crowned our new queen." She cried tears of joy and pride.

Chapter 54: Revenge of the O'Bell

Lem Lothe sat on his horse watching his men work. This was the third pass since leaving the border that had been intentionally blocked. The O'Bell women fell trees across a vital part of the road, then set them on fire. The options were to wait a day or two for the fires to burn out or have teams of men with shovels try and extinguish the fires. *Every minute that we're delayed gives these warrior women time to tighten their defenses. The Gahrenna are potent, but they are not immune to arrows and there are not nearly enough of them.*

There were still about two hundred of the Gahrenna. After feasting on the flesh of the women of O'Bell, they were hungry for more meat. When around the men, they paced awkwardly on all fours. Most of the time, they took to the woods to look for any kind of prey. Lem knew that his control over the creatures was razor thin. *Any mistake and they'll be free of my control, and their duty to not kill and eat all of us.* He thought to himself.

"How long till we can pass?" he asked what passed for an engineer.

"At the rate the men are workin? Three more hours, maybe four."

"About what I thought. Crack the whip, get them moving! We have the holy scripture to spread, and this is a waste of time!"

The country of O'Bell was set in what looked like a giant teacup. Its borders, including the side facing the sea, followed the tops of mountains. The peaks looked down on the center of the country that was flat and had excellent land for farming. Castle O'Bell was set on top of the mountain range along the Northern coast. The castle was the highest point for many hundreds of miles. From the observation deck in the Queen's Tower, you could see a great deal of the country on one side, and far out to sea on the other.

Lem Lothe saw the steepness of the few roads that led up to the castle and cursed his luck. The Gahrenna could probably get up there fine; but his men would have a very difficult time to climb while under fire. He'd learned a lesson from the disastrous attack on the Ammun temple. The bulk of his army was still south of here, they were roaming around parts of Kees and Wingard blowing through little towns, murdering for sport. He wondered if he should wait and have them move north so he could strike with a much larger force. Then he thought again about the Gahrenna, and he knew that he had to use them now, or soon he would be feeding his own men to them to keep them docile.

Dellan pulled even with his leader and gazed up at the Castle. "We could starve them out, we're out here with the supplies. How much could they have moved inside before we got here?"

"We could, but we'd be sending our troops out all across the country looking for scraps and that's when they would come down and attack. Besides that, the Gahrenna won't wait, you can see it in their eyes, they're just barely under control."

"You think the beasties can get up and over those walls before the witches cut em down?"

"You saw the way they took out the border guards, and the temple." He looked carefully up at the hill before them, "They can do it, but there aren't enough of them. Not enough of them to get the gate open before getting cut down with arrows."

"Well, what if there were more of them?" Dellan asked.

Lem looked at his second, and for once, he was speechless. His men were setting up their camp, convinced that they might be there for days, if not weeks. He had no love for the others, not even for Dellan. They were followers of Quell, but that didn't make them interesting companions. Their sacrifice would be the highlight of their existence, it would surely guarantee them a place in the great beyond. The stakes were high, but their sacrifice would be worth it.

"How many to do the job? A thousand?" he asked his second.

Dellan smiled widely at his master, "That should probably do it."

They picked out one thousand of the weakest and most useless of their number and herded them into a large circle in the middle of the field. Four thousand men formed a ring around them, and with their shields and swords at the ready, kept them from breaking free. The men in the middle were very late to the realization that something was afoot. They had no idea what was going on, but they started to panic and tried to break out of the circle. Lem Lothe stood on a special platform that they had constructed for him. It was a wood frame, twenty feet high with guard rails and stairs. He calmed the crowd with a few gestures, then began speaking.

"Brothers! We are all here for the same reason! We are here to spread the word of Quell. All that oppose him must die! All who are followers of the 'Old Gods', must convert or die!" the crowd cheered at his words. "Up on that mountain are women. Women who think that they are the equal of men! They act like whores, speaking whenever they wish, they order men around! They need to be taught a lesson. They need to know their place!" the crowd was getting charged up by his sermonizing.

"A frontal assault on their walls would be hopeless, even with the size of our army. Our allies, the Gahrenna are more agile and can climb and jump like we cannot. They can breach the walls and open the gates for the rest of us to flood in and kill these godless women!" he waited for them to settle just a bit. "The problem is, we need more of the Gahrenna. I have asked the commanders to choose men especially suited for this mission. We are going to have you join the ranks of the Gahrenna. You will have the glory of being the first over the walls, you will be the first to taste the sweet blood of the women who are hiding up there!" The men in the middle grew scared. They redoubled their efforts to escape.

Lem grasped his medallion and held it out for the Gahrenna to see. He used his most commanding voice, "Beasts, servants of Quell, infect these men, and have them join your ranks!" He indicated the ones inside the circle, "Do not *eat* them, just infect them so that they too will become Gahrenna!" he ordered. The leader nodded, then howled to his brothers. Soon they were all howling. They stood on their hind legs and pushed their way into the center of the circle where the helpless men waited to be infected.

When they were inside the circle, the human followers of Quell closed the ring. The leader of the Gahrenna walked in his strange half-human gait towards the nearest man. The man was skinny and short, his face was a mask of terror. The creature lifted the man to his dripping muzzle and took a vicious bite at the man's neck. The man instantly started shaking uncontrollably as his lifeblood squirted from the bite wound. The creature tossed him to the side and repeated the actions with the next man in line. The other Gahrenna followed suit, attacking the terrified men, and passing on their curse. Men were screaming like little girls as rabid creatures waded into the crowd, biting everyone they could catch. The blood on the ground became a shallow pool, and blood coated every man who was helping to maintain the circle.

In less than an hour, it was done. The ground was littered by what at first glance appeared to be the torn and dead bodies of hundreds of men. They were face up, face down, arms and legs splayed carelessly. Then they began to stir. Some of the first that were bitten were the first to turn. Everyone stared in amazement as a man would roll to his knees, then cry out as his bones and tendons were stretched. Hair sprouted from every surface of their bodies, and their faces lengthened and became wolf-like. It took hours till the last of them completed their transformations.

A few that had been attacked too violently died. Lem gave his permission, and they were eaten by the new pack of Gahrenna. The few who had died were just a snack, the creatures were becoming restless for real meat. They growled at their human allies and looked at them as if they wanted nothing more than to devour them, drink their blood, and gnaw on their bones. Lem loved how well his gambit had turned out. He started to plan the invasion, the part where he rode victoriously through those nigh-impenetrable gates. The time was now, time to release the creatures to do his dirty work. Lem leaned over the rail on his platform so that he could speak directly with the leader of the Gahrenna. He held his amulet out to amplify his command. "Storm the walls, do whatever you can to get the gates open. We will be right behind you!"

The creature growled, then let out a terrifying howl that caught the attention of the others. He fell to all fours and charged up the road toward the castle. The rest of the Gahrenna dropped in behind him and they became a river of fur and teeth, flowing up the road toward the main gate of the castle. They hit the snow line and kept running till they were almost out of sight.

"Form up, prepare to march!" Lem ordered. "Let's take this castle and teach these women their proper place!" They all cheered and followed their leader up the long steep trail that led to the home of House O'Bell.

It was eerily quiet. They had expected much more noise from the road up ahead. Unlike the border gate, there were no sounds of women screaming, or of wolves howling, no clashing of weapons. Lem rode ahead of his troops up and up the steep grade till he was almost in the shadow of the castle. He found a dead Gahrenna in the middle of the road, with no blood, and there was no sign of violence. He found it odd; but kept the group heading upward and onward.

A hundred feet away were a couple more of the dead wolf-like creatures. No blood, no arrows in their sides, no visible cause of death, aside from some frothing at their jowls. Lem felt a tightness in his stomach; he had the sinking feeling that something had gone tragically wrong. Soon he came to a clearing where there were literally hundreds of the dead Gahrenna. Then he started to notice that around the bodies were hunks of meat. He thought that he saw chickens, goat meat, and even some donkey haunches. It soon became clear that all the Gahrenna had succumbed to the siren song of raw meat, and that they were not able to detect the poison until it was too late.

Lem heard some of his own men screaming and looked up just in time to a see cloud of arrows heading for them. He turned his horse quickly and made to force his way through the crowd, knocking over his own men in his haste to escape. The first volley of arrows hit with great effectiveness as dozens of the invaders were struck. Lem felt an arrow pierce his lower back. He snapped it off a few inches from his side and kept riding down the hill. Seeing their leader turn and run, the men also turned to run down the hill. The troops near the bottom were in no danger, the men at the top were fleeing a storm of arrows, and the men caught in the middle were trampled by the men above them on the trail, while also being riddled with arrows.

When they were out of range and back down at the camp, Lem estimated that he had lost every single one of the Gahrenna, and several hundred men, to not a single loss by the O'Bell. He searched out the surgeon and had the arrowhead in his side removed and the wound stitched up. He cursed his luck and cursed the O'Bell.

Chapter 55: Repelling the Quell

When the fleeing forces of the Quell reached the bottom of the mountain, they collapsed into their tents and awaited orders. Lem Lothe was suffering from his arrow wound and had taken a draught of a healing elixir to soothe the burning pain in his side. Dellan was glad to be alive, though he was visibly shaken by his near-death experience and their incredibly one-sided defeat. It had been a long day, and everyone was ready to rest and regroup in the morning. Unfortunately, the O'Bell had other ideas.

The cook fires were burning out, and the only stirring was the men on guard duty around the perimeter of the camp. Well-aimed arrows from the tree line took out each guard before he even knew he was in danger. With the camp unguarded, a whistle rang out letting the O'Bell riders know that it was their time to attack. Two hundred women, armored and on horseback, charged down the remaining distance into the clearing where hundreds of tents were set up. The clatter they raised got some of the men out of bed. Before they could realize what was going on, much less arm themselves and stand ready, the O'Bell Calvary swept through their ranks, torches in hand. They set as many tents on fire as they could in the first sweep, and on the way back, they cut down the few men who were up and ready to defend the camp. With just a couple of passes, the camp was on fire. Hundreds of tents were burning, and sparks were floating over to set other tents on fire. The night was filled with the sound of men screaming as they burned alive in their shelters.

As quickly as they had come, they rode back up the road to the safety of their castle walls and gate. Lem looked at the aftermath in disgust. He was a second-rate military leader at best, and his 'troops' were basically conscripts that believed in the cause, and him. He had another fifteen thousand men that were coming together in southern Wingard. He decided that he would take what was left of this army and march south to meet up with them. With the combined forces of the various factions, they would be unstoppable.

Of the five thousand men he had marched with, Lem Lothe only had about half that number now. There were a thousand that had been infected with the Gahrenna curse, only to be poisoned and left on the ground, to rot in the sun. Several hundred of his men had been sitting ducks for the O'Bell archers and more than a thousand died screaming, trapped in burning tents. Now he had a shade over twenty-five hundred men, with no food, and now no shelter. The best idea he could come up with was to force march them out of this female-led purgatory, and south to greener pastures.

Their destination had them passing through a different gate out of O'Bell lands, and this time, the gate was unmanned and open. It took a couple of days to reach the border, and when they saw the open gates, the men were thankful, despite their fatigue and hunger. They were able to travel another two days without seeing a soul. They passed the border between Kees and Wingard without any events. The defeat still a bitter taste in all their mouths as they marched on and on. They had encountered a few small villages and farms, and they raided and consumed everything edible. They were not as desperate as they had been while running from the O'Bell troops, but they were at the end of a long day of marching and were dog tired.

Their column had come out of some hills and were now on a long open plain. It was like being in the middle of the ocean, the horizon seemed to be a million miles away in every direction. Lem Lothe and his minion Dellan were riding in the middle of the long line of men. A scout on a tired horse came up to them, both the man and his mount were out of breath.

"Brother Lem, there is a force behind us, they must be following us!" the man reported.

"Did you see how many they were?" he asked.

"I got as close as I could, but out here, you can easily see a rider for a couple of miles. Several thousand I would guess."

"Are they moving?" he asked the scout.

"They weren't but they saw me and sent out riders after me. They dropped off a couple of miles back," he said breathily.

Lem turned to Dellan while pulling his spyglass from his breast pocket. "Dellan, send about four men with the tallest ladder that we have over there," he pointed due west. "Then have them circle around till they can just barely see the enemy in this glass. Then have one climb the ladder and have the others hold it. They can use a horse to help steady it. When he gets to the top of the ladder, have him give us an accurate estimate of how many horses and how many troops."

"Yes Brother Lem," he said before riding off to choose the work party.

Lem thought to himself, *finally, a fair fight. If there are too many, we run back to our lands in the West. If there are less than... say, fifteen hundred, we attack!* He had no idea who was ahead, but he longed for the moment when the smaller armies his commanders had assembled would come together. He prayed to Quell for more help; but today, Quell must have been busy.

"Brother, they are still following, and they are slowly gaining on us. There are probably three to four thousand of them, about half are the women from O'Bell, the rest are men," the scout reported.

"Very good," he replied. "Dellan, we are not going to run away, there is nowhere to go. Have the men set up whatever defenses they can. Most likely, the enemy will be trying to attack us from the rear, so concentrate the men with shields there."

"Yes Brother Lothe," he said as he ran to get the men ready.

Chapter 56: The Princess and the Warlord

Renata Rin rode up to Princess Lydia O'Bell. Their combined armies were chasing after the Quell and had them on the run. They had ridden together for the last day and a half since the princess and her army passed near Inram. Though she was now the Queen of Inram after evicting the Laima family, she still had feelings of loyalty to House O'Bell where she was born and raised. How strange she thought, chasing after an army of men who treated women like dogs and sex slaves, with a combined army led by two women.

The princess had grown a lot since the last time they had met. Unfortunately, they had not found time to really talk with each other. Renata remembered leaving O'Bell as a very young woman, and Lydia was a young girl at that time. She had visited every couple of years and her cousin had really grown both physically and emotionally. Now, instead of seeing men as only servants and generally as being useless, she had children of her own. Queen Vandressa should be leading this army, yet her daughter was already stepping into her mother's boots. After the routing of the Gahrenna, and pushing the Quell out of their lands, she offered to lead the effort to chase them down and exterminate them.

"Are you ready for this Lydia?" she asked.

"Of course, why not?"

"Picking off these stupid men from behind gates with longbows is much different from taking a short sword and jamming in his gut."

"I hear what you're saying, sister, but we'll never know for sure till I'm tested by fire."

"True enough. I'll lead the attack if you don't mind. I'll attack from the front. I want you to split your force and attack both sides at the same time that I attack the front."

"Are you scared?" she asked the older woman.

"Scared? No. As usual, I'm nervous, but scared. No." They were both lost in their own thoughts for a few minutes. "There they are, you can see them now on the horizon. Looks like their scouts got back to them and they've decided to stop and fight it out," she said looking with her battle trained vision. They have a rough shield wall; but it won't stand up to our initial cavalry charge. Go now! When you hear the trumpet, split and have your warriors double time to charge them from both sides."

The princess rode off to speak with the women whose lives were her responsibility. Renata watched her ride off for a second, taking stock of this new warrior princess. She decided that she was ready, and even if she wasn't, it was too late now. Ahead was a wall of shields with hungry, tired men behind it. They don't just want to kill her and her countrymen, they want to exterminate every trace of the Kronos culture and replace it with some twisted belief system. A system where women were objects to be used, then tossed aside. She knew that she had to win, and that under no circumstances could she be taken prisoner. She would do what great generals had always done; she would lead her men into battle. They would be the tip of the spear, and if the gods wanted this day to be her last, then so be it.

The followers of Quell were as ready as they could be. They formed what they thought was the standard shield wall that all armies often employed. What they had was several hundred men with mis-matched shields forming a wall with holes and weak spots all throughout. Behind them were many hundreds of men armed with a mixture of swords and farm implements. At a command from their leaders, they steeled themselves for the initial charge. Two hundred riders with full armor, armor for their steeds and ten-foot lances crashed against the wall and found it to be as porous as a sponge. The wall had almost no affect, the riders knocking men aside as if they were not even there.

At the head of the men was a woman in the colors of Inram, though House Laima was defunct, they still sported their banner. She was the fiercest warrior present, her battle scream made a man's testes retreat up into his torso, her bloodthirsty grimace made them question their faith. Renata Rin had a reputation to uphold. Where a man in her place would be called 'General', she was known as 'the Warlord'. She embodied the God of War in both her demeanor and her actions. Her horse easily crushed the few men that tried to block her path, she concentrated on swinging her perfectly balanced sword to relieve enemy heads from their shoulders. Within a minute of the battle commencing, she was already covered chin to toe in the blood of her enemies. The horse's momentum carried them through the weak front line and into the heart of the Quell's defense.

From her perch, she kept swinging downward, each chopping motion of her arm taking a life. Blood sprayed upward, looking like scarlet rain in reverse, as she hacked at an opponent, then moved on to the next. Easily a dozen men had perished before her horse's forward momentum was halted. The press of bodies forced her from her mount, but her petite size allowed her to still maneuver while in the press of bodies. She took comfort when she looked to the side and saw her second, Sir Dorman Cole. He was still tall in his saddle, swinging his longsword like a scythe, splashing buckets of blood like a washerwoman tossing out dishwater.

The men she faced were fanatics; but thankfully, they were ill-equipped and hardly trained at all. The only way she could be defeated by them would be for her to tire from swinging her sword. She would chop down an opponent and he would fall to the ground between them, then another would crawl over the body to get to her. Fights going on behind her were pressing against her back, forcing her forward. Axes and swords, and even the handles to shovels and rakes were swinging at her from all sides. For close combat like this, she often went without a shield, today she had lost it when she lost her horse. She carried a long dagger in her off-hand that she used to block attacks, the long sword to bring down the most dangerous opponents.

The next hour was a flurry of murder and mayhem, and only her nervous energy allowed her to keep up the pace. She would block an axe aimed at her neck, while simultaneously skewering a man in front of her. Then she would lash out with the dagger, leaving a deep gash on the axe man's arm. She would duck a swing meant to take her head off, then kick a man in the jewels. She chopped at a young man's neck, cutting deep into his shoulder till the blade hit his collarbone. She saw his face go white with fear and pain, then she saw him cry as he fell beneath her relentless attack.

No more than two hours after the initial charge, the battle was over. The Warlord was finally able to take a breath and assess the situation. Her men, along with the O'Bell women had clearly won the day; but there were still many losses on both sides. Dorman was still alive and no worse for wear. She walked over to him as he was taking reports from some of the troop leaders. He straightened up as he saw Renata come in his direction.

"My queen!" he said, "You've won the field of battle and by a respectable margin!"

"Indeed. How are the losses of our people, Sir Cole?" she asked of him.

"Not all of the reports are in, but it seems we are less some seven hundred souls, and the O'Bell have lost about as many."

"Terrible that we should lose so many good men to the likes of these," she said with contempt, waving at the bodies of Quell that were all around.

"It could have been much worse, had we not brought the Warlord," he said in all seriousness. She grew angry, thinking that she was being mocked, till she saw the lack of humor on his face. He pointed to where she had been, there was a giant ring of Quell bodies, stacked as high as a horse, all the way around except for an opening in the back. "You killed more of the buggers than any five men. If I ever doubted your reputation before, I now know it is well deserved. You are truly an army unto yourself." He leaned in, "It is a pleasure to serve you, my queen."

"Where is the princess?"

Looking confused, he searched around and finally flagged down a couple of mounted O'Bell soldiers. "Where is Princess O'Bell?" he asked. They both looked down in utter shame.

"She has been taken, your Lordship," one of them answered.

"Taken?" he asked incredulously.

"Yes, she was following their leader who was trying to escape on horseback. He was riding so fast that he was in danger of killing his mount, and she was hot on his trail, till he reached the very rear of their lines. There he had a dozen or more men waiting. They overpowered the princess, then rode off with her towards the south."

"Towards the South?" Renata asked.

"Yes, we questioned one of their survivors, and he said that they have a huge army forming to the South. Once this Lem Lothe character reaches their armies with the princess in tow, there is little hope of rescuing her."

Renata looked crushed, despite the huge victory that she had just won. Dorman came and put his gloved hand on her shoulder, "I don't think they will kill her, not when they find out who she is." He was an island of calm in a sea of turmoil. "They will of course demand some ridiculous ransom."

"Send word to King Syphon. I think he might be passing through Northern Khatuna by now."

"Yes, my queen."

Renata was kicking herself. They had won the battle, but potentially lost a friend, cousin, and future ally. Not exactly the outcome that she was hoping for as her first real test as queen. Her people would only see the win, but Queen Vandressa would never forgive her if she couldn't get Lydia back.

Chapter 57: The Prisoner

King Syphon marched East picking up armies as he went. He now had more than ten thousand warriors under his command, and they were passing through Northern Khatuna near the Margera border. The Iron Road made it easier to move men and wagons because of its quality of construction and upkeep. His advanced scouts let him know that he was within a week's march from the enemy. Word had it that they had upwards of fifteen thousand, though the quality of their troops was questionable at best.

A messenger from the Warlord, Renata Rin, let him know that Princess Lydia O'Bell, heir to House O'Bell, had been taken prisoner. He knew that they were going to try and exact a heavy price to get her back, a price that a good general would not be willing to pay. Against his better judgement, he let a group of individuals from different factions go out and try a rescue. This was the most that he was willing to do. Otherwise, he couldn't let one person's fate deter his plans. They left more than a day ago, and he might not know if they survived or not till after the war was over. He prayed to the gods that they would be successful.

From the top of a large sand dune, the crew could see the camp below. Thousands of tents for the main body of the Quell army. Hundreds of cook fires made it look like a bustling town from this distance. Somewhere down there was Lydia O'Bell. An odd group had volunteered to sneak in and bring her back.

Landis was the last to join; but somehow was almost instantly promoted to leader. Prince Herron joined because he knew it was something his father would have approved of, and he needed the experience. Roku and Melina of the Ammun volunteered because they were quiet when they fought, and this mission would require stealth. The first to volunteer was Timo, the Emar assassin. He knew that his ability to become invisible in shadow would be invaluable.

"How long has he been gone?" Landis asked.

"Couple of hours now. He said it could take this long. We should probably eat and maybe get some rest," Gabriel said.

"I hate waiting for someone else to do their job, while I'm just standing around."

"Always go with the best man for the job, my father always says," Gabriel offered. "Those Emar are almost invisible at night, and this one's trained as an assassin. Did you see the way he backed into the shadows and just disappeared? Spooky. I'm glad they're on our side."

For another hour, Gabriel and Melina fixed a meal of wild pheasant, while Landis continued to stare at the lights of the enemy's encampment. Then Landis felt a hand on his shoulder and turned to see the dark face of the Emar Assassin. The man's white teeth were the only thing that showed on his blue-black face. His bulging eyes were squinting, hinting that he had some interesting information. Landis tried to not show how startled and surprised he was by Timo sneaking up on him.

"Thank the gods, you're back!" he said only loud enough for the five of them, "You look like you have news."

"It took a while. There are many campfires down there, making it hard to find shadows to shift into," he said as if it meant anything to the rest of them. "They have her tied to a pole outside the commander's tent. She seems to be in good health, though she is beaten up a bit. Not sure if it's from the battle, or mistreatment after her capture."

"Any idea of what they have planned?"

"I heard that they sent a ransom demand; but I think whether they get their demands met or not, they are planning on a public execution."

"Friends, gather around," Landis said to the group, "There are still six hours till morning light. I say we move now, have Timo lead us around obstacles, and take us on the best path to where the princess is being held." They all agreed and began packing up their gear. Most of it they left in place, deciding to take only their weapons, or in Roku's case, nothing.

Timo led them down the sandy hills till they were at the border where the Indigo Desert met the Phister Swamps in northern Laurens. The various factions of the Quell had crossed the desert to meet here, because if they could invade the main church in Lourens, and wipe out the High Father, they would be much closer to wiping out the religion of the Old Gods.

When they reached the tree line, the group was hiding in the shadows not a hundred feet from the closest sentry. Timo raised his hand in a gesture for them to wait, then he disappeared. As the sentry walked past the shadow cast by one of the closest tents, two arms reached out and pulled him into the inky blackness of the tent's shadow. A second later, Timo was again next to them and waved for them to follow him. Landis and Gabriel gave each other a look, noting how the Emar could seemingly transport himself from shadow to shadow. They all crouched and ran as fast as they could across the small open area. When they were all in the shadows, they could see the sentry with his throat cut, laying in a heap next to the tent.

As a group, they moved from tent to tent till they got to where the princess was tied up. She looked up at them, not knowing who they were. She was dirty and had blood on her face and clothes, both hers and that of her enemies. Landis dropped to one knee and sawed away at the ropes that bound her.

"Princess, we are here to recover you. We received a message from the Warlord."

"Thank you, but how will we get out of here? There are more than fifteen thousand of them by now."

"A future queen of O'Bell is worried about a mere fifteen thousand 'men'?" Landis asked while cutting through the last of her bonds.

"It is true, they are not very bright." She stood up and followed the group led by Timo.

They were working their way back to the trees when they saw a commotion ahead. Someone had found one of the sentries that they had dispatched. Timo looked back at Landis with a question in his eyes.

"Make for the open desert. They won't expect it," he said to the Emar. With the alarms starting to sound throughout the camp, they relied less on stealth and more on speed. Timo was very sure of foot and tried to guide them along the path of least resistance. It worked till they were near the edge of the camp where they were met by a cluster of twenty or more Quell fighters.

Roku covered half the distance to the men, bowed, and assumed a fighting stance. The fighters hesitated for a moment, then charged him. He blocked their initial attacks while grabbing the arm of the man closest to him. His hands and feet moved as fast as lightning, he struck his enemies before they could react, breaking bones and causing concussions. His rock-hard fist crushed the nose of another man, sending blood flying everywhere. From over his shoulder, Melina launched a series of knives. One at a time; but in rapid succession and with deadly accuracy. Each knife found an eye or an exposed throat.

"I like her!" the princess exclaimed, then went to the ground to find an abandoned weapon.

Landis stepped in front of her and met the charge of two men intent on cutting her down. For stealth reasons, he didn't wear armor, but he did bring his buckler to block at least some attacks. With his blessed sword, he hacked and slashed at the men who were stupid enough to challenge him. For Landis, the art of sword fighting was intuitive. He never had to plan his moves, everything just flowed naturally without his having to think about it. On his off hand, he wore a small oval buckler, which when worn by him, was as dangerous as a club. He would block a chop at his shoulder, then smash the other fellow in the face. He would kick one man, then run the next man through. On his backswing, the pommel of his sword would crush the skull of an opponent behind and to the side. He was just getting used to his new sword, Soulbane. The blade was light when swinging but landed like a much heavier weapon. The enchantment on the blade caused it to change direction just a bit, enough to make a potentially damaging strike lethal. Almost every swing of his blade took a life or caused a debilitating wound. Lydia and Gabriel watched from the protection he provided and marveled at his skill.

"Here, milady," Gabriel said as he offered her a short sword.

"Who are you people?" she asked.

"I'm like you, next in line for the throne. Gabriel Herron of Khatuna, at your service." He offered his hand, which she accepted, "This wall of steel that we are hiding behind is Landis Stone, he comes highly recommended and now I see why. The Emar is named Timo and the others are Roku and Melina of the Ammun," Gabriel said as he lashed out at one of the Quell.

"Landis, this is going well enough, but I think we've overstayed our welcome," Gabriel shouted.

"You're right kid. Everyone, follow me!" Landis bowled over two men, and then with a running start, ran over another four. The monks followed in his wake, followed by the prince and princess. The Assassin brought up the rear. They ran towards the deep desert, and soon the lights of the enemy camps were far behind them. Landis took a rope and had everyone grasp on to it. He had the Emar in front leading the way and soon, they were far from the Quell and far from the cover of the trees.

Chapter 58: Desert Storm

The wind was beginning to kick up as it did most nights. The stifling heat of the day disappeared and gave way to the cool of the night. Far off in the distance, they could hear the shouts of the search parties. They had lost their prize and they wanted her back. The group could hear them but couldn't see them. Visibility was nearing zero due to the sand that was carried by the growing wind. It was becoming a raging sandstorm, and no one could see more than a foot or two in front of them.

"We should probably try to find some kind of shelter!" Melina shouted over the howl of the wind. "Whether they find us or not, we won't survive till the morning if we stay out here." She held her scarf across her nose and mouth to keep out the sand.

They walked around for several more minutes till they came across a spindly sapling of a tree. Though it was only two inches in diameter, it was holding its own against the blasting sand. Melina took the Emar's cloak, which was the largest, and tied one corner near the ground and the other as high as she could reach about five and a half feet. The third corner, she secured to the ground with a long dagger. Along with Landis' and Gabriel's cloaks, she was able to fashion a tiny shelter. Melina and the Princess were inside, the men could only fit their heads inside; but at least everyone could breathe.

They had been inside the makeshift tent for more than an hour. The Princess was anxious to get away from enemy territory, as was Landis. The Assassin was listening for pursuers, the monks were calm and meditative, and Gabriel had fallen asleep.

"Gabriel said that your last name was Stone?" Lydia asked.

"Yes, that's right."

"Are you related to Jarrod Stone? I may be crazy, but there seems to be some resemblance."

"He's my younger brother; but if he owes you any money or an apology, you're going to have to get it from him."

"I'm sorry to say this, but your brother is dead. He was killed by the Quell in Kees less than a week ago."

Landis was stunned into silence by the news. They were closer than he would admit to anyone, his brother dying was a blow to him in a year that had dealt him many blows.

"He died while protecting his lover, and my best friend, Meisha Bannon. He was charming enough, for a man. I'll always be indebted to him for saving my best friend's life."

"Funny," Landis said. "I would have bet anything that I would have been the first to go."

There was a very faint sound of people shouting, Timo was the first to hear it and let the others know. Soon, they could all hear a small group of men moving in their direction.

"I'll take care of this," Roku told the group. Melina handed him a scarf without being asked. He tied it around his mouth and nose and withdrew from the safety of the tent.

"Why did he go?" Landis asked.

"He is silent, no metal on metal. He can kill a man with a well-aimed punch," Melina explained. "If the visibility is still poor, he will have the advantage, he will kill the one in the rear, and the rest won't know till 'they' are the one in the rear."

As advertised, fifteen minutes later, he poked his head back under the cloaks. "There was a group of six that were looking for us," he said as he threw a few water skins into the tent. Everyone took a drink, no one asked how he could be so casual about taking out six enemies and finding his way back so quickly.

Another hour and the storm had tired itself out and stopped blowing sand about. Timo looked around to gather his bearings, looked at the stars, then made his decision.

"I will go bring horses. You go another mile into the deep desert, then a sharp left. That will take you away from the desert and towards the trees that mark the edge of Phister Swamp. I will meet you before you reach the swamp."

They agreed to the plan, and he was off. The group headed out into the desert, then turned the corner that would take them around the Quell's encampment. Less than two hours later, they heard what sounded like the breathing and walking of several horses. It was still more than an hour till dawn, and the Emar, for all intents and purposes, was invisible. The princess was not thrilled that she had to share a horse with the female monk, but being rescued was better than the alternative, so she decided not to complain.

They had barely gotten underway when they heard the sound of pursuit. A handful of riders had been circling the camp and had finally found them. They urged their horses forward and the chase was on. One turned to report back to camp, and the rest maintained their pursuit. The group followed Timo who seemed to know the way. They made good time, but the men following were slowly gaining ground on them. They were still out of bow range when Timo and Landis crossed into the swamps. The ground became soggy and wet, there were clumps of trees and brush that only got thicker the deeper that they went into the swamp.

The Quell decided that the odds were not in their favor, and they were not about to pursue their enemies across country borders without orders from above. A single rider was sent back to inform the leader, the rest sat on their horses and watched. They wanted to make sure that this enemy would not circle back. Lem Lothe would know what to do, following them or not would be his call.

Chapter 59: Calm before the storm

Word spread around the camp like wildfire. Princess Lydia O'Bell had been rescued from the heart of the Quell encampment. The troops all knew that they were going against a larger army and that the Quell fanatics were not afraid to die. Their defeat at the hands of the O'Bell and the rescue of Lydia O'Bell did a lot to boost everyone's morale.

The princess reported directly to King Syphon at his command tent. He looked up when she was announced and was happy to see that she had survived her ordeal. They had met at the King's Table, but they knew each other by reputation only. He was younger than she thought he would be, no grey hair yet. He offered her a seat and a cup of tea.

"I hope you don't mind, but I couldn't spare a whole brigade to go and get you."

"Of course not sire. I'm embarrassed to have been captured. I have no doubt that my mother will never let me forget this," she said dropping her gaze to her lap.

"More importantly, what is the status of their northern army? How many more men will they add to the main body?"

"Sire?" she asked. "You don't know? By the time I was captured, the battle was essentially over. We threw poisoned meat to tempt the wolf creatures that they sent against us. They foolishly ate it and died just outside the walls of our castle. We chased the rest down the mountain and out of our lands," she was reliving the events as she shared them. "We met up with the Warlord, and together with the men of Inram, we pretty much wiped them out. There may be a couple thousand of our troops still coming, but their Northern army was decimated."

King Syphon's mood lit up at this news, though he would have to find out why his staff was not giving him all the information that he needed to lead the army. So much good news at one time, he pulled out the wineskin and two glasses. He smiled for the first time in a long time and shared a drink with the princess from O'Bell.

Landis felt a hand on his shoulder, it was light, and it almost didn't register that someone was trying to get his attention. He turned around to see a young twenty-ish woman with long flowing black hair. She started with an expression of anger that almost instantly changed to one of relief.

"I'm so glad you made it back!" Danika exclaimed. "You didn't even say goodbye before you left, and I was terribly worried about you!"

"Sorry, Mother. I wasn't aware that I had to check in with you before doing what I do best," he laughed.

"Well... now you know. Try not to scare me like that again."

"I'm surprised that you remember me. Before last month, I haven't seen or heard from you and Jorn for almost six years!"

"We've been in Argus' home the whole time. You knew where we lived. You could have visited." Her scolding expression gave way to a wide smile. "I don't have many friends, so I value the few that I do have."

"I hate to tell you, but you have one less friend. That princess told me that Jarrod was killed last week. Killed by the Quell while defending an O'Bell that he had fallen in love with," he said in a tired and utterly crushed tone. He couldn't meet her gaze as he finally allowed the loss to sink in.

"By the gods! No!" she wailed. Instantly she was crying and sobbing uncontrollably. She went to Landis and threw her arms around him, burying her face in his chest and crying for a long time. The emotion was too much for him, he joined her, and they wept over their loss together.

"This war that we've all committed to could start any day now. It's going to be very dangerous around here," he said to her. "I hope that you and your brother aren't planning to move with the army. There's no telling how things will go."

"Argus didn't come with us, he said that he had something very important to deal with. He told us to be careful, but he didn't seem too worried. I think he's starting to have some confidence in our abilities."

"That could be." He looked down at her innocent face. She was no longer a child, but she still had an innocent quality about her. Her body had become a woman's body, and despite living in an old castle with a thousand-year-old mage, her brother, and a Telnor manservant; she had learned how to dress like a woman. Just when he was wishing that he could feel her touch again, she lifted her hand with its long, graceful fingers and brushed his cheek.

"We are going with the army. Say that you will stay close and keep me safe," she said in a honey-sweet voice that caused his knees to weaken. He still remembered her as an adolescent. *Why is she having this effect on me?* he thought to himself.

He had no option, "Of course. I'll be by your side and will protect you against the Quell and anyone else who would be stupid enough to try and harm you."

"I heard we leave at dawn. I hope you are using a horse these days," she said smiling at him, before spinning on her heel and gliding away. He sighed, *by the gods, that girl is going to be the death of me.*

The guards announced Prince Herron and Jorn Anant who were ushered into the king's tent. The older man was having his dinner while staring at the map in the middle of a large folding table. He waved the two young men over and offered them seats near him.

"Gabriel, I see that you survived your first mission," Kel said.

"Yes Sire, I did as you suggested. I watched and mostly kept my head down."

"You look familiar, have we met?" he asked Jorn.

"At King's Table, my Lord. Jorn Anant."

"You're the young mage that Prince Herron speaks so highly of. I pray you can help us to win the coming battle." He turned to face Gabriel, "What did you learn during your adventure?"

"Well... first and foremost, I'm very glad that the Emar are on our side. Especially at night, they are bloody scary."

"That's good to know," the king mused.

"Landis Stone is by far the most dangerous fighter I have ever witnessed. Watching him fight is better than any ballet you could ever hope to see." He waved to a servant to bring two more plates. The men sat quietly eating, each of them lost in their own thoughts. The king had much on his mind; but he liked the young prince who would soon be a king.

"Gabriel, where will you be when arrows begin to fly?"

"Where I belong Sire, leading the men of Khatuna. They won't be thrilled to see me there; but I'll be the first Khatuna man on the battlefield. They'll see that, and they'll follow me."

"Very good! If we both survive this, I hope you and I can become friends." He turned to Jorn, "Where will you be, son?"

"I don't know yet milord. I don't claim allegiance to any country. My sister and I are living in the southern part of your country, maybe I could stay near you?"

"You're most welcome. Unlike Gabriel here, I can't be in front of my army. I have to control things from a bit of a distance. You can stay with me and my staff."

"Thank you, sire, I'll try to stay out of trouble."

Chapter 60: Final March

Lem's mind was racing as he marched his men southward. His scouts had confirmed that the first few hundred men were establishing a camp just south of the swamps. *They must think that the swamps are too difficult to navigate, that they can leave that direction practically unguarded and still be safe. The fools! They don't have their backs to a wall, a swamp may be hell to cross; but we will trudge through the swamp and flank them! Only I have the vision to launch such an attack. I might lose many brothers; but when we have crushed the combined armies of the nations of Kronos, I will surely be rewarded by Quell.*

It was early in the morning, and the sun was slowly crawling into the sky. Now that they were out of the desert, it was much cooler at night and in the mornings; but as the sun rose, the humidity rose, and it soon became sticky, and the air was thick. There were parts of the swamp that were above ground, some patches of dirt here and there, the occasional exposed tree roots. In some areas the water was deep, over a man's head deep. Most of the swamp though, was waist deep water, with a mucky bottom and there were slime covered trees and thorny bushes everywhere. The men would take a step, and the thick mud under the water would suck at their boots. Every step was a chore, and it was tiring them out quickly. As usual, he rode a horse, so Lem had no firsthand knowledge of how difficult the march was.

"Master!" Dellan called as he rode up to Lem. "Even if we catch them totally by surprise, the men are going to be too tired to attack."

"What would you have me do? We're in the middle of this damned swamp! It's the same distance to go forward as it is to go back!" he replied irritably, "We can rest the men when we are an hour away. We just have to kill any scouts that would let them know that we are coming."

"What does Quell think we should do?" Dellan asked without the same degree of respect that he had usually had.

"It has been some time since the Lord has answered my prayers. Perhaps he is unhappy with our recent defeats," Lem said.

"I wouldn't blame him for abandoning us completely," Dellan said a bit too loud.

"Keep your voice down or face my wrath!" Lem hissed at the man.

"I begin to wonder if Lord Quell has ever spoken to you!" Dellan was fuming, the troops around them were marching painfully through the swamp, hanging on every word, "I'm not sure…," his rant was cut off by the long sword that Lem had pushed through his chest. The blade passed through him and exited his back, causing Dellan's life blood to drip into the murky water. The look on Dellan's face was a mixture of betrayal, disbelief, and defeat. Lem pulled the sword out and allowed his long-time Lieutenant to fall to the sodden ground. He fell face forward and sank below the surface, and only a few bubbles marked where a man had been a minute ago. The troops marched around him, and no one attempted to lend him any assistance.

Most of the troops refused to look at Lem. If he could casually execute his second in command, then none of them were safe. When he had regained his composure, he looked for one of his other commanders. He found a man who was marching the troops through the muck and mire.

"You there! Grab that horse. You are now second in command of this army."

Chapter 61: The Swamp

King Syphon was walking amongst the tents with Prince Herron, visiting with the men to making sure that their spirits were up. It was a cloudy afternoon; but the air was dry and there would be no rain today. To the north were the swamps, hundreds of square miles of quagmire. West of them lay the Indigo Desert, and to the east was the Kanto Sea. If they needed to flee, the only sensible direction would be to go South, deeper into Lourens territory.

Some troops had arrived weeks ago, others had arrived in the last two days. Together, they were the best of the men who were of military age. Some men were ready; but most were either too ready or the kind who would never be ready. They looked up at their leader and saw in him an experienced soldier who was not afraid, who was ready to do what needed to be done to protect the people of Kronos.

"I'd say we're ready, my liege," the prince stated. "Look at these good men, I'd take a hundred of them over a thousand of those Quell bastards!" he said loud enough for the men nearby to hear. A messenger rode up, dismounted, and bowed as he handed his message to the king. After reading it, Kel broke into a wide smile. He dismissed the messenger, who mounted and rode off.

"Great news, Gabriel," he said to his junior. "It looks like the Quell are falling into our trap! Even now, as we speak, they are making their way through Phister Swamp. When they arrive at our camp, they'll expect to meet with an unprotected flank; but we'll be waiting in force!"

"Let's get over there and see to the preparations. If we can surprise them, we could greatly change the odds in our favor," Gabriel said happily.

Jorn was jogging around the camp nervously looking for his sister. The camp was subdivided by kingdom, but Jorn and Danika didn't claim citizenship to any of the kingdoms represented here. The news was out that things were going to be happening soon. The camp had been still for days, some of the men were becoming restless; but now there was activity everywhere. Canteens were being filled, arrows and bowstrings checked, and there was plenty of last-minute work to be done. No one was ever without his boots on.

He found her near the king's tent chatting with Landis. Relieved that he had found her, he slowed his pace as he walked towards them. He was about to call out when he saw something in his sister's eyes that he had never seen before. He was not sure what it was; it was like a sparkle. He looked at Landis who was listening intently to Danika's stories. He loved his sister; but in his opinion, she was not very interesting. Inexplicably Landis seemed fascinated by her story. Very strange.

"Jorn!" Danika said as he drew nearby, "I'm glad I found you. I heard that the enemy is very close and that the fighting could start at any time!"

"Well, ok. What should we do? Wait here with King Syphon or are we going to march along with the knights?" he asked her.

"Well, I've already agreed to protect you two, so I have a thought. We should hang back with the command staff," Landis said.

"I suppose that would be okay," Jorn replied.

Prince Herron walked up to the small group, smiling as always. He clapped Jorn on the shoulder, then checked out the others.

"Jorn, I'm getting ready to move my men out. We are going to set up a defensive position at the edge of the swamps. Looks like the men of Khatuna get the honor of being our army's shield. Want to ride with me?" he asked.

"He is 'not' going to join you at the front!" Danika yelled.

"You must be Danika. Nice to finally meet you," he held out his hand. She looked at it like it was a week-old dead fish.

"So, you're going to be in the front, eh?" Jorn asked his friend. Going on one mission doesn't necessarily qualify you as a combat veteran. What's your plan to stay alive? Your people are going to need you someday soon to become their king."

"Well..., I figured if I had a high-powered mage at my side, I might have a decent shot at surviving this whole thing."

"They're still just children," Landis cut in. "They don't belong in battle."

"Children!" Danika raged, "You're only a few years older than us, and this prince is about the same age as Jorn and I," she said, turning red with indignation.

"You're all invited. I think that with Mr. Stone... should I knight you?" Everyone looked confused. "If we all live through this, remind me to knight you. Anyhow, with your sword between us and the Quell, I would feel much safer."

Jorn summoned a sphere of water, he felt a vision coming on. Every other time, he sought out the visions that came to him. This time, the vision came looking for him. Alone in his tent, he stared at the glistening bubble of water before him. It hung still in the air and the surface took on a glassy finish. In the reflection on the water bubble, he could see the battle between Argus and the demon Qaumon. The idea that witches were creating doorways to let evil flow into his world scared the young mage. He now knew the impetus behind the rise of the Quell and he feared that he wouldn't have the skills needed to stop future incursions of demons and monsters into the world of Man.

Several hours later, scouts returned to report that the enemy was now only an hour's march away. The good men of Khatuna waited in formation behind their prince and his officers. Tension was high and they all knew that they were not only outnumbered but that they were going to be the first to enter the fray. The Quell were notoriously reckless with the lives of their followers. Men hoping to get rewards in the afterlife were less concerned about their safety in this life.

"Jorn, Danika, Landis, come here please." He waved them over. They dismounted and walked over to join him, "I have a plan that might work wonders. Or it could be a disaster, but I think it's worth considering." Making sure that no one else was near, he proceeded to go over the details. They were skeptical at first, but he soon had them persuaded. The four of them left their horses behind and together, they walked into the swamp.

The ground became soggy, and the trees got thicker as they trudged deeper into the swamp. Soon it was difficult to see for even a short distance. They walked on, Landis and Gabriel in their full metal armor, Jorn in bright blue pants and a dark blue shirt. Danika at first tried to hold up her bright red dress, but it got wet, and she soon gave up and let it drag in the muck and mire. The four of them didn't speak at all, they were intent on listening for the enemy. Birds called out from branches high up in the treetops, frogs croaked, and insects buzzed; otherwise, it was just the sloshing of their boots in the knee-deep mud and stagnant water. Twenty minutes of walking, and now they were up to their mid-thighs in the scummy green water. Gabriel held up his hand for them to stop.

"This should do," he whispered to the group. "I thought that I heard something."

They all waited in silence for several minutes till they heard the tramping of feet in muddy water and the rattling of weapons and gear on the backs of the Quell fighters. There were hundreds of them, and behind them, thousands more. Soon, they could see the enemy. Unhappy, unwashed, ultra-religious zealots who looked forward to the killing more than the conquest itself. Their leader sat high up on a horse that was having its own difficulty navigating the uneven and flooded ground. When he saw the twins and their armed escorts, thinking that they were scouts, he sent a small group of men to silence them.

Ten or so men tried to pick up their pace and run towards Landis and Gabriel, who were in front. They had swords drawn and ready and it was almost comical how long it took them to cross the divide. When they were in range, Landis drew his longsword, Soulbane. Gabriel shot three of them with his bow before switching to his long sword. They waded forward as the twins stood their ground and waited.

Soulbane was like an extension of Landis' arms. He reached out and with strength and precision, he carved his opponents into lifeless heaps. The blade shone brightly, despite the dim light that filtered down through the trees above and it whistled as he swung it in the heavy, wet air. The sword was not as long as a two-handed sword; but was so light that he used it like a bastard sword, equally adept with one, or both hands. The sword's special properties made Landis even faster than he would have been with a normal sword. It also altered his swing ever so slightly, so that almost every slash or stab was a life-taking strike.

Gabriel struggled to take on two of the fighters, but eventually won without taking any damage. When he had finished, he looked over at Landis who was putting the finishing touches on a fifth opponent. At this point, the twins felt comfortable enough to slog their way up to where their protectors were standing.

Seeing that the men and woman were going to stand their ground and that they would not be so easily beaten, Lem ordered everyone to continue moving forward. The army's forward motion had backed up while the fighting had gone on, and now Landis could make out what looked to be many hundreds of men, perhaps thousands or more, and that was just what he could see through the mist and the trees.

The Quell surged forward slowly and methodically and were still out of arrow range when Jorn stepped to the front. He started chanting a spell that enhanced his natural ability. It was too far for the Quell to see or comprehend, so they continued to close the distance. The air around Jorn became filled with powerful, mystical energy. The air before him started to glow and took on an almost metallic smell. His friends were behind him, so they didn't see how his eyes began to glow like radiant suns, his brow furrowed in concentration, every muscle in his body tensing… then he released the energy of his spell. Holding his hands just above the murky swamp water, he directed his ability to summon cold. The water directly in front of him froze, and it worked its way away from him in a wave. The water between the two groups froze, then the water that the Quell were standing in froze.

The Quell had never heard of much less seen magic on this scale. For as far as the eye could see, Jorn froze the swamp, trapping men and horses alike. The men screamed in panic, even though they were not yet experiencing any pain. They were scared... as they should be. When he was done, Jorn stumbled and almost fainted from the exertion. Landis caught him and pulled him back. He marveled at the raw power of the boy.

"My turn," Danika stated. She stepped forward so that Jorn and the others were safely behind her. She looked over at the men across the swamp. She recalled the many tales that she had been told of how they killed the sick and the disabled, how they tortured and brutally slaughtered men who loved other men, and how they raped any woman who had the misfortune of just being female. She remembered how they were responsible for the death of her friend Jarrod. All the emotions that these horrors stirred up in her were channeled into her spellcasting.

Like her brother, she drew in energy causing the very air in the forest to come alive. She held her hands out, and flames seemed to pour from her outstretched palms. It built up in front of her until she released it. A wave of fire shot forward and spread out as it moved till a huge pie-shaped section of the swamp in front of her was washed over by the flames. She heard them scream, but it bothered her not in the least. She followed the initial wave of fire with individual fireballs. As fast as she could imagine them, she launched fiery death at the enemy. The swamp was not as flammable as a typical forest; but in the end, they are both made of wood. There was no way to tell; but more than likely, all of the men who had been snared in her brother's ice were now burned from the waist up. The rest who were beyond Jorn's range were now running from the rapidly spreading forest fire.

They were all ready to turn back to camp when the twins both grew faint and almost lost their footing. Landis looked at how they both swooned at the same time and was concerned.

"What happened?" he asked as Danika walked over and embraced her brother.

"It's Argus. He's dead," Jorn stated.

"How can you know that?" Landis asked.

"We felt him die," Danika said through tears. "We can feel when major events happen in the magical realm, just like he felt our awakening." She held Jorn closely, "He's gone, brother."

"I believe it's time to leave," Gabriel said somberly. They all agreed and made their way out of the swamp.

Chapter 62: War

Lem Lothe saw the ice spreading towards him and his men, and before he could process in his mind what was happening, his horse was hopelessly trapped. Not wanting to find out what else the mage had in store, he dropped down from his saddle onto the ice. He began running to their rear. It was a very long way until the ice gave way to water again. He heard a commotion behind him and stopped to see what was happening. He looked back to see waves of fire and then balls of fire setting his men aflame and then burning the trees and brush around them. He barely escaped death, and he was haunted by the screams of thousands of his men burning alive.

He urged his men who were not trapped in ice to reverse course and head back in the direction from which they had come. In the confusion, many were trampled or drowned; but the majority were able to turn back and avoid the fire that was still heading in their direction. Almost all of them dropped their weapons, dropped their supplies, and did their best to flee from the firestorm.

It was at that moment that Lem Lothe knew that Quell had abandoned him and that his cause was a lost one. He began to question his faith and the belief that murdering and enslaving non-believers was justified by their god. What god would allow, much less condone such behavior?

King Syphon was waiting when Prince Herron and the group walked out of the woods. He was confused and was looking for answers.

"Prince Herron, what's going on?" he asked.

"I had an idea to slow down the enemy. Can you see the fire over there?" he pointed towards the heart of the swamp where the trees were still burning.

"How did you do that? the King asked.

"It wasn't that difficult, old man," Danika replied as she created a flame and let it dance on her palm.

"I don't know for sure, but I think we may have killed as many as a couple thousand of them," Gabriel said. "Jorn froze them in place, and Danika torched them, then she set the swamp on fire for good measure. I'm sure that what's left of them is headed back towards the desert with all possible speed."

"That upsets the plan a bit, but I like that the odds are more in our favor."

"I have another idea. All it would really take is the use of a couple of your Ravens," Gabriel said.

The Quell had been trudging through the swamp for most of the day and now all through the night. Half their number were now safely back in the Indigo desert. Lem Lothe was in his tent contemplating running away, but there was nowhere to go. He was easily the most hated man in all of Kronos. He still had ten to twelve thousand men, maybe if he could address them, re-instill their desire to get the spoils due conquerors. A messenger was announced by his guards and let in. The man was wet with perspiration and nervousness, which made Lem think that he must be bearing bad news.

"What is it now!" he demanded.

"We were attacked, Master. After the sunset, a full brigade of Emar troops landed on the East side of the swamp."

"Landed? Where did they come from?" he raged at the poor messenger.

"Hundreds of ships entered the Kanto Sea, and they dropped them directly into the swamp, right where our people were passing through," the man said shakily.

"Were passing through?" Lem asked.

"There must have been several thousand of them, all highly trained elite troops. You know how those creatures can almost disappear in the dark. They massacred all of the men who had not yet gotten out of the swamp, three to four thousand men."

"Thank you. Have all of my commanders that are left report to this tent immediately!" he ordered. The man saluted and ran out.

Lem Lothe had finally come to the realization that he was no tactical genius. It was easy to win a battle when his forces were double that of the enemy, but now he was running out of men to throw at the combined army of Kronos. King Syphon had maybe twelve thousand troops with him along with at least two very powerful mages. The inhuman Emar had come from somewhere across the sea to join the fight. He was now severely outnumbered, and he would be pitting tired hungry, poorly trained men against hundreds of knights and thousands of professional soldiers. It was time to retreat. Lem turned to his generals and gave the order that they all knew was coming, "We must withdraw to our own lands and regroup. Prepare the men to leave immediately." The beat-down men grumbled and left his tent to start tearing apart their makeshift camp.

Lem was deep in thought when he heard a loud sound, like thunder but louder and more ominous. Poking his head out of the flap of his tent, he could see a dust cloud forming to the South. Thousands of riders were heading for the Quell encampment at full charge. The Quell were at their weakest and it was the perfect time for the armies of Kronos to attack. Leaving all of his possessions, Lem strapped on his sword and cloak and was in the process of mounting his horse when a young officer approached.

"Brother Lem, we are being attacked by the army of King Syphon from the South!"

"I can see that, get ready to defend yourself."

"We are also being attacked by the O'Bell combined army, from the North!"

"Join your company, grab a sword, and prepare to die for the glory of Quell!" he commanded the young man. The officer looked very skeptical but ran off to join his assigned group. Lem knew that if the women warriors were attacking their exposed flank while they were busy defending against a superior force from the South, they would be completely wiped out. He briefly thought about sending a messenger to inquire about terms of surrender; but he had no intention of standing trial for war crimes. Instead, he mounted his horse, threw his hood over his head, and slowly rode out of camp. The West was wide open and as soon as he was clear, he whipped his steed and urged it to run as fast as it could.

Gabriel walked into the twin's tent after being announced. He was all smiles as he sat down a keg of wine. Jorn and Danika were there, along with Landis, and Father Sebastienne.

"I bring good tiding, my friends! The war is over!" he called for a steward to bring glasses.

"Over? What news do you have?" Father Sebastienne asked.

"I rode with King Syphon ahead of the army. We coordinated our attack with the O'Bell and the Warlord. We ran them over with our calvary while the ladies took out their flank. It was set to be a massacre; but their leader fled their camp just before the battle started. Without leadership and being outnumbered, they were tired, and they lost the will to fight," Gabriel said as he poured the first few glasses.

"I thought that they were all preferring the afterlife to this one. Rewards in heaven and all that?" Landis asked.

"When their god died, they lost hope. They would pray, and no one answered," Jorn said.

"When their god died?" Gabriel asked, seeming confused by the statement.

"They thought that Quell was a god; but he was really a demon, summoned to this plane to bring hell to Kronos and replace the 'age of man', with the 'age of monsters'." Jorn told the group.

"How do you know all this?" his sister asked him.

"I felt a vision coming on and I saw a battle between our master, Argus, and a demon that was thirty or forty feet tall. It was a terrible fight; but in the end, the demon was defeated and banished to the hell he came from."

"That why the old mage didn't ride with us?" Father Sebastienne asked.

"He couldn't be here because he's dead," Jorn said numbly. "He fought a witch that brought the demon to our world. After he defeated the demon; she attacked him and won because he was in a weakened state." Jorn was not much of a drinker, but he took a long pull at his wine glass. "When we return to Chuo, we'll have to properly bury him." Jorn took another drink, "This is a time to celebrate; but you all must know that the followers of Quell were the precursor of what's to come. They were not the storm; but the wind and rain that precedes the storm. This Winter Witch has opened a door to our world and gods only know what will come through."

"What about their leader, that crazy Lem Lothe character?" Danika asked.

"He knew after the debacle in the swamp that Quell was no longer on his side, and that there would be a price on his head. He stuffed a couple of saddle bags with coins and took off towards the West," Gabriel answered.

"I think that I won't be able to rest till he has paid for his crimes," Landis said bitterly.

"That's for another day. Today, we are alive and together, and at least for now, Kronos is safe."

King Syphon sat alone in his tent. The good news had reached him first, now he would have the privilege of returning the various armies to their countries, mostly intact. There was a push for Kronos to have one king that would stand above all the others. A King of Kings. He was not sure that he was worthy of such an honor; but it would definitely come up at the next King's Table.

Kell Syphon was not an overly religious man; but he did believe in giving credit where credit was due. He looked at the statue of Magnus that he had brought with him from his castle. He knew that the gods must have intervened, and that with Magnus' blessing, they were able to conclude this war with far fewer casualties than he thought they would incur. The young mage warned that harder times were in the offing, and he knew that regardless of who was on his side, he would not get off so easily again.

There was rustling behind him, the sound of a tent flap opening. A man entered his tent without invitation, looking like he didn't have a care in the world. Kell was in the middle of his prayers, and his usual genial nature gave way to anger. He turned to see the stranger close the tent flap after entering. He grabbed a chair and pulled it over till he was just a foot or so away.

"I don't know who you think you are, but its rude to interrupt a man when he is giving his thanks to the gods."

"Well, I'd apologize; but you basically invited me in, so in that case, I guess that it's not that rude."

"What do you mean? I won't be plagued by your riddles!"

"No riddles then." He picked up the statue, rolled it in his hands, "Doesn't look a thing like me, you know," he commented. The king went as white as a black man can.

"I have always allowed other religions in my world. Most of them are from different cultures trying to describe me and the others in their own ways. Look at their holy books. They have so many names for me; Tanus, Dorn, Lady Draco, Yob. Many wonderful and fascinating stories; but in essence, they're all trying to describe me." He set down the statue and looked at the

Kel, "This 'Quell' business was different though. Men were worshipping a demon and harming each other in the most inhumane ways in 'his' name. That, I could not allow."

The stranger smiled to himself, "I saw the way you defeated those beasts that killed your friends and took your hand. You have the spirit of a fighter in you, and the wisdom of a man many years your senior. I see clouds on the horizon, and you're still the man to lead my people. I'll do what I can to make sure you are named King of Kings."

"Thank you, Lord Magnus," the King stuttered. "I'll serve to the best of my ability and to my last breath."

"Of course, you will, that's why I chose you. From time to time, I or one of the Old Gods will impart gifts to people who are meant to participate in the events yet to come. I have already given one of the six Blades of the Colossus to one of your fighters. He has no idea what it is capable of, but he will learn in the hard days to come. Other champions will emerge and together, they will stand against the evil that is coming, and coming soon." The young stranger reached for the fake hand of the king, pulled it off, and tossed it into the fire. "This is a gift that I give you for your loyal service." When Kell took his eyes off his burning prosthetic and looked down, he saw that his missing hand had been restored. He flexed the wrist, and moved the fingers, testing their flexibility.

"Thank you, Lord. I will do all that you ask of me, without hesitation."

"Very good. I know you will. We are almost done here. You need to unite all of Kronos under your rule. Soon you will discover that this beautiful land that I have crafted for all of you is but one of many. When your people are ready to sail the deep oceans, you will find other lands to the North, to the East, and to the West. It's my hope that you can save them from the onslaught of evil that is trying to enter this world."

He got up and walked to the tent flap. "When and if you see me again, I will appear as someone else, or possibly I'll be a whisper in your ear." With that, he winked at the king and was gone.

Author's Note:

I'd like to thank a couple of people who made this book better.

Thanks to Author Sean Hall for helping me with writing structure and for feedback on how to get my writing 'out there'. Doesn't matter how good your book is if no one knows about it.

Thanks to my girl Hoàng Nhi. Not for supporting my writing per se, but for believing in me and kicking me in the butt.

This book is the first in a series of 4 books and counting. I re-wrote this from scratch and know that it is a quantum leap improvement from the original. I hope you enjoyed it, and if you did, please leave a review at the link listed below. I have also put in links to my professional social media contact information.

Check out my website: MarkRGoodrum.com

Email: markgoodrum@MarkRGoodrum.com

Instagram: **mrgintl**

Facebook: https://www.facebook.com/profile.php?id=100094028413995

Twitter: @MarkRGoodrum

Made in United States
Orlando, FL
07 December 2023